FIGHT FOR LIBERTY

THERESA LINDEN

PRAISE FOR FIGHT FOR LIBERTY

"… book three in the Liberty trilogy climbs to a dazzling climax, filled with plot shifts that will tantalize adult, juvenile and YA readers. Liberty 554-062466-84 of Aldonia resembles a Marvel Comic Book hero, without superpowers. Tough and accomplished, she comes into her own as a role model for girls and women, following that inner voice calling them to greatness."

~Amazon review

Fight for Liberty is beyond the cherry on top; it's the ever-awaited melty delicious ice cream at the bottom of your bowl as you slurp up every last drop. Exciting beyond measure from front to end. You will not only love this book, it will make you think and learn stuff you didn't realize before. A must read for any generation!"

~Amazon review

"*Fight for Liberty*, just like the first two books in the trilogy, is a fast-paced page turner, and brings a fantastic and satisfying conclusion to the story! Linden has an amazing ability to build characters with such depth and put them (and us) in rich, layered and realistic environments. She is a pleasure to read and I'm looking forward to diving into the rest of her books! Highly recommended!!"

~Amazon review

"If we were to do a direct comparison between L'Engle and Linden then the Chasing Liberty Series would be the Kairos series This is an excellent conclusion to the trilogy, and an incredible read."

~Steven R. McEvoy, Top 1000 Reviewer

BOOKS BY THERESA LINDEN

CHASING LIBERTY TRILOGY
Chasing Liberty
Testing Liberty
Fight for Liberty

WEST BROTHERS SERIES
Roland West, Loner
Life-Changing Love
Battle for His Soul
Standing Strong

NEW ADULT FICTION
Anyone But Him

SHORT STORIES
"Bound to Find Freedom"
"A Symbol of Hope"
"Made for Love" (in the anthology *Image and Likeness:*
Literary Reflections on the Theology of the Body)
"Full Reversal" (in the anthology *Image and Likeness:*
Literary Reflections on the Theology of the Body)
"The Portrait of the Fire Starters"
(in the anthology *Secrets: Visible and Invisible*)

FIGHT FOR LIBERTY
Copyright © 2016 by Theresa Linden
www.theresalinden.com
Print ISBN-13: 978-0-9968168-8-5
eBook ISBN: 978-0-9968168-9-2
First Edition: Silver Fire Publishing, July 4, 2016
Second Edition: Silver Fire Publishing, June 27, 2018

Cover: Theresa Linden
Editor: Elizabeth Brenneman

SILVER FIRE
PUBLISHING

DEDICATION

This book is dedicated to all who seek true freedom, not only for oneself but for all. In a special way it is dedicated to the men and women who have served and are serving in our military. Thank you for what you have done and are doing for us so that we may enjoy the freedom we take for granted. Those who have lost their lives in this service are not forgotten.

ACKNOWLEDGMENTS

I am sad to see this trilogy close. The characters and their story have become very dear to me. There are so many people who have helped, encouraged, and supported me along the way, from my aunts and fellow homeschooling moms who keep asking when the final book will be done to my editor, Elizabeth Brenneman, who shared her exceptional talents without receiving the full compensation she deserves. I further wish to express my gratitude to beta readers Carolyn Astfalk, Don Mulcare, and Dan Cunningham, each of whom brought their unique talents and insights to this story. I wish to thank John Paul Wohlscheid for his contribution in creating the character Grenton. I love this character he created and see a possible short story in the future. Above all, I want to acknowledge the love and support of my husband and boys, who inspire me and keep me going. This book would not be possible without them. To all my readers who have stayed with me throughout this trilogy: thank you!

FOREWORD

When thinking about the concept of liberty, what comes to mind? As our societal norms continue to change, this is a question we should ask ourselves. In the United States, liberties that citizens of many other countries can only long for from afar are taken for granted every day. This is an unfortunate fact.

True liberty, or freedom, is slowly becoming a thing of the past in America. I have watched it happen, slowly but surely, ever since I began paying attention to current events on September 11, 2001.

If you are a reader of dystopian fiction, have you ever wondered why so many authors are writing dystopias? And what is a dystopia if not the opposite of a utopia, something that many people in America believe is possible to create for themselves at this time? Could it be that creative Americans are writing dystopias as a way to convey what they see coming down the pike? And is it possible that American citizens are reading dystopias because they, too, feel a sense of unease?

I believe this is the case. After all, I have written my own dystopian series with many of the same themes as Theresa Linden's Liberty Trilogy. Other authors of my acquaintance have done the same. Though the stories are set in vastly different worlds, they are all variations on the same theme: the replacement of unalienable rights with top down regulations issued by an out of control State in order to create their vision of utopia.

If I may, let me spell it out for you in four simple words: There is no utopia. And though no country is perfect, the closest thing to a perfect society exists right here in the United States. So we should do everything in our power to preserve our freedoms if we don't want our descendants to exist in a dystopian nightmare.

Just such a nightmare is portrayed in horrifying detail in Theresa Linden's Liberty Trilogy. Aldonia, the repressive city from which Liberty risks her life to escape, is something that will become reality if we don't step up and stop the erosion of our rights.

In Liberty,

Daniella Bova, author of the Storms of Transformation series
Landenberg, Pennsylvania
June 11, 2016

Is true Freedom but to break
Fetters for our own dear sake,
And, with leathern hearts, forget
That we owe mankind a debt?
~James Russell Lowell

1

Keep trying. Follow the clues and you will gain wisdom.

"Easy for you to say. You're in my head." I leaped for an overhead branch. Again. My palms smacked it, conveying a stinging sensation via the 3D gloves, and I stuck. I laughed, pleased with this little victory and glad I didn't slide back down this time.

My name is Liberty. And *My Friend*, as I called him, had been in my head since childhood, since my first traumatic experience at age five when I transitioned from the Breeder Facility to one of Aldonia's Primary Facilities.

"Why can't you just tell me?"

Experience is a better teacher.

I pressed the toe of my shoe to the thick tree trunk—really the climbing wall, but it seemed realistic enough. A bead of sweat dripped down my chest and ran along the edge of my bra. I couldn't have sweated any harder if I'd been experiencing this in reality.

I had once been known as Liberty 554-062466-84 of Aldonia, when I was a child of the Regimen Custodia Terra. But now I was simply Liberty. I longed to have a second name, like my friend Abby and all the colonists did. Their second name showed that they belonged to a family, to people who loved them in an exclusive way. While I felt a connection to everyone in Aldonia, I belonged to no one. I wouldn't complain, though. Unlike the majority of Aldonians, *I* was now free.

Keep climbing. You're almost there.

My Friend had never spoken to me as directly as he had these past several weeks, since Re-Education. He led me to believe I would be instrumental in changing Aldonia and gave me hope that freedom would win out against the all-controlling government, the Regimen Custodia Terra. They controlled every facet of life from population numbers and education to ideologies and individual vocations. Considering all life equal in value regardless of species, but considering humans akin to parasites, they had corralled people into cities and forbade entry into the Fully Protected Nature Preserves.

The urgency I felt for my real mission made playing this 3D game seem childish. Pointless. I needed to understand the message *My Friend* had for me then get to work in the real world.

A folded piece of paper, my next clue, sat wedged between branches and almost within my reach.

A swish of grass warned me that someone approached. It had to be my yellow-eyed opponent, a kid who had been dogging my steps through every level of the game. I didn't know the kid in real life, but the cocky attitude he had every time we crossed paths irritated me. I wished I'd played privately instead of entering an online game room. Computer-generated characters could be wicked and annoying, too, but at least they weren't real. Someday I might actually run into this kid.

Clutching an overhead branch, I forced myself up the final distance. My heart pounded against my ribs. The dark second-story windows of a nearby shop came into view. My fingertips brushed the edge of the note. I tried snatching it but found resistance.

"Let it go, shrew." My opponent's voice grated like sandpaper. "It's mine."

~~~

A short hike later, I stood before a narrow three-story brick house trying to catch my breath. The sun had edged closer to the horizon but still provided ample light. A breeze kicked up and cooled my sweaty neck. The smell, spring flowers and dead fish, made me gag. Light showed in one of the two windows on the second level, but the first level had a single dark multi-pane window with white shutters. I wished I could peek inside and get a clue as to why I was here, but wooden interior blinds blocked my view.

I slid the note out of my skirt pocket and unfolded it, wanting to confirm that I had read everything there was to read and wishing that I could figure out the rest of the message. I reread the curly handwriting. *Go to the Ross house on Arch Street. It is imperative that you . . .*

Yellow Eyes, winner of the other half of the note, would know what imperative deed I was supposed to do here. I hoped he hadn't followed me. I needed the points to complete this level. If I logged out and started over, I might be able to avoid him, but I didn't want to waste more time.

"*This* feels like a waste of time," I shouted to *My Friend*.

All is not as it seems. Do not lose sight of your goal. Amusement came with his message, something bordering on laughter.

"I don't even know what my goal is." I jerked my hand up and waved the ripped note. "What am I supposed to say or do here?"

After a moment without a response, I took a deep breath and lifted my fist to the white wooden door.

Voices came from inside the house, muffled and feminine.

I reached up to fix my hair and found the knot had fallen out and my auburn locks hung freely down my back. Using both hands, I stuffed my hair into my white cap so I could make a decent impression. Was I even supposed to make contact with the occupant of the house? Maybe my mission was to spy.

I glanced up at my points, the glowing numbers hovering above my head. I had noticed a slight increase when I reached the house, but now they remained constant.

As I tucked in the last curl, the door creaked open and my points ticked up. A woman older than me but still in her early twenties with ruddy cheeks, a narrow nose, and big, beautiful eyes, stood before me. Dark hair peeked out from a white cap, one similar to mine. She wore a yellow patterned top and a full dark skirt, and she held an apron.

"I am sorry," she said, "but the shop is closed for the day, and we were on our way out." She tossed the apron onto a cluttered table just inside the door.

"Um." No other words came to mind. Did I need to see her? Did I have a message for her? Did she have something for me?

Giggles, footfalls, and other feminine voices came from inside. Was she even the owner of the shop?

"I-I'm looking for, I mean, I need to speak with . . . Are you the owner of the shop?"

She smiled, her big avatar eyes twinkling in the light from a lantern inside. Then she gave me a studied glance, probably noticing the dirt smears on my skirt that I had gotten earlier while in a fight.

"Yes, I am," she said. "I am Miss Ross. Did you need work done or have you a message for me?"

"Um, actually . . ." I tried to look friendly, but I could feel my eyes opening wide and my eyebrows lifting. My avatar's eyes must've looked huger than huge. Should I have a message for her? The goal of this phase of the game was to energize the movement. How could that be accomplished? I had to think. I needed time.

"May I come in?"

Miss Ross glanced over her shoulder at the girls inside, I presumed. They had all quieted down. She peered over my shoulder for a moment, seeming to scan the street. Then her gaze returned to me and she swung the door open wide. "Why, of course. Do come in."

She scooted back, giving me room to step inside, and closed the door behind me. My attention drifted to a cluttered worktable in the middle of the room. Scissors, spools of thread, a yardstick, a ceramic jar of pencils and other strange instruments, and folded fabrics with loose threads showed this to be some kind of sewing shop. Checkered, striped and flowered fabrics in greens, off-whites, and reds hung from posts on one wall. Neat shelves with bolts of fabric, brown packages, and spools of ribbon hung on another wall. A third wall displayed three different styles of curtains on either side of a paneled fireplace. Baskets of fabrics here, piles of cushions there . . . All of it made for too much color for so little a room.

"Prudence." Miss Ross faced an open doorway next to a window on the far side of the room. Three young women stood there staring, each of them holding a brown package tied with twine. "Be so kind as to bring us tea." Miss Ross waved her hand sideways, as if indicating for all the girls to go with Prudence.

"Yes, Miss Ross." Prudence, the tallest of the three, turned and stepped into the next room.

Once the girls moved from view, Miss Ross whispered, "Did someone send you?"

"Yes," I blurted out without thinking. Maybe Miss Ross was expecting me.

"Who?"

"Uh . . ." I couldn't answer her, not without knowing if she was a Patriot or Loyalist. "I can't say."

"You can't say?" Her big eyes narrowed with suspicion. Again, she glanced at my soiled skirt. "Are you in trouble?"

I wiped a dirt smear on the skirt but it accomplished nothing. Avatars did not always respond in predictable ways. "No, I'm fine."

"Are you here for a delivery?" She made a sideways glance at the doorway where the girls had stood.

"Um . . ." That was a good possibility. The girls had each held a brown package and they were on their way out, as Miss Ross had said. Maybe it wasn't safe and I was here to make the delivery for them. Or maybe I was here to intercept the delivery. I wish I knew which side she was on. Maybe if I knew more about her . . .

"Is your husband here?" I said.

"My husband?" The color flickered in her big eyes. She gave a sad smile and averted her gaze. "I am a widow."

"Oh, I'm sorry."

"We began this business together." Her eyes now held a strange look as if she saw things present and past, and her gaze flitted around the shop. "We met as apprentices to the same upholsterer. I was twenty-one when we married." Her face fell. "Then the unrest began, and John . . ." She gave me a fleeting glance. ". . . my late husband, was a member of the Pennsylvania militia. He died in a gunpowder explosion."

"Gosh, I'm sorry." Okay, he was with the militia. Most likely, we were on the same side.

"May I enquire? Was it your husband who sent you?"

"My husband?" Heat slid up my neck and to my cheeks. Dedrick Ryder's face popped into my mind. *We stood alone in a dimly lit hallway. He had stopped me on my way to the Mosheh. "Don't make promises to them," he had said, his brown eyes peering into the depths of my being. "Make promises to me."*

I shook my head a little too vigorously. "No, I'm not married. I don't plan to be. Not for a while, anyways." My tone and choice of words made me sound defensive. I had no reason to feel this way. I only needed to figure out my mission.

"Well, once the right man comes along . . ." Miss Ross smiled. ". . . your plans will change. You can start a family. John and I never had children, and I came from a big family. Fifteen children—"

"About the delivery," I said, taking a step toward the doorway through which the girls had disappeared. I glimpsed a shadow moving. Someone whispered. Another giggled. "What is it? What am I to deliver?"

"Oh, well . . ." Miss Ross paused. "I have curtains and cushioned chairs that need delivered to two separate addresses, both a good distance away, but I . . . I'm sorry. I didn't get your name."

"Oh, it's Liberty. I mean, no, my name is Amity." I couldn't get used to my avatar's name. It showed above me, above the points, but characters rarely asked for it.

"Amity." She appeared thoughtful for a moment. "What are you here to deliver?"

"Uh . . ."

A knock sounded on the door and I jumped. My points climbed like crazy. A smile stretched across my face. This was it, the reason for my visit.

I held my breath as Miss Ross swung open the door.

Three men in their forties stood outside mumbling warm greetings to Miss Ross. Like the rest of the men in this level of the game, they wore stockings and pants that came to the knee. But these men also wore military coats with shiny gold buttons.

Miss Ross stepped aside and let them in.

"Betsy, I am glad we caught you at home," said a man with an oval, boyish face.

"Yes, you almost missed me. If not for Amity here . . ." Betsy Ross made a sweeping gesture, drawing everyone's attention to me.

I attempted a curtsey, bumped the cluttered worktable, and sent the yardstick clattering to the floor.

The man with the boyish face chuckled, but the tallest of the men, a man with a dignified demeanor, peered at me through narrowed eyes as if he didn't trust me.

I gasped, recognizing him. He was the commander-in-chief of the Continental Army. We had met by the Delaware River in another game. The same game, really, but at a different point in history. I had since started the game over and hadn't reached that point yet, so George Washington wouldn't know me.

"You must be the messenger," the third man said. He had a double chin and hard eyes, but his smirking mouth made him seem friendly. He stuck out his hand, palm up. "Robert Morris at your service."

I grabbed his hand, ready to shake it, but he yanked my hand to his mouth and kissed it.

"And I am Colonel George Ross," said the man with the oval face, "Uncle to Betsy's late husband and part of this committee."

"She is one of ours?" George Washington said, still eyeing me. I understood his hesitation to trust me. One never knew friend from foe in this game.

"Yes," Robert said. "She was sent ahead to ensure we would find Miss Ross at home."

"Very good." George Washington gave me a dignified nod and the hint of a smile. "Thank you for your service, Miss . . ."

"Amity," I said, though I knew he wanted my last name. I smiled, glad to have discovered my mission—keep Miss Ross at her shop—and gladder to know that I accomplished it.

"Won't you come to the parlor?" Betsy said to the men just as Prudence appeared in the doorway with a serving tray. "We shall require more tea and cups."

Prudence mumbled something and slipped from view.

I followed the men into the parlor, another small room that barely accommodated us. A circular table with three chairs stood before a dark, tile-framed fireplace. Elegant curtains partially covered the three windows in the room, leaving glimpses of a blue gray evening and shadowy trees.

Betsy and I drew the curtains closed while Washington slung a leather satchel onto the table and seated himself. The other two men remained standing, Robert by the fireplace and Colonel Ross by a large walnut chest.

"We are a committee of Congress, appointed to prepare a flag for the United States." George Washington spread several sheets of paper on the table. Betsy stood beside him and studied them. Washington tapped one of the papers. "I created several drawings, but I lean toward this one."

"Hmm." With lips pressed together and concentration in her eyes, Betsy ran a finger over the lines of the drawing.

"It's a rough design," Washington said. "The thirteen stripes represent the thirteen colonies and are to be red and white."

Betsy's gaze snapped to him. "Like the Grand Union flag?"

"Well, yes, but there is a difference." He pointed to a circle of stars in a rectangle in the top left corner of the drawing. "You see here . . . We do not have the symbol for Great Britain but rather a circle of thirteen stars representing the union of the colonies. The circle shows that all colonies are equal. They will be white in a blue field, which will represent a new constellation."

"Here, here," Colonel George Ross said. "We no longer accept Britain's rule. We shall rule ourselves."

"Red stripes to represent our mother country," Washington said, locking onto Betsy's gaze. "White stripes to show we have separated from her. The white stripes shall go down to posterity representing liberty."

I sucked in a breath at a sudden memory. Everyone looked at me, making me feel the need to explain. "I've seen a flag like this before, only I think it had more stars." I'd found it in the bunker we discovered in the outskirts of Aldonia.

That day had changed my life. I had realized there was more to life than I'd ever imagined and that life had once been very different. People once lived free. And it could be that way again.

"You've seen this pattern?" Washington's eyebrows drew together.

My points flashed and clicked down. I had said something wrong. I needed to fix it.

"Um, no. Never mind me." I smiled, folded my arms across my chest, and backed up, bumping the walnut chest. My points stopped their freefall. Everyone still stared. "It-it was a dream, I think, but it felt like a very significant dream." My answer worked. My points crept up.

Gaining confidence, I stepped forward. Something about this meeting would give me the "wisdom" *My Friend* had promised. "Maybe one of you can explain to me the importance of a flag."

Washington and Robert exchanged glances. I just realized that their coats matched. They both wore blue while Colonel George Ross wore dark green.

Washington straightened. "People need a symbol they can rally behind." His expression showed his conviction. "Every detail, shape, and color of our flag will have meaning. Red for valor, white for purity, and blue for loyalty. This flag, our American flag, will stand as a symbol of freedom and justice."

He faced Betsy. "Do you think, Miss Ross, that you can make this?"

"Well, sirs . . ." Betsy glanced from one man to the other, a look of anxiety washing over her. The look ebbed to one of confidence. She must've felt the weight of this task: sewing the flag of a new nation.

Standing taller, she articulated her answer. "I do not know, but I can try. I've never made a flag before, but with this pattern, I do not doubt my ability to do it." Quote marks glowed above her, showing that her words came right out of history. The historical Betsy Ross had given just this answer.

The men smiled, exhaled, and exchanged looks of satisfaction.

"I have one question, though," Betsy said. "How attached are you to the six-pointed star?"

"Hey, Liberty."

Goosebumps popped out on my arms at the sound of my real name. I glanced at the doorway. The three girls stood there, two of them holding trays, but none of them appeared to have called me. One glanced over her shoulder as if wondering what I looked at.

"Hey," came the voice again.

Then I felt a whack on my arm and realized who called me.

"Hold on." I raised my hand in the air, drawing everyone's gaze, and tapped the virtual "pause" button overhead. George Washington, Betsy Ross, and all the others froze in place, confused expressions on their faces. I peeled the 3D helmet from my head and blinked as my eyes adjusted to the dark game room and the angry, tiger-eyes of Alix.

"I should've guessed you'd be in here." She snatched the helmet from me, stomped across the mat, and fidgeted with the control panel on the wall.

My heart raced, disturbed by the sudden transition from 1776 to today. I believed I had won the level and I needed to analyze the ideas. Washington thought a new flag would motivate the colonists and make them ready to fight for freedom. How could that work today?

"What's with the obsession?" Alix strutted up to me and folded her sinewy arms.

"I'm not obsessed." I peeled motion sensor pads from my wrists, ankles, and knees. "I'm trying to get ideas, answers. I can't help but think that the solutions for today can be found in our history."

"Yeah, well, your solution for today is to get your tail to the Mosheh meeting."

"The meeting? Oh." I glanced at the time display on my TekBand. The meeting was to have begun ten minutes ago. "Who's gonna be there?"

She smirked, as if reading my mind, as if fully aware that I had been avoiding Dedrick for the past three months. "Everyone."

2

Alix walked ahead of me, her lanky arms swinging in time with her strides. We neared the ramp that led to the Mosheh Control Center. Dressed in black from head to toe, Alix appeared as a silhouette before the light that came from the lower level. I assumed she was leading the way to the meeting room, but she passed the ramp.

"Where's the meeting?" I doubled my steps to walk beside her.

She turned her angular face toward me, her tiger-eyes almost glowing. "Dining hall. Meeting room's too small for today's gathering." A smile slithered across her face and disappeared. "Everyone's here."

Did Alix know why I'd been avoiding Dedrick? Who would've told her? Dedrick? *No way*. She must've had other reasons for the sneaky smile.

"Do you know what the meeting is about?" I said. The elders had held private meetings day after day all winter long. Occasionally, they invited one person or another. No one I had spoken with knew what they discussed. I got the impression that something big, something transformational was about to happen.

"Not exactly."

"So . . . sort of?"

She smiled and lengthened her stride, passing me.

Voices and a buttery-yellow light traveled over the makeshift half walls that separated the dining hall from the rest of the darkness on this level of the converted parking garage.

As we approached, a layer of sweat formed on my palms and my inner chains started slipping off their sprockets.

Dedrick would be here.

Working in Gardenhall and studying the history of America in Bot's 3D game, I had avoided crossing paths with him for the past three months. My favorite pastime had been working on false walls and hidden doors in the tunnels. Manual labor fulfilled an inner need to work with

11

my hands and make things come together, but I couldn't shake the feeling I would run into Dedrick, who practically lived in the tunnels. I never did, so I assumed he made an effort to avoid me, too.

Granted, I couldn't avoid him forever, but I wasn't ready to see him yet. I didn't know how he'd handled my rejection. I hadn't wanted to hurt him. I hadn't really wanted to say *no* to his marriage proposal, but I had work to do. I couldn't say *yes*.

Alix, a few steps ahead of me, darted into the dining hall.

People crowded together at long bench tables, the flickering light of thick candles dancing on their arms and faces. A few young adults at one table greeted Alix then scooted closer together to make room for her. Several people stood leaning against the half walls.

Not sure where to sit or stand, I scanned the room for a colony boy with Aldonian hair, dark with blond tips. He had colored it as part of his disguise many months ago, back when he'd rescued me from the Breeder Facility.

My gaze passed over him but then doubled back.

My inner chains slipped again, and I sucked in a breath to compensate.

Dedrick looked different. His hair, super short and jagged on top, hadn't a trace of blond. He wore camouflage pants and a brown leather jacket with a crudely mended tear in one sleeve. Sitting hunched on the half wall, his arms on his thighs, he spoke with Fulton.

Neither of them looked my way, so I scooted between tables on the opposite side of the dining hall.

"Liberty." Bolcan's voice boomed, quieting the chatter of those nearby. He rose from a row of tables closer to the front. Bolcan, a golden-haired hunk of a man, had his sights set on me.

"Hey." I gave him a little wave as I found a place along the wall. My gaze snapped to the opposite side of the room, to Dedrick whose eyes had turned to me.

Bolcan lumbered up to me and folded his arms across his bulging chest. He wore an off-white shirt made of a homespun cloth. A colonist had probably given it to him. "You're late. The elders have been waiting on you."

"Sorry. I lost track of time."

The room had quieted, but he blocked my view of the front, so I couldn't see why.

"Everyone is here, I do believe." Elder Lukman's voice came through speakers that hung above the netting that served as a ceiling.

"Come." Bolcan jerked his head to one side, indicating for me to follow.

"No, I'm fine here." I leaned my backside against the short wall to demonstrate my satisfaction with the location.

Bolcan's mouth curled up on one side, and his eyes flickered with humor. Then he unfolded his arms and took my hand, his grip warm and firm.

"So we will begin," Elder Lukman said.

I imagined Dedrick was still watching me, but I didn't want to look. Elder Lukman may have been watching me, too, wishing I'd sit down. Not wanting to draw more attention, I let Bolcan lead me to his table. We sat squeezed between others on a bench seat, our backs to the table so we could face the front of the room.

Peering past the heads of people sitting in front of me, I was able to glimpse the elders. Elders Lukman, Rayna, and Dean sat at a long table, front and center, directly before the counter that separated the kitchen from the dining hall. Screens hanging above them on either side showed Mosheh members at remote locations.

"Our colonists have a ritual." Elder Lukman spoke with a rough old voice that soothed and promised wisdom. "When our young people approach the age of adulthood, they have the opportunity to sneak into Aldonia and experience the world of the Regimen. They come in groups. They explore." He glanced at a few people in the front. "I daresay they have fun."

A few chuckles came from around the room, from young and old.

Elder Lukman, grinning behind his white beard, waited for silence. "Most return to the colonies, but a few feel compelled to remain, to consecrate themselves for the work of the Mosheh. Fewer still have made lifelong commitments. Those who have been rescued from Aldonia have also been given the choice. Almost half of them choose to enter colony life, while the other half—you—remain here with us."

Bolcan's chest rose and pride showed in the tilt of his head.

I felt good, too, though I had yet to make my promises. The last time I had spoken with the elders, I had made known my desire to join. I wanted to take the vows and dedicate the next four years of my life, if not more, to working with them. They'd told me to wait. Could today be the day?

"You," Elder Lukman said, "you are the Mosheh. Whether you work hidden in our underground network or venture into the city, you are the rescuers. You work to make the world a better place, for one person here, one person there."

Elder Rayna nodded and glanced from face to face, showing her appreciation to individual members. Elder Dean, who had been sitting with his head down, swiveled his wheelchair to face the monitor nearest him. He lifted a fist and gave a nod to recognize the remote members. A camera, I assumed, picked up the gesture.

"The mission of the Mosheh," Elder Lukman said, "since its founding, has been to rescue individuals who are unable to conform to the ways of Aldonia, who are rejected by the Regimen Custodia Terra. We have done well, but we have not done enough. Recently, we have been convicted. Events and signs have led us to believe that we are called to something more. Today, our mission changes."

Gasps and indistinct speech arose on all sides. People turned to one another with whispered questions.

The dream that had haunted me last fall rushed in vivid color to my mind. *Dark clouds rolled over a vast stretch of land. An emaciated figure flung tares to the wind and watched them take root. Soon, weeds overran everything. Then another figure came with tiny wheat seeds. He tossed them onto the few bare patches of soil he could find, desperate to have them take root. His desperation became mine, and I had awoken from the dream covered in sweat.*

"Fear not, friends," Elder Dean said, rubbing his smooth, bald head. His hand dropped to the table, and his expression grew hard. "We will not abandon Aldonians in need, individuals in critical situations."

Elder Lukman mumbled something to Elder Rayna. Elder Rayna replied to him and turned to face us. Candlelight played on her dark-chocolate skin. "We plan to integrate many of our members back into Aldonia."

The gasps and chatter swelled, filling the room. I said nothing, wanting more of an explanation.

"What?" Bolcan's leg bumped mine as he stood. "How can we help anyone if we're out in the open? We'll be as helpless as babies in a Breeder Facility, back to living under the control of the Regimen without freedom."

"We've spent the past several months working out the details," Elder Rayna said, her sonorous voice drowning the last few mumbled comments. "And many of you have been training over the winter. This may seem like a daunting task, but we know you are ready. And we are ready. We need those who know freedom and truth to plant seeds. You are called to bring the wheat that must conquer the weeds. You are called to *be* the wheat."

I jerked back then sat stunned. Last fall, I had told them my dream, sensing it held importance for others besides myself. Elder Dean, an Interpreter of Dreams, had said, "This dream is meant for us. We are not to remain separated from Aldonians. We are to come out of hiding and live among them." Was this how they planned to do it?

"Not me." Bolcan folded his arms over his chest and dropped down to the bench, bumping me again. "I'm not going back in. They know me. I'll be back in Re-Ed."

We exchanged glances. I didn't want to go back either. Sneaking in and rescuing a person was one thing. Living there again? Being watched day and night? Having to guard every action and even your tongue? No thanks.

"No one will force you," Elder Rayna said. "That is not our way. This is voluntary only. We have created new identities and have the ability to replace the records connected to your individual retina patterns. Your appearance will be altered, your hair and eye color. You will select an identity, complete with a past and a vocation."

"You're not going to pick the vocation for us based on our skills?" Alix said, smirking. For the first time, I wondered what vocation the Regimen had given her before the Mosheh had rescued her from Aldonia. I could picture her with the Unity Troopers.

"We are not like the Regimen," Elder Lukman said. "You always have a choice with us. But keep in mind, Aldonians need us. You. Me." For a moment, I imagined that he planned to volunteer, but I erased the thought from my mind. The elderly would not last long above, especially if they needed medical care.

"Those who feel called," Elder Rayna said, "will slip back into Aldonia within a few days, into a new life."

"I like it." Camilla sat at the table nearest Dedrick, though I hadn't noticed her until now. Did colonists always sit together? Had she and Dedrick grown close over the winter?

"How do we plant seeds?" she said.

Elder Rayna tilted her chin, admiration written on her face. "You will seed the words of truth and freedom through literature and messages and the example of your lives. Bot's 3D game has spread across the continent, but not everyone in Aldonia has experienced it. Do your part to create interest in it. The more people learn about the values of the past, the more they will long for it today."

I found myself nodding in agreement. She worded it well. That was exactly why I spent so much time in Bot's game. Which reminded me . . . I needed to understand the importance of the flag and the importance of having a symbol. Maybe we needed something like that today.

Right then, I made up my mind. Others could volunteer to go back in, but not me. I would work behind the scenes. I would use my time to learn our history. Maybe I'd find answers for everyone. Answers for Aldonia.

Just then, my vision clouded over and a tingling sensation overwhelmed me, *My Friend* making himself known. Though I did not like when He spoke with me in public, I had no choice but to close my eyes and attend Him. Sitting still, I tried to focus on the message.

No words came, but I got the impression I had overlooked something. Then a face appeared in my mind, blurry but coming into focus. A woman with dark hair. No, not a woman. An avatar from the 3-D games. Ruddy cheeks, a narrow nose, and big, beautiful eyes. The Betsy Ross avatar hovered in my mind!

Disgusted, I huffed and opened my eyes. I had obviously been spending too much time in the game. Perhaps it hampered my ability to hear the voice that I needed for guidance, the voice of *My Friend*.

"You okay?" Bolcan stared with golden eyes that pierced through me, making me feel exposed.

"I'm fine." I shifted to reduce the amount of contact my arm and leg made with his, then faced forward.

Elder Dean had been speaking to a captivated audience. I wished I hadn't missed what he said. He was a man of few, carefully-chosen words. "A big part of this," he said, "will involve secret assemblies and talks."

Silence followed the comment, all eyes locked on the baldheaded man in the wheelchair, all minds trying to decipher the importance of his words.

Someone finally spoke. "What secret talks?"

Elder Dean grinned. "Ours is not the only hidden community in Aldonia. We do not pursue this mission alone. In fact, I believe we play a very little part."

Another moment of silence had me, and probably everyone else, wondering if he had actually answered the question.

"What talks?" I said.

"Others in Aldonia have taken on that initiative," he said, again leaving the question unanswered.

I turned to see Dedrick's reaction. Maybe he knew more.

Dedrick's gaze flitted to mine. He shifted, looking uncomfortable, then scooted off the half wall. I couldn't imagine how, but the talks had something to do with him.

"We will provide the time and location of the talks," Elder Rayna said. "You need only give the invitations."

"I can do that," someone said.

"Meeting in public," I blurted out, "knowing the Regimen watches everything . . . it sounds risky." I couldn't count how many times people had told me to watch what I was saying when I lived openly in Aldonia. The Regimen listened through the mandatory flexi-phones and watched through surveillance cameras.

"Yes, it is risky," Elder Lukman said. "The folks at the Citizen Safety Station will continue to search for rebels, for those with ideologies that do not conform to theirs. You will risk very much. But we will always have our eyes on you, too. We will protect you."

While I believed in his goodwill, his answer did not comfort me.

"I hope us brown-eyed colonists aren't left out of this game," Camilla said. "I mean, I don't look too Aldonian, but I want in." Not all, but most of the colonists had brown eyes, a color unheard of in Aldonia. She would stand out.

A few kids near her laughed. Everyone knew Camilla's love of risk taking.

"We can take care of that," said a kid at a table in the front of the dining hall. He sat before a handheld computer, facing us. He leaned forward and turned to the elders. "We ready to sign people up?"

I glanced to where Dedrick had been standing.

He was gone.

3

The beam of the hands-free flashlight secured to Dedrick Ryder's belt plowed through the darkness. Shadows stretched and twisted, swallowing up the tunnel behind him. His footfalls made little sound on the concrete as he strode toward his destination. Fulton had said someone came through one of the warehouse entry points. Probably another false alarm.

Dedrick checked the time on his TekBand. He had two hours to investigate the entry points before he had to get to the location of the secret assembly, an abandoned alley outside a Gray Zone. He'd have just enough time. Andy, his younger brother, had said he didn't need to worry, didn't have to show up every time Andy sneaked out of the old courthouse. How could he help but worry? Andy was just a kid, too young to be involving himself in the fate of Aldonia. Andy should be with Mom and—

Something in the distance clanked.

Dedrick halted, flicked the light off, and flattened himself against a cold brick wall. Unsure as to which direction the sound came from, he peered into the darkness on either side. He forced himself to breathe slower so he could detect noises other than his breaths and heartbeats.

A gust of cool air carried a damp, earthy odor to his nose. Water dripped somewhere. Not near. He caught the faintest scraping sound, probably rats scurrying to a sewer pipe. Nothing else.

He turned the flashlight on and resumed walking, picking up his pace. He'd been searching for signs of an intruder for the past three months or so, ever since video surveillance picked up that woman in their tunnels. Liberty had said her name was Silver.

Liberty.

Dedrick ran a hand through his hair, and his thoughts locked up for a second or two. Liberty's face hovered in his mind like the afterimage caused from glimpsing a bright light. She had looked at him twice in the dining hall . . . while she sat next to Bolcan.

Footsteps sounded in the tunnel behind him, a faint sound. Getting louder. Then a man called, "Hey, wait up."

Dedrick cringed. *Bolcan.* He'd seen enough of Bolcan for one day.

Now the tunnel amplified Bolcan's footfalls. Dedrick imagined a lion closing in on its prey. A few seconds later, a bulky figure appeared in Dedrick's peripheral vision.

"You shot out of there in a hurry," Bolcan said.

"Yeah, so?" Dedrick remained face forward.

"Aren't you signing up?"

Dedrick spared a glance.

Bolcan grinned. "Me neither. I cherish my freedom too much to sacrifice it for the cause." Under a long denim jacket, he wore one of the shirts made by the colonists, a rough off-white thing that Dedrick's mother could have made. It was not his typical sleek Aldonian style. What was he trying to prove?

"I think the elders are making a mistake," Dedrick said, "and I want no part of it. This will be the downfall of the Mosheh."

"Your service has ended, hasn't it? If you're that worried, why you still hanging around? You could be living it up out in a colony."

The sly tone got Dedrick's hackles up. "Why are you hanging around, around me? I've been sent to check out a couple of access points."

"Me, too. Apparently, they don't want you going alone."

"I always go alone." No one knew the tunnels the way he did. He knew the shortest route to get anywhere. He could walk them blind.

"They've found more images, more signs of an intruder. Maybe they're worried you'll run into Silver."

"Like I can't handle her?" He had never faced an opponent he couldn't handle. Well, except for Bolcan. Bolcan's massive size, skill, and savage qualities gave him the edge.

"Maybe you can't."

"I took care of her before, and she wasn't alone. It was me against two." It was the day he'd first rescued Liberty from Sid, a boy who'd been obsessed with her. No man, no woman of any size could've kept Dedrick from protecting Liberty. "I'm sure I'll have no problem if I meet up with her down here."

"Apparently, the elders don't share your confidence. That's why they told me to go with you. And gave me a taser." He tapped his jacket even though the taser was not visible.

Dedrick let the insult roll off him and gave Bolcan a studied glance. "Do you know Silver?"

"Yeah. We were in the same secondary, for a few months anyways."

"Before you got sent to Re-Ed?" He regretted his comment as the words left his mouth. Bolcan had always seemed uncomfortable with the subject, never wanted to talk about it. The place must have really jacked him up. "I'm sorry I mentioned that place."

"Right. Well, one day I'm gonna blow that hellhole to bits." He clenched a fist. "But that's not why. She's four years older than me, so she transitioned out a few months after I transitioned in."

"Oh, got it."

"A few months were long enough to learn what she's capable of. She spent all her spare time lifting or picking fights. The girl is driven."

"She fight you?"

He gave a confident nod and flexed his deltoids. "I can handle her."

Dedrick wanted to ask who'd won but decided against it.

They walked to the sound of their footfalls for a whole minute while they neared their turn off, an intersecting tunnel with walls that curved overhead.

"You should start training someone," Bolcan said. "Make sure one or two kids know their way around the tunnels like you do. I mean, if you're really done with your service to the Mosheh." He turned to stare, but Dedrick pretended not to notice. "Although . . . I think you're hanging around for a particular reason. And I think you'll stick around as long as she does."

Dedrick's head turned on its own, his gaze snapping to Bolcan and catching his snide grin.

"You think no one knows?" Bolcan said. "What I can't figure out is why you've been avoiding her. Not that I mind. She's been hanging out with me a lot. In fact, I'd say we—"

"No, she hasn't." Dedrick regretted replying, regretted falling for Bolcan's bait. He did not intend to share his feelings for her with anyone. It was bad enough Miriam knew. Fortunately, she wasn't around to bother him about it.

"Sure she has," Bolcan said. "Maybe it's because we're both Aldonian and we both like to rescue people and we both suffered through . . . well, you know, Re-Ed." His eyes flickered as he said the word. "But we really hit it off. She's gone on two rescues with me, and I've joined her in the training room I don't know how many times. We even eat together."

"Everyone eats together or you get stuck with scrapings."

"Not you. Where do you go when you're avoiding her?"

A cool sweat broke out on Dedrick's chest. He felt the urge to scrap with Bolcan, but he hadn't a good reason to do it. Neither of them had actually mentioned Liberty's name. He needed to play it cool. "Who are you even talking about?"

Bolcan laughed. "I saw you a few months ago, the day after Liberty escaped Re-Ed. You were talking to her in a dark hallway, standing real close, probably thinking no one saw . . ."

Dedrick felt as though he'd just walked out of his clothes and stepped in his undershorts into a Mosheh meeting. Who else had seen? What had they seen? Had Bolcan seen the kiss? Had he heard anything? Had he heard Dedrick propose?

"What were you guys talking about? It seemed personal."

Dedrick bit back the defensive words that wanted to fly from his mouth and took a second to formulate a controlled reply. "I don't remember, exactly." The word "exactly" was meant to keep it from being a lie, but he did remember *exactly*, word for word, emotion by emotion. Yeah, he had just lied. "We were all pretty worried about her, weren't we?" That was true. "I was just checking on her, making sure she was okay." Not trusting himself to speak more about her, he tried to think of something else to talk about.

"I don't buy it. It looked deep to me. I think you were telling her—"

"So . . . has anyone heard from Miriam?" It was a reasonable thing to talk about. When the Torva had decided to remain with the Rivergrove Colony, Miriam had chosen to remain with them. That was over three months ago.

Bolcan laughed. "That was an abrupt change in topic."

"She coming back anytime soon?" Dedrick cemented himself to the subject. They were not saying another word about Liberty. "The Torva may have done the colonists a favor, but they're still wild men. There's no reason we should trust them."

"I heard a rumor the Torva were on the move."

"Yeah?" Dedrick exhaled, relieved that Bolcan stuck with the new subject. "That's good. It's spring. They can wander back to their own lands. I suppose Miriam will be returning to us, then."

"I get the feeling you have a history with these wild—"

The hair on the back of Dedrick's neck stood up an instant before he heard it.

From behind them came the mechanical chink-clack of a shotgun being racked.

Dedrick and Bolcan froze. Dedrick's hand snapped to the Beretta in the holster under his jacket.

"Uh uh uh," came a woman's taunting voice from several yards back. *Silver*. She had found access not only to Aldonia's tunnels but also to the ones known to the Mosheh alone. "Hands up and clasped behind your head, boys."

Dedrick's mind flipped through a speedy assessment of the situation. Guns were illegal in Aldonia, and the Regimen only used nonlethal weapons. Would she have access to ammunition? Could she be bluffing?

"Better listen to her," Bolcan said, exchanging glances with Dedrick and raising his hands. The posture of surrender did not look natural to him.

Seeing no alternative, Dedrick released his grip on the pistol and withdrew his hand from his jacket. He did as told and clasped his hands behind his head.

"Don't do anything stupid. I'm coming for your guns." The sound of her voice showed that she approached Dedrick first. She came up behind him and patted both sides of his jacket. "Ease the gun out, set it on the ground, and kick it aside," she said, stepping back.

Dedrick obeyed, kicking his pistol toward the wall of the tunnel rather than toward her.

"You too," she said to Bolcan.

"I ain't got no gun," Bolcan said, turning his head to face her or maybe to communicate to Dedrick. He did have a gun. He had the taser. And he must've known she would check.

"Face forward," she spat. "You think I'm gonna believe that?"

Taking Bolcan's lie as a signal, Dedrick readied himself. He glimpsed Silver in his peripheral vision as she came up behind Bolcan.

Like a lion pouncing on prey, Bolcan twisted around and sprang into action.

Dedrick had spun around, too, the beam of the flashlight on his belt finding the muscular woman with the silver mane of hair.

Bolcan's left elbow cracked against the shotgun Silver foolishly held with one hand. His right fist made contact with her chin.

Dedrick swung a leg out. His boot finished the job of disarming her, sending a Mossberg tactical shotgun clattering to the ground.

At the impact of Bolcan's punch, Silver's head jerked to one side. Her hand shot up and landed on Bolcan's shoulder. Then she shoved, forcing him off balance.

As Bolcan fell, he latched onto her other arm.

Unable to resist the inertia, she went down with him.

They landed together, Bolcan throwing an arm out to protect his face from the ground, Silver smacking down on her side. Bolcan pushed his torso up and wrestled to get hold of her arms, probably wanting to pin her. She wrapped her legs around one of his legs and thrust her shoulder up as if to sweep him into an inferior position. Appearing equal in strength and ability, they struggled against each other, each grappling for the advantage.

Dedrick stepped back. Bolcan would win this. He wouldn't want Dedrick to cut in.

The shotgun lay at a distance, too far for Silver to reach at the moment. Dedrick went to the wall to retrieve his pistol. If Bolcan didn't own this in a minute, Dedrick would end it.

The instant he turned his back, one of them grunted. An electrical clicking noise sounded. Then there came a thud.

Dedrick swiped his gun from the ground and spun around.

Metallic silver strands of hair, illuminated by the flashlight on his belt, swooshed toward his face. Then crack. Silver's head slammed into his cheekbone.

He reeled back and stumbled into the brick wall of the tunnel. Before he could regain his senses, Silver rammed the heel of her hand into his forehead and smacked his head against the wall.

The impact brought a flash of hot white, a jolt of pain, and blackness.

~~~

Cold. His cheek burned from icy cold. Dedrick blinked his eyes open and realized he lay prone, his cheek pressed to the gritty cement floor. His arms were bent behind him and restrained. Someone with hard hands was binding his wrists together with tape or something.

"I can't believe you don't remember me," Bolcan said, his voice coming from directly above Dedrick. Bolcan was binding his wrists?

"Why should I remember you?" Silver stood at a distance in the shadows. "I haven't given one thought to anyone from Secondary. Besides, four months to freedom from that place, my mind was somewhere else." She paused. "Him, I know."

Wanting to assess the situation, Dedrick lifted his head. Pain rushed into it. He laid his head back down on the cold cement. "What are you doing?" he muttered to Bolcan through clenched teeth. Why was Bolcan helping her? Was he not really Mosheh? Was he a mole? If so, for who? Not for the Regimen.

Bolcan leaned closer. "I'm doing whatever the girl with the gun tells me to do."

Dedrick forced himself past the pain to lift his head and glance over his shoulder. "I thought you had this."

Bolcan shrugged. "She got me with my taser."

"Good. You're awake." Silver stepped into the beam of a flashlight that lay on the ground. Her black and gray sneakers glowed and light reflected on the shotgun that dangled at her side, but her face remained hidden in darkness. "Tape your wrist to his, then make him sit up."

"What?" Bolcan said, incredulous.

"Just do it." She jerked the shotgun up and leveled it at Bolcan.

He huffed. There came the ripping sound of unrolling tape. Then he fidgeted with Dedrick's wrists.

"I love duct tape, don't you?" Silver paced. "There're a hundred and one things you can do with it."

Bolcan clasped one of Dedrick's bound hands and grabbed his bicep. "Roll over and I'll help you sit."

"I got it." Dedrick sat up with assistance anyway, the throbbing in his head making him wince. He rested with one leg stretched and the other bent, feeling uncomfortable in every way. He needed to generate a plan. Having his hands duct-taped behind his back and attached to Bolcan wasn't going to make it easy. Maybe Bolcan could grab Dedrick's pocketknife from his belt when Silver wasn't looking.

Bolcan sat beside Dedrick and rested his free hand on his raised knee. "Now what, Silver? What's your game?"

"My game?"

Dedrick turned a hard gaze to Silver, though he couldn't make out her face because of where she stood. "Yeah, what do you want from us?" The girl was dangerous. How much did she know about the Mosheh's underground network?

"I just wanna talk." She stepped into the beam from the flashlight and squatted, light finally falling on her face. Her black pupils expanded, making slivers of her strange silver irises. Scrapes covered her prominent chin and one cheek. Blood streaked her swollen lips.

"I've been exploring these tunnels ever since I learned about this place, whenever I get the chance, anyway." She motioned with the shotgun. "One day, I found a hidden door that led to more tunnels, these tunnels." She paused and studied Dedrick's eyes. "What's down here?"

"What do you think is down here? Tunnels and more tunnels, sewage and power lines."

"You," she said, glaring at Bolcan, "sit back to back."

Bolcan let his irritation show with a few choice cuss words as he scooted into position. "You gonna leave us like this?"

Setting the shotgun down, out of reach, she grabbed Bolcan's free hand and the duct tape, but her gaze remained on Dedrick. "You took the runaway teens down here. I know because I followed you." She gave the hint of a grin. "Where'd they go?"

"There's more than one Gray Zone in Aldonia." Dedrick hoped his answer would satisfy her. It was true and she knew it. "And there are more in Jensenville, and all across the country, for that matter." The Regimen Custodia Terra believed they controlled everyone, but people still found places they could go to avoid surveillance. Kids on the streets called them *Gray Zones*. Andy would be holding a meeting in a Gray Zone right about now, in an abandoned building near the old city center. And Dedrick could do nothing to see to his safety.

"So you took them to a different Gray Zone?" Having taped Bolcan's wrist to Dedrick's, Silver sliced the duct tape with a pocketknife and slid the roll onto a strap on her belt. "That's what you use the tunnels for?"

"It's better than traveling above. Surveillance is everywhere." Dedrick glanced at her wrist. The Citizen Safety Station listened to conversations through a person's flexi-phone. Fortunately, she didn't wear hers. But she did have the implant, and if a drone passed by for a read, it might pick her signal up.

His gaze latched onto the pocketknife in her hand. He spotted a name etched in the side. His name. It was his pocketknife! The one his father had given him when he was a boy. "Hey, that's mine." He leaned forward, accidentally tugging Bolcan's hands.

"Knock it off," Bolcan said, jerking his hands to one side.

Grabbing up the shotgun, Silver stood and stepped back. She slid the knife into a jacket pocket. "Last fall, when we ran into each other at the bunker, where did you come from, you and Liberty?"

"What?" Dedrick couldn't focus on her question. "Hey, that knife's kinda important to me." He leaned against Bolcan, thinking they could stand up together.

"Knock it off." Bolcan slammed his back into Dedrick's.

"You were outside the Boundary Fence, weren't you?" Silver said.

"Those fences are charged with electricity," Bolcan said.

"I found a way out," Silver said, her eyes still on Dedrick. "I think you were out there. So tell me what's out there."

Dedrick shook his head. He had nothing to say to her.

Bolcan laughed. "There's nothing out there. Why do you think they came back?"

Silver slinked forward and squatted by Dedrick again, closer this time. "I want answers. I want in. Whatever you got going on, I want in. If you don't let me in, I'll expose your secrets." She stood and left the way she came, with silent footfalls and trouble no doubt brewing in her mind.

"So, you got a knife or something?" Dedrick said to Bolcan.

"Yeah." Bolcan twisted his wrists, twisting Dedrick's, too. "Don't know how either of us can get to it. It's in a leg pocket."

4

Men shouted all around us, barking out commands, calling for help, cursing. A thick fog transformed moving figures into the things of nightmares, creepy humanoid blurs staggering through the night. A few meters away, an untended campfire blazed, one of several the general had told us to make in order to deceive the enemy. Smoke billowed from damp branches between realistic, mesmerizing flames.

I tightened my grip on the soldier at my side. He had a gunshot wound in his thigh, and his head rolled forward every few steps as if he kept dozing off. Devastated by our defeat, I struggled to keep my thoughts on the present moment. My mind refused to stay focused—a side-effect of Re-Education—and kept jumping back to my early days in Secondary.

"I can't believe she threw you out of class for suggesting there was a supreme creator." I sat with my legs stretched out before me, my back up against a cool wall in the deep end of a dry swimming pool. Afternoon sunlight streamed in through high windows, making trapezoidal shapes on the small square tiles of the pool floor.

"Yeah," Sarkin said, his head bobbing with his sarcastic attitude, "and if you noticed, no one seemed interested anyway. It's not like my ideas have ever influenced anyone. Nobody cares what I have to say." The empty pool amplified his voice even though he whispered.

"I care." My whisper traveled. I imagined it reaching the dark corners of the natatorium and bouncing off windows and doors, threatening to expose us.

Sarkin locked eyes with me for a long second, the sunlight behind him, shadows on his face. His pupils dilated, shrinking his irises to deep red rings. The color reminded me of the scarlet tanager, a bird that had almost gone extinct during the time of rampant logging, a time before the

Regimen Custodia Terra. They looked striking with his deep caramel skin and black hair.

"I can't believe you're skipping class," Sarkin finally said, his appreciation for having an accomplice evident in his tone.

I loved how he contemplated life independently of the ideologies pounded into us since Primary. He alone stood up to the teachers, voicing his own opinion. His ideas made me think, made me hope for more. I felt honored to be at his side.

I giggled. "Do you think anyone's noticed?"

He smiled then shrugged and lifted his right hand, displaying the fingerless makeshift foil glove I had made for him. "Do you think this'll really block a read of our implants?"

"Of course." I fidgeted with the glove on my hand, smoothing the edge at my wrist. "The RFID readers in the building can't communicate with the transponders in our hands, not through all this foil."

"How do *you* know how it works?"

"If you weren't so busy philosophizing, maybe you'd learn a thing or two in class." I gave him a look of challenge.

He didn't smile. "I don't want to learn what they're teaching. Why does it bother them that I have my own ideas?"

"They've got it all figured out. Why question them?" Keeping a straight face, I punched his arm.

He narrowed his eyes as if he took me seriously. Then he rammed his shoulder into mine, knocking me over. He laughed.

I laughed, less conscious of the sound now, and rammed back.

"I'm going to dig this thing out of my hand one day," he said, "and get away from here."

"You'll trigger the anti-tamper device. You'll lose your hand." We learned this in health class, each year getting more detailed information. Since the ID implant was vital to our society, scientists designed it to have an anti-tamper device that would discourage individuals from attempting to remove it. Tampering with it released a toxic chemical that would spread from your hand to your entire body. The only way to stop it would be to remove your hand.

"That's what they say," Sarkin said. "Maybe they're lying."

"Maybe, but what if—"

The creak of a door then the clack of high heels on the hard floor sounded above us.

I gasped. We exchanged wide-eyed glances then peered up to the top of the pool wall. We'd been made.

Sarkin had left Secondary soon after, a transfer no one ever explained. We assumed they sent him to Re-Education. They kept a closer eye on me from that day forward, so I gave up rebellious behavior and never skipped class again. Nonconforming thoughts and ideas I kept to myself. I lived without hope.

Without hope . . .

Still supporting my companion in the 3D game, I plodded forward.

This level of the game felt that way, too: hopeless. We'd made a mistake, not exploring the lay of the land. The British had found an unguarded path and came up behind us. They'd outnumbered us two to one, and they surrounded us on all sides. We'd had no choice but to retreat. My group had plowed through a mosquito-infested marsh. Surrender seemed inevitable.

"Let me rest." My companion slid his arm from my shoulders and doubled over.

"Almost there." I peered into the fog. I couldn't see our destination, the East River, but we had to be close.

Breathing hard and dripping with sweat, he shook his head. "No. Must rest."

"General Washington said we have to reach the river before the first light of day." I glanced back the way we came. The campfires appeared little, like points of light. The British must've seen them like that, too, only from the other side. They probably assumed we would rest tonight and surrender tomorrow.

"Don't care." My companion lowered himself to the ground, favoring his wounded leg. "You go. I'll catch up."

"No. Rest for a minute. I'll wait."

This losing battle resembled the fight for freedom in Aldonia. The Regimen had us surrounded and outnumbered. They saw and heard everything. Worse yet, most people didn't seem to care. They seemed content with government care from cradle to grave, satisfied with receiving the bare minimum as long as it included entertainment credits.

There was a lesson in all this for me, for Aldonia. I could see the parts and almost put them together, but not quite. I needed a little more.

Men passed by, more or less visible through the fog, some walking alone, others in twos or threes. One approached at an unusually quick pace, heading directly for me. Clouds of fog gave way and the figure emerged. Dressed in the uniform of a Continental soldier, a blue coat trimmed with red and buckskin breeches, Alix halted a meter away from me.

"Hey, girl, I need to talk to you."

"Wow. You came into the game instead of just whacking me on the arm."

She shrugged and adjusted her three-point hat. "I figured I'd join you in here since I'm about to ask you to join me out there." She grinned.

"Out there?"

"In Aldonia."

"Oh."

"Yeah, oh." She glanced at a group of men as they staggered past us. "What's going on here? Level description says you're defending New York ports. Looks like you guys lost this one."

"Yeah, we did."

My war buddy groaned and raised a hand to me.

I glanced at Alix, wanting to ask her to help lift the man, but she'd already reached for his other hand. We eased him up and each took an arm, dragging it over our shoulders.

The fog still shrouded our surroundings.

"We're going that way." I used my chin to indicate our direction. "Crossing the East River."

"So we're running away?" Alix said.

"We're following orders. George Washington wants us across the river before break of day."

Alix said, "Oooh," stretching the word out for a whole second.

"Okay, we're running," I said. "It's better than surrendering. Sometimes you have to get away from the conflict and regroup."

"Is that what you're doing?"

The wounded soldier tipped his head forward, giving me a clear view of Alix. I stared for a moment, realizing she no longer spoke about the game. "No. Or yes. I don't know. I mean, I hate the levels where we fail or it seems like nothing important happens, but I think there's something to it that I'm not quite getting. There's something in the details, in the struggle, maybe even in the failure. I mean, I know we win in the end. The United States won freedom from Great Britain."

She stared, as if not getting my meaning.

"I think I need to learn something here. It's important for me, maybe for Aldonia."

"Well, when you're done learning whatever you think is so important, why don't you come up and actually *do* something with the rest of us."

"I am doing something. Immediate action isn't always the answer."

"Immediate? What are you talking about? The Mosheh has taken months to put this plan together. And your silly dream was the motivating force. You should be up there helping. You wanted to join the Mosheh. Remember? And you're perfect for this assignment. You know the streets of Aldonia as well as—" She gave a sly smile. "As well as Dedrick knows the tunnels under Aldonia. Besides, I need a roommate and I don't want it to be a stranger."

"What job did you sign up for?"

"Unity Trooper."

I knew the answer even before she gave it.

"Hey, if I'm going to be living above ground," she said, tilting her chin up, "I'm going to have weapons. Sure, they're all supposedly nonlethal, but it's better than nothing."

Our pace had picked up, the wounded soldier using us like crutches, hopping along on his good leg. The sounds of the river came to us, water splashing, soldiers boarding boats we could not yet see through the fog.

"You can't waste all your time in a game." Alix stopped and released her hold on the soldier. "These things suck your brains out."

"Yeah, you're right. I'm almost done for today. I'll come up tonight, but I'm not staying up. I'm not getting a job or a new ID yet."

"But that's the way we roll."

"I know and I'm almost ready. I'm this close." I showed her a three-centimeter gap between the tips of my index finger and thumb. The message was within my grasp, I was certain. Maybe once I wrapped my mind around it, I would join her, but I needed more time and direction.

The soldier's arm slipped from my shoulder. He collapsed to the ground with a thud.

"There's a talk tonight, right?" I squatted by the soldier who now lay sprawled on one side.

"Right. Alley south of Vibrant Street, west of the closed Secondary School."

"I'll be there."

Alix reached overhead and tapped the image to end her participation in the game. She faded from view as she spoke. "Try to find me tonight."

"Okay." I looked at the fallen soldier and gasped.

Pale irises showed through half-open eyes on a frozen face. He was dead.

5

Dr. Supero slid a tray of sample tubes into the refrigerator. As he swung the glass door shut, the pallid face of a haggard man swiveled into view, gawking at him. Whiskers on a jaw where a meticulously-manicured goatee had once grown. Circles under tired eyes. Pale violet irises, a cruel reminder of his former self, surrounding black windows to a betrayed soul. A stocking cap over a bald head, covering a sloppy scar that would never heal.

Sickened and angry, Dr. Supero averted his gaze. Gone was the man of power and success, the man who had control over his life and over a great many other lives. Traces of that man remained, pinned down by weakness and failure. Would he ever regain the fight he needed to get back on top?

The first of the double doors to the laboratory slid open, then the second, and heels clicked on the floor.

Dr. Supero adjusted his black stocking cap. It was about time one of the student assistants arrived. Without glancing at the student, he returned to his workstation, to the microarray scanner where he'd been analyzing data for so long that he saw spots even before images appeared on the glossy desktop.

"The lab is in need of a good cleaning," he said, still without glancing, with only the slightest interest in which student it was. They all irritated him equally. They all made him feel old and decrepit.

"Hi, Professor." Cam—the new girl—stepped into his space and leaned a curvy hip on the desktop, an outdoorsy scent accompanying her. Her lab coat hung open, revealing a flashy pink and blue shirt that complemented her tan skin and royal-blue eyes. Her eyes intrigued him. He'd never seen eyes so dark on an Aldonian.

"Are we still analyzing DNA from cancer tissues?" she said, slipping a hand into a pocket of her lab coat.

"*I* am analyzing DNA. *You* are cleaning the lab." Dr. Supero waved a hand to indicate a table where he had extracted and isolated RNA from tissue samples. He had used and abandoned solutions, labeling mixes, and pipettes . . . admittedly sloppy technique for a geneticist of his experience.

Cam bounced to the table, her brown- and black-streaked ponytail swinging behind her. Her moves, playful and sexy, appealed to him. If he did not feel so pieced together and freakish, he would pursue her. He could expect no more than friendship from a girl now. And she was a *girl*, quite young, actually. Could a friendship not based on physical attraction and self-gratification develop into something more? No, that did not seem possible. No female would want him.

Humming a soft tune, Cam slid one of the centrifuges forward and opened it.

Dr. Supero winced. He had forgotten about that set of samples.

"How long have these been in here?" With a bounce that made her ponytail swish, she dropped her hand back into her pocket. "Oh, I forgot. I have something for you."

As she approached, she withdrew her hand from her pocket and turned her palm up, displaying a tarnished coin.

His blood iced over. He shrunk back, slipped off his stool, and froze in an awkward position. "No!" The utterance came from a deep place.

"What?" Cam glanced from him to the coin, her royal blue eyes appearing to detect humor.

"Who gave this to you?" Breaking down the wall of fear, Dr. Supero snatched the coin and waved it in her face.

A scowl replaced her tittering laughter. "I don't know. Some kid. He came up to me in the courtyard."

"You don't know? Really? What did he say?" Every muscle in his face had tightened. His left eye twitched. He could only imagine how grotesque he appeared to her.

"He said to give that to you."

"Specifically. Tell me word for word." The twitching continued. "What did he say?"

She opened her eyes wide and bit out each word. "Give this. To Professor. Supero." She huffed then tugged her lab coat, straightening it. "That's what he said."

"Certainly, you can tell me more than that." Dr. Supero took slow steps, creeping closer and closer like a beast moving in on a vulnerable child. But he could not stop himself. "You are a student of genetics. You cannot succeed in this field unless you are attentive to detail."

She closed the centrifuge and pushed it to the back of the countertop. "I'm not working today." She turned away, flipping her ponytail. "I'm sick. See you, professor."

As her heels clicked across the laboratory and the door slid open, his gaze fell to the tarnished coin in his hand. On one side, the words "United States of America" curved around a figure with a torch and crown. Years ago, while sifting through files he shouldn't have had access to, he had stumbled across a similar image. A statue with the same torch and crown—but crumbling from age and the assault of nature—stood somewhere in the Nature Preserves, he believed, on an island where no one would ever see it.

Dr. Supero gripped the coin tighter, his hand trembling and his fingers turning white. Then he whipped the accursed thing across the room. It struck the door of the microbiology safety cabinet and ricocheted to the floor where it spun in place for a few seconds.

He stood transfixed, his head spinning with the coin, as if he had been sucked into a giant centrifuge for the purpose of separating the sane and insane parts of his psyche.

Before allowing him to leave the old city center in the Gray Zone, Guy had shown Dr. Supero coins . . .

"Do you know what this is?" Guy had said, a twisted grin on his face. He displayed a tarnished coin between his finger and thumb, holding it level with Dr. Supero's eyes. His other arm, the one without the hand, he held behind his back.

Too tired to get up from the make-shift examination chair, Dr. Supero flicked the coin with the back of his hand, sending it flying. It clanked against a metal cabinet then hit the floor, skittered a short distance, and fell silent. "Of course, I know what that is. It is a form of currency from our primitive past." No one cared about coins today. If a person found one, they'd simply turn it in to a recycling center, hoping to gain a few credits.

A gleam of demented delight flickered in Guy's eyes. He shook his head and withdrew a second coin from his pocket. "Nope. It's a message." He waved his eyebrows, smirking. "It means I need to see you." He strolled to the metal cabinet and leaned against it, resting his stump of an arm on it and bending one knee in a casual way. "So, when you get one of these . . ." He turned the coin over and over in his hand. ". . . you'll need to stop what you're doing, gather a few medical supplies, and come to me."

"Come to you? Just like that?" Dr. Supero swung his legs off the chair. Head aching, he sat forward and glared. "I am recovering from brain surgery, and you expect me to sneak through the streets of Aldonia undetected, climb fences, and whatever else it takes to reach you?"

"Good, you understand." Guy slid his arm off the cabinet and sauntered to Dr. Supero, his earthy odor preceding him. Placing his stump on Dr. Supero's shoulder, he grabbed Supero's arm and helped him to his feet. "I'll give you a day to gather the supplies." He gripped rather than relinquished Dr. Supero's hand. "And I'll expect you the following night. Understand?"

"Yes," Dr. Supero seethed, wriggling his hand free. "I understand that you want me to add to my crimes. In addition to supplies, what else will you want from me?"

Brushing wrinkles from Dr. Supero's shirt with his stump, Guy shrugged. "Little favors. Nothing you won't be able to handle."

Dr. Supero had made a commitment to himself that day. Once back in the real world and fully healed, he would find a way to report the miscreants to the Citizen Safety Station without incriminating himself. The miscreants had evidence against him, though, so it would not be easy. He could not allow anyone to know he had gone there for surgery or he would end up in Re-Ed with them.

Dr. Supero dropped his flexi-phone into a drawer, grabbed his hooded jacket, and shuffled to the door. He could not live like this.

6

The ear-piercing wail of a siren brought me to my knees. I couldn't get caught. I couldn't go back. I couldn't live through Re-Ed again. Trembling and sweaty, I crouched behind a dumpster, covered my ears, and gulped down rancid air.

Seconds later, blue and orange light flashed on the cracked pavement under my gaze. A black Unity Trooper vehicle sped past, and then the blare of the siren abated.

Relief shuddering through me, I exhaled and forced myself to stand.

They were not looking for me.

Of course. They had no way to track me. I did not have an implant or flexi-phone. And since I had emerged from the underground ten minutes ago, I hadn't crossed paths with anyone who could've given me a retina scan and I hadn't passed a single functioning surveillance camera. Most likely, the Mosheh had caused a disturbance to draw the Unity Troopers away from the illegal assembly.

Regaining my resolve, I shoved my hands into my jacket pockets and resumed walking down a street as dark as spent motor oil. I was going to be late for the assembly. I had played Bot's game longer than I intended to, but I felt close to gaining understanding. The message from the game was about perseverance, I thought.

Walking at a steady pace, I could still feel the wounded soldier by my side. But he had died. He wasn't with me. He'd died by the river, and we had lost the battle.

I should really stop playing the game, but I needed answers. I almost had them. I would know the time to quit.

I picked up my pace, jogging now. If I hurried, maybe I wouldn't miss much of the assembly.

Cool air hit my face and neck. Having worked up a good sweat under my hooded windbreaker, I welcomed it, but it made me shiver.

Once the shiver ran its course, an image flashed in my mind. The gray overhead light of my cell in Re-Ed.

A wave of panic overcame me.

Pale walls surrounded me.

I shook my head and blinked, but the image remained. This was not real. Not real. My mind took too many detours since my stay at Re-Ed.

Trying to focus on my inky surroundings and my footfalls on the pavement, I shivered again. Uncontrollable trembling overcame me, making me hug myself.

I lay curled up on a mat. Coldness bit my hip and arm through my thin gown. How long would I remain here? How long could I handle this without cracking?

A distant light drew my gaze. Figures strolled toward it. Five, seven, ten figures.

I was no longer in my cell. Where was I? Who were they? Had I been taken to the Lesson Room for the History Lesson?

Reluctantly, anxiety making a rock in my chest, I strode forward.

Music traveled to me. The strumming of a guitar. A strong male voice singing.

I knew that voice, that song, didn't I?

A longing tugged at my heart, but apprehension weighted my steps. Still I moved forward, converging with the other figures. I had to know where they headed and who they were.

Voices, eerie and indistinct, replaced the music. Then they grew silent and a man spoke. My mind would not hold onto his words. I needed to understand something first.

After rounding the same corner as the others, I froze and sucked in a breath.

Black bodies huddled together, half-naked slaves crammed into the small compartment under the deck of a ship. Groups and groups of them, filling every centimeter of space between walls. They barely moved. Couldn't move.

Sorrow ripped at my heart. They would move once they reached the New World. From sunup to sundown, they would work the fields and plantations. They would live with little but suffering. People without a strong, controlling government did this to them.

One man staggered past, his white eyes on me.

I stared, confused. How had he found the space to move?

"What's the matter with you?" he said, bumping me as he passed.

"We want truth!" a slave shouted. Others repeated him until a chant began.

Something didn't make sense.

I squeezed between two dark-skinned women in rags and pushed deeper into the crowd. Fires burned in metal garbage cans, one here and one there, making shadows snap and twist, distorting images. Sparks and smoke swirled upward. The smell of wood smoke and body odor . . . no, of *cigarettes*, wafted to me.

Anger replaced sorrow. Something wasn't right.

This isn't truth, a voice said. The voice came from within and reverberated through me. *My Friend?*

The chanting ceased. The man spoke again, his voice strong and clear. He said something about lies and truth, something about freedom.

"We want truth!" The chant began again.

A moment of clarity came to me. White slaves and black slaves . . . black masters and white masters . . . men fighting to keep them, to free them . . . men dying . . .

"I remember," I said, though the thought had begun to fizzle out, my mind shutting down like a dying engine.

A young black man turned to me. Shaking his head, he narrowed his eyes and said something. I couldn't hear him, but I read his lips. "You talking to me? What are you on?"

I pushed past him, immersing myself into the mix of slaves. I needed to figure this out, to find the missing part and get the engine working again.

Slaves were treated like objects, not people. Yet, the degradation of one person for the benefit of the other was the spirit of the age, not the spirit of this land. Slavery existed all over the world, even in the earliest known civilizations. Yes, I remembered . . . the conscience of the people of this land, of the Americans, had brought it to an end. Two million soldiers laid down their lives to bring an end to slavery. Three hundred sixty thousand died.

That was the truth.

The dark figures in rags transformed into people of every shade dressed in neutral-colored, eco-friendly tops and jeans. A few kids wore bright colors, extras they must've used entertainment credits to get. *Aldonians.*

I heaved a sigh, relieved to find myself in the real world. Not in the History Lessons. Not in Re-Education. Free . . .

My heart twisted with renewed sorrow. Aldonians had no freedom. The Regimen kept them like slaves, ignorant of the truth, not free to live as they felt best. Not free to grow and reach higher. Forced to remain below the deck.

Still unable to focus on the speaker, I studied the assembly. More people had come than I'd expected. Less than I'd hoped. Maybe two hundred kids, mostly straight from Secondary, I guessed, stood in groups in this alley marked with urban decay. The greatest concentration crowded under a fire escape that zigzagged between broken and barred windows of an abandoned, ten-story apartment building. The lowest steel-grating platform served as the stage. LED lanterns hung around it. Crates had been stacked to provide access to it.

"So give us the truth," the boy in front of me shouted, pumping his fist in the air. At that moment someone strolled past and yellow light from a portable lantern fell on him. The sleeve of his jacket slid back, revealing a pale band of skin on his bare wrist.

Glancing from one person to another, I checked other wrists. No flexiphones. People had left them home. This was good. If they hadn't and the Citizen Safety Station did roll call, the group would've been discovered. Everyone here would lose entertainment credits, at the least. The Regimen forbade assemblies.

The speaker said a final word, and applause and various chants erupted. The energy of the crowd moved like a wave that passed through me, recharging me.

A smile crept onto my face and hope crept into my heart. Could this be the beginning?

The strumming of a guitar began, fast and with an energy level that matched the mood of the crowd. The clapping and cheers lessened. People bounced to the music. A man sang. "There's a tire swing in the backyard of the house my father built . . ."

"This is truth," *My Friend* said deep in my heart, stirring my emotions.

I peered toward the stage but couldn't see the musician. I knew the song. I knew the singer. Andy and Dedrick had sung this in the old courthouse last fall. They sang about living in America back in the time of families. Families lived free, worked their own land, and directed their own lives. My heart had ached back then, when I'd first heard the song. My heart ached now. Dedrick had wanted to make a family with me.

"Liberty?"

The low voice rippled through me, deepening the longings of my heart that the song had evoked.

I turned to face Dedrick.

A few meters away, he stood with his arms at his sides and one foot behind him, as if he had seen me and stopped dead in his tracks. He had an ugly bruise on his forehead . . . from an accident or a fight? With parted lips and concern in his brown eyes, he looked surprised, maybe even overwhelmed with emotion.

"You're here," he said, though I had to read his lips to know it. He closed the distance between us and stuffed his thumbs in the front pockets of his jeans.

My heartbeat quickened. His gaze unsettled me, almost compelling me to walk away without speaking. But we weren't enemies. I had simply said, "no" to his marriage proposal. I didn't hate him. In fact, my feelings for him had intensified. But I couldn't say, "yes." Slavery still existed in our world, and I could not live as though it didn't. I needed to fight for the freedom of Aldonians. My desires came second.

He smiled. "I didn't think I'd see you—"

"Hey, you made it." Alix weaved through a group of girls and strutted up to us. She wore high boots and a shiny black jacket over a short orange jumper. Her eyes, no longer the colors of coal and fire but instead striking blue starbursts, flashed with approval. She slapped me on the shoulder. "I knew you'd be here." She nodded to acknowledge Dedrick.

"Nice hair," Dedrick said, smirking.

"You like it?" she said. Her hair, while the same short length, no longer fell in layers that framed her face. It stood on end, dark with spiky red tufts. "Wait till you see what Liberty's going to look like."

"She's not going undercover." Dedrick's eyes narrowed to slits. He stepped toward Alix, angling away from me. "Not everyone needs to work out in the open. There's other work to be done."

Alix gave a crooked grin and shifted her gaze to me. She knew . . . I knew Dedrick felt protective over me.

"So what do you think of our assembly?" Alix said to me. "These people are all here by invite. Our people, undercover, got the word out. And it spread."

Dedrick stepped back and took a breath that made his chest rise and fall.

"It's great," I said. "Think it'll do any good?" A sprinkle of rain hit my cheek, so I glanced up at the dark sky. Clouds had covered it all day. We'd have no moon or stars tonight.

"Sure," Alix said. "It's just the beginning. We've got people undercover in Primary and Secondary facilities, in commissaries and malls, in practically every vocation. We've sent cryptic messages to attract everyone from the recycling worker to the Unity Trooper." She scanned the crowd on either side. "I mean, not the higher government officials and bosses and whatnot." Her blue starburst eyes returned to me. "Word will spread. We'll have double, triple this at our next assembly."

"Yeah?" Dedrick said. "So, where's a group that big going to assemble? This is dangerous. Unity Troopers could show up any minute." He scanned the crowd, turning full circle.

"The Mosheh will warn us." She tapped her ear, probably her earphone. "We'll have time to disperse. People can race to the mall or to apartments."

"You *hope* there's time," he said. "If people get caught coming to these assemblies, they'll stop coming, maybe even report future events to CSS."

Two more raindrops hit me.

"Nah. I know why you're worried, why you're here." Alix gave a crooked grin, the one she gave too often lately, and she turned to face the musician.

I strained to see him.

I should've known—Andy, Dedrick's brother, sat on a crate on the steel-grating stage. With head tipped forward and hair in his eyes, he strummed the ending notes of a song. Was he the speaker, too?

Running a hand through the jagged hair on top of his head, Dedrick glanced in Andy's direction then up at the sky. His commitment to the Mosheh had ended, but the dangerous activities of his younger brother no doubt forced him to stay active. If Andy decided to remain permanently in Aldonia, would Dedrick renew his promises to the Mosheh?

The music stopped. Andy stood and handed the guitar to someone, a woman with blonde hair. The poised way she carried herself told me it was Angel, Guy's girlfriend whom I'd met in the old courthouse in a Gray Zone. Andy leaped off the steel-grating platform as a man in a black robe and yellow straw hat climbed up.

"Our next speaker we call John the Baptist," a man—it was Guy— shouted. Did he let the audience see the stump where his hand should be? I guessed he did. He had never seemed shy about it.

Applause and shouting began. The man in the black robe raised his hands as if wanting to thank or silence them.

Dedrick leaned close and mumbled, "Father Damon, he shouldn't be here."

"Why did Guy call him John the Baptist?" I said, an icy raindrop landing on my face. The man reminded me of the straw-hat priest from the Maxwell Colony, the one who'd stood between an armed boy and a Unity Trooper, the one I found all but naked on the floor in the Re-Education Facility. It couldn't be him. After the rescue, he had probably gotten as far from Aldonia as possible.

"Uh . . . well, it's from the Bible," Dedrick said, squinting as if he found this hard to explain.

I knew what a Bible was. I'd seen people read them during my stay in Maxwell.

"Father Damon gets around, preaches in alleys and all over. And I guess you could say he's got a way with words. A lot of Aldonians are drawn to him. They risk coming to him again and again, eventually seeking baptism."

I nodded even though I didn't understand.

"Hey . . ." He stared for a moment. "Uh, sometime . . . can we talk?"

"Talk?" My heart flipped. From the question? From the sudden change of subject? From how close he stood?

He nodded, his eyes holding a gentle, apologetic look. "I need to talk to you but not here."

I opened my mouth to reply, but then someone shouted my name and I turned.

A young dark-skinned man rushed toward me, waving people out of his way. "Liberty!" He wore black pants and a black jacket over a gray shirt, a modest outfit that probably related to his vocation.

"You know him?" Dedrick said over my shoulder, caution in his tone.

"I . . ." More droplets of rain fell, one landing right in my eye. Motionless, I stared as the man closed the last few meters between us. Did I know him?

He put on his brakes, bouncing to a stop that barely saved him from crashing into me. A smile stretched across a face that had the hint of a beard. He lifted his arms. "Aw, come on, Liberty. It hasn't been that long. Two years or so." As his gaze bounced around my face, Dedrick bumped my arm and a beam of light crossed over and illuminated the man's eyes . . . his scarlet eyes. Scarlet like the endangered tanager!

My heart did a summersault. I lunged for him. "Sarkin?"

He hugged me with strong arms as he spoke in my ear. "Yeah, how've you been? I thought you were destined for the Breeder Facility. How'd you get out here?" He pushed back but gripped my arms as if worried I might run off and disappear into the crowd. "And you know what this assembly is about, don't you? If they catch you, you've got double trouble."

"Yes, I know. It's why I'm here. But forget about me. What happened to you? One day we were sitting next to each other in Secondary, next day you're gone." I kept myself from blurting out how lonely I'd felt after he left. It wasn't his fault.

He laughed, giving me that lovable smile that had always transported me out of bleak Secondary days. "Yeah, I got sent to Re-Ed. You had to know it would happen. I was always getting reprimanded." After glancing to either side, he leaned close. "But I never made it to Re-Ed. The bus broke down. Next thing I know, these people with guns are boarding it. They overpowered the security guards and escorted me off the bus." He paused. "I was rescued." Releasing his grip on my arms, he lifted his hands. "I'm free now. No implant. No flexi-phone. No one telling me what I can believe."

"Wow, you were rescued." Joy filled my heart while more raindrops sprinkled my face. This was the best news ever. I glanced over my shoulder to see if Dedrick knew Sarkin. Maybe he had rescued him.

Dedrick stood with Alix several meters away. He was talking and gesturing with agitated movements, complaining to her about something. His gaze snapped to mine, but then his hand shot to his ear . . . to his earphone?

Alix spun to face Dedrick. Then she turned away and shouted, "Assembly's over!" She waved her hands in the air. "Move it out, people. Unity troopers are headed this way."

What did she say?

Heads turned. Eyes locked onto her. Gasps, shrieks, and chatter filled the air. Everyone moved at once.

"Get to safety," Sarkin said, patting my arm. "I've got to help some people." And he took off.

"Unity Troopers?" As if jumpstarted like a dirt bike, my heart started racing and my stomach sank. Raindrops kept falling. I looked to Dedrick for confirmation. I couldn't let them get me. Not again. I couldn't go back.

Dedrick rushed to me, grabbed my arm and yanked.

My body slammed his, our lips nearly touching. I tried to back up, but his hand sank into my hair.

He pulled me closer, his gaze shifting away from me. Raindrops gathered on his nose and mouth, on his beautiful pink lips. "Let the mob pass."

I relaxed in his arms, pressed my lips together and tasted raindrops. He would keep me safe.

The crowd stampeded past us, behind him, behind me. Somewhere, glass shattered. Bodies bumped me, pressing me to Dedrick. Bodies bumped him. The chaos intensified for a few seconds and then diminished.

A far-off siren wailed.

I pushed away.

This time he released me. "Unity Troopers are four minutes out. Don't panic, just go back the way you came." He stepped away from me. "I have to see to . . ." He jabbed his thumb over his shoulder in the direction of the stage, of Andy.

"I know." As I spoke, I walked backwards, crunching over broken glass. "I'll be fine." I would be fine. I didn't need him to keep me safe. I needed to run. I had come through an access point in the basement of a closed Secondary facility a good ten minutes from here.

Dedrick turned and weaved through the remaining stragglers, towards Guy, Angel, Andy, and the rest of their group.

Raindrops splattered my face and my neck. Gentle and cleansing, a spring rain usually gave me hope. The last stragglers cleared the alley. Garbage lay everywhere, wrappers and cigarette butts. Fires, undaunted by the rain, still burned in the metal cans.

I stood alone, shivering. A rivulet of rainwater trickled down my forehead and dripped off my nose. I needed to run. My mind felt like cracked glass sometimes, ready to shatter at a single touch.

Run! the inner voice said.

I turned and dashed into darkness.

7

Light flickered in the distance where the beam of Bolcan's flashlight bounced off pipes and puddles in a low, wide tunnel. Breathing in the odor of soil and stagnant water, Dedrick jogged a few paces behind Bolcan. They stomped to the same beat, retracing steps so they could access a different section. They'd been searching for Silver all afternoon, finding no trace of her, not a strand of metallic hair, no empty cartridges, not even a food wrapper.

A tune played in Dedrick's mind, one of the songs Andy had strummed last night at the assembly. His heart warmed with the deep feelings he got whenever he thought about Liberty. Seeing her last night had thrown him for a loop. Knocked him off his edge. He'd heard she wasn't going undercover, so he hadn't expected to see her at the assembly, to see her gazing up at him through misty green eyes . . .

He hadn't stood that close to her in months. Being near her had messed with his mind. His thoughts kept jumping back to last fall, stirring up unwelcome feelings . . . the protectiveness he'd felt working with her on rescue missions, the desperation from searching for her after she escaped Re-Ed, the vulnerability and hope when he'd asked for her hand in marriage. The intimacy of their kiss.

Alix had brought him back to reality last night, what, with her talk of Liberty joining the Unity Troopers. That was not going to happen. Not if he had any say in it.

He didn't need to worry. Liberty showed no interest. She seemed to think she had a different role to play, some message to decipher. It was that dream of hers, the one about the wheat and weeds. A part of him wished he hadn't suggested she tell the elders about her dream. Maybe the elders wouldn't have come up with their dangerous plan of integrating back into Aldonia in the hopes of changing the culture. Maybe the

Mosheh would still be rescuing one at time as they had from the beginning.

An unwelcome image of strange red eyes invaded Dedrick's mind.

Liberty had thrown herself into that kid's arms last night. She'd never looked happier to see anyone. She must've known him in Primary or Secondary, maybe both. They must've been pretty close, her hugging him like that.

Dedrick had seen him a time or two before at Guy's place, but he hadn't considered why he looked familiar until last night. Once his flashlight had revealed the kid's eyes, Dedrick placed him. The kid dressed nicer and had grown the hint of a beard, but it was definitely a boy Dedrick had rescued years ago. *Sarkin.*

Dedrick had snatched him right off a bus headed for Re-Ed and escorted him to Maxwell. Other colonists had led him to another colony, a more distant one. Why would *a rescue* return to Aldonia? He hadn't come back for Liberty, had he?

Bolcan slowed and glanced at Dedrick over his shoulder. "This sucks."

Dedrick shrugged. Bolcan used the tunnels, but he never seemed to appreciate them. Even now. He helped search for Silver, but he didn't perceive the depths of the threat she caused. The network of tunnels, once a safe refuge and underground route, had now become vulnerable, open to an intruder and at risk of exposure to Aldonia's government.

"If the elders were smart . . ." Bolcan said.

While hearing him insult the elders struck a nerve, Dedrick welcomed the break from his thoughts. "Yeah?"

"They'd send more than just us. They'd have teams searching down here. She could be anywhere. She could be one step ahead. Or she could be on our tail again." He turned and, squinting, shined his flashlight down the tunnel behind them.

"How much trouble you think we're headed for with Silver?" Dedrick brushed a finger over the sore spot on his forehead, the bruise she had given him. A headache lingered. He needed to take something before it got worse.

"Who knows?" Bolcan turned around and walked alongside Dedrick. "They ought to send one of ours to work in CSS and track her with her flexi-phone."

"We've had members in there in the past. It's too dangerous."

"Nah. We have people everywhere else. Got Camilla working at the university with that crazy doctor, for earth's sake." Bolcan laughed.

"He's harmless now, but he's a good one to keep an eye on."

Neither spoke for a moment, but Bolcan didn't walk a step ahead, the way he typically did. Dedrick trained his attention to distant sounds, isolating each one: a pipe creaking, a faint hum, a rodent scurrying along cement . . .

"I'm thinking of joining the Unity Troopers." Bolcan's tone held a hint of uncertainty, as if he actually wanted Dedrick's opinion. He portrayed himself as fearless and invincible, but he probably wrestled with anxiety about returning to Re-Ed if something went wrong.

"Thought you treasured your freedom too much to live undercover in Aldonia."

Bolcan cocked his head, flipping his shoulder-length golden mane. "I'll be incognito. Besides, it'd get me closer to destroying the Re-Education Facility. Maybe I could get Liberty to join me."

Dedrick bristled. "Join you as a Unity Trooper?"

"That. And I'm sure she'd help me blow up Re-Ed."

"You know that's not gonna happen."

"What? Blowing up Re-Ed or getting Liberty to join me?" With a sly grin on his face and attitude in his step, Bolcan looked at Dedrick. "Think she's remaining below because of you?"

"I didn't say that. I just don't see her stepping out in Aldonia dressed as a Unity Trooper. She has her own goals, her own vision of what needs done to save Aldonians."

Bolcan swiveled the beam of his flashlight to Dedrick's chest. "You're lying to yourself if you think you can win her."

Dedrick's hackles rose. He swung the beam of his flashlight to Bolcan's smug face. "What?"

Bolcan smacked Dedrick's arm, forcing the flashlight down. "She's Aldonian. You're a colony boy. You might as well come from two different planets."

A sharp inhale gained Dedrick an ounce of self-control. This was not a subject he wanted to discuss with Bolcan. "You don't know what you're talking about."

"Meaning? Are you saying the differences don't matter to her, or are you saying I'm wrong, that you're not even interested?"

To keep from blurting out the first thing that came to mind, Dedrick clenched his jaw. He would win her. One day. Living without her no longer seemed like a possibility.

His thoughts snapped back to the assembly. The crowd faded away, leaving only her. Dark hair cascading over her shoulders. Misty sea green eyes turning to him. A fire had ripped through him and settled in his heart, in the hole she'd left there. He'd missed her. A part of him regretted having avoided her for so long, though he'd needed it to temper his feelings. Now he wanted to, *needed to* see more of her.

He still couldn't believe he had actually asked if they could talk sometime. The question had flown out. What was he going to say when they talked? He wanted to make sure they were good. He wanted to ask her to see him. What if she said *no*? She'd made it clear she wanted to devote herself to saving Aldonians. Maybe she didn't feel for him the way he did for her. No, when he'd kissed her that day, three months ago, she'd kissed him back. She loved him, too.

"No comment?" Bolcan said.

It took a second for Dedrick to remember Bolcan's last words. "Sounds like you're the one with the crush. You really think she'd be interested in you?"

"She *is* interested in me. If you ever see us together, you'll see what I mean."

Dedrick struggled to suppress his jealousy. He knew they got along, but he did not want to see them together. Bolcan flirted like an Aldonian. More than that, though, they related to each other in ways he could never relate to. Bolcan had an easy way about him, and he had strength and looks that might appeal to a girl. But she didn't love him or feel that kind of attraction, did she? Besides . . .

"You've taken vows," Dedrick said. "Do they mean that little to you?"

"Hey . . ." Bolcan raised a hand, palm out. "I didn't say we were romantically involved. But we're close. I know she wants to join the Mosheh, so we'll work together. That's enough for me. For now. When her time is up . . ."

"Don't even go there."

Dedrick's earphone clicked in his ear and an urgent voice came through and broke his stride.

"Dedrick, Bolcan, return to the Control Center at once."

Dedrick's gaze snapped to Bolcan. The elders did not typically contact them personally via phone. Much less Elder Lukman.

"Copy that," Dedrick said.

"Guess we better turn around." Bolcan flung his arms up and slowed to a stop, looking like a guy who hated wasting his efforts. "Maybe they found her."

"Nah. They'd tell us where she was." Dedrick checked his TekBand for further communication but found none. He reversed course. "Something else is up."

~~~

A foot ahead of Bolcan, Dedrick emerged from the tunnel into the Mosheh Control Center. His headache had intensified, making him long for a bed. As he crossed the dark expanse, his attention snapped to the commotion at the island of workstations and to the elders in the midst of it.

The hanging overhead lights and array of wall monitors gave Elder Lukman's hair and beard a heavenly glow. He gave instructions to one person then another, his powerful voice carrying throughout the cavernous underground. He had an air of an immortal about him. An immortal with an immense burden.

Elder Rayna, Elder Dean, and three communications specialists had formed a circle around Fulton, whose hands flew back and forth over his workstation.

Bolcan passed Dedrick and met Elder Lukman at the edge of the island of workstations.

"Good, you're here," Elder Lukman said, glancing from Bolcan to Dedrick.

"What's the problem?" Dedrick feared hearing the answer. If something had happened to his brother . . .

"The Torva are coming," Elder Lukman said, composed but communicating urgency with the look in his eyes. He directed Dedrick and Bolcan to the group by Fulton.

"The Torva? Coming where? To Aldonia?" Dedrick rubbed his aching forehead. He couldn't grasp the idea. What madness would possess them?

Elder Rayna looked at them as they approached. Her mood did not show on her chiseled brown face or in her dark eyes. "Glad you came quickly." She stepped back and made room for them in the little group. Fulton greeted Dedrick with a nod.

"The Torva," Bolcan said, glancing from face to face and then staring at Dedrick. "The clan of wild men in the Nature Preserves? Why the earth would they want to sneak into Aldonia? And how?" Bolcan snorted, sounding incredulous. "It's not that easy."

"They discovered the sinkhole on the Breeder Facility grounds," Elder Rayna said.

"Sinkhole? What sinkhole?" Bolcan searched faces, again pausing when he came to Dedrick.

"It's behind the Breeder Facility." Dedrick averted his gaze as his thoughts returned to the night he sat around a campfire with the Torva, the night he told them about the sinkhole. He had been careless discussing Mosheh business with Miriam in the presence of the Torva. He had been foolish. This was his fault.

"Why don't we get it closed," said a short dark-haired woman, one of the communications specialists. "We can report it anonymously to the Citizen Safety Station, and they'll take care of it. The Torva will have no way in."

"No," Dedrick said. "It's our only way in and out right now, until we find another way."

"How many of them and when?" Bolcan's eyes narrowed with a calculating look.

"Thirty-five, forty," Fulton said, adjusting his baseball cap. Challenges usually brought out his sense of humor, but he had the attitude of an elder today, all serious and official.

Bolcan nodded, his eyebrows climbing up his forehead and disappearing under his mane of hair. "Forty Torva men."

"Let me talk to them," Dedrick said to Elder Lukman. He'd messed up. He needed to fix this. He would talk to Grenton, who was probably leading this mission. He and Grenton had seemed to get along last time they saw each other. "I'll go out there."

"It's past that point." Elder Rayna gave him a hard glare as if she blamed him. She couldn't have known.

"Miriam's with them," Elder Lukman said in his grandfatherly way. "She's been talking to the Torva, trying to work with them. She's the one who told us."

"Miriam? What else did she say?" Dedrick wished he'd been present when she'd contacted them. He could read things in her tone and choice of words. Maybe she even had the seeds of a plan.

"She said the Torva want our help," Elder Lukman said.

Bolcan laughed. Alone. Everyone but Elder Dean threw him a wary look or an outright glare. Elder Dean sat with elbows on the armrests of his wheelchair, hands clasped on his chest and head down, as if he were resting.

"This is perfect," Bolcan said. "You want to take Aldonia down, close up the Breeder Facility. They count on a specific number of births each year, you know, to keep society held together. Take away their breeders, they'll fall apart." He glanced at everyone in turn as if searching for an ally. "Are we gonna help them? We could interrupt surveillance."

"What're you thinking?" Dedrick spoke harshly, glaring at Bolcan. "Are you suggesting we help the Torva kidnap the girls from the Breeder Facility?"

"Sure, they'd have a better life," Bolcan said.

"No," Elder Rayna and Dedrick said together, each with force. Then they looked at each other.

The rest of Dedrick's retort died in his throat. He couldn't stop staring at the elder. He typically found himself on the opposite side of issues with her.

"The young ladies are not property to be given to a group of wild men," Elder Rayna said with a stern look for Bolcan and a nod of approval for Dedrick.

"W-we could always ask them." Dedrick said, surprised at himself for saying it. But it was an idea.

"Ask who?" Elder Rayna's eyebrows lowered over hard eyes, making her look ready to shoot down his suggestion.

"The girls. We could send someone in to talk to them." He knew Elder Rayna would oppose his idea and they'd be back on opposite sides, but the more he thought about it, the more he liked it. "There's a lot of discontent in that place ever since they learned they carry their own babies. Maybe some of them would want to take their babies and go where they can raise them."

"Oh, so rather than rescue all of them, you'd take a few," Bolcan said, smirking. "And you'd figure out which babies belonged to which girls." He huffed and rolled his eyes. "You'd never be able to organize that. No, you'd have to take them all. And do it in one night. You'd need those Torvah men. Go in big and get out."

"The Torva must not come into Aldonia." Elder Lukman raised his voice. "Citizen Safety Station no longer searches the wilderness. If, however, the Torva come in, the drones will go out. They will search far and wide. All our colonies will be at risk."

"Dedrick is right," Elder Rayna said.

Dedrick's gaze snapped to her. His mouth fell open. She agreed with him?

"We will present the opportunity to the women." She glanced at each person in the group, sounding like she had come up with the idea. "Those who wish to raise their own children and are willing to leave the comforts of Aldonia will have the chance. We will take them ourselves and sneak them out over time. The Torva must agree to remain outside the Boundary Fence. And they must respect each woman's choice. The women will decide if they want to remain with the Torva or live in a colony."

"Yes." Elder Lukman nodded. "We will contact Miriam." He nodded to Fulton, who then turned to his station and grabbed his headset. "Miriam will convince the Torva. And we can continue to use the conflict between Jensenville and Aldonia as the scapegoat. We will give the Regimen no cause to turn their eyes to the Nature Preserves." The hint of a smile peeked from between his mustache and beard. He glanced at Elder Dean.

Elder Dean had lifted his head at some point. He nodded at Elder Lukman. "Yes. We can work out the details in a day or two. This is a good plan."

"Okay." Bolcan slouched and rested a hand on his hip. "So who's going to deliver the message to the breeders?"

"It should be a woman," Elder Rayna said. "The girls would relate to a woman on this subject."

"Everyone's undercover in Aldonia," Bolcan said, a hint of irritation showing in his eyes. Did he dislike the idea because it was Dedrick's, or had he really liked the idea of closing down the Breeder Facility?

"Not everyone's undercover," Dedrick said. "We have Liberty."

8

Standing on the front step of the finest two-story brick house in Mount Holly, I dropped my makeshift sack next to a slim bundle of firewood and banged on the door. A few snowflakes drifted down from a gray sky despite the mild temperatures. Must've been a glitch in the game.

Months ago, when playing with Bot on this very day in history, I couldn't stop trembling from the cold. It was Christmas day and George Washington was motivating his troops, preparing to cross the icy Delaware River in order to take Trenton by surprise.

"The hour is fast approaching on which the Honor and Success of this army and the safety of our bleeding Country depend. Remember, officers and soldiers, that you are free men, fighting for the blessings of Liberty— that slavery will be your portion, and that of your posterity, if you do not acquit yourselves like men."

His little talk had moved men to tears.

My admiration for the commander-in-chief gave me an almost obsessive desire to fight for him. But the game took me to Mount Holly. Maybe if I completed this mission, I could still join them at Trenton.

I pounded on the door again. "Open up!" My breath formed a cloud before my face. Impossible with these temperatures. It had to be sixty degrees out.

This level bored me. I couldn't imagine what I needed to accomplish to complete it. It began in a house that the Hessians had ransacked. I found a note on a rickety table, the sole piece of furniture that remained in the house. The note listed supplies and gave an address. Wasting no time, I had gathered all the supplies—blankets, bread, canned goods, and a load of firewood—from four different houses, all of which Hessians had picked over. I also found some boys' clothing that fit me. If I made it to Trenton, I'd need to dress like a boy so I could fight.

The door creaked open and a middle-aged, long-faced man peered down at me. His eyebrows lifted to a worried slant. "Have you not departed with the other women?"

"Huh?" I lifted the blanket that held the goods. It felt like it weighed twenty pounds. I had yet to wrap my mind around the technology behind gaming gloves that allowed players to experience temperature, weight, and texture. "I'm here with supplies."

He glanced at the bag and the firewood at my feet, and then he looked over his shoulder. The coarse laughter of men came from somewhere inside. The long-faced man closed the door around himself and spoke low. "You know this house is occupied by Hessians, then?"

"That's fine with me." I itched for the challenge of this level. It must've been here, at this house. "Let me at 'em."

His eyebrows slanted even more, one of them climbing higher than the other.

I laughed. "I'll be okay. I was told to bring these here, so let me in."

"Very well." Resignation in his movements, he opened the door wide and stepped outside for the firewood.

I hefted the bag over my shoulder and stepped inside.

Two doorways, two staircases, and a hallway came off the dimly lit foyer. Savory aromas teased my nose, and warm air kissed my cheeks. Laughter and manly voices traveled from the room to my right. I took a few steps in that direction.

"Hold it there, young lady." The long-faced man grabbed my wrist and stopped me. "You will want to take that down to the kitchen." Releasing me, he pointed to a dark, descending staircase. "No doubt, Miss Ross is awaiting the items."

"Miss Ross? Betsy Ross?" I almost laughed, glad I'd find a familiar character in this level. "What's she doing here?"

He shushed me with a wide-eyed expression and a wave of his hand. "Perhaps you should discuss that with her. Aside from a few servants, she is the only woman who remained behind when the militia left town."

"They abandoned the entire town?" Judging by the ransacked houses I'd come across, I understood that the militia had taken a hit. I hadn't thought they'd fled, abandoning the town entirely.

"They had no other option." He backed up and then turned and stomped away, his shoes clomping on the hardwood floor. He headed for the laughter, warmth, and light.

I headed for the dark staircase. One hand to the handrail, I galloped down the stairs to a hot, smoky kitchen with a stone floor. Gray light streamed in through narrow windows high on opposite walls, revealing smoky clouds that rolled over wooden tables and hutches that held jars and utensils on open shelves.

Two women worked at a large rustic table in the middle of the room, arranging dishes on trays. A man sat on a stool near a big brick hearth, turning a plump bird on a spit. On the opposite side of the hearth, a black pot hung over a crackling fire. Another pot sat on a tripod.

A young, slender woman stood beside the man, making wild gestures as she spoke. Her clothes did not befit one working in the kitchen. She wore a yellow dress with a high waist, low neckline, ruffled sleeves, and a full skirt that made her look like an upside-down tulip.

She turned. It was Betsy! Her gaze landed on me, and her big avatar eyes grew two sizes.

"I know you." She squinted as she approached. "Miss Amity, right?"

"Yeah, that's right." I was glad she mentioned my name before I did. I hadn't broken the habit of giving my real name. "Was that your list I found?" I lifted the sack of goods. "I think I got everything."

"My list?" She took the sack and peeked inside. "I sent Martin Goodworth to get these. Has something happened to him?" She withdrew the loaf of bread and handed it to one of the women at the table.

"He fled, I guess." My mission had been to fulfill the duties of a Patriot who had gotten scared and deserted. Here, they had all deserted.

"Oh, well, I don't blame him." She leaned and whispered, "The Hessians have taken over the town."

I nodded, the gears in my head turning, trying to solve this level. "So, why are *you* here?"

"I am entertaining our guests." A sneaky smile played on her lips. "I plan to keep them here for as long as I can." She pulled jars of fruit and sauce from the bag and lined them up on the table.

"Why bother? The others have abandoned this town. We should, too. Or maybe we should be trying to get them back here." That had to be it!

A glance up at my score—glowing green numbers partially obscured by the smoke—told me nothing. I sighed. It may have been the answer to this level, but I probably needed her cooperation to see a point change. Or maybe it wasn't the answer.

Anxiety or the heat in the kitchen had me clawing at the buttons of my jacket and pacing to and from the stairs. "Have you ever thought of joining the fight?" I said.

The Battle of Trenton had been a pivotal battle. It restored momentum to the cause. Nothing was going on here. Maybe I needed to get her to understand that. Maybe she played a key role. What about that flag Washington had asked her to make? Maybe the troops needed to rally around it.

"Fight? Me?" Betsy folded the blanket I had used as a sack and laid it on the table. "No, I don't belong on the battlefield."

She turned and watched me with undivided attention. As I peeled off my jacket, her eyes flickered with disapproval.

"What?" I said, wondering if she didn't like my simple dress. "It's hot in here."

"Amity." Betsy took my jacket and draped it over her arm. "We each have our own part to play. You may think that ours is a little part, but that does not mean it is less important."

A silent moment passed, then she smiled and walked toward the staircase. "Which reminds me of something I once read in Poor Richard's Almanac." After hanging my coat, she beamed at me. " 'Little strokes fell great oaks.' " She took my arm. "Come now. You shall need to freshen up before dinner."

"Dinner? With the Hessians?" Stifling further complaint, I let her guide me up the stairs. I couldn't fathom eating dinner with the Hessians. These men were the mortal enemy of our freedom. This would not gain me points or send me to the next level.

A few minutes later, Betsy had me washed clean and my hair pinned up except for a few loose curls. I wore a silky blue dress with ruffles and lace that made me into another upside-down tulip. I felt pretty and ridiculous at the same time, not to mention comforted that no one in the real world would see me. Not even Yellow Eyes. He probably lucked out and got sent to Trenton.

Once in the dining room, Betsy indicated the chair I should take, the one next to hers, but I stood frozen in the doorway. Portraits hung between glowing lamps on the walls. The stern-faced people in the pictures joined me in glaring at the enemy seated around the exquisitely-adorned long table.

The Hessians, all chatting amongst themselves, had features as harsh and crude as their strange guttural language. They wore dark jackets with buff-colored leggings and vests. The Hessian at the head of the table, an attractive blond with an irritating air of confidence, noticed me with a lingering gaze and said something to me in a smooth, foreign language. He glanced at the other men around the table, said something in a harsh language, and they all laughed.

It occurred to me that I had gained a speech translator, a reward earned on an earlier level, so I reached up and tapped the overhead control panel to activate it.

"I am afraid I don't know English," the blond Hessian said, "so if you understand neither French nor German, we shall simply have to stare at one another. Or, perhaps, find another way to communicate. One without words."

The men laughed again, one of them muttering something to his neighbor.

"I understand your language just fine." I stomped to my place at the table.

A soldier jumped up and pulled out my chair.

I should've thanked him, but it annoyed me.

"This is Colonel Carl von Donup." While looking at me, Betsy gestured gracefully toward the blond man. ". . . the senior officer in New Jersey." She faced him. "Colonel, this is my friend Amity from Philadelphia." Leaning over my shoulder, she whispered, "I did not know you spoke French."

"Me neither," I said. Was I speaking French? The words sounded no different. And who was von Donup? His name meant nothing to me. He couldn't have been important.

Colonel von Donup cleared his throat, silencing the others. "We welcome you to our Christmas celebration. Sadly, if you have come to spend the holidays with Jersey folk, I am sorry that your friends will not be joining us."

My jaw clenched. I knew that colonists had fled various towns at the approach of Hessians like these. "Gee, I wonder what happened to them," I spit out.

"We found them at Petticoat Bridge," the bearded man across from me said, "the Jersey militia, that is. Exchanged a few balls, we did."

A rugged man farther down the table winced, convincing me that they, too, had lost men in the skirmish.

"Then they took off," a man with a high voice said and snickered into his glass.

"They ran so fast," the bearded man across from me said, his lips trembling as he contained his laughter, "we had not the opportunity of killing any of them."

Everyone laughed, including Carl von Donup. Wine sprayed from one man's mouth. The high-pitched man slumped over his plate. Fists pounded on the table.

My blood boiled.

Betsy grabbed my arm. "Easy," she whispered.

I dropped the knife I hadn't noticed myself clutching and took a deep breath. "How can you stand it?" I muttered to her.

Out of the corner of my eye, I glimpsed movement in the doorway to the hall. A dark-haired man with an athletic build strutted into the room and stood with legs spread. "Excuse me," he said in a low, familiar voice.

With great effort, I turned to look at him.

The guest, dressed in high boots and a long black jacket, resembled Dedrick.

I sucked in a breath and held it as I considered the possibility. My mind had generated his image in other virtual realities. No, this wasn't really him.

I exhaled, slumping forward a bit. Then I looked again.

He approached the table, his brown, bigger-than-life eyes fixed on me, his stylized mouth curling up in a half-smile.

Straightening, I sucked in another breath. This was not Re-Ed where my mind generated the appearance and mannerisms of characters. The characters in Re-Ed always appeared lifelike, not stylized as in other

games. No, my mind had not generated Dedrick. Either the game had or
. . .

Or Dedrick was in the game.

"Pardon or excuse me, or whatever," he said, glancing at the men around the table. The soldiers' confused expressions showed they didn't understand him. "I need to speak with her."

Dedrick grabbed the back of my chair and leaned over me. His breath warming my cheek, he whispered, "Can we talk?"

"Now?" Overwhelmed with conflicting emotions—excitement, irritation, embarrassment—I got up and followed him to the doorway that led to the hall.

"Who is this? What does he want with the girl?" A Hessian pushed out his chair and stood, a look of challenge on his face.

Dedrick stopped and turned around. "What's his problem?" He glanced in the direction of the table then his gaze roved all over me and my upside-down tulip dress.

"He wants to know who you are." I felt a soldier come up behind me but didn't bother to look.

"Um . . ." Dedrick peered upward, either at the overhead virtual controls or at his points. "I'm a messenger." He patted his jacket pockets.

The men at the table quieted. Another chair scraped out.

"I probably have . . ." Dedrick slid a hand inside his jacket at the chest. "Here it is. A note!" With a triumphant grin, he slipped a paper from an inner chest pocket and unfolded it.

The soldier behind me bumped my shoulder and snatched the note. "For Colonel von Donup, I assume."

"What'd he say?" Dedrick raised his eyebrows at me. "Is he speaking German?"

"You're really in the game?" I asked.

Dedrick glanced at his outfit and shrugged. "Well, yeah."

"Oh, when you said you wanted to talk, I didn't realize it was urgent."

"I . . ." He seemed to be studying me or trying to recall something. "This is something different."

The soldiers mumbled behind me and another chair scraped on the hardwood floor.

"Okay. So, what's up?" I said.

"We need your help."

He had my full attention, though I wasn't sure if he was referring to the game or real life.

"The Torva are coming."

"What?" I jerked back. The Torva had never seemed real to me, but this was real life.

"They want the girls from the Breeder Facility."

I'd heard about the Torva from Dedrick and Miriam. I remembered the bruises they gave Dedrick and how he helped them anyways. But I'd never seen one in person. Why would anyone risk their life breaking into Aldonia?

"How can they get through the Boundary Fence?" I said. "They'll get caught."

"There's a sinkhole behind the Breeder Facility." Dedrick lifted his hands as he spoke, moving slowly and not stopping until they reached shoulder-height. "They'll come in there. Then they expect the Mosheh to help them avoid detection."

"The Mosheh's not going to do it, are they? I mean, that's crazy. All those Torva men, all those girls, there's no way the Mosheh can pull that off."

Still standing with his hands up as if he were surrendering, Dedrick's gaze shifted to a point behind me. "Can we talk about this outside or—or pause the game?"

I turned.

Three Hessian soldiers stood behind me, one of them with a pocket flintlock pistol leveled at Dedrick.

A giggle escaped me.

"Are you a spy?" one of them said.

"What'd he say?" Dedrick glanced at me.

"He thinks you're a spy."

"I think he's going to shoot me." Dedrick squirmed. "That might hurt."

I suppressed another giggle, remembering that he once told me the games felt too real to him. "I guess I'm done here, anyway." I reached up and swiped a glowing control button to end the game. "We can end this."

"*I* will end this." The soldier sneered and cocked his pistol. Betsy, Colonel von Donup, and all the others in the room gave puzzled looks. Then the entire scene froze and faded.

Dedrick and I stood alone, facing each other in the dark. The purplish lights that shined low on the walls of the game room reflected on his face and our bodies, giving us form. Dedrick removed his helmet and padded across the mat to the sunken shelves on the far wall.

Remaining in the big tread area in the middle of the room, I removed my helmet, too. The air felt good on my sweaty head.

"That level was a big waste of time." I tucked the helmet under one arm and peeled off the gloves.

"You think so?"

"Yeah, I didn't do anything. Betsy wasn't doing anything. We were just sitting down to a cozy dinner with our enemy. I probably lost points for that."

Dim overhead lights flicked on.

Standing by the shelves, Dedrick twisted toward me and smirked. "Betsy wasn't doing nothing. She was keeping von Donup and the Hessians out of the Battle of Trenton. If they'da shown up, Washington wouldn't have won."

"Oh." Betsy's big-eyed avatar popped into my mind. "Little strokes fell great oaks," she had said. I huffed and shook my head, impressed. She knew what she was doing.

"That was a pivotal battle, you know," Dedrick said, stripping off his gloves. "The Americans needed that win to recharge their enthusiasm."

"Yeah, I know." Peeling sensor pads from my arms, my mind turned to our present battle. "So what do you need me to do?"

"We think we can stop the Torva, but we need to get a message to the girls in the facility." Dedrick ripped game sensors from his arms and legs and dropped them into a bin. "They now know they each carry their own baby, one that's developed from their own egg, anyway. And they're feeling possessive. Causing all kinds of trouble in there."

"Yeah, Alix told me months ago. She rescued the guy who discovered that little secret and told all the girls."

"Right."

"So, what do you need me to do?" I stooped to peel the sensors from my feet.

"We need you to go in."

Crouching and peeling a sensor, I lost my balance and threw my arms out. The helmet tumbled to the mat. I caught myself before falling flat on my face.

Amusement flickered in Dedrick's eyes. "Don't worry. We'll keep you safe. In fact, I'm going in with you. You'll change your appearance and dress the part. And we'll be in constant communication with Fulton. He'll control the surveillance cameras and give us a specific route through the facility to reach the nursery. That's where you'll deliver the message."

"Hold on a minute." Helmet and sensors in hand, I stomped up to him. "I'm changing my appearance? You're going in with me? Then what? Are we breaking girls out? Are we actually giving them to the Torva? That's wrong."

He took the game accessories from me and dropped them into the bin. Eyes still on me, he strolled to the door and reached for the knob. "It's not like that. Come on. I'll explain everything."

I took a step and then stopped. "Wait. You had something else you wanted to talk about."

Dedrick blinked. His hand slid from the knob.

"Yesterday, at the assembly, you said—"

"I know." He dropped his gaze. "I wanted to ask you something." Eyes to the floor, he drew near, coming so close I imagined I could feel his body heat.

His gaze slid up to meet mine. "It probably seems like I've been avoiding you."

I pressed my lips together. Did he know I had been avoiding him? "I- I thought maybe . . ."

"I haven't, actually, well . . ." He stepped back on one leg, rolled his eyes, and sighed. "Okay, I have. I've been avoiding you. When you . . . rejected my offer . . ."

A wave of heat rushed through me.

"I needed some space." His voice and the look in his eyes softened. "But I miss you." His hand brushed mine. He pressed his lips together.

Was he going to kiss me?

I glanced in five different directions, my gaze unable to find a resting place until I returned it to him.

"So, can I see you?"

"I . . ." My mouth went dry. I didn't know how to answer. If I made a commitment to the Mosheh, I couldn't be romantically involved. Is that what he wanted, or did he mean *as friends*?

"I know you want to be, but you're not Mosheh yet," he said, reading my mind and unsettling me. He brushed my arm with the back of his fingers, took my hand, and then released it. "Before you make your promises to them, let me see you."

"Then what?"

He shrugged. "I'll respect your promises. I won't make it hard on you."

I opened my mouth but had no answer. I needed to think about it.

9

Clutching the strap of a backpack bulging with stolen medical supplies, Dr. Supero paced back and forth. He scanned his surroundings but found nothing familiar. Shadowy bushes and tangled weeds grew throughout the area and especially along a six-foot-high chain-link fence topped with barbed wire. Cloud cover made the night as dark as it had been three months ago when he had left this place. This Gray Zone. He had crawled under a mangled part of the fence, but where?

Dr. Supero put a hand to his stocking cap, applying pressure to his scalp. He was wasting time. Did Guy expect him at a certain hour? What would Guy do if he were late? Would he give him the benefit of the doubt?

Knowing the answer, he huffed and approached the fence. Knee-high thistles grew against it here, near a slanted vertical pole. The vertical pole . . .

Dr. Supero flung a hand out and clutched the cold pole. Yes, he remembered crawling under the fence near one of the vertical poles. His rude escorts had drawn his attention to it.

"Don't hit your head on the pole, man," one of them had said, his voice nasally. He'd shimmied under the fence first. "Your skull might split back open."

"Could his brains slide out?" The other kid had sounded young, twelve maybe. But that couldn't be true. During Dr. Supero's entire recovery time, he had not seen anyone that young in the condemned building.

"He should be wearing a helmet," the nasally kid had said. Both boys laughed.

Dr. Supero did not look at either of them, had not looked at them once since they had been assigned to walk him home. Pain penetrated through his skull and brain, his head throbbing to the point of madness. Angel had withheld his Morphine, claiming they could spare no more. She just wanted him to leave, he suspected. Now he could only move forward, eyes to the ground, taking one step at a time on an endless journey through a cold black night with the hope of arriving at his apartment before he lost consciousness.

The twelve-year-old had guided Dr. Supero to the ground and pointed to where he should crawl through. "Get on through, Sparrow."

As Dr. Supero stood clutching the pole, he could still hear the squeaky voice of that irritating child. He kicked the weeds aside and stooped for a better look.

The fence dug into the ground here.

He straightened and traipsed to the next pole. Several poles later, he found what may have been the spot. Cut and twisted at the bottom, the chain-link fence left a good-sized gap between it and the ground.

Dr. Supero adjusted his stocking cap, squatted, and eased down onto his abdomen. Careful to keep his head down, he crawled under the fence and into a cool patch of dirt . . . no, of mud. Of course, he had to crawl through a wet patch of mother earth!

Ten minutes or so later, after hiking down various crumbled streets and stumbling into potholes, Dr. Supero managed to find the old courthouse. He remembered that an old air-conditioner unit sat somewhere in the way, so he waved an arm before him as he crossed the patio to the back door.

His knuckles cracked against a cold metal door. It hung open a bit, enough for his fingers to slip inside.

His scalp crawled as it often did since the surgery, and he longed to scratch it. He had wiped most of the mud from his hands onto his black cargos, but he could still picture opportunistic bacteria racing around his hands, desperate for entry into his body. No, he would not scratch his head.

Shrugging the backpack onto his shoulders, he stuck his thumbs in the straps to give his hands something else to do. In the process, he shed a few globs of mud. He had never felt more disgusting in all his life. Had he? Perhaps. Regardless!

Thanks to Guy, he would have to return to his apartment on the university grounds looking like a drug addict. Many students did not sleep in the wee hours of the night. They would see him tonight like this, desperate and filthy. He, the head of the Department of Genetics at Aldonia's RCT University. So much for his image.

Dr. Supero slid his fingers around the edge of the cracked door and swung it open, revealing a dark, silent room that reeked of mold. How foolish of them to leave the door open.

He leaned in. "Hello?"

A smirk started to form on his face but then stopped. No, how *unlike* them. They were a cautious, paranoid band of miscreants. Had something gone wrong? Perhaps the Citizen Safety Station had raided this Gray Zone. Perhaps the miscreants had been found.

The thought should've given him relief. He would have nothing hanging over him again. Instead, panic seized him. The miscreants . . . *Guy* would not fall alone. He would suspect Dr. Supero of reporting them and bring him down, too.

Peering into blackness that relinquished nothing, Dr. Supero took one step, two steps into the room. "Hello? I am here as you requested." His voice fell dead.

A swishing came from behind then a thud as the door slammed shut.

Dr. Supero's stomach leaped into his chest. He spun around and banged into the door, bringing a moldy, metallic odor to his nose. The doorknob wouldn't turn. "Open the door. I am not here for games." The foul odor intensified.

He turned his back to the door and leaned against it for safety.

"Turn on a light," he shouted. "I have what you asked for. Do not toy with me." He should've brought a flashlight. Next time he would. No, there would not be a next time. This was the last time. He would find a way to destroy these people.

Orange light flashed in the hall, illuminating the doorway and traces of pipes and bulky rectangular units in the room. A monstrous unit, its tubular arms reaching in every direction, towered to his left.

Shadows shifted and the light ceased.

Dr. Supero envisioned the monstrous unit coming to life. He dragged in a breath, flailed an arm out, and stumbled in the direction of the doorway.

Reaching the doorframe, he shuffled into a pitch-black hallway and peered in both directions.

"Give me light," he shouted, aware of his voice traveling a good distance to each side. A far-off shuffling sound came from his left, a click from his right. "Take the supplies and let me go." He shrugged the backpack off and, gripping it with one hand, thrust it into the darkness on his right.

A light flashed to his left, about midway down the long hallway.

"So I must play your game, eh? You have all lost your minds." He put a hand to the wall and touched something rough and crumbly. He shivered. Using the wall as a guide and trying not to think of what his fingertips brushed, he crept down the hallway. "You feel free here, living apart from society, free to do as you please. But you are living in buildings long since condemned, living without the comforts and benefits that the Regimen provides. How can you hope to avoid mental illness? You live on the edge, knowing that any day . . ."

His fingertips skimmed something sticky. An involuntary moan escaped him. He jerked his hand back and shook it, unable to release something from his middle finger. Losing his grip on the backpack, he wiped his hand on his pants. The backpack rattled and clanked as it hit the floor.

"Pick up the goods. This way." The childish voice came from a floor above.

Dr. Supero obeyed and reached an open foyer area. Muted orange light appeared on the second landing of a staircase, shining through the balustrade and falling on a few top steps. It gave a slight impression of the rest of the staircase and showed the beginning of the handrail to be eight meters or so from Dr. Supero. Then the light went out.

"You expect me to climb the stairs in the dark?" Knowing they did, he put a hand out and shuffled forward. The eight meters stretched out as if he had inadvertently turned. But then his shoe cracked a marble step, bringing both pain and satisfaction. The sooner he met with them, the sooner he could go.

Finding and grasping a cold wrought iron handrail, he climbed. He expected, once he reached the second floor, they would direct him to the rope ladder and force him to climb to the third floor. He'd undergone his surgery there, and his two-week—if that—recovery.

A surreal image of Angel's face, hazy and glowing, appeared in his mind. The day Dr. Supero had opened his eyes for the first time since the surgery, Angel had hovered over him, her wavy dark-blonde hair hanging free around her heart-shaped face. She gazed at him, concern and kindness in her almond-shaped eyes. Her thin, curvy lips stretched into a smile. Dr. Supero had wanted to speak to her, to ask her who she was—in his drugged state he could not remember—but his raw, aching throat prevented him from speaking. Nor could he think clearly, but he knew he owed her a debt of gratitude. He felt it in his entire being. She had done a great favor for him, one that he would never be able to repay.

Dr. Supero reached the end of the handrail. Weak light broke the darkness, pouring from a room halfway down the hallway ahead. It spilled onto dirty flooring, illuminating wayward yellow caution tape. Good. They did not want him to climb to the third floor.

As he picked up his pace, he set his jaw and collected himself, preparing for whatever they would do to him. He would get this over with and go.

Voices came from the room, whispers and stifled laughter. The shuffling of feet.

Dr. Supero stepped into the doorway and the room fell silent.

Several makeshift LED lanterns glowed amidst piles of rubble, slabs of drywall, rotting boxes, and splintered wood beams. A shaggy blanket weaved from recycled plastic bags covered the window—Dr. Supero had seen many of those during his stay. A young man slouched against a wall in a spot where drywall still hung. An overweight man in a muscle shirt sauntered up to Dr. Supero, glared, and came around behind him.

In the middle of the room, on a red, upside-down milk crate, Guy sat poised with one leg bent and the other stretched out. He wore the heavy black boots of a Unity Trooper, shorts that came to his knees, and a Regimen official's jacket over a bare chest. He looked Dr. Supero over, his gaze creeping down then all the way up to the stocking cap. Grinning, he stood and extended his hand as he approached.

"Well, hello, Dr. Supero. You're right on time. This being your first call to duty, we weren't sure what to expect from you."

"As if I had a choice." Dr. Supero bit back the edge in his tone.

"You have your life, Dr. Supero." A woman spoke from the shadows in the far corner.

Dr. Supero held his breath. Angel?

As she sauntered from the shadows, the amber light of a lantern fell on her, revealing a shapely figure in a long, frayed sweater and black leggings. It was Angel. She wore her dark-blonde hair in a loose braid draped over one shoulder. Slinking up to him, she smiled. "Your life. Doesn't that mean anything to you?"

"I . . ." As she stepped into his personal space, his thoughts jumbled. "Yes, and I am not ungrateful."

She lifted a delicate, feminine hand and touched him, stroked his unshaven jaw, then traced a finger up the side of his face.

As her fingertip neared his temple, he leaned back. "I-I am not ungrateful." He shifted his gaze to Guy, who stood smirking with one hand on his hip. Dr. Supero's inner strength returned. "You have saved my life, but you have kept a part of it for yourself. I am your indentured servant."

Angel touched him again, her thumb sliding under the edge of his stocking cap.

Skin crawling, scalp tingling, his arm jerked up. He latched onto her wrist.

As his fingers tightened around her tender flesh, someone grabbed him from behind. Someone wrenched Dr. Supero's arms behind his back and kicked his legs out from under him.

With a jolt of pain, Dr. Supero crashed to his knees on the gritty floor. He resigned himself to her examination.

"Isn't that what the Regimen does to everyone?" Guy squatted before him and gestured with his one hand. "They act like they own you. Tell you what to do, what to think, where to go. You should be used to it."

Angel peeled the cap from Dr. Supero's head, exposing his ugliness and frailty to all. She traced a finger along his scar.

Deep feelings of inexpressible gratitude coursed through him, shivering across his skull and down into his brain. His hands trembled. He could not bear this. He needed the hat back on.

As if sensing his discomfort, she pressed her palm to his head for a moment.

Her touch soothed him and made him realize that he had missed it. She had visited him several times a day as he recovered, running her fingers across his scalp, talking to him, smiling. Two others came, too, bringing food and liquid, but they were rude and he did not trust them. For days he found himself unable to complete a sentence or follow a thought, loopy from the medicine. Unable to stay awake for more than a few hours at a time, he kept dozing off. His sense of smell had heightened, allowing him to detect every unwashed body that entered the room, every chemical, even dust. Her scent alone had pleased him.

"You should get a second hat and wash this thing." She handed the black cap to him and smiled.

"I would," Dr. Supero replied, "but I do not have the credits."

"So steal one." The brute behind Dr. Supero said this.

"They are sold at the mall." He made a sideways glance but could not see the man. "My criminal act would be caught on surveillance."

Angel continued her examination, pressing his scalp and the sides of his head.

"What happened to your credits?" the man leaning against the wall said. His nasally voice . . . yes, he had been one of Dr. Supero's escorts three months ago. "You're a doctor. You guys get extra credits."

"He's a professor now," Guy said, smirking and wandering around the room. "When he learned of his vocation change, he redecorated his old apartment and office. That can be costly. Isn't that right, doctor?"

Dr. Supero glared. Guy referred to the tantrums Dr. Supero had thrown. He'd destroyed everything in his old apartment and office.

"The deep tissue seems to be healing," Angel said, stepping back. "Any more seizures?"

"No, none." He wouldn't have had seizures to begin with, or the infection, if the surgery had been performed in a sanitary environment and by a proper surgeon.

"So what do you do at that college anyway?" Guy stopped before Dr. Supero and offered his hand.

"*That college* is Aldonia's RCT University." Trembling and irritated, Dr. Supero eased his stocking cap back on and struggled to his feet without assistance. "You seem to be keeping close tabs on me. I am sure you already know that I am head of the Department of Genetics."

"But you were at the hospital," the nasally kid said. "You were a doctor, right?"

"I was Aldonia's Head Physician."

"You like titles, don't you?" the brute behind him said.

"So you should be able to perform surgeries," Guy said.

"What surgeries?"

"Some of our girls want to get pregnant." Guy paced again and gestured with his stumpy arm while he spoke. Something from the ceiling fell at his feet, but he didn't seem to notice. "Of course, they've been sterilized. You can fix that, right?"

"Yes, the doctor can fix that." Angel straightened Dr. Supero's cap. "We need tubal ligation reversals."

"Reversals? Are you mad?" Dr. Supero tensed and glanced from face to face, causing Angel to back up. "The population is strictly controlled for a reason. Do you not understand that? The earth cannot sustain erratic population growth. We've been there before. We've done that. Do you know how many years it took to restore balance?"

He looked specifically at Angel now. She, most likely, wanted this. "Besides, you have no guarantee that the babies you produce will be healthy. Do you not know what we do in the laboratory, how many imperfect embryos are discarded? What measures we take to ensure that every baby born is healthy?"

"Oh, we know what you do." Guy put his stumpy arm around Angel's shoulders and leaned his head against hers. "We don't care. We want a baby." They bumped noses, kissed, then Guy leaned toward Dr. Supero. "I'll even let you in on a secret. Angel and I, we're getting married."

"Married? What is that? An archaic custom that enslaved generations of men and women and stifled progress? You *have* gone mad." Dr. Supero turned to the muscle shirt behind him, looking for a single sane person among them and finding none.

"Maybe we have gone mad," Guy said, "but we're okay with that. Screw the world government. We want to be a family."

"What do you know about being a family? Would you sacrifice the whole of society for your selfish little family unit?"

Angel shrugged. "Don't worry about us, doctor." She stepped away from Guy, letting his arm fall from her shoulders, and approached Dr.

Supero. "So, that's what we need you for. You're going to perform reversals on a few of our women."

"Including Angel." Guy came up beside her.

"I'll go last," she said. "And I'll help you with the others."

Dr. Supero gave reason another attempt. "Do you not realize the risks involved in a surgical procedure? Besides, there is no guarantee that it will succeed, that you will conceive. Especially here in this condemned building? Why, the risk of infection—"

"Oh, that reminds me." Angel pulled a sheet of paper from Guy's back pocket and handed it to Dr. Supero.

"What is this?" He unfolded and peered at it, unable to decipher the sloppy hand-formed words on the stained page.

"It's a list of supplies we'll need for the surgeries," she said. "I thought old-fashioned paper would work better than sending a list to your flexi-phone. You know, CSS might catch it and pin the thefts on you."

He studied the page and the words began to make sense: operating microscope, microhemostats, micro needle holders, babcock clamp, uterine cannula, sutures, anesthetics . . . "I am supposed to steal all of this?"

Angel shrugged. "Get them whatever way you can."

Dr. Supero opened his muddy jacket and stuffed the paper into the chest-pocket of his shirt. He would get the items. But he would also research when the sterilizations began in Aldonia and why. Specifically, *why*. Perhaps, he could bring reason to these headstrong people. They were fools to think they could bring healthy babies into the world without the aid of science. He would show them.

Dr. Supero turned to go.

"Oh, there's one more thing." Guy swung around and stretched out his arms, blocking the door with his deformed body. "I need you to arrange a meeting with someone."

"Me? Certainly you can do that yourself."

"No, I need you to do it. I'll need it at a location without surveillance. We haven't decided where yet. And we can't arouse suspicion, so you'll have to act like it's a date or something. Maybe you should start working on that now."

"And who is my date?"

"Her name?" Guy exchanged glances with someone behind Dr. Supero. "Well, she's the governor."

A hard lump formed in Dr. Supero's throat. He struggled to swallow. Not her.

10

I followed Dedrick up a cold rung ladder, trying to avoid looking at him. I did not have the inner conviction that I belonged on this mission.

Light from his flashlight bounced between the cement block walls of our narrow passageway, illuminating cracks and debris caught in webs. We had taken a short drive in a tunnel kart to get to this rung ladder. Now we needed to take an elevator to the floor of the Breeder Facility nursery.

"Almost there," he said, drawing my eye upward toward his voice, and to his bare legs and sandaled feet.

Feeling like I had invaded his privacy, I snapped my gaze to the next rung.

He climbed up, out of view, and said something I didn't catch. If he were speaking to our guide, Fulton, I would've heard him through the earphone.

Reaching the last rung, my head emerged from the dark passageway. Humming and sliding sounds echoed off four close walls of rails and brackets. The cool air reeked of hydraulic oil. We had reached the elevator shaft.

Dedrick stood a few meters away, near a pair of car buffers in the middle of the floor. He directed the beam of his flashlight overhead toward the first set of elevator doors some two meters above us. He glanced at me then used the flashlight's beam to indicate a ladder and light switch attached to the wall next to the first set of elevator doors.

I pressed my palms to the edge of the cold cement floor, swung a bare knee up, and hoisted myself into the elevator shaft. Standing, I tugged the knot out of my dress and let the skirt fall free to my ankles.

Dedrick glanced again, his gaze dropping to my flowing skirt.

The elevator squeaked and hissed, snapping our gazes upward.

"It'll be a minute yet." Dedrick came toward me without making eye contact. "We'll stand back here. When Fulton gives the go-ahead, I'll climb the ladder and flip the switch."

I had the impression he didn't like the new me. A team of Mosheh women had transformed me in a matter of hours. They dyed my hair blondish, an unnatural shade that I could only compare to the color of yellow zinc hardware. They let me choose the color that would replace my green irises. A set of scarlet lenses had reminded me of Sarkin, my friend from Secondary, so I picked them. The women did my makeup to match, making it dark and shocking. I hated wearing makeup.

Fulton gave the signal. Dedrick scrambled up the ladder, and I pointed the flashlight at the light switch target. With the flip of the switch, LED lamps illuminated the elevator pit.

Except for an occasional glance, Dedrick seemed reluctant to look at me. But the behavior may have been due to his own embarrassment. At the Mosheh Control Center, as we had prepared for this mission, he'd stepped out of a back room dressed for the job and been met with laughter and taunts. He wore a creamy white dress—a mini-toga, the guys had called it—that fell halfway down his athletic thighs. A bandage covered one shoulder—not part of his costume. I assumed he wore it to cover the s-shaped scar he hadn't wanted me to see. Someday I would ask him about that—and a long belt and sandals completed the look. With a threat in his eyes, he had given his tormentors a fake smile, glaring at everyone who noticed him. Then he'd strode with purpose to my group.

I had stood with Bolcan, Fulton, and Elders Rayna and Lukman. The elders had only glanced, seeming pleased, but Bolcan stared, examining Dedrick from head to toe. As Dedrick neared, Bolcan's expression had transformed from shock to amusement. A grinning Bolcan welcomed Dedrick to our group, saying, "Wow, look at those legs. Did you have to shave them?"

Dedrick's jaw had twitched, but he'd made no reply. He'd given me the once-over and then averted his gaze.

Feeling awkward in my getup, a low neckline on a flowing dress that gathered under my breasts and fell to my ankles, I sympathized. I decided not to say a word about his outfit. Unless he brought it up.

He did have nice legs. Even now, as Dedrick climbed back down the ladder and returned to me, I almost couldn't stop myself from checking them out.

Fulton's voice came through the earpiece. "Stay alert. Here it comes."

Dedrick's hand shot to my arm, as if he thought he needed to prevent me from lunging forward to my death.

A creak and swishing sounds accompanied the descending elevator car. A gust of air made our skirts flap against our legs. My yellow zinc hair blew into my face and strands stuck to my lipstick.

When the elevator stopped at the first-floor landing, we crossed back over to the ladder.

Dedrick climbed up first then hoisted himself to the top of the car. Something slid and creaked. More light came from above.

I hiked my skirt up again, tied it in a knot around my thighs, then climbed up after him. He had made it look easy, but my sandals slipped and my hands grew sweaty and tingly every time I grabbed a new rung.

"Here." He appeared above me and reached down. A braided, brown leather bracelet slid down his wrist and dangled over his hand.

Gripping his hand, I couldn't help but wonder why he'd accepted the extra adornments for his disguise. Who would've noticed?

With a bit of effort, I reached the top. Releasing his hand, I clung to the safety rail and climbed up beside him.

The emergency access door stood up on its side, allowing light to escape from inside the cabin.

Dedrick lifted his gaze to me. "After you."

I scooted to the opening, gripped the edge, and swung down into a comfortable elevator cabin. The light made me squint at first, but my eyes soon adjusted. I glanced up.

Dedrick's bare legs dropped down, his sandals loose on his feet. He hung there for a moment while he pulled the trap door into place.

My eye caught something that made me look twice. Amused and oddly touched, I smiled. He wore a braided, brown leather anklet that matched his bracelet.

He thumped to the floor and tapped his earpiece. "We're ready to roll," he said to Fulton, his voice coming through my earpiece, too.

"Trap door secured?" Fulton said.

"Of course."

"All right. I'll have you guys to your floor in a few seconds. Hold tight."

We stood in silence for a moment, both of us facing the door, staring at the numbers above it, me feeling slightly self-conscious. I still hadn't answered his question about seeing me.

"So." I glanced at him. He glanced back. "You told me this was a low-risk mission. Why do you think that?"

Eyes to the numbers over the door, he said, "Eh, the staff are all in a meeting. That gives us about an hour, and all we need is ten minutes, fifteen tops. Plus, Fulton has control of surveillance. We just need to stick to his route, follow his directions." He glanced and tapped his earphone.

The elevator moved, making my stomach jump. The numbers over the door glowed: one, then two, then three . . .

I had prepared for this mission, going over all the details with a team and rehearsing what I would say to the breeders. But I didn't like the idea of returning to the Breeder Facility for any reason. And I didn't like the idea of giving women to the Torva in order to prevent the Torva from sneaking into Aldonia. Let them get caught trying. But that wouldn't be good either. The Regimen would know that people still lived in the Fully-Protected Nature Preserves. They would increase their search, putting other colonies in danger.

"These girls will not become the property of the Torva," Elder Rayna had said with authority and fire in her dark eyes. "You know that is not our way. Every girl, every woman, must be free to make her own choice. To assure this, a representative of the colonies is on her way to the Torva . . ."

"My sister Ann," Dedrick had whispered to me through gritted teeth.

". . . to ensure that the girls are given the choice: life with the Torva or life in a colony."

The girls would have a choice. I could live with that plan. Ann had been staying at the Rivergrove colony, so it would take days for her to reach the Torvah. Would the Torva wait for her arrival? Would they respect each girl's choice?

I pressed my lips together, thinking it over. The Mosheh must've seen this as the best, maybe *only* option. Was *I* really called to deliver this message?

The elevator stopped and the door slid open. Dedrick and I stepped out together into an empty hallway with bright LED panels high on the walls. We turned to the right, walking in-step, our sandals padding along on the shiny floor.

"So, how did you get paired with me for this mission? I mean, you're not Mosheh anymore."

"I'm not Mosheh?" He glared, blinking. "I'm not *not* Mosheh."

"Oh. Did you renew your promises?" I hoped he wouldn't sense the shot of disappointment that hit me. The thought had never occurred to me that he might renew. I had always taken for granted that he'd be free of commitments.

"No, I didn't renew."

"But you're going to?"

"No."

"Oh." A moment of silence passed. "So, I don't get why the elders chose you to go with me."

Jaw set, glaring, he faced me. "Wishing they would've sent someone else?"

"Just wondering." I now wished I hadn't asked.

Two breaths later, tension showing in his stride, he said, "So . . . you and Sarkin . . ." He cut a glance to me but added nothing to his sentence.

It seemed like an odd time to bring him up, though I had wanted to ask Dedrick something about Sarkin, too. "Uh, yeah, were you the one who rescued him?"

"Yeah, that was me. Did he tell you?"

"No, he just said he'd been rescued."

"Mm."

"I'm so glad you did. I never knew what happened to him. I mean, we all thought they took him to Re-Ed. It made me sick to think about him having to go there just because he'd voiced his opinion."

"You were pretty close?"

"Yeah. He was never like the others."

He gave a nod and looked away.

A clicking sound came from around the next intersecting hallway. We stopped. It wasn't the clicking of heels, but it reminded me of getting caught skipping class in Secondary. The clicking of heels on the hard floor that day had signaled inevitable doom.

Dedrick crept to the intersection and peeked around the corner. Then he stepped out, walking casually, not appearing worried at all.

I still approached the intersection with caution but saw no one either way. "What if we come across someone?"

He turned around and spread his arms out. "I'm not wearing a dress for nothing." His jaw twitched and a hint of irritation flickered in his eyes. Then his gaze rested on my dress for a moment, making me self-conscious. "We're undercover. No one who sees us will think twice."

"I don't know about that."

He huffed and faced forward, slowing to walk beside me.

Fulton directed us down two more halls before I spoke again. "Where will they think we're going? I don't think breeders are free to roam the halls. I'm pretty sure they're escorted from one place to another."

"So, I'm your escort. And stop calling them *breeders*. They're women, some of them only girls."

"Okay. You're my escort, so where're we going?"

"I don't know."

"Well, what if someone isn't in the meeting? What if we cross paths? And what if they ask?"

"We're going to your room."

"Oh? Why?" I smirked, wondering if he had thought through that answer. Of course, anyone would believe it. It was the Aldonian way. In both Primary and Secondary, our teachers encouraged sexual exploration and promiscuity. I stubbornly refused. I wasn't the only one. There were a few of us. I didn't know their reasons, but mine had to do with a deep conviction. *My Friend* had filled my heart with a promise that I hadn't quite understood—still didn't understand—but that I cherished. I was special, like a precious stone, not to be given away in bits and pieces but to be kept whole.

Dedrick gave me an intentional stare. "I'm not naïve. I know what services the guys provide here."

Heat slid up my neck and burned my cheeks. He *had* thought his answer through. I guess it shocked me to hear him say it because colonists didn't behave that way. "It's so different in the colonies. Why is that?"

"Why? Aldonian girls are sterilized, but you all know the natural outcome of sex, right?"

Since I *was* Aldonian, the way he worded his question, lumping me in with Aldonian girls, shouldn't have offended me. But it did, so I didn't answer.

He acted like he didn't realize he'd offended me and continued talking. "We make promises, commitments, before we get that close."

"You colonists are all about promises." I emphasized "you colonists" and I didn't look at him.

"Yeah, we are."

I felt his gaze fixed on me, as if he wanted to communicate something without words.

When I finally looked, he said in a low, flat voice, "When we're in, we're all in."

His manner and words left me unable to reply, but then I forced myself to act unaffected and challenged him. "What about you? You're here, but if you're not renewing your commitment, you're not all in. You want to return to the colonies, don't you? You're straddling a fence, Aldonia's Boundary Fence."

He looked away. "I'm all in. Just not for the Mosheh. I'm all in for the people who are important to me."

"You mean Andy?"

He glanced but didn't answer. I knew he meant Andy, but he also meant me.

We turned down a long, curvy hallway with ceiling-high windows that overlooked the Nature Preserves. The feeling I'd had when I first gazed out these windows returned to me, a feeling of longing for something that I could see and never have. Then, I had wanted to experience the wilderness and I wanted freedom. Now . . .

"Okay, you're there." Fulton's voice blared through my earphone.

We neared a door marked "Nursery." Dedrick unclipped a device from his belt and brought it up to the scanner then hesitated.

"You ready?" he said.

Wondering if I should be here at all, I took a deep breath and nodded. My heart raced. "Please, help me," I thought to *My Friend.*

"I'll wait out here, but I'll be listening." Dedrick tapped his earpiece. "Let me know if you need me."

The door slid open and I rushed in before I changed my mind. I needed to deliver the message and go. I could do this.

Young women, some with round bellies, all in flowing gowns like mine, stood at cribs, sat in rockers, or lay stretched out on the floor of a big, crowded room. Babies cooed and cried and giggled. Girls talked over them. The odor of soiled diapers and vanilla air-freshener hit me.

The nearest girl lay on her side on a play mat. With an air of boredom, she flicked a monkey on a rainforest mobile that curved over a chubby baby. She turned her head and looked me over.

I smiled but remained frozen where I stood. *How should I begin?*

"Who are you?" A girl with shoulder-length golden hair sauntered toward me, glaring through golden eyes.

I sucked in a breath. I knew her: we'd met the first time I came here. Her name was Topaz. She had resented me because I had been given her room. She would not be open to the message, not coming from me. The mission was falling apart before I even spoke a word. I shouldn't have been here.

"Please," I communicated to *My Friend*, "don't let her recognize me." She shouldn't. I did not look the same. She hadn't even seen me in a dress. I still wore my street clothes when she had confronted me last fall.

"Do I know you?" Standing before me, she propped a hand on her hip and her gaze flitted around my face. "Yes, I think I do. Where do I know you from?"

Many of the other girls stopped talking and peered at me through suspicious eyes, reminding me of the Hessians with Betsy Ross in the game. If they had weapons, they would've drawn and leveled them at me. Even the babies quieted.

Betsy Ross had managed to accomplish her goal despite the difficulties. I could do this.

"I'm here to deliver a message." I stepped around Topaz, my confidence returning. "For the moment, no one is watching us." I nodded to indicate one of the surveillance cameras. "This message is just for you."

The looks in their eyes told me I had their attention but not their trust.

"You've learned that you carry your own babies, and your hearts go out to them. You want to hold them, nurse them, care for them. And you should. This is natural." I weaved around the room, looking into the eyes of every woman I could. A few pulled their babies closer. One got teary eyed. Their eyes followed me around the room, every girl transfixed.

"The Regimen doesn't want you to bond with your own child because *they* want to form your children. Our society depends upon the indoctrination of each generation." To my amazement, Andy's talk at the assembly came to mind, so I relayed parts of his message. "They've lied to you about many things. It's not right. And you don't have to accept it. You can have the truth."

"What are you saying?" Topaz stood with her arms loose at her sides and confusion glistening in her golden eyes. "Who are you? Who let you in here?"

"What can we do about it?" another girl said with an exhausted sigh. She repositioned the baby she held, snuggling it up to her chest, and pushed up from a rocking chair. Other girls stood, too, some of them creeping toward me.

"I'm here to invite you to live in a secret community. A place where you can keep your babies, your children. Where you can raise them as your own."

"Where?" A round-faced woman glanced at the two security cameras in the room then returned her tired eyes to me. "They know everything we're doing. All the time."

Topaz moved closer, still looking me over as if determined to identify me. She could become a threat to the success of this mission.

My heart pounded in my throat. I imagined Topaz running from the nursery and calling for help.

"I-I can't say where, but it's safe. You would have to leave Aldonia. Life won't be as comfortable. You'll have to work and make sacrifices. But you'll be free. I believe you'll find it's worth it." As the words passed my lips, my heart stirred. I *was* called to do this, to speak these words at this time to these girls. My words would make a difference.

"We can't just walk out of here," Topaz said. "People would stop us."

"I know." Sensing that she held sway over some of the others, I faced her directly. Maybe I needed only to convince her and the others would follow her lead. "But you can trust me. We have a plan. You only need to follow my directions. And to spread the word. Secretly. No one can know but the other girls." The word "breeders" was on my lips, but I knew Dedrick listened to me through his earphone. He wouldn't have liked to hear me say it. And he was right. A person did not receive their true identity or purpose from the Regimen.

"Whoever wants to go, needs to give us a sign. The cameras in this room are off, but they'll be on in a few minutes. Sometime today or tomorrow, and without looking at the camera, do this." I made a c-shape with my hand and formed a fist. I repeated the signal, turning so everyone could see. "Try to be inconspicuous and don't all do it at once. We don't want CSS getting suspicious."

The girls threw more questions at me. "Where will we go?"

"Will I have my own room?"

"How will we get out?"

I gave a few vague answers, hoping it was enough. But then time ran out. I had done my part, and now I had to go.

I raced through the doorway and turned without looking, slamming into Dedrick.

He grabbed me by the arms and steadied me.

I couldn't stop smiling. The girls had welcomed my message. My few words would make a difference in their lives. Many would leave this place, changing the dynamics of Aldonia.

Little strokes fell great oaks.

But something else had occurred to me, too. I could make no more excuses. My little words, along with the little words of others, could fell the great oak in Aldonia.

I had work to do.

11

The day I discovered the bunker in Aldonia, *My Friend* had given me a message. Secrets made known. Cages bursting open. Walls coming down. Chains broken. Light piercing the darkness. Waters and sky, pure and endless. That day I knew freedom could be mine . . . would be mine.

After gaining my freedom, I'd dreamt of a man scattering wheat in a field of weeds. This dream forced me to realize freedom belonged to everyone though few possessed it. And I, as one of the free, had a responsibility to help others claim it for themselves.

In Re-Ed, *My Friend* had deepened my understanding. Freedom could not stand alone. It must be braided to truth and goodness. Still, I wrestled with how to help others claim freedom. Using Bot's game as an instrument, *My Friend* seemed to be telling me that hard work, perseverance, and faithfulness to my little part was the answer. All this together led me here. I knew this.

So why did my legs tremble as I stood here in formation listening to our captain?

Unity Troopers surrounded me, at least twenty on either side, eight rows in front and one behind. We wore shiny black helmets and scaly, surprisingly light-weight metallic armor that made us look like dark reptilian humanoids up on hind legs. We stood motionless in a hangar near a fleet of drones.

The drones . . . Financial restraints had caused the Regimen to ground them, or they'd probably be using them now to scan the Nature Preserves for other off-grid communities or even to gather information from Jensenville.

With my scarlet eyes, yellow-zinc hair, and a new history attached to my retina file and ID implant, no one would recognize me. But I couldn't override the fear that someone someday, maybe even today, would turn to me and say, "Hey, you're not a Unity Trooper. You're Liberty 554-

062466-84." Then everyone would face me, leveling guns and accusing glares. They'd move in, a hundred pairs of hands reaching to restrain me. I would have no chance of escape. By the end of the day I would be sitting half-naked on the cold floor of my Re-Ed cell, the guard with the potato chin smirking down at me.

Trying not to move, I sucked in a deep breath and slowly exhaled. I had to shake the feelings of fear and hopelessness. As overwhelming as it all seemed, I had to cling to the seed of hope *My Friend* had placed deep in my heart. *We will overcome.*

". . . each one of you is here . . ." Fillida, a fifty-something, stern-faced woman, the commander of our unit, paced before the array of troopers, shouting in a rough voice. ". . . because the Regimen has determined that you possess the ability to do this job. The Regimen has analyzed everything about you, your aptitude, your physical abilities, your habits, even your mental state, and found you . . ." She jabbed a finger at five different troopers. ". . . specifically suited for this job. I don't want to hear about some of you complaining."

She stripped her helmet off, revealing cropped black hair, and stood with her legs spread and helmet tucked under her arm. Her voice rose. "We can't have some of you falling behind and letting others do all the work. When you're sent to a location, press the pedal to the metal and get there. When you're told to watch the mall or a neighborhood, keep your eyes off your flexi-phones . . ."

Since arriving undercover this morning, I had heard two similar speeches from two different senior officers, though this was the longest. We were also reminded of the Unity Trooper's mission statement:

The mission of Unity Troopers is to safeguard unity among Aldonian citizens, providing preventive, investigative, and enforcement services in order to ensure that the actions of people are in keeping with the ideals embraced by all world citizens: respect and protect the environment.

When I had volunteered for this assignment, I hadn't imagined a Unity Trooper's job could be so boring.

I had volunteered two days ago. Once Dedrick and I had returned from the mission at the Breeder Facility, before I'd even changed out of my gown, I'd announced to the elders my desire to go undercover as a Unity Trooper.

Dedrick had been walking away, probably anxious to get out of his mini-toga and into his jeans, but then stopped and spun to face me. "You're doing what? Now? Why? I thought—"

"This is her decision to make," Elder Rayna had said, lifting a hand as he approached. She turned a softer expression to me. "You've taken your time to respond to the call, so I trust much thought has gone into your decision."

"This is suicide," Dedrick had said, shifting toward and away from me, seeming unable to hold still and unsure of what to do with his hands.

"I have to do this, and I'm ready." The fear of returning to Re-Ed hovered in my mind, but I trusted that *My Friend* would protect me. I had only to do my little part, to spread the word about the assemblies and help as many as I could to consider the possibility of a different way of life.

The preparations had begun at once. Elder Lukman had detailed the rules and regulations that troopers followed, stressing the parts I should memorize. The women who had dressed me for the Breeder Facility mission fitted me for Unity Trooper armor and prepared outfits, which they then sent ahead to my apartment. Alix would be happy to learn I was her new roommate. Bolcan had spent a few hours with me in the training room, going over the techniques I should know, moves we had gone over several times during the winter. We routinely practiced the training that the CSS and Unity Trooper received so we could prepare for future conflicts with them.

"Good move, Liberty," Bolcan had said before we parted. He'd stood opposite me on the mat in the training room, dragging a beefy arm over his sweaty forehead and giving me one of his crooked smiles.

I'd bent over to catch my breath. I thought he was talking about my last takedown. It wasn't often I threw Bolcan onto the mat. I assumed he let me.

"I knew you'd go on this mission." He'd tapped my arm with his fist and leaned over, too, resting his hands on his thighs and bringing his face near mine. Sweaty locks framed his face and his manly scent filled the space between us. "It's risky, but you're brave."

My face burned at the compliment, or maybe from the closeness. "Just trying to do my part. I care about Aldonia. Besides, the Mosheh has us covered."

"We hope." He took my hand and straightened. "I'll be joining you soon. Look for me. I'm taking the name D. Stroy."

I laughed, slipping my hand from his. "That name won't draw attention."

His smile faded, a grim look replacing it. "It's the reason I'm going out into Aldonia. I'm going to destroy Re-Ed."

We stared at each other. The fierce determination in his golden eyes both bound me and startled me.

I tore my gaze from his and moved to leave the room. "Maybe you'd better settle for the name Troy."

He laughed, a good sound that calmed my fears about his reckless nature.

Elder Rayna had created my new profile, the details that would now be linked to my retina scan, including my new name. She let me pick, so I decided to use my game name, thinking I would more easily remember it. Not that I often remembered it in the game.

My name is Amity 254-060965-101 of Aldonia. I have been a Unity Trooper for two years, working on the opposite side of Aldonia, transferred today to work with Troop 9.

Commander Fillida stopped pacing and lowered her voice, the scolding tone gone now. "You will likely be called to respond to riots on our border with Jensenville. Jensenville's Unity Troopers are weak and unable to control uprisings. We must be prepared to defend Aldonia."

~~~

After the talks, four officers called out our assignments and dismissed us. My partner, a trooper with fifteen years' experience, had told me to wait here. He had something to do before we left for patrol.

I removed my helmet and turned in a circle, gazing at the chaos around me. Troopers had broken formation and now traipsed through the hangar in every direction. Some stood in groups, talking and laughing, their voices distorted by the acoustics. Many walked alone with their heads down, their attention on their flexi-phones. I needed to make a few friends so I could begin my work.

"Amity!" A trooper bolted toward me, bumping into people as she peeled her helmet off. A head of spiky hair, dark with red streaks, gave her identity away . . . to me anyway.

I smiled, glad to see a familiar face. "Hey, Alix."

Still a few meters away, she slowed her approach, and her blue starburst eyes narrowed. When she reached me, she punched my shoulder. "Get the name right. It's Lex."

The armor had softened the blow, but it still smarted. "Oh, sorry."

"I heard you were coming. You're just in time."

"For what?"

She glanced over her shoulder. "I've made a few friends. Come meet them." She motioned with her helmet.

We walked between groups of troopers, more troopers crossing our path or striding in the opposite direction. The hangar didn't seem any less crowded than when we'd stood in formation. Apparently, no one was eager to get to work.

"My new friends are on our side," she said, her voice almost too low to hear over the chatter and the electronic beeps and sounds from various flexi-phones.

"Already?"

"Yeah, they're totally in." She leaned and glanced past me. "And they want to help spread the message."

"Great. And you haven't been up here that long. Just think what we can accomplish in a few months."

She bumped my shoulder and tilted her chin, guiding me around a group of troopers just as a trooper burst into laughter and staggered back.

I swerved around him.

"My friends have ideas, too," Alix said. "One of them thinks we should get everyone to request a vocation change. We flood the Vocational Department with requests."

I laughed. "They'd just deny them."

"Sure, but they'd see our discontent." Her starburst eyes swiveled, her gaze connecting with a trooper who stood in a group a few meters from us, close enough to hear her speak. "And even better, it'll get people thinking about what they *want* to do, considering the possibility of making their own choices. Maybe a nanny would rather be a trooper, or a trooper wants to work in medical. Maybe a teacher would rather be out on the farmland." Her voice had risen, making me fear her comments would be picked up by her flexi-phone.

The group of troopers she'd been staring at approached, three men and two women, all but one carrying their helmets.

Alix glanced at each of them and nodded as they formed a circle with us.

"Maybe I don't want to live in Aldonia at all," a male trooper said, gaining our attention. About my age, he had skin as dark as Sarkin's, the hint of a mustache, and curly black hair. His comment shocked me because the Regimen traded people with other cities a few times a year, but no one wanted to be traded. No one wanted to *have to* leave Aldonia. We considered it more of a punishment. Now that I thought about it, I didn't know why.

"I want to go somewhere else." The trooper moved with rhythm, gesturing with both hands, even with his helmet tucked under one arm. "I'm sick of Aldonia. I need outta here. High fences all around me, living in fear. I mean I'm glad we're doing our part to keep the world safe, but, man, I need to stretch my legs. Get out of this place."

He turned to the female trooper on his right. Clutching their helmets with two hands, they cracked them together.

Alix rolled her eyes. "I know that's not enough, barraging RCT with vocational changes. It's just an idea. But listen to this." She grabbed my arm and pulled me to face her. The color of her irises intensified like hot blue flames. "Neeva has a great idea." She glanced at one of the female troopers, the one who still wore her helmet. "She thinks we should broadcast the next talk."

"Broadcast?" I looked at Neeva. The enthusiasm of Alix's friends gave me hope. The Mosheh may have been the only group actively rescuing people, but they weren't the only ones who wanted more for Aldonians. And they weren't the only ones with ideas.

I had wanted to make a commitment to serve the Mosheh, to make my promises last fall. They'd asked me to wait. And maybe that was a good thing. Maybe there were other ways I could help Aldonia, bigger ways that would affect more people.

While Neeva continued to explain, my gaze traveled to the trooper with skin the same caramel shade as Sarkin's.

Sarkin . . . Dedrick had rescued him and would've taken him to a colony. Why was Sarkin back in Aldonia? True, some rescued Aldonians chose to remain here, but they worked for the Mosheh. Sarkin did not work for the Mosheh. What reason did he have for coming back?

The answer came with the question: Sarkin wanted to help Aldonians. He felt the same call I did. But what did he do?

New purpose came to me. Before I decided to go "all in"—as Dedrick had worded it—with the Mosheh, I needed to talk to Sarkin. He'd seemed to know all about the assembly and wanted to make sure I knew the risks for being there. My guess: I'd find him at Guy's place.

"Yeah," Neeva said, still sharing her idea. "We'll let everyone hear the next talk on their flexi-phones and workstations."

"No, we won't *let* them." The dark-skinned trooper jabbed his hand in the air as he spoke. "They'll have no choice. We've got to own the Internet. At least for an hour."

Voices quieted throughout the hangar and movement caught my eye.

Four Unity Troopers in helmets and with hands hovering over the weapons at their hips marched toward us.

My mouth went dry and I shrunk back, bumping Alix. The troopers headed directly for me. Something must've went wrong with my transfer. One thing out of place, one little detail amiss, and they knew. They knew I was not Amity.

They knew I was Liberty.

My heart pounded against my ribs, threatening to burst from my chest. Unity Troopers would soon surround me. I had nowhere to hide. I was going back to Re-Ed.

"Chill, Amity." Alix jerked my arm. She turned me to face her and grabbed my helmet. At some point she had put on her own helmet. "Get a hold of yourself," she whispered in my ear, "or you'll be of no help to the movement." She put my helmet on my head and straightened it.

The hangar amplified the footfalls of the approaching troopers.

My skin crawled. My legs trembled as I turned to face them. My work had ended before it even began. Dedrick was right. This was suicide.

They stopped a meter from me, the nearest one looking me over.

"Are you Wick 576-122266-79?" This trooper directed his question to the guy who wanted to leave Aldonia. The other three troopers surrounded him, even the one who had looked me over.

Wick laughed and glanced to each side, but his friends had backed away. "That's my name. What of it?"

A trooper lifted his arm and shoved a small canvas case at Wick's face. "This was in your locker."

Wick's gaze snapped to the case, and his mouth fell open. He jerked back, bumping into the trooper behind him. "That ain't mine. I don't do drugs."

I couldn't stop trembling, even as they took him away. It irritated me that one of our new recruits was now out of the picture, though I knew it was his own fault. Maybe they would only discipline him by withholding credits. We needed every Aldonian we could get.

"Here comes your partner." Alix smiled, more like smirked at me. "Keep it together, alright?

I nodded, willing my body to stop trembling.

"See you later." She took off.

"Okay, Amity. Ready to go?" Holt, my partner, towered over me. A man in his thirties, with fifteen years' experience as a Trooper . . . Would he listen to what I had to say? Would he be open to the truth?

Maybe I shouldn't have been here. Maybe Sarkin would show me a better way.

12

The dank tunnel air penetrated to the bone, and the tangy, rotten smell made Dedrick breathe through his mouth. Until he imagined he could taste it. Drips and clanks sounded in the distance. Spring, with its constant rain, gave life to the tunnels.

Dedrick and Bolcan stood side by side, gazing at the graffiti on a cement tunnel wall. Someone had scrawled the words "I want in" and "yes or no" over a big letter "S."

"Silver?" Bolcan said.

"Who else?" Dedrick rubbed his shoulder, the one with the s-shaped scar from when the Torva girl Shaneka had branded him. Which would he rather be dealing with today, Silver or Shaneka and the rest of the Torva? Neither. Rescuing specific women and children from the Breeder Facility and entrusting them to the Torva was going to be bad enough.

Dedrick slipped his hand into his jacket and through the neckline of his shirt. He touched the edges of the scar. He still hadn't told Liberty about it. Would she care? Would she want anything to do with him, knowing the entire Torva tribe considered him Shaneka's property?

"Guess we'd better report it," Bolcan said, fumbling with his TekBand.

"Yeah, I'll do that. You capture the image." Dedrick pressed a button on his TekBand and turned from the wall.

"What's up, Dedrick?" Fulton's cheerful voice sounded through Dedrick's earphone. "You guys find her?"

"No, but she left us a message. Bolcan's getting an image of it. He'll send it to you."

"What's your location?" Fulton said.

"Five minutes out from Gardenhall."

"That's dangerously close. What's the message?" Fulton mumbled something. One of the elders probably stood near him.

"Words 'I want in' scratched in the wall," Dedrick said.

"I want in? Think she tried the door to Gardenhall?"

"Don't know." Dedrick combed a hand through his hair. He dragged in a deep breath of raunchy air. Silver had said the same thing to them when she met up with them the other day. She wanted to know what they used the tunnels for. She wanted in.

"I'll talk to *the man*," Fulton said, referring to Maco.

"I'm sure Maco would've contacted you guys if he knew anything." Maco, Gardenhall's chief of security, was ever-vigilant for the safety of the community. He spent all his time guarding the main door. Ate all his meals there. Found ways to entertain himself while keeping guard. He even slept in a ratty cot nearby.

Dedrick turned around.

Bolcan stood hunched over, staring at his TekBand.

"Okay, Elder Lukman wants you guys back here." The cheerfulness had left Fulton's voice. "And send that image."

"Gotcha," Dedrick said. "I mean, copy that."

~~~

Forty-five minutes later, heart racing faster than usual, Dedrick lengthened his stride. Bolcan had a thing about walking a step ahead that ticked Dedrick off.

Thinking about Silver's message also ticked him off, and knowing she had access to so many tunnels. If she knew what to look for, she might discover their entire network. The elders wanted to believe that Silver had stumbled into the tunnels by accident, found them useless, and moved on to other pursuits. Now that they realized this was not the case, they had one more thing to worry about. They probably had a team considering options. What could they possibly do about her? They couldn't give her what she wanted. What would she do once she realized that?

"You send that image yet?" Dedrick said with impatience.

Bolcan fidgeted with his TekBand, his thick fingers tapping its glowing face. "I keep putting in the wrong code. It didn't send. Oh, wait . . ." He grinned. "Got it."

He dropped his arms, letting them swing at his sides, and tread faster.

"You know Silver better than anyone," Dedrick said, increasing his pace to walk in step. "Is there a way to redirect her?"

"Nah, we need to find her and bring her in." Bolcan sped up, jogging now, his hair flapping with every step. They could've taken a tunnel kart earlier today. They'd be back by now. But Bolcan had insisted they walk so they'd make less noise and avoid detection.

"Bring her in to where?" Dedrick jogged, too. "She can't be trusted, and it's not like we have a jail cell."

"We could make one."

Dedrick shook his head. "That's not right." The Mosheh made it their mission to free people. The elders would never agree to lock a person up.

"Maybe we should hire her." Bolcan, two steps ahead, glanced back. "Let her help with missions. She could do the dirty work, like taking down troopers or blowing places up. The elders don't like the use of violence any more than the Regimen, but sometimes it's necessary."

"Can't you think about anything else? The Mosheh's not going to approve blowing up the Re-Education Facility. And letting Silver help us is not a good idea. She could be dangerous to our entire mission, not to mention all our communities. She'd work for us today and expose us tomorrow."

"No, she wouldn't. Not if she felt like a part of things."

"If she wants to join us, she can do what our undercover members are doing. Above ground. She can get people to the assemblies or whatever they think they're doing." Dedrick considered what he'd just said. No, he didn't like that idea either. That would put her close to Andy, who spoke at the assemblies.

"Besides . . ." Bolcan glanced. "I'm not the one who knows her best. Liberty is."

Dedrick had no comment. Bolcan just wanted to get her name in the conversation, probably had something to say about her, something else to tick Dedrick off. One of these days Dedrick would lose control and throw a punch.

"I noticed you didn't see Liberty off this morning." Bolcan fell back, jogging alongside Dedrick. "Not too happy about her going undercover, huh?"

Dedrick forced an even tone. "Like Elder Rayna said, it's her decision." No, he wasn't happy. Now, in addition to serving the elders and watching out for Andy, he had Liberty's safety to worry about.

"You'd rather keep her where you can see her."

"I'm not her keeper."

The end of the tunnel came into view, a small rectangle of light bouncing in his vision. Dedrick fastened his gaze to it.

Yeah, he'd rather have her stay where he could see her, where he could protect her. As much as he had hated wearing the dress, he'd liked working the Breeder Facility assignment with her. She had seemed to like it, too. After giving the message, she'd rushed out of the nursery. He could still feel the impression of her body slamming into his and see the joy of accomplishment on her face. They had laughed like two kids, racing back to the elevator to make their exit.

At what point did she lose her mind and decide to return to life in Aldonia? Did seeing Sarkin at the assembly have anything to do with it? Had she no fear of getting caught and thrown back in Re-Ed? He wanted to keep her safe, but she'd made it near impossible. All those Unity Troopers . . . He'd have to keep his distance to avoid getting a retina scan. If it ever came to it, he couldn't sneak into a den of fully-armored Unity Troopers to save her.

Yeah, he could. He'd put on the uniform and do what he had to do. He was done pretending to himself that he could live without her. Not that he was ready to share that with Bolcan or anyone else.

"We could use Liberty's help, that's all," Dedrick said. "Especially with the Breeder Facility rescues. That's going to be a job."

"Yeah, you just want her back in that gown." Bolcan shut off his flashlight and picked up his pace, jogging in the whisper of gray light from the Mosheh Control Center. "You didn't look so bad in your mini-toga, but, man, she was hot in that long white thing."

Dedrick clenched a fist and took a long, deep breath. "Better the dress than a UT uniform."

His hand went to the leather bracelet he'd worn ever since that assignment. The dark brown color had reminded him of Liberty's hair, her real hair color, and now he couldn't get himself to take it off. He'd seen the women fitting Liberty for the uniform, her dyed blonde hair cascading over the metallic scales and glowing under their work lamps. Sadness made him look away. He missed her dark hair and misty green eyes. Badly.

"Yeah, well," Bolcan said. "I think she made the right choice, going undercover. She'll be fine. She's tough. Trust me, I know."

They both stopped jogging and fell into an even pace.

Dedrick shot a glare. Was Bolcan purposely taunting him? Dedrick knew full well that she trained with Bolcan for hours yesterday. To keep himself from barging in, he had thrown himself into working with a team on the plan to rescue the women from the Breeder Facility.

They had their work cut out for them on that one. Within the first two hours after Liberty had left, a dozen girls had given the signal that they wanted rescued. More signaled later that day. The team had already identified their respective babies. Some kid had gained access to the files that showed which babies belonged to which girls, but you could pretty much tell without the documentation. The girls gave most of their attention to their own anyway.

Bolcan cleared the tunnel first and peered over his shoulder. "You really think you have a chance with her?"

"I've got more of a chance than you've got." Dedrick scanned the Control Center. A dozen people stood or sat at the glowing island of workstations, a relaxed scene. His gaze snapped to the white-haired man standing over Fulton. Elder Lukman. He held his beard with one hand, the other hand clutching the back of Fulton's chair. Something about his posture made Dedrick worry.

"You're wrong." Bolcan said, taking long, casual steps. He also headed for Elder Lukman, staying two steps ahead.

"Have you got her?" Elder Lukman's voice traveled.

Fulton, tugging on the bill of his baseball cap, glanced at the elder and mumbled something.

"Put her on speaker when you do," Elder Lukman said. "Something's wrong." Looking up, he caught sight of Dedrick and Bolcan and motioned them over.

Dedrick followed Bolcan though the workstations. His ears had perked at the word "her" but his heart tensed at the elder's last words. Something was wrong? With who? Liberty? He had begged Fulton to keep an eye on her for him and to contact him if anything looked suspicious.

"Got her." Fulton sat back and nodded to acknowledge Dedrick and Bolcan. "You're on speaker, Miriam. What's the problem?"

"Miriam?" Dedrick felt no relief learning this didn't concern Liberty. He leaned in, anxious for Miriam's reply.

"I did what I could." Miriam's voice, strained and heavy with urgency, came through the speaker. "But they won't listen to me. They're coming. The Torva are coming."

Dedrick's gaze snapped to the access chutes on the far side of the Control Center. He could get above ground and to the sinkhole behind the Breeder Facility in a matter of minutes. He lunged.

Bolcan's hand slammed against his chest, a brute force breaking Dedrick's momentum. "What are you thinking? You can't go out there alone."

A surge of adrenaline made Dedrick's fist fly up, but he stopped himself from swinging.

"He's right," Miriam said. Then she sighed—or someone did—the hint of a whimper followed. "They're forty strong, and they'll be to the sinkhole within the hour."

"Miriam, are you okay?" Dedrick leaned over Fulton's desk, resting a palm on each side.

"Fine, I'll try to—"

Fulton pushed Dedrick back and tapped controls on the glassy desktop. "We lost connection."

"Well, what are we gonna do? We gotta do something." Dedrick glanced from Fulton to Elder Lukman to Bolcan, who stood beside him.

No one replied.

"Come with me," Dedrick said to Bolcan, stepping into his space.

"Will we be armed and prepared to stop them?" Bolcan cocked a brow, challenging Dedrick. "Or are we just going to talk?"

"We'll do whatever it takes to keep them out." He gave the elder a sideways glance, not sure that he'd like the attitude. "Yes, we'll be armed and we'll . . ." The fault of his plan became apparent to him. Even with guns, two of them could not subdue every one of the forty Torva men that approached the fence. Depending upon their weapons and the level of chaos, surveillance equipment might pick up the noise, at the least. Attention would come to the Breeder Facility and to the woods outside the fence. But the biggest flaw . . . Dedrick assumed that Grenton, the firstborn of Takomo, chieftain of the Shikon Tribe, led this group. His savage strength and determination would win against two men whether they were armed or not.

"What about a team? We go out as a team." Dedrick knew he grasped at straws. If they wanted to prevent the Regimen from turning toward the wilderness and putting all their colonies at risk, they had only one option.

"No, we can't stop them in time." Elder Lukman turned to Fulton. "We need to make them invisible."

Fulton nodded and snapped into action, running his fingers over controls. Maps and surveillance videos appeared on the array of wall monitors.

Bolcan stepped forward. His chest swelled. He probably thought they would finally welcome his ideas. "We need to act fast. Take surveillance down in the whole area. Take all the power down. It'd be as simple as blowing up a few transformers, and I know right where they are. We can come up with an explanation for the power failure later, but now we need to move."

Elder Lukman studied Bolcan.

Dedrick held his breath, watching wisdom wrestle with folly. Bolcan's plan would give the Torva exactly what they wanted. The Torva would have the women, whether the women liked it or not.

"I don't know, Bolcan," Fulton said. "The instant the power and surveillance go out, we got the Citizen Safety Station on high alert. No way the Torva get in and out before Unity Troopers arrive."

Elder Lukman continued to hold Bolcan under his gaze, as if telepathically testing his mettle.

"We have to do something," Dedrick said.

Eyes still on Bolcan, Elder Lukman lifted a hand. "Go. Take it down."

Bolcan ran a hand through his golden hair and stepped back, the hint of a smile flickering on his lips.

"Dedrick," the elder said, "you're with Bolcan. Gather supplies and get to the transformers but wait for my mark. We must synchronize our moves." He turned to Fulton. "The Torva will come, but we will not let them leave. Not today. We'll need to call in some of our undercover agents. And we'll need a bus, two buses . . ."

Dedrick and Bolcan took off, heading for the WAG room, the storehouse of weapons and gadgets. Bolcan tapped his TekBand and inserted his earphone, then gave a list of what they'd need. Behind them, red lights flashed and the chatter elevated as Elder Lukman barked out commands and questions and others replied. Dedrick thought he heard the elder say Liberty's name, but he didn't look back. They had all shifted into emergency mode. For the safety of all, they had to succeed.

13

Dr. Supero tramped across the empty campus courtyard, gripping his jacket shut at the neck. He hadn't expected the temperature to plummet over the last few hours of sunlight. This morning he had strolled late to his first class under a blue sky with a few ragged clouds. Now brisk winds and a wet cloud layer threatened snow or icy rain. Either way, he did not want to be caught in it.

He wanted to complete this dreaded task and return to his new project, researching the reasons genetic engineering had become vital to the health and welfare of the human race. A few things he'd found had left him confused.

He had not been able to access the files on his own. Only those high in government could view them. Dr. Supero had needed to ask one of his students for help. The student, Rhom, owed him.

One day Rhom had left his bag on a counter in the lab and Dr. Supero, irritated to find it there, had shoved it to the floor. Drugs fell out, bags and bottles of illegal substances. The boy raced to pick them up. Dr. Supero simply stared down at him.

"They're not mine," Rhom had said. "Someone asked me to hold them. I-I didn't even know—"

"I don't care," Dr. Super said, and he'd meant it. "Do whatever you want to your body, to your brain. Just keep your belongings out of my laboratory."

Rhom had been grateful, more attentive in class and cooperative in lab. Dr. Supero had him working on sorting records and soon realized he knew his way around the servers. He'd kept him late one day in the lab, saying a deadline approached. Once alone, he admitted what he really wanted. "I need access to files that are locked. You can get me in." The boy did not question the request, and within minutes Dr. Supero sat down to study top-secret records.

He needed proof that would convince Guy and his people of the error of their ways.

A gust of icy wind blew, and the strap of Dr. Supero's bag slipped off his shoulder. He whisked a hand down, catching the bag before it hit the ground. The contents shifted. Suture packs, gloves, gauze pads, and bottles of methylene blue dye . . . nothing easily damaged. The toe of his shoe cracked a cement step he hadn't seen, throwing him off balance. An awkward step and one hand to the ground saved him.

Heart pounding in his throat, he straightened and scanned the grounds for spectators. A few windows glowed on each level of the three- and five-story buildings that towered over the courtyard. Solitary figures with hoods up and heads down, too far to notice him, rushed to their destinations.

Taking a deep breath, he slung the strap over his shoulder and walked on. He had not obtained all the items on Angel's most recent hand-written list, the one she'd given him after a full day of tubal reversal surgeries. She wanted things he would need to get from the hospital. Would they still allow him onto the premises?

"Professor, wait!" The feminine voice came from behind him, the wind stealing its uniqueness and preventing Dr. Supero from identifying the speaker.

Dr. Supero quickened his steps. He had no desire to talk with any of his students. Or any of the teachers. Or anyone at all.

He cut between buildings and the Collins building, the home of his laboratory, came into view.

Footfalls sounded behind him. And panting.

"Hey, Professor, slow down." Cam bounced up beside him.

Not breaking his stride, he glanced. She wore a sweater, too thin for the falling temperature, and a fluorescent pink band around her head. He wished she would wear her hair down now and then instead of always in a ponytail. "You should be in your dorm studying or out partying with the rest of the student body."

She smiled, a look that warmed him. "Are you going to the lab? I missed you earlier. I cleaned out the lab refrigerator and sterilized—"

"Good, good. You are done for the day." He waved a hand. "Now, if you'll excuse me, I have my own business to attend to."

"Well, I left a few things out that I didn't know what to do with." Her gaze dropped to the bag under Dr. Supero's arm. "Oh, did you get the slides and labeling mix we need? I can help—"

"No, that will not be necessary." He clutched the bag to his side, hoping she didn't recognize it. Unwilling to waste the credits on another bag—Angel had kept his last one—he'd taken this one from a student. The kid had left it on a bench while he stepped over to a group of friends. Dr. Supero had merely to reach down and swipe it as he passed. It contained nothing of value . . . a change of clothes, a gram of cocaine, a few snacks. The boy would learn to keep track of his things.

Cam sprinted on ahead, her boots clomping on the cement. Reaching the door, she waved a hand over the implant reader.

The glass doors made a clunking sound and slid open. One day they would give out, stopping halfway or not opening at all. Dr. Supero would probably be trapped inside with supplies stolen from both the university and the hospital. CSS would send someone to investigate. His life would be ruined. Further ruined.

Before Dr. Supero could stop her, Cam, ponytail swinging, clomped down the hallway and into the genetics laboratory. His lab. Where did she get all the energy? She even volunteered at the hospital, if he was not mistaken.

Irritated, he dragged in a breath and sighed as he passed through the double doors. He would not be able to unload his stolen supplies into a desk drawer with her here. But he needed to. The bag would draw attention at the hospital if he stuffed it to capacity by loading the medicine on top of the other supplies.

"See, it's all these." With her back to him, Cam spread her arms wide, indicating whatever lay on the workbench before her. "I know you don't want them in these drawers. I mean, I guess that's why they're all over the place. But where should I put them?"

He gasped. In his search for the tools Angel had wanted, he'd yanked instruments from various drawers and flung them on the countertop.

Dr. Supero slid the bag from his shoulder and let it drop onto his desk. He darted to her side and reached for the instruments.

She grabbed his hand, encircling it with cold fingers and keeping him from touching anything.

His gaze snapped to hers, and his heart skipped a beat. He had never allowed himself to stand so close to any of his students, to anyone, really, since the operation. Her feminine scent, fresh air and the hint of a flowery perfume, teased him.

Amusement flickered in her eyes then faded, the look children give when they watch a video of playful animals and realize that species has since died out.

"I got it." She released her grip. "I'll sterilize them and put them in cases."

"Yes." He stepped back. He needed her to leave but had no idea what to say. Maybe he could unload the bag discreetly while she sterilized instruments. She liked to talk. She might not hear the noise he made.

"What's that?" Cam lifted her cold, slender hand. Her royal-blue eyes shifted. Taking him in? She opened his jacket and touched his shirt at the chest.

Heat, flames, fire spread through his body. He stepped toward her.

Her hand jerked back. "Oh, this is paper, right?" She turned Angel's note over in her hands and unfolded it. The use of paper had died ages ago. It must've interested her. "I didn't think you guys had paper. I mean . . ." Her eyes widened. "We . . . we don't have paper here in—"

Dr. Supero's head spun. He snatched the note and stuffed it back into his chest pocket. Exhausted and frustrated, he staggered to his desk, dropped into the chair, and dragged the bag onto his lap. He buried his face in his hands and pressed a finger to the scar on his head.

He had too much to do. He still needed to contact Governor Yancy and arrange a meeting. He needed to get into the hospital and steal the last items on his list. He needed to continue his research.

The research . . . Yes, he had to look deeper into the files he'd found. They documented the progression from chaos to the order that the Regimen Custodia Terra had brought about in the world. But something he'd read led him to wonder. Had the government implemented human genetic engineering to ensure the health of future generations? Or was it implemented simply to control population numbers? He gleaned that it was part of a several-step plan. But he needed to find out more.

Perhaps he should visit the hospital later, with fewer staff present, and continue the research now. Taking the supplies to Angel and getting back to his apartment would make for another late night. Did she really need the supplies tonight? Perhaps it could wait.

Either way, the girl needed to go. "Please leave," he said into his hands. "Complete the work tomorrow. I don't have time—"

"What's wrong?" Cam had approached without him knowing. She knelt beside him and rested her hand on the arm of his chair, locking her royal blue eyes onto his.

He sat back and gave a little headshake. Her behavior . . . Did she like him? No, that could not be possible.

"If there's anything I can do to help . . ." She smiled, straightened, and rested her bottom on the edge of his desk. "If you're not doing anything Friday, maybe you could go somewhere with me."

Dr. Supero shook his head again, dumbfounded. She could not mean a date. "Where? Go where?"

"Well, it's a secret, so you can't tell anyone."

"A secret?" he said mindlessly. Was the fabric of his sanity ripping apart? He gripped the bag on his lap.

"Yeah." She smiled and slid off the desk, standing before him.

Slender, tan, and all curves, she was so young, perhaps half his age. So pretty. And he . . . scarred, unkempt, and with bald patches on his head, he had become a monster.

"I feel like I can trust you." She squatted and touched the bag on Dr. Supero's lap.

His heart raced. Did she know what the bag held? Did she know he'd stolen things? Did she plan to report him to gain credits?

"I don't think you're happy with the way things are." She pulled the zipper of the bag, easing it open.

He found himself powerless to stop her. Whatever she planned to do to him—report him, humiliate him, bribe him—he would let her.

She lifted the bottle of methylene blue dye, looked at it, and put it back. "Things can be different. We don't have to go along with the Regimen." She zipped the bag, grabbed the strap, and slung it over her shoulder. "What else do you need? I volunteer at the hospital. I can get it."

Dr. Supero shook his head. Again. This was not happening.

"I saw medicine on the list."

"No." Finding the strength to move, he stood and wrapped his fingers around the strap, brushing her shoulder. She didn't flinch. Didn't release her own grip on the bag. "I am not obtaining these things . . . ethically . . . as a professor."

"Oh, I know. You're stealing them." She smiled and took two steps away from him. Then her flexi-phone played a bouncy song and she stopped. She inserted an earphone into her ear and turned away.

Dr. Supero's heart had not slowed. Nothing felt real. Was she really going to help him?

A moment later she turned and stuck the bag out to him. "I have something I need to do, but I'll get what you need and bring it back here tonight." She smiled. "Then you have to go somewhere with me this Friday. Deal?"

Dr. Supero nodded. Guy may have had other plans for him, but if he could—yes, he would go anywhere with her.

14

Under a gray sky of sailing clouds, hoping no one would notice me, I sprinted across the field that grew around the fenced-in Gray Zone. Long blades of grass brushed my pant legs and made my shoes damp. Green blades grew between clumps of old dead ones, making me think of wheat overtaking weeds.

After work, Alix had dropped me off at our apartment building and said she'd be back soon. Once the bike had disappeared from view, I had taken off. I passed others coming home from work, but the closer I got to the Gray Zone, the less people I saw. No one stirred on the nearest street. The chilly weather had probably driven everyone inside to play 3D games or wrap themselves in blankets on the couch. Just in case anyone watched, I wore my hood up and jogged around to the least visible section of the six-foot-high chain-link fence.

Gripping a cold metal link, I turned and took in my surroundings with a sweeping gaze. Certain that no one saw me, I climbed up, swung a leg over the sagging barbed wire, and jumped down with a thump.

It was weird seeing this Gray Zone in the light. I had only been here in the black of night, fearing for my life, running to and from the old courthouse.

Houses lay in flattened heaps with boards and shingles splayed out in interesting patterns, as if a hurricane had come through here. Spiky weeds with purple, yellow, and white blooms grew between cement blocks and bricks from crumbling foundations. Everywhere I looked, I found a striking combination of ugliness and beauty, decay and new growth.

Wasting no time, I sprinted toward eroding buildings, then down one block and another. But then I had to stop in the middle of a broken road.

Two wiry kids appeared in my path. Two more came up behind me, clubs in their hands.

I gulped in air for a few seconds, trying to catch my breath. Then I stuffed my cold hands into my jacket pockets and shouted, "I'm looking for a friend."

"Hands where we can see 'em," a boy said, his stringy hair blowing in his pimply face. He seemed young, too young to have graduated Secondary.

I dropped my hands to my sides, rolled my eyes, and pushed back my hood. "Look, Guy knows me. And . . . well, my hair's different, but you probably saw me last time I was here. Wasn't that long ago. We were looking for a group of runaways from Secondary. Remember?"

The two in front exchanged glances. Then the young one looked over his shoulder, in the general direction of the city center, and gave a nod to someone I didn't see. The other spoke into an old-fashioned two-way radio. A garbled voice came back.

"What's your name and who are you looking for?" the one with the radio said.

"I'm Liberty. And I'm looking for a friend." I hesitated to give his name. What if he wasn't with this group? Deciding it wouldn't matter either way, I gave his name.

"Nah. There's no one named Sarkin at Guy's place," the radio boy said.

The sound of heavy breathing came from over my shoulder.

I shivered, stuffed my hands back into my jacket pockets, and glanced over my shoulder.

The two men behind me had drawn near, too close for comfort. The wind rattling through debris must've masked their footfalls. Was I wrong to have come here tonight? I was, after all, a Unity Trooper. What would happen if I got caught in a Gray Zone?

I sighed and raked my fingers through the hair the wind had blown into my face. "Look, I just want to talk to Guy. Or Andy. Yeah, I want to talk to Andy. I know he's here. Most of the other Secondary kids left, but not him."

The radio boy turned his back on me and spent a ridiculous amount of time talking on the radio, the garbled voice speaking whenever he stopped. The young one alternated between staring at and chewing his fingernails. The two behind me . . .

Uhg. I turned away from them. Still clutching their clubs—rough things they'd probably chiseled from part of a building frame—they stood too close and stared at me through grim eyes.

The radio boy finally turned back. "All right. Come on."

I walked between two of them, the other two on our heels. None of them spoke as we crunched down one street and then another, moving along much slower than I would've on my own. We finally reached the front steps of the old courthouse.

"Wait here." Radio boy and the young one went around the side of the building.

A minute later, a lone figure came from the other side of the building. Andy!

Dressed in jeans and a mottled jacket weaved of recycled materials, he walked toward me with slowing steps. Then he stopped about three meters away and squinted at me. "Liberty?"

I turned my hands up and laughed. "Yes, it's me. Good disguise, huh?" I twirled a lock of my yellow-zinc hair.

Hands stuffed in his pockets, eyes still like slits, Andy crept closer. "Your eyes . . ."

"I know. They're red. I'm undercover, so I needed a whole new look."

"Looks weird on you. I've only seen one other person with eyes like that."

"Who?" I stepped closer, hopeful. He had to mean Sarkin.

"His name's Silas. He's a seminarian. Anyway . . ." He smiled. ". . . your voice is the same." He turned and seemed to be searching the area. "Where's Dedrick?"

I looked where he looked. My two grim-eyed bodyguards had backed off and now stood relaxed, smoking cigarettes and talking. "I don't know where Dedrick is. I came alone."

He gave a partial nod, still looking suspicious. "Does he know you're here?"

"What?" I blinked a few times. "No. I'm here on my own. I needed to talk to someone."

"He's not gonna like that."

Frustration built in my chest. "So? He's not my brother. Or my . . ." Did Andy think I needed to ask Dedrick permission just because he'd rescued me a time or two. I was not accountable to him. I had my own life to lead and my own choices to make.

I closed the distance between us and grabbed his arm. "Listen, I don't have all night and I need to talk to someone. His name is Sarkin. I saw him at the assembly. I'm hoping he's here, that he's working with you guys."

"Sarkin?" Andy shook his head. "Sorry, Liberty, there's no one . . ." His gaze snapped to some point over my shoulder. "Why don't you ask Father Damon. He knows just about everybody who's passed through here."

I turned to see who he looked at.

Two men stood in a grassy area a stone's throw away. One wore a long black robe and had a neatly trimmed beard on his pale face, Father Damon, I assumed. He swung his arm out, pointing in one direction and then another, indicating something on the ground. The other, a younger, dark-skinned man in a black jacket and black pants, nodded. He shook something in his hand. A can of spray paint?

"Father's with one of the seminarians," Andy said.

"Sarkin wore clothes like that at the assembly." My heart leaped. It was him; it had to be. I took off toward them.

"Hey!" someone hollered, probably one of my bodyguards.

I didn't care. I bolted across weedy, debris-littered terrain until I reached them.

They both turned to me at the same time, one with brown eyes, the other . . . red. It was Sarkin!

"Sarkin!" I said, resisting the urge to throw myself into his arms the way I had at the assembly. "I found you."

Father Damon looked from me to Sarkin. Sarkin squinted at me the way Andy had.

I tugged a lock of my hair. "It's my disguise."

"Liberty?" The corners of his mouth turned up and recognition showed in his scarlet eyes. He handed the spray can to the priest and opened his arms.

I flung myself at him and exhaled.

"Wow, what a transformation," Sarkin said, stroking my hair.

"Do I know you?" Father Damon said.

I released Sarkin and stepped back. "I . . ." At this moment, realization struck me. I knew the priest. He was the one who . . . My mind returned to the day I'd rescued him from Re-Education. The beam of a flashlight had first revealed him to me in the dark Lesson Room. *A man in nothing but undershorts sat slumped in the corner, his arms hanging loose at his sides, his chin resting on his hairy chest.*

After what he'd been through, I could hardly believe he was still in Aldonia and that he was actually one of the speakers.

"Yes," I finally said, "we've met." I didn't want to explain further.

He didn't make me. He simply nodded and blinked his eyes, the look in them saying he now remembered, too.

"I will leave you, Silas. We'll meet for Vespers and start the walkway tomorrow." Father Damon rubbed Sarkin's shoulder and then mine. He nodded, his eyes showing a heart filled with emotion. Then he strolled away, a slight limp visible in his gate.

Regaining my calm, I turned to Sarkin. "Silas, huh?"

He smiled. "I took the name when I was baptized." He motioned for me to walk with him. With the wind at our backs, we headed toward a pile of broken concrete.

"We didn't have much time to talk at the assembly. What are you doing here? I mean, you were rescued, so you've lived in the colonies, right?"

"Yeah, that's right. Over two years. But I'm living here now, studying under Father Damon."

"Studying? Are you here to help bring freedom to Aldonia? Because that's why I'm here." The words tumbled out, my thoughts a jumbled mess. "I had this dream. It meant something . . . then I got this message about the importance of symbols, or I think I did . . . and I'm working with the Mosheh, undercover now, but I wanted to know what you were doing. Because maybe there's a better way. Maybe there's something else I should be doing."

I shut my mouth and took a breath, hoping what I'd said made sense. If he felt the same, he'd understand.

We reached the pile of cement chunks. The remains of an in-ground fountain basin lay behind it, most of the floor and two-thirds of the walls still intact. All cleaned out.

"You're with the Mosheh, huh?" He hopped down into the meter-deep basin and offered his hand.

I took it and hopped down, too. We sat beside each other on the cold concrete floor, the wind no longer reaching us. "Yeah, I'm with the Mosheh for now. I haven't made a commitment yet. Still thinking about it. Trying to figure out the best way to help Aldonia."

He nodded. "They do a lot of good."

"So you were at the assembly. Do you give talks?"

"Me?" He smiled and leaned back against the cement wall. "No, I'm still learning."

"I remember you were always searching."

He nodded. ". . . for the Creator. Well, I found Him." He looked me in the eye. "The Creator I always spoke of, He's real. And everyone in the colonies knows Him."

"You talk as if He's a person and they've all met Him." I smiled, amused at his choice of words. "So where is He now?"

"Well, He's everywhere. And we're all meant to come to know Him. We're meant to be His children, and I want the world to know that."

Something stirred in my heart, *My Friend* maybe wanting to tell me something. But I couldn't listen now. I had only this moment to speak with Sarkin, and I didn't want to lose focus.

"Okay, but you and I both know Aldonians have no freedom to believe that. So, first things first, we need to bring freedom to Aldonia. Isn't that why you're here? I mean, I could've remained safe in a colony. You could've remained there, too, but we both came back here. These are my people and I want them all to have what I have: freedom."

"Yeah, I guess that's why I'm here, too . . . why I'm studying to be a priest."

"Studying? How does that help?" A gust of wind reached me, blowing my hair and chilling my neck. I put up my hood and stuffed my hands in my pockets. "You should give talks. Remember the things you spoke of in Secondary? You made me think beyond what we were taught, longing for more. Maybe you got others thinking, too."

"Thus, the transfer to Re-Ed." He chuckled. "No, Liberty, I only had questions then."

"They're teaching you, so don't you have answers now?" My jacket no longer kept out the cold and I shivered.

"Sure, but I've got even more questions."

"Does it ever end? You'll always find more you're curious about. Eventually, you have to stop learning and do something."

Alix had said something similar: "When you're done learning whatever you think is so important, why don't you come up and actually *do* something with the rest of us."

She must've felt the way I felt now. We didn't have time to sit around and think about it. Troubled times called for swift action.

"I know," Sarkin said. "I've got two and a half more years in seminary. I'll be ordained a priest. Then I'll *do* something." He pressed his lips together, a strange look of longing passing across his face. "I'm hoping to go to Jensenville to share the Good News there."

"What? Jensenville?" I couldn't believe my ears. "Why not stay here and help your own people?"

"Ever heard the saying: a prophet isn't welcome in his own town?"

I shook my head and my heart grew heavy. "So, then what am I supposed to do?"

He stared at me for a moment. "Do whatever you're called to do."

I let out a sarcastic laugh. "Right. That's sort of why I'm here. I was hoping you had something big going on, something I could take part in. But you're only focused on yourself."

"That's not true." He paused and stared again. "I've got another saying for you. Be who God meant you to be, and you will set the world on fire."

I smiled, visibly shivering now. "Says who?"

"Saint Catherine of Siena."

"Who?"

"Never mind. But it's good advice." He put his arm around me and pulled me close. "You're cold."

We had often sat beside each other in the past, but never like this. Maybe due to the rampant promiscuity of most of the others, we had an unspoken rule that we never touched each other. But this felt good. Safe and pure. Leaning against the remains of a concrete wall and against Sarkin's warm body, I wanted to stay here as long as I could and remember the friendship we once had.

The sky grew darker and darker, threatening rain or snow. Then the sound of boots clomping on cement rose above the wind's wild rampage. My escorts approached, probably ready for me to go.

Sarkin and I looked at each other. A memory from Secondary came vividly to my mind and maybe to his, too. We both laughed.

"Do you remember that day?" I said.

"In the empty swimming pool?" he said.

I nodded. The clomping of high heels on the hard floor of the natatorium had warned us that we'd been caught skipping class. "That was one of your last days with us in Secondary." Remembering that day had always made me sad, but now it made me happy. That was close to the day the Mosheh rescued him.

A hand to the top edge of the cold, rough cement, I pulled myself up and brushed off the seat of my jeans. "I guess I should head back."

He glanced at the dark and moody sky. "I hope you don't have far to go. Looks like rain."

On impulse I reached for his shoulders and pulled him into a hug. We promised we'd get together again. Then I jogged away with my escorts on my tail until I reached the fence.

I was glad to have seen Sarkin and happy he'd found answers to his own questions, but he had no answers for me. I'd come to a dead end. Or maybe this was confirmation: I was meant to make promises to the Mosheh.

15

Hands on his hips and head cocked to one side, Dedrick stood before an eight-foot-high chain-link fence waiting for Bolcan to do his thing. Several rusted safety signs hung at eye level: WARNING, CAUTION, DANGER, HIGH VOLTAGE . . .

Bolcan clung to the fence, the toes of his boots stuck between links and one arm draped over the top horizontal bar. Indirect light from a high floodlight shone on his work and illuminated his unruly yellow hair. He wielded a cable cutter awkwardly, trying to cut one of three strands of barbed wire.

He should've let Dedrick do it. They'd be over the fence by now.

Dedrick adjusted the strap of the AR-15 slung over his back and dragged an arm over his forehead. Despite the low temperatures, he had worked up a good sweat hiking down roads without surveillance and cutting across fields to get to the electrical substation that distributed power to a quarter of Aldonia.

A bead of sweat ran down his back, the cool air turning it to ice water. All the low temperatures and rain they'd had lately . . . spring seemed to have no intention of giving way to summer this year. He still couldn't believe he would never spend another summer back home in Maxwell. He'd probably spend this summer here, keeping watch over Andy and Liberty.

Dedrick peered across the field behind him at a quiet road a hundred yards back. Quiet because it was past curfew. If a vehicle came by, it'd likely be a Unity Trooper. They'd be caught.

Bolcan snapped a strand of wire, the new ends popping up and swinging down.

"You know," Dedrick said, "it would be way easier to blow up the transformer outside the Breeder Facility. And faster." Fulton would be calling them any minute now, counting on them to have the power down.

"No way." The chain links rattled. Bolcan grunted. "These things are flipping dull." He adjusted his grip on the cutters. "Wouldn't be good enough. Might not get all the security cameras."

"Do you know how many apartment buildings and other facilities this will affect? A lot of people are going to be cold tonight, and tomorrow, and for however long it takes them to repair the damage."

"Better a few cold Aldonians than colonists in the hands of the Regimen." The last row of barbed wire snapped and split apart, springing in either direction. Bolcan ducked his head and the cable cutter clattered to the concrete just inside the fence.

"Yeah, just toss it when you're done. Who cares about the Mosheh's tools?" Dedrick reached under the fence and snatched the cutters. After locking it, he secured it to his belt.

"What can I say? It slipped from my hand." Bolcan climbed over, rattling the fence, and dropped to the ground with a solid thud. "Hey, grab me my bag."

With one hand to the web sling of his semi-automatic, Dedrick hoisted Bolcan's backpack from the ground. He judged it to be a good twenty pounds, not the five he expected. Bolcan had ordered the supplies for this job and gone to the WAG room alone. Putty explosives didn't weigh that much. "What'cha got in here?"

"Toss it over." Bolcan spread his arms, ready to catch it. "You stay on that side of the fence. When we get the *go*, we'll have to be clear of here anyway."

"No, we need to move. The two of us can work faster." Dedrick tossed the bag over the fence and into Bolcan's waiting hands then shoved a foot into the chain links.

Bolcan set the bag down, squatted, and unzipped it. "How far apart do you think those transformers are?"

Dedrick scaled the fence and leaped to the ground, the fence quivering behind him. The rifle's strap slid off his shoulder, but his hand snapped to the rifle, catching it.

A few yards away, five cylindrical transformers lay on their sides atop blocky enclosures. Steel lattice structures supporting high voltage lines and metering apparatus towered over and behind the transformers, gleaming under a few well-spaced floodlights.

The hum of electrical power made Dedrick shudder. The hairs on his sweaty arms tingled. He imagined electrical currents and stray magnetic fields penetrating through his body and destroying the integrity of his cells.

"About two yards, I guess," Dedrick said.

Bolcan straightened with a coil of detonator cord and three blocks of Semtex, each the size of a pound of cheese. "You mean two meters?"

"No, I mean two yards." Dedrick turned up a palm. "I'll wind the det. cord. You place the other two explosives."

Bolcan, apparently not one to be bossed, handed Dedrick two blocks of Semtex. "Go set those on the farther transformers. I'll take care of this one." He shoved the end of the primer into the putty and started winding the cord around it. It would need to be well wrapped for Dedrick to detonate it with his AR-15 from fifty yards away.

Dedrick tossed a block of Semtex in the air, caught it, and strolled to the farthest transformer. This assignment wouldn't give him the satisfaction he usually got rescuing people. He hated the idea of helping the Torva kidnap the women, but they had to do something. They couldn't sit back and let the Torva get caught sneaking under the Boundary Fence. The Regimen would know people still lived out there, putting all the colonies in danger.

"Dedrick, Bolcan . . ." Fulton's voice blared through Dedrick's earphone.

Dedrick set a block of Semtex on a transformer and tapped a button on his TekBand to communicate. "Hey, Fulton, we're almost ready." He peered back at Bolcan to see if he had spoken truthfully.

Still winding the det. cord, Bolcan strutted to a transformer. He gave Dedrick a confident nod.

"Okay, but it's not time yet," Fulton said. "Don't blow nothing up without my mark."

"Gotcha." Dedrick threw a warning look to Bolcan.

Bolcan shook his head. "Don't worry about me." He set the block on the transformer and unwound more detonator wire as he paced to the explosives on the next transformer.

"We're waiting for the girls to get the babies on the bus," Fulton said. "Elder Lukman wanted me to check on you. Seems Unity Troopers are suspicious about activity in a nearby neighborhood."

"We're fine," Bolcan said. "Got the explosives in place. Another minute and we'll be ready to detonate."

"What are you talking about?" Dedrick asked Fulton, heading for the fence. He trusted Bolcan would get the third block of Semtex connected to the wire. "What do you mean *girls on the bus?*"

"Oh, I guess you left out of here before getting the plan. We're having a fire drill at the Breeder Facility."

"Huh? That sounds like a bad idea. Won't CSS be all over that?" Dedrick reached the fence and grabbed the cold links, but then his gaze shifted to Bolcan's backpack.

"No," Fulton said. "We contacted CSS to let them know we were doing it."

"Are you crazy?" Dedrick squatted and unzipped the backpack. Not sure he saw what he thought he saw, he leaned to get his shadow out of the way. Ten or so blocks of Semtex, neatly stacked, and a big coil of detonator wire filled the bag.

"Kind of risky," Fulton said, "but we convinced them we were legit. Told them the girls needed to work on their emergency evacuation routine. They're past performances, dragging their feet, talking, going back for things, would've left half of them dead."

"Zip that up and give it to me." Bolcan stood behind Dedrick, legs spread and arms tensed.

Without zipping or lifting the bag, Dedrick straightened and stood face to face with Bolcan. "CSS bought it?" Dedrick said to Fulton while glaring at Bolcan.

"Guess so. So far so good. They want us in constant contact, though, telling them how it's progressing." Muffled voices came through the earphone, then Fulton said, "Hey, I'll contact you when it's *go* time."

"Copy that," Dedrick and Bolcan said together.

Bolcan stepped past Dedrick, bumping his shoulder, then bent over his backpack and zipped and lifted it with one hand. He slung it over a shoulder and grabbed onto the fence.

"Got a lot of Semtex in your bag." Dedrick leaped and gripped the top horizontal bar of the fence.

Bolcan leaped, too. The links jangled under them as they raced each other up and over. Their feet pounded to the ground at roughly the same time.

"I'm gonna need it," Bolcan said. "Probably need more than that."

Dedrick shook his head to convey his disapproval, but Bolcan turned before seeing it. Bolcan's obsession with the Re-Education Facility would get him in trouble with the Mosheh. He had to know that.

The two of them trekked across the field, a lawn in need of mowing, getting their fifty-yards distance. Dedrick swung the AR-15 off his back then took a magazine from his belt and slapped it into place.

"Where do you think they're taking the girls?" Bolcan said.

"Good question. And what'll they do with the Torva?" Dedrick preferred the idea of having the women in the care of the Mosheh, but he couldn't imagine the Mosheh welcoming the Torva to their underground network. They didn't typically open their doors to anyone except the few selected for rescue from Aldonia.

Figuring they had gone about fifty yards, Dedrick slowed.

"Here's good," Bolcan said, stopping.

"Yeah." Turning to the substation, Dedrick pulled back the charging handle and chambered a round. Then he got into position, dropping onto one knee and tucking the buttstock against his shoulder and cheek. He peered through the scope, sighting steel lattice structures, the chain-link fence then a transformer, but not the right one.

A light flashed behind him and a siren bleeped.

Dedrick and Bolcan dropped to the ground simultaneously, Bolcan facing the street, Dedrick the substation.

Dedrick's heart thumped against his ribs. Blades of grass tickled his ear. The long grass wouldn't completely hide them, but they both wore black, so they might go unnoticed.

"They're moving real slow," Bolcan said. "But I don't think they see us."

Dedrick jerked a hand to his TekBand, ready to contact Fulton when Fulton's voice came through his earphone.

"Unity Trooper in the area."

"Yeah, we see 'em," Bolcan said.

"Stay hidden," Fulton said. "They're not looking for you. Just some trouble in the area. As soon as they're gone, Dedrick, you're up. Then you two will have to beat it out of there. Head for the Breeder Facility. We may need you there."

"Copy that." Dedrick, lying prone, swung the rifle into position and dug his elbows into the ground. He took a few breaths, trying to calm himself, then peered through the scope and sighted the target. One shot was all he'd need.

"Okay," Bolcan said. "They're gone, outta view."

"Take the shot and run like hell," Fulton shouted.

Dedrick steadied himself, sighting the transformer, sighting the block of Semtex . . . He had to shoot between the chain links. *Easy now* . . . He squeezed the trigger.

Before the spent case hit the ground, the first transformer exploded into a ball of blinding white light. Then the second and the third.

"Let's go." Bolcan was on his feet, poised to run but looking at the spectacle.

Dedrick jumped up, swung the rifle over his back, and charged with Bolcan across the field. The electrical hum intensified, making Dedrick glance back.

Another explosion. Then another. Bolts of electricity ripped through the air, arcing and cracking with a sound that tore through Dedrick. Severed high voltage cable ends jumped and danced. Flames consumed the transformers and the boxy housing units under them. Rolling black smoke . . . shooting sparks . . . he would've liked to stay and watch.

Except for the Unity Troopers screeching onto the scene.

16

I sat on the weathered brick wall of an empty flower bed outside my new apartment, gazing off into the distance. A few street lights, half as many as before curfew, illuminated portions of the empty street. Someone shouted from a top floor of the towering apartment building across the way. Someone from a lower floor answered. Lights shone in two-thirds of the windows, giving us a bit of light down here.

A young man with a round face, cocky smile, and yellow eyes sat beside me with his legs stretched and crossed at the ankles and his bare feet twitching every now and then. He reminded me of the kid in Bot's game, but I didn't dare ask him. Our competitive relationship had stirred up feelings of hate. I wanted him to like me, to trust me now. Besides, he probably didn't recognize me with my yellow-zinc hair and scarlet eyes.

The wind had died down, making the air warmer. I had managed to get several neighbors to join me outside. So now seventeen of us hung out, some drinking, others pacing, and a few talking. We had all left our flexi-phones inside in case the Citizen Safety Station did roll call. If a vehicle approached, we'd have to bolt for the doors and take the party inside. CSS discouraged loitering and after-curfew excursions.

"How do you know they lie to us?" Yellow-eyes said. "Why would they? And who are they? There's no *they*. We're all in this together." He took a swig of his drink, some volatile concoction that his friend had distilled in his bathtub. He had offered to share, earlier, but I had declined.

"We're all trying to do our part to care for Mother Earth," a girl said. A hint of sarcasm in her tone? She glanced up from the mouse or rat or whatever quivered in her hands. Alix had told me she took the thing everywhere she went, storing it in a pocket or her purse, sharing her meals with it.

The girl bent over and let the rodent scamper on the ground. It didn't go far. Eyes on the little thing, she straightened and stuffed her hands into her jacket pockets. Her unusual height, towering over every kid in our group, made me wonder if scientists had tried something new with her genes and now secretly studied her.

"Come to the assembly Friday," I said loud enough for everyone to hear.

As a few of them glanced, everyone suddenly transformed into shadowy figures. We all gasped.

The street lights had blinked out. Again. Apparently, it happened often in this neighborhood. The nearly-full moon peeked from behind heavy clouds but then disappeared. People clapped. More shouts and laughter came from the apartments across the street, from windows that had also gone black. A few points of light flickered on in several windows, light from their flexi-phones.

"Come here, Whiskers," the tall girl said, her form a shadow blending in with more shadows.

"Why do you keep that thing?" someone asked. "It's wrong to interfere with other animals."

"I'm not interfering," she said. "He's my friend."

My eyes began to adjust, allowing me to locate everyone in our group. A couple stood hugging or kissing. A few others huddled in a circle. The rest stood where they had before the power outage.

"Come to the assembly, you guys. You won't regret it." I figured I had their full attention now, since we couldn't see anything. "There's more to life, but the Regimen has kept it from us. And they have secrets they don't want us to know." I had invited the group when we first got outside, but only two seemed interested.

What could I say to get more to come? This little way frustrated me, inviting one here and one there to a talk they might not even agree with. I wanted to do something bigger, to be part of something pivotal like the Battle of Trenton in the fight for independence. Still . . . a part of me felt good about attempting to make a dent, even if nothing came from it. Another part of me felt fake. Maybe because I worked undercover, never revealing my true self, but also because it went against my nature to talk so much.

"Aren't you a Unity Trooper? You and your roommate?" Yellow-eyes stuttered a laugh and scraped a bare foot back and forth on the cement.

"So?" I couldn't imagine sitting outside barefoot in these cool temperatures. The alcohol must've warmed him.

"I don't know how I feel," he said, "about living in the same building as Unity Troopers, and rebellious ones at that."

The front door of the apartment swung open and Alix stomped out with a flashlight. She wore her Unity Trooper uniform, minus the helmet. Everyone quieted and stared. While a person might consider an off-duty Unity Trooper a friend, the instant the uniform came on, wariness, even hostility surfaced.

She strode toward me, her expression hidden by the dark.

I scooted off the brick wall and wiped the seat of my jeans. "What's with you?"

"Where you been? I came looking for you earlier. You go somewhere after our shift?"

"I . . . I just had to check something out. I'm here now. What's up?"

"Come on. Get changed." She grabbed my arm and tugged, not allowing me to protest. "I volunteered you for extra hours. We need to go now."

"What? Why would you do that? I thought we were supposed to—" I pointed to Yellow-eyes.

Alix dragged me up the steps and to the heavy front door. "This power outage, it's big. Apparently, an entire electrical substation exploded."

I stopped at the door. "A substation? Why do they need troopers for that? They need electricians."

Once inside the foyer, she flashed the light up and down the stairs then yanked me close and whispered, "The Mosheh want us at the Breeder Facility. Troopers have been called there."

"Breeder Facility? Something go bad with the rescues?" My stomach leaped into my chest. Dedrick had been working with a team, preparing for it. The Mosheh usually dragged their feet approving a plan. Had the rescues begun already? Was Dedrick in trouble?

With only the handrail and the beam of her flashlight to guide us, we tramped up the stairs side by side, one flight, two flights . . .

"No," Alix said, her voice low, "this has to do with those wild men. They crawled in under the fence anyway."

We stepped onto our floor.

"The Torva? They were supposed to wait." So many of the breeders seemed to welcome the opportunity to live free and raise their own children. I thought for sure the plan would work.

"Yeah, well, they didn't wait." Alix swung open the door to our apartment and pushed me inside.

"Were they caught coming in? Did they get into the Breeder Facility?" Steering around boxes of clothes and supplies in the living room, I stripped my sweatshirt off over my head. Not having undressed in front of anyone since Secondary, it made me self-conscious. Even in the dark.

Alix went ahead of me into my bedroom. "The wild men are in the facility. That's all I know. The message was brief. Urgent."

Hangers clanked in my closet then Alix flung my armor onto the bed.

"What are we supposed to do?" I envisioned Unity Troopers, me among them, storming into the Fully Protected Nature Preserves, searching until we found every colony.

"The Mosheh will instruct us once we're there." She tossed me my uniform shirt, a snug black pullover worn under the armor.

I wrestled the shirt on over my head and fixed my hair up in a ponytail. "What else did they tell you? What are we going into?"

While I changed into the pants, she loosened the straps of my scaled ballistic vest.

"Quit with the questions. The plan changed earlier today." She helped me into the vest. "The Torva decided not to play by the Mosheh's rules. That's all I know."

"Then we're all ruined. They'll find out where the Torva came from. They'll search the—"

"Get a grip." She slapped my helmet into my hands. "The Mosheh will break in and give you messages through your helmet, just like our captain does. But you can't reply to the messages or else our captain—and whoever else is listening—will hear it." She put her own helmet on. "Got it?"

I nodded and followed her out the door, down to the first floor, and out back to her UT-issued motorcycle. No, I didn't get it. How could I follow the Mosheh's instructions and still come off as a faithful Unity Trooper? I would probably blow my cover tonight. Then what?

17

Jogging at a pace that bordered on sprinting, Dedrick pushed himself. Bolcan stayed a few steps ahead, as he had from the beginning, apparently too competitive to run side by side. Irked, Dedrick kept trying to catch up. Which explained how they got to this unsustainable pace.

The sound of Bolcan's heavy footfalls accompanied by the thudding and jingling of his gear kept Dedrick on track. Without them, he'd have stumbled into a curb by now. They ran through darkness almost as thick as in the tunnels, using the flashlight infrequently to avoid notice. A sooty sky, a shade lighter than their surroundings, hid the stars and moon. On either side, buildings towered above them, ominous shadows with a scattering of dimly-lit windows.

Bolcan's footsteps faltered then his hand landed on Dedrick's chest. "Let's . . . take it easy. We're over halfway there . . . I think." He flicked on his flashlight and slowed his pace. The beam of light showed their turn a half-mile ahead. It also revealed Bolcan's heaving chest and his sloppy stride.

Heart pounding and sucking in deep breaths of cold air, Dedrick worked on regulating his breathing. He could outrun Bolcan if he wanted to.

At this slower pace, the chirp of a cricket came to his ears, and then a man's voice from an upper window. A campfire burned, visible between apartment buildings, the work of an Aldonian taking a risk out past curfew.

Bolcan shut off the light. They walked blindly again, this time with the impressions of buildings and their general direction in their minds.

The campfire scent took Dedrick back to last fall, to the endless walk through the woods on his search for the Maxwell colonists. Grenton had come up behind him. *"You there."*

A shudder ran through Dedrick, accompanied by an involuntary groan. He could hear Grenton's disturbing baritone voice in his head.

"Problem?" Bolcan switched on his flashlight and shined the beam at Dedrick's gut.

"No, just hoping this goes down smooth."

"Think the Torva will accept the change of plans?"

"I don't know." Knowing Grenton, he could not imagine unquestioning compliance. As firstborn of Takomo, chieftain of the Shikon Tribe, he probably deemed it necessary to come across hard and unflinching, at least around his men. Plus, he had a reason to hate the Regimen. They killed his mother, he had said. Maybe he even *wanted* to confront them. If he wanted that, he'd get that. But he'd never win. Miriam had tried to tell him that.

It was the night Dedrick had inadvertently revealed the way into and out of Aldonia. Dedrick, having slept all day, had finally woken up. He'd joined Miriam and his sister Ann around a bonfire with several other colonists and more than a few Torva. Including Grenton, who sat next to Ann.

Dedrick hadn't realized anyone listened while he and Miriam discussed their way out of Aldonia, the sinkhole behind the Breeder Facility.

"What do they breed?" Grenton had broken into their private conversation with his baritone voice.

Miriam explained, telling him and all the Torva about the twisted reproductive methods of the Aldonians. Without realizing it, Dedrick had brought the seed of an idea into the open. Miriam had planted it, and Grenton would make it grow.

Grenton had played with a tuft of his hair, one directly over his scar. "You say there's an easy way into this Breeder Facility."

Miriam had shown her disapproval with a headshake. "Don't get any ideas. They've got surveillance and security. You'd never be able to steal a girl from there." Growing up in a colony, she had experienced Torva raids. She should have known their recklessness and determination.

"We wouldn't steal *one*," Grenton had said. "We'd take them all. They shouldn't live like that. It's inhuman." Grenton had obviously justified the idea in his own mind; they'd be saving the women.

"They have babies," Miriam said. "You can't take the girls and leave the babies with no one to care for them."

"Then we will take their babies, too."

"Forget about it," Miriam had said. At this point, she may have realized the seriousness of the threat, but it hadn't shown in her manner. "Your weapons and numbers don't compare to the strength of Aldonia. And their girls like it in there. It's the most desired vocation."

"They have never met us," Grenton said, "us wild men."

A hand landed hard against Dedrick's gut, taking his breath away and snapping him from his thoughts.

"Look up," Bolcan shouted as he dove off the road.

Dedrick glanced up to see headlights on the road before him, several blocks away but moving in their direction. He darted off the road, grabbing his flashlight from his belt.

"Over here," Bolcan said, shining his flashlight at Dedrick then shutting it off. He squatted behind an unkempt hedge that grew in front of an apartment building.

Dedrick joined him and watched as two pairs of headlights approached.

"It looks more like a bus than a trooper's vehicle," Bolcan said.

"Two buses," Dedrick said, noticing the strings of lights that ran down the sides of them. He tapped his TekBand to talk to Fulton. "Fulton . . . we've got company."

"You on 44th Street already?" Fulton's voice came through Dedrick's earphone. "I was getting ready to contact you. We've got two buses, and we need one of you on each. I'll tell our drivers to expect you."

"Copy that." Dedrick jumped into action first, bolting for the road.

The bus barreled toward him. The strips of LED headlamps became visible over each headlight, giving the bus two angry eyes.

Standing in the middle of the street, he waved his arms. A thought crossed his mind. These might not actually be the Mosheh-controlled buses. These might be Regimen, and he'd be caught. He'd have to run.

Bolcan jogged toward the street.

The bus's low beams found Dedrick. He flung an arm over his eyes to block the glaring light. The bus screeched to a stop and the door squeaked open.

Dedrick cut around to the side and laid eyes on the driver.

"Come on up," Camilla said with a smile, her face illuminated by the glowing gauges and controls on the dashboard. Leaning forward with her back straight and one hand to the door controller, she managed to look at ease in a cockpit designed for a bigger person.

"I thought you were at the university." Dedrick thumped up the steps.

"Yeah, I needed a change of pace, something more exciting." She closed the door and shifted into drive, the interior lights dimming.

Dedrick latched onto the vertical bar behind the driver's seat and glanced at the passengers on the dark bus. Women in robes and nightgowns with infants and children piled on their laps. A few men sprinkled through the group. Little children standing in the aisles. Almost everyone stared at him, eyes round, confusion on their faces. They probably had a time cramming onto two busses, probably wondered what happened next.

What did happen next?

"So what's the plan?" Dedrick leaned against the pole to come closer to her.

"The Mosheh didn't tell you?"

"No, we've been busy with other things."

"Due to the, uh, *situation* at the Breeder Facility, the residents are being transferred to emergency housing." She glanced. "An old Secondary school not far from here."

She peered in the rearview mirror then spoke in a quieter voice. "Now that you're here, you can sedate the staff." She reached into a side pocket in the driver's seat, pulled out a canvas folder, and handed it to him.

Dedrick opened it, finding several black cylinders—Mosheh-designed sedation misters.

"Once we arrive at the facility," Camilla continued, "we'll see which of these mamas want freedom." A glint of pleasure flashed in her eyes.

Dedrick understood. It gave him a rush, too, rescuing people, bringing a person to a life they've never known about but should've had all along. A life of freedom.

"They'll stay on the bus," she said. "The rest get booted off at the facility. Including the staff. Guess we'll have to carry them in ourselves. Hope you're ready for a workout." She glanced, grinning. "Then we'll confiscate flexi-phones from our freebirds and remove implants so no one is tracked. That's going to bring some tears to the babies." Her gaze shifted from the road to the rearview mirror. She grew up in a big family. She knew all about babies' tears.

"Then we get to an access point," Dedrick concluded, liking the plan more and more. "Every girl who wants it will be free."

"Yup, you got it." She smiled.

Dedrick scanned the passengers. Most had turned their attention to the children. A few still watched him. "How do I know which ones are staff?"

"May I have your attention, please," Camilla shouted, glancing in the rearview mirror. She flipped a switch and overhead lights came on.

Dedrick slid one of the misters from the folder and turned to the passengers.

"Citizen Safety Station needs to ensure that we are proceeding according to regulations," Camilla said.

"Is that me?" Dedrick smirked at her over his shoulder. "I'm with Citizen Safety?"

She shrugged, a light-hearted grin stretching across her face. "Sure, why not? They're all yours now."

"Thanks."

Stepping around toddlers and glancing at faces, he took a few steps down the aisle. How could he accomplish this? He didn't want to reach over anyone when he sprayed the sedatives. And he couldn't have babies sliding from the arms of sedated staff.

A few steps later it came to him. Yeah, he knew what to do. "Staff members, please stand." He stood tall and tried to sound official. "You must be seated on the aisles, and you need hands free so you can be of assistance when needed. So pass the children to one of the . . ." He struggled to get the next word out, hated to use it. It was degrading. ". . . to one of the breeders."

Ten people stood: one older man, three young men probably fresh from Secondary, and a group of middle-aged women. As they handed off infants and toddlers, a baby burst into tears, a toddler called for a nanny, and chatter began. Girls stood to switch seats with staff members. More babies cried. The chatter grew louder.

"You can shut out the overhead lights," Dedrick called back to Camilla.

The lights went out.

Pleased with the semi-darkness and commotion—it would keep people from noticing the staff members passing out—Dedrick maneuvered to the back of the bus. He'd start there.

The staff member farthest back, a fortyish woman, leaned over a toddler who lay in the aisle throwing a tantrum. "Settle down," the woman said, trying to grab a flailing arm. The girl beside her worked on comforting a crying baby, paying no attention as Dedrick drew near.

"Hey, sit up," Dedrick said in a low voice, hoping to draw only the woman's attention.

As she lifted her head, Dedrick sprayed the sedative.

"What are you . . . doing?" she said, her voice weaker on the last word and her eyes glazing over. The toddler stopped his tantrum and lay flat on his back, his wide eyes locked on Dedrick.

Dedrick pushed the woman back into the seat and buckled her in so she wouldn't topple into the aisle. He smiled at the toddler. "You don't have to stop your tantrum on my account."

He came up behind the next staff member, this one a boy. As he sprayed the sedative, the bus slowed, whining as it decelerated. It decelerated more urgently, rumbling, the engine groaning.

Grabbing a seatback to steady himself, he peered out the front windows of the bus.

A row of flashing orange and blue lights stretched across the road.

A roadblock of Unity Troopers.

18

Surrounded by darkness, cool air rushing by, the rumble of the motorcycle vibrating through me, I sat behind Alix, balancing on the back half of the seat and clinging to her armor at the waist. The lack of street lights due to the power outage had no effect on her speed. She meant to get us to the Breeder Facility in record time.

The slope of the seat put me a bit higher than Alix, so I kept my head tucked and my eyes closed. I typically enjoyed a bike ride, but riding through darkness with Alix as the driver was not the same. Glimpses to each side had given me vertigo and made my stomach flip. We appeared to race through nothingness. No ground beneath us. No buildings. No horizons.

Even with eyes closed, the vertigo gripped me, the world tipping . . . or maybe vanishing, leaving me to drift alone through space.

I opened my eyes and peered over Alix's shoulder to gain some impression of reality.

The beam of the headlight revealed gravel and cracks in the road, a weed here or there that had fought its way through a curb, and impressions of high rises ahead.

I still felt like a comet soaring through space, a tail of excitement in my wake. I was a tiny comet in the vast solar system, trembling as I approached the sun. Or rather, I was a Patriot, small and uncertain, coming up against the greatest world power of the day.

This wasn't an open battle, though. I didn't need to feel this way. Maybe we would find the Torva before other troopers did and we could direct them to safety. I had no need to fear, I simply needed to figure out my little part.

We rounded a corner and darkness gave way to glaring white and flashing blue and orange lights. About eight Regimen vehicles, Citizen Safety Station and Unity Trooper, were parked every which way in the street. Two had even pulled up onto sidewalks. A few troopers stood by various cars and equipment, none looking our way. Searchlights cut through the night, sweeping over sidewalks, doors, low windows, and lawns between the towering facilities. Light glowed in several hospital windows, probably powered by backup generators. A few dim lights showed in the Breeder Facility windows, at least one on each level.

Alix slowed the bike and leaned into a tight turn. She parked at the end of a row of six Unity Trooper motorcycles and scooters. She shut off the engine and we dismounted at the same time.

"We should . . ." Alix lifted her visor and turned her icy blue eyes to me. Now that we wore the helmets, we'd have to watch what we said. "I'm going in, to see where we're needed."

"Me too." We cut across a lawn, making a bee-line for the open front doors of the Breeder Facility.

"Remember they are always watching," Elder Lukman had said to me before I left the Mosheh Control Center. I wouldn't forget. The elders had gone over this several times. Devices in the trooper helmets sent audio and video to various Regimen offices. UT commanders used the live feeds to guide troopers on duty. Citizen Safety Station used the information in their continuous search for terrorists—meaning those with opposing views.

"Once you're on duty, you can't simply remove the helmet either," Elder Rayna had told me. "If the need arises, you will have to be creative and find a reasonable explanation for why the helmet comes off."

"Pretend someone comes up behind you and cracks you in the head," Bolcan had said, his golden locks flying into his face as he demonstrated. "Or throw yourself on the ground and roll around a bit." He dropped onto the floor right in the middle of the Control Center and thrashed his arms and legs. Then he rolled over and sat up, grinning. "They'll assume you're in a fight."

Elder Rayna had covered her mouth and turned away, attempting to conceal her amusement. "You're creative, Liberty. You will know what to do when the time comes."

~~~

"You there. Troopers." Hurried footfalls sounded behind us.

With less than twenty paces to the open doors of the Breeder Facility, it took effort for me to stop. Alix and I looked at each other before turning to face Commander Fillida.

In a scaly UT uniform draped with weapons—a bulky rubber-bullet rifle, a holstered stun gun, two tasers, and a tactical gas gun—she stomped up to us and took a wide-legged stance. She wore her visor and gas mask up and the helmet strap dangling freely. Her hard eyes assessed us for a moment.

"You, Lex, get inside." She lifted the strap of the tactical gas gun over her head, grabbed a taser from her hip, and handed both weapons to Alix. "We believe there are intruders in the Breeder Facility." She withdrew a 20-centimeter sheathed knife from a thigh pocket. "They may be armed, so use whatever force necessary to subdue them."

After packing the other two weapons, Alix grabbed the knife. She unsheathed and inspected it then nodded but didn't take off.

"You." The commander's eyes narrowed as she looked me over. "What is your name?" She stepped closer, probably identifying me herself with a retina scan.

"Huh? I . . ." My mind could only pull up my real name.

"That's Amity," Alix said. "She's a new transfer, but she's not new to the job. Send her in with me."

"Who's your partner?" Commander Fillida said, tilting her chin so that she glared down her nose at me.

"Holt, Commander." I stood as straight and tall as possible. "But we're first shift. I don't think he'd be here."

"Holt's here. He came in." She turned and scanned the area. "He's outside somewhere searching the perimeter. Find him." Her attention snapped back to Alix. "I gave you your orders. Go."

"Yes, Commander," Alix shouted. She gave me a nod and took off for the open doors. I wondered if the Mosheh had given her instructions.

The commander stormed away, heading towards troopers who operated a searchlight.

I took off for the perimeter, jogging across the lawn, when a voice came through my helmet. "Liberty . . ."

The feminine voice did not sound familiar, but the speaker used my real name, so it had to be Mosheh. Remembering Alix's warning, I forced myself not to respond.

"We need you inside. Once your commander is out of view, get there."

I glanced over my shoulder then spun full circle. I spotted Commander Fillida a stone's throw away leaning in the open door of a trooper vehicle near the searchlight.

I bolted for the facility.

The doors stood open wide. A portable lantern on the floor of the entranceway gave gray light to walls, shiny plaques, and huge prints of extinct animals and organisms.

"You've been through the access point in the crematorium," the Mosheh woman said. "Go there now."

Three hallways branched off from the entrance, dim light showing at the end of one, darkness in the others. Not having spent much time here, I amazed myself at what I remembered. Elevators straight ahead. Offices to the right. The left hallway led to the hospital, but the stairwell also came off it. I switched my visor to night vision and took off.

"With the power out," the Mosheh woman said, her voice something of a comfort, "you'll need to climb inside the cremator and manually switch to connect to our tunnel. Then we need you to get as many Torva to safety as possible. They rejected our first attempt, but with the troopers on to them, they may listen to you."

I clomped up the dark stairwell, the walls, rails, and steps appearing greenish through my night-vision visor. The crematorium was on the fourth floor.

As I neared the third-floor landing, a burst of lime-green light flashed. Flickering light followed. I pounded up the last few steps. Flames and a figure showed through a square window in the door. The figure disappeared. Torva?

I grabbed the doorknob but then froze. I would have to watch myself. The Regimen would see what I saw and hear what I heard.

Twisting the knob, I opened the door to blinding light, flames in the nearest open doorway. I threw an arm over my eyes and lifted my night-vision visor. Ghost spots hovered in my vision. Blinking them back, I stepped into a smoky hallway on a residential floor.

"Not here," a man called from a distance but directly ahead. Torva or Unity Trooper?

I dashed past the burning room with its sour chemical smell and came to intersecting hallways.

Water droplets landed on my face, raining down from overhead fire sprinklers. To my left, smoke billowed from a half-open door. A blazing torch lay on the floor at the feet of two fighting figures, one a bearded man in primitive clothing, the other a fully-armored trooper. Swinging a knife, dodging, kicking . . . the Torva seemed to have the upper hand. The trooper's rifle lay on the floor, closer to me than to him. He must've dropped it in the skirmish.

"We've found none! This is a trap!" The gruff voice came from the opposite end of the hallway. A group of men, five or more, emerged from the smoke.

This was my chance. If only the trooper weren't here, I could lead these men to the crematorium before more troopers arrived.

I jogged toward the rifle and leaned for it.

The trooper spun toward me and I stopped. "Behind you," she shouted then charged toward me.

She sounded like Alix, but why would Alix be fighting instead of trying to save them?

Heart racing and unsure of what to do, I left the rifle and turned toward the approaching men. I needed to convince them they could trust me. I needed to save them.

Hands landed on my back and shoved me forward. My helmet cracked the wall and slid off my head, the strap cutting the skin on my chin. I smacked hard onto my knees and threw out my hands, stopping myself from landing on my face. The armor protected me from the pain I expected.

Feet shuffled. Something slid along the floor and cracked into a distant wall. Men shouted.

I jumped up, gulping in smoke so thick it burned the back of my throat.

Two Torva held Alix. She doubled over coughing, her hair hiding her face. She wore no helmet.

I wore no helmet! I glanced all around but couldn't see where they lay. This was my chance.

"Where are the girls?" A man with chest muscles at my eye level shoved me against the wall. A dozen or more men crowded into the hallway, the smoke hiding their features.

"You must come with me," I said, peering up at the man who'd shoved me. The smoke brought tears to my eyes. "I'll take you to them." Did the Mosheh have the girls, or was I making a promise I couldn't keep? Either way, if they came with me, they'd remain free.

The muscular man turned his head, facing the others. He laughed, a sound so deep it made me cringe.

"We must go," another man said. "More are coming. We blocked doors, but they will get through."

"Come with me." Desperation or maybe smoke constricted my throat. I blinked to see through my watery eyes. "You can't fight them. There will be too many. I can take you somewhere safe."

"Listen . . . to her," Alix struggled to say. "We're with . . ." A coughing fit erupted.

"We're with the Mosheh," I said.

"Why should we believe you?" The man brought a knife to my throat then dragged it backwards through my yellow-zinc hair. "You are Aldonian. And you wear the armor of the enemy."

"Let's go," another man said, slapping this man on the arm. More had crowded into the hallway on either side of us.

A hissing came from the far end of the hallway and a loud bang that made me jump. A split-second later, an explosion with a flash of light showed through the smoke. All heads turned as Unity Troopers thundered toward us.

"Please." I grabbed my captor's arms. This was the last chance. If we ran to the stairwell, if we blocked the door, if troopers didn't already swarm the 4th floor . . . "You must come with me. I can get us out of here."

"We don't want out of here," my captor said, stepping away from me. "Not without the women." He turned toward the troopers. Like a fool.

I grabbed his arm, a sweaty, muscular thing that slipped from my grip. "I know what you want. Come." The Unity Troopers had probably drawn near enough to make me out through the smoke. They couldn't have heard me, though.

Alix broke from the Tova that held her and yanked me by the arm. Men shouted and rushed forward. Alix dragged me back the way I had come, through a crowd of shouting wild men and toward the stairwell.

"No, this is crazy." I twisted my arm, trying to break free of her grip.

She forced me past the burning room to the stairwell door.

The shouting continued. Then shots rang out.

One, two, three, four . . .

A wave of despair washed over me, leaving me sick and trembling.

We both grabbed the knob together, I to stop her from opening it.

I held her gaze for a moment, neither of us forcing our way.

"Turn and move forward," a man shouted. "Resistors will be shot."

I looked over my shoulder. Through rolling black smoke and hazy gray, I saw them.

The Torva. They marched down the hall, hands restrained behind their backs, flanked and driven by Unity Troopers.

Wild men. Captured by the Regimen.

We'd failed them.

19

"Good, you're right where I told you to be. This time." With a grim face and her helmet dangling from her hand, Commander Fillida emerged through the open front doors of the Breeder Facility. She operated controls above the implant scanner and the doors slid shut.

Heavy with defeat, I forced myself to stand tall and combed a hand through my hair. My ponytail had fallen out, and I had nothing with which to fasten it back. Didn't matter. I couldn't look worse in her eyes. She had caught me stumbling from the building an hour ago, knowing I had disobeyed her direct command to find my partner, Holt.

Standing face to face, Commander Fillida stared me down through cold salmon-colored eyes.

I dropped my gaze to her flaring nostrils to keep her from reading my mood.

"I don't know how they do it in your old troop." Arms behind her back, she circled around me. "But here, we follow commands."

"Yes, Commander!" I expected to receive a good scolding. She'd already forced me to remain outside while other troopers searched the building, while the firefighters came and went, and while troopers conducted the Torva past me and to a prisoner bus.

The man who had held a knife to my throat had noticed me leaning against the wall, his gaze connecting to mine as he passed. Tall and muscular, with self-assurance in his step, a scar over one eye, and bare-chested except for a vest made of animal hide, he struck me as their leader.

Anger at their stubbornness had brought tears to my eyes as I watched. They would go to Re-Ed. Each of them would suffer. How would we ever rescue so many from there again? The Regimen would not be fooled the same way twice.

Alix had marched out last, her movements swift and her attitude serious. She had the air of a seasoned trooper who hoped for advancement. "Building's clear," she had reported to Commander Fillida, not glancing at me at all. They exchanged a few words then she strode to her motorcycle and waited while the rest cleared out, leaving me and our commander the last ones here outside the Breeder Facility doors.

The commander continued circling and berating me. ". . . would never have sent a girl like you in alone. You're too new."

A retort floated in my mind. *I have more training than any of your troopers, except for Alix. And I can handle myself.* I bit my tongue to keep from saying it. The comment wouldn't have earned me any points with her. For the sake of Aldonia, I needed this job.

"Do you understand me?" She faced me again.

I nodded, though I hadn't been listening.

"You newbies think you can run roughshod over our rules." The raw quality of her voice made me think she'd been yelling all day. "Think you know better? You will do things our way, or I'll be filling out a Vocation Change Request form on your behalf."

Maybe I needed a change of vocation. Maybe Unity Trooper was not the best job for me. If I had a more laid-back job, I could easily make friends to invite to the assemblies. But I wouldn't have had the access I had today, to help—

Sadness twisted my heart and my eyelids fluttered. No, I hadn't helped anyone.

Why wouldn't the Torva listen to me? They would go to Re-Ed . . . more people trapped in Aldonia instead of more people free. And the breeders, the women . . . the Torva men had said they couldn't find them. What had happened to them?

"Where are you?" I asked *My Friend*, speaking internally. Caught up as I had been in this mission, I couldn't remember the last time I'd turned to Him or even felt His presence.

He had done this before, abandoned me. *Abandon* was probably the wrong word. He probably meant this as a test or a way to help me grow. Losing a battle didn't mean losing the war. I needed faith. I needed to believe without seeing, without feeling. Amid failure, I needed to trust that somehow this would work for good.

Or maybe I had taken a wrong turn. Maybe I shouldn't have been doing this.

The twisting of my heart increased. We failed. I failed.

". . . return to the station and file a report with Captain Erran. You will explain yourself . . ."

As Commander Fillida paced behind me, my gaze caught movement in the distance. Across the street, in an alley between tall administration buildings, a bus with dark headlights rolled forward and then back out of view.

Our bus? Could the women and children be on it waiting for the Unity Troopers to leave so they could return to the Breeder Facility? Why would they return? Maybe they had to. The Mosheh may have only had them removed to keep them from the Torva. Or maybe they planned to use the access points in the Breeder Facility to bring them to safety.

I sucked in a breath, my failure striking me hard. The crematorium! I should've gone there first and manually switched the tunnel access. It was the only command they had given me before I lost my helmet.

My helmet! I could use that as an excuse to go back inside.

"Is that your ride?" Commander Fillida squinted over my shoulder.

"Um." I glanced.

Alix sat on the curb near her motorcycle leaning back on her arms, her legs stretched out before her. She wore her helmet, so if the Mosheh had given a command, she'd know it.

"Yes, Commander, it is."

"Then get to the station." She stepped away, turning toward the last UT vehicle in the street.

"Wait!" I almost grabbed her arm but thought better of it. "My helmet. It's inside the facility. I know where I dropped it."

She looked me over, her eyes narrowing. Then she stomped back to the main doors. "Never leave things behind." She tapped a code on the control panel above the implant reader then scanned her implant. "Retrieve your helmet and get to the station."

The door slid open.

"Yes, commander." I dashed inside and the door slid shut behind me.

~~~

I stood stunned for a moment holding a flashlight in a trembling hand and staring at three waist-high doors in the steel wall of the crematorium. Dedrick and Miriam had brought me here almost a year ago to save me. I hadn't recognized them or known their intention. Dedrick had to beg me to trust him.

There was a control panel off to the side. Dedrick had used it to open one of the doors. I would have to do it manually.

Taking a breath, I clipped my flashlight to my belt and pressed my palms to one of the cool steel doors. I pushed as hard as I could.

It budged.

Leaning my body into it, feeling a strain in my arms, I pushed again. It slid up easier now. When I got an opening wide enough for my hands, I gripped the bottom edge and forced the door the rest of the way.

A deep, foul odor hit me.

Gagging, I stumbled aside. A charred face popped into my mind, a hideous thing drawing near. Hollow eyes, burning limbs, haunting movements. More burning bodies. They pointed at me. This was my fault.

Guilt clawed at the core of my being. I edged back. This was my fault. I did this to them.

More and more gruesome figures appeared in my mind, surrounding me, reaching for me, and leaving me no way to escape.

I backed into something hard and reached behind me.

A table, flat, cold . . .

Faces appeared inside the hollow eyes, dark hair, pale green eyes—

I gasped. My face!

"No," I shrieked, swinging my arms for protection. "Not real. Not real." I breathed and turned away, bumping a stainless-steel body cart behind me. Body cart. Crematorium.

I rubbed my face with cold hands and sucked in a deep breath. I needed to rein in my thoughts. The images . . . they were from the History Lessons, the lessons on the destruction resulting from overpopulation and rampant industrialization. This was not real.

Hands trembling, I rolled the cart to the open crematory. As I climbed onto the cart, the odor brought the haunting images back, but I worked to ignore them. I got on hands and knees, bringing my face up to an imaginary charred face. Then, with a final push, I crawled through it and onto a track of steel plates in a narrow, metal shaft.

The odor of burnt flesh made me gag again. The imaginary figures surrounded me.

With my flashlight strapped to my shoulder and the beam bouncing, I crawled forward. I remembered how the tracks had moved my body along and how I'd felt the heat on my bare feet. So the flames must've been farther down the shaft, but the floor had shifted before I got there, transferring me to a smooth surface in a sloped tunnel, the Mosheh access point. Dedrick had used the control panel to save me. I'd need to do this by hand.

Staying low to avoid bumping my head, I had crawled forward about three meters when the beam of my flashlight revealed two diagonal slits in the smooth metal walls. The slits, about a meter apart, angled away from me. A bit farther down on the opposite wall, two vertical slits ran from top to bottom of the shaft.

I envisioned the mechanics of it. The vertical lines were the edges of the door to the access point. I would need to force the door up or down. The diagonal lines were the edges of a panel that would lay across the tracks and angle a person to the access point. It would probably have a raised lip on the far side, something to guide the body off the crematory track.

Excitement raced through my veins, subduing the haunting images and propelling me into action. I could do this.

Within a minute, I figured out how to lower the diagonal panel. Latches at the top held it into place. As I expected, it had a wide lip on the far edge. Within another minute, I gripped the bottom of the door and pushed upwards, lying awkwardly because of the lack of space but giving it everything I had.

Cool air assailed me, blowing my hair as the door slid open and disappeared overhead. The beam of my flashlight showed bricks arching over a sharply-sloped metal slide that dropped down to darkness.

A falling sensation overcame me. I shrunk back.

The first time I'd been here, moving through the tunnel, I believed that I had somehow chosen death over life in Aldonia, that only death could bring freedom. I was wrong. I had chosen life. Life that most Aldonians never knew.

Whispering voices traveled down the shaft, interrupting my thoughts. Were they from the History Lesson or were they real?

I crawled back the way I had come. Movement showed through the door to the crematorium, shapes and colors and patches of light. Faces. A baby's soft cry.

I moved faster, pulling myself with my forearms, pushing with the sides of my feet.

A face appeared in the opening then a ball of blinding light in my eyes. "Got it?"

The sound of Alix's voice brought joy to my heart and made my eyes water. I found myself laughing and crying at the same time as I emerged from the shaft and swung around onto the body cart.

A crowd surrounded me. Women, girls really, with babies strapped to their chests. Others clutching the hands of the toddlers at their feet. All dressed in nightgowns. Eyes round with fear, excitement, apprehension . . . they didn't know what they were getting themselves into, but they wanted to love and raise their own children. They were willing to take the risk. They were brave.

"You can do it." I scooted off the table and patted it, inviting the nearest girl to climb up. These women and children would have to go on faith, like Sarkin, believing in something they couldn't see, trusting that it would lead them to something better.

My heart swelled near to bursting with my joy for them. I had failed the Torva, but these women would live free.

"Freedom lies at the end of a dark tunnel," I said. "Don't be afraid."

20

"Coming soon . . ." The face of an ageless woman with hair pulled back and perfect features seemed to pop from the TV screen. ". . . the 6-6-6 plan for ongoing formation."

Dr. Supero slumped down in a molded plastic couch until his neck rested on the curved rim and his face angled toward the ceiling. He had taken the couch at the back of the CSS waiting room because three or four people sat in each of the other three. Each could seat five or six comfortably, but he had no desire to socialize.

"Six times a day, six days a week . . ." the cheerful voice went on, ". . . you will receive a six-minute lesson on such topics as history, ecology, and nature equality. On the seventh day you will have an opportunity to win credits. That's right. Six days of six six-minute lessons and a chance to win credits that you can use anywhere, for anything. And who said learning can't be fun!"

Dr. Supero's flexi-phone buzzed. He lifted his wrist so he could identify the caller without moving his head.

Words scrolled across the screen: *The 6-6-6 plan, coming soon!* Then a 3D image appeared. Several tiny balls seemed to shoot from the screen toward him. They burst into red, yellow, and green fireworks. The woman on the nearest couch giggled as she watched the firework display coming from her flexi-phone.

Dr. Supero sighed, disgusted by the propaganda, and covered his phone with his hand. He bumped the cut he'd gotten climbing a fence last night and winced. If he were at home or the lab, he would rip the flexi-phone from his wrist and whip it across the room. He had no intention of playing their educational games regardless of the credits he could earn.

The door beside the computer screen on the far wall—the virtual receptionist—slid open. "Nova 554-062472-25?"

The boy on the nearest couch stood up.

Dr. Supero sighed and closed his eyes. He hated waiting. The governor herself had called him here. Eleven o'clock sharp, she had said.

He yawned and felt his eyeballs relax behind his eyelids. He could use a nap. He'd been running himself ragged. Ever since the day wasted doing tubal reversals, he'd spent his free time deep in research. His biggest discovery came last night after Cam finally left the lab saying she'd get his medicine.

She had come through for him, to his surprise.

Sitting at his desk, several top-secret files open before him, Dr. Supero had brought a mug to his mouth and drained the cold remains of coffee. He'd shuffled to the empty coffee pot to fill it a third time. The door to the lab slid open, making his stomach leap. He'd expected troopers to collect him that night and for Cam to receive the reward.

"You're still here." Cam had clomped into the room. Face flushed and ponytail disheveled, strands now framing her face, she'd come up to him and set a bulging canvas sack by his feet. It rattled with the familiar sound of pills in plastic bottles.

Dr. Supero had exhaled a sigh of relief and set the empty coffee pot back down. Thankful, stunned, struggling to believe, he'd whispered, "You . . . came back."

She nodded, her serious expression and quick breaths saying something went wrong. "I said I would."

"It's so late," he said, wanting to know what had happened but not sure he should ask. Perhaps she'd been careless and CSS would come for her instead of for him.

"Yes, you should get to bed." She had smiled, a weak thing that did not hide the trouble in her eyes. Then she turned and bolted from the lab.

He should've gone at that moment and taken the goods to Guy, but he continued his research until the wee hours of the night then dragged himself home to his apartment. He had paid for that mistake in the morning.

The sound of people talking had woken him. With all the coffee he'd drunk the night before, his bladder screamed for relief, but his heavy eyelids wouldn't lift.

"I brought what you asked for. I want to meet the surgeon."

Dr. Supero's eyes had snapped open at the sound of his own voice.

His voice came again, but it had turned harsh and desperate. "Take this!"

Dr. Supero had bolted upright in bed, flung back the covers, and nearly wet himself.

There on the floor, a 3D image hovered above the face of the flexi-phone he had cast aside before bed. It played the video of that dreaded transaction. He would never forget the night he'd brought Guy and Angel stolen supplies in exchange for a surgeon, or how they had recorded the moment for blackmail.

Holding himself like a little boy who couldn't control his own body, Dr. Supero had scooted to the bathroom. *Who else would they send this recording to? Was this just a warning?* He should've delivered the supplies last night, despite the late hour. He would call for a substitute teacher, get dressed, and do it now.

As he'd relieved himself, taking longer than seemed humanly possible, his phone had buzzed.

He cut short his stream, raced to his bedroom, and snatched his flexi-phone from the floor. "Wait! I am here. I got your message." He grabbed his navy dress pants from under the bed, the ones he'd been wearing for the past three days because he had no time to do laundry. "Do not do anything foolish." Gripping his flexi-phone in one hand, he sat on the edge of his bed and shoved a foot into the pants. "I will deliver—"

"Dr. Supero?" A woman's voice.

Dr. Supero froze then glanced at the caller ID. *Yancy, governor of Aldonia.* "Dr. Supero?"

He could not get his mouth to move, the words to come out. What would the governor want with him? Guy had wanted him to contact her, but Supero had delayed that action. Perhaps Guy had moved things along.

He took a breath. "Yes, this is Dr. Supero. I am a very busy man. What is it you want?"

"Aldonia needs your services, Dr. Supero."

"Aldonia benefits from my services daily here at the university through my teaching and my research. What more can I do?"

"I am glad you ask. There is a small matter which would benefit from your attention. Well, not . . ." Her voice faltered, a sign of weakness or desperation. "Maybe it's not so small. There was an incident at the Breeder Facility last night, and we need a team to consider the best course of action."

"What incident?" He could not think of the Breeder Facility without thinking of Liberty. Perhaps they had another Liberty at the facility. He wanted nothing to do with her.

"We will meet at the Citizen Safety Station," Governor Yancy had said, "eleven o'clock sharp."

"I am a professor. I have classes to teach," he said, having every intention of skipping classes and no desire to meet with her.

"Find a substitute."

"Very well." He ended the call and sat stunned, exhausted, one foot in his dress pants. He would need to hurry to get the supplies to Guy and return for the meeting. He would not have time to shower, but perhaps a shave.

After yanking the pants up and tightening his belt, he'd staggered shirtless into the bathroom and commenced his five-minute grooming ritual. He added another five minutes to tidy up the whiskers, then grabbed a shirt and Angel's supplies.

Guy had been pleased with the news. Oddly, he had met Dr. Supero outside under a cloudy sky near the ruins of an old church building where people had once worshipped their imaginary deity. He had taken the backpack from Dr. Supero and set it on a cement block. "A meeting with the governor at CSS, huh?" He'd slid his arm around Dr. Supero's shoulders and walked with him.

"Yes, so I must be going. I do not wish to arouse suspicion."

"Understood." Brow lowering over eyes filled with mock-concern, Guy nodded. He straightened Dr. Supero's stocking cap using both his stump and his hand, then he rubbed Dr. Supero's chin which now sported manicured stubble and a chin strip. "I like what you've done here."

Dr. Supero gave him a hard, cold glare. "I am glad of that, but I must go."

"And I won't keep you. But here's what I want you to do . . ."

~~~

A figure sauntered into the waiting room, coming from the entrance way, a tall, muscular man in sweats and a tank-top that showed off his biceps.

Wild silver hair hid his face and fell past his shoulders to his well-developed, almost feminine appearing pecs.

Dr. Supero looked again and jerked back. No, it was a woman. *That* woman. What was her name? Oh, yes . . . Silver.

She stood by the virtual receptionist on the far wall. After touching a few controls on the screen, she stepped back and glared at the surveillance camera over the door. "Hey! I need some help here. Now!"

If she received attention before he did, he was going to lose control.

The door slid open and two armed officers stepped out. "Once you've registered, you'll have to take a seat."

"I don't have time to take a seat," she said. "I have clients. And I've had my credits docked twice last month. Can't afford to let it happen again."

Dr. Supero remembered her from an interview last year when they had searched for Liberty. She was one of Liberty's acquaintances, worked at a Rehabilitation Center, took steroids . . . brought Chief Varden to his knees.

"Take a seat," one of the officers said, stepping toward her. "You'll be called—"

Dr. Supero had turned away but now glimpsed sudden movement. Two people in the waiting room gasped. Somehow Sliver had managed to take the stun gun from the officer and get behind him with her meaty arm around his neck.

The other officer leveled his own stun gun at her. "Release him and drop the gun."

"You're crazy," Silver said, grinning and aiming at her hostage's chest. "You drop the gun and get Chief Varden. He knows me. He'll be happy to hear what I have to say. Tell him I have information that may be of interest to him. Tell him I know about a secret community . . . and I want a reward."

The officer lowered his gun and backed through the door he had emerged from.

The blood drained from Dr. Supero's face. The scar on his head pinched. What secret community did she mean? Did she know about Guy and the other miscreants at the old city center? Would she betray them? Would that be good news? Dr. Supero would no longer be enslaved to them. Or maybe he would fall with them. They would assume he turned them in. Then they'd share the videos they'd made. Unless he told Guy about Silver first. Maybe . . .

Dr. Supero stared ahead without focusing until something moved in his peripheral vision.

The woman nearest him gasped. "Look," she said to no one in particular.

Four troopers stormed in from the entranceway, tranquilizer guns leveled at Silver.

A man who carried himself like a person of importance stomped into the doorway where Silver waited, a grimace on his freckled face. *Chief Varden.* "You do not come to CSS demanding to be seen." He snatched the gun from Silver.

"I have information you want," she said, apparently undaunted by the show of force. "And I want a reward."

"We're not interested. We have other situations that require our attention." He turned away from her and scanned the waiting room, his gaze stopping on several people, including Dr. Supero. With a tilt of his square jaw, he invited them all back.

~~~

In a large conference room with ambient lighting, seven people sat around a long glassy table, Governor Yancy at one end and Chief Varden at the other. The others included the new Head Physician of Aldonia's hospital, a fifty-year-old man with perfect hair and a devious glint in his eyes; a young blond male geneticist, a recent college graduate who was supposedly something of a prodigy; and three middle-aged women who organized the day-to-day operations at the Breeder Facility.

Dr. Supero seated himself last, ending up with the seat next to Governor Yancy.

Governor Yancy concentrated on whatever computer images she had brought up on the tabletop, reading and flicking through files with an annoying jerk of her hand. Her hair, the same orange color but shorter than when he'd seen her last, stood straight on top and formed flat curls against her neck. She wore lipstick to match and a burnt umber pantsuit.

He had always despised her, the way she brushed his projects aside for her own, the way she stared without flinching when opposing him.

However, her ability to rise to positions of power, he had to admit, impressed him. She had gone from Regional Secretary of the Department of the Environment to President of Aldonia's City Council. To governor. He would have to keep that in mind when trying to speak civilly with her.

Governor Yancy glanced up, raising her penciled eyebrows and giving a fake smile. "Okay, well, let's get started. Some of you may have heard . . . last night, the Breeder Facility was attacked."

"Attacked?" Dr. Supero said with emotion, as if he cared, but his heart had grown cold to that place. He never wanted to set foot in there again.

No one else flinched. Perhaps they already knew. It may have been on the news, which he rarely watched.

"Yes, attacked," Chief Varden growled, twisting in his seat. "There have been attacks all over Aldonia, and we have our hands full at the Jensenville border. They're throwing explosives over the fence, or at the fence. I think they want in. Where are the Jensenville Unity Troopers—"

"Chief Varden." Governor Yancy slapped a hand on the table, making files and icons flip. "We are meeting for a specific reason. Without breeders we do not reach the annual population numbers. Our society dies."

"Our society grows smaller," Chief Varden said. "It doesn't die."

"Oh, but it does die," Dr. Supero said, still feeling apathy. What did she mean by *without breeders*? "Scientists, environmentalists, economists, and a team of other specialists determined the exact numbers required to sustain our society. Every baby born is needed. Every breeder is needed." He glanced at the blond boy across the table. ". . . every geneticist . . ." His gaze slid to Chief Varden. ". . . every trooper, security officer, and chief . . ." He eyed the three Breeder Facility workers. ". . . every caretaker in every facility . . ."

His thoughts took him to his current findings. The world they knew today had not come about the way they had been told. Population numbers had not decreased drastically through wars, overpopulation, and industrialization. He had stumbled upon secrets. Perhaps, if not for the tumor changing the direction of his life, he would've been made privy to these secrets at some point in his career. He may have viewed them differently in that case. But now . . .

The Regimen's plan, which began unfolding about a hundred years ago, seemed quite sinister. They had introduced contraceptive chemicals to the drinking water, making couples childless. In grossly overpopulated parts of the world, they forced immunizations that actually damaged people's immune systems and introduced diseases like Ebola and HIV. It took little time to attain the desired population numbers, but then the world government had a new problem. Sustaining the human race on the earth.

The earth did need protected from man, though. Didn't it? Perhaps he would've agreed with the methods, had he lived in those turbulent times.

Chief Varden sat back and rubbed his stubbly hair. "Well, then Aldonia's screwed because half your breeders are gone. I say, let the next generation deal with it. We've got enough to do. We need to stabilize our borders."

Dr. Supero shook his head, trying to rid himself of the apathy. Yes, this was important. He should care. "What do you mean the breeders are gone?"

"Last night," Chief Varden said, leaning his arms on the table, "they were taken."

"Taken where?" Dr. Supero said.

"We don't know who took them or where they are," Governor Yancy said. "They got on a bus which was later found by the Jensenville border."

"And you can't guess where they are?" Chief Varden huffed and rolled his eyes.

Dr. Supero did not ask why Jensenville would want them. The answer was obvious. Their high suicide and infant death rates had wreaked havoc on their city.

"Maybe so," Yancy said, giving the chief an icy glare. "But we found men vandalizing the facility, men not in our databases. And they had no implants."

A smile crept onto Dr. Supero's face. The men had come from the wilderness. He'd known more were out there. Chief Varden should've listened to him and aggressively searched the Nature Preserves. This would not have happened.

"We traced them to an abandoned neighborhood," Chief Varden said, "one we haven't bulldozed yet. If we had the funds . . ." He glared at Governor Yancy. "But that's another matter."

Dr. Supero, seeing his chance, spoke with emotion he did not feel. "What are you doing now to ensure the safety of the rest of the breeders? Safety for all in Aldonia?"

He glanced from the chief to the governor and back to the chief, his expression as dramatic as his tone. "Am I safe? Are my students safe? I should like to know. In fact, I want detailed information about the safety measures you will be taking."

Dr. Supero didn't want to know. Guy wanted to know. Let a scourge take over the earth for all he cared. He only wanted to be left alone, to heal, and to figure out his life.

"I don't give a crap what you want, Dr. Supero." Chief Varden stood and jabbed a finger to the table, inadvertently interfacing with the computer, making icons appear on his side of the desktop. "You don't need that information any more than I need to know what you're doing with human DNA. What I'll give you—"

"Chief Varden!" Governor Yancy pounded the table with her fist, all the icons zipping to her. "You will give Dr. Supero whatever he requests. He has proven himself as Aldonia's Head Physician and now as the university's Head of the Department of Genetics."

Dr. Supero stared, unblinking. Governor Yancy had never liked him, had challenged him at every council meeting. Why had she taken his side now? Perhaps arranging a meeting with her would be easier than he expected. Maybe she pitied him because of the tumor she assumed he still had, or maybe she found him attractive. He shuddered at the thought, but he could use that to his advantage.

Chief Varden growled. "If that's the way you want it. But I make my objection known."

"Your objection is noted," Governor Yancy said, tapping a file. Her gaze clicked to Dr. Supero.

Snatching the opportunity, Dr. Supero gave her the hint of a smile and a leering look that made her blush.

"We have doubled security at all Breeder, Primary, and Secondary Facilities," Chief Varden said. "We're increasing surveillance outside all abandoned neighborhoods. Because of budget restraints, cameras will be in continuous operation during the night but not during the day." He shrugged, giving a sheepish look. "Unity Troopers make their rounds, so no one's gonna try anything during the day. We have also tightened our computerized search for terrorism in speech and . . ."

Dr. Supero's ego inflated as he filed away every detail. He had not lost his ability to get what he wanted. No, this was what *Guy* wanted: security status and the private meeting with governor. Still, Dr. Supero had gotten it.

21

Dedrick strode two steps behind Bolcan down the middle of a decaying road in a fenced-off and abandoned shopping area. Oppressive gray clouds drifted away, giving the evening sun freedom to shine. Angled sunbeams glinted off broken glass, puddles, and a buckle on Bolcan's boot. A blue bird with a black mask, possibly a Blue Warbler, flew overhead.

Birds. The Regimen couldn't keep them from Aldonians the way they kept the rest of nature from them with the electric Boundary Fences. The birds came and went as they pleased, flying between high-rises and Regimen buildings, making nests on surveillance cameras and official building signs, fluttering over the Boundary Fence and through woods . . . all the way to the colonists' spring gardens of red and yellow tulips and purple hyacinth blossoms, drawing the eye of children that lived free and children confined to government facilities alike.

Dedrick and Bolcan crossed into the crumbling parking lot of an abandoned retail warehouse, the location of the first ever above-ground Mosheh meeting.

Dedrick sighed. This was a bad idea. But what could he do about it? He wasn't officially Mosheh anymore, and his heart was somewhere else.

"This meeting will be like no other," Bolcan said over his shoulder, still walking ahead, attitude in his steps.

"Why's that?" Dedrick kicked a chunk of asphalt and watched it skip several yards away.

Bolcan turned and walked backwards, flexing his arms. He wore a brown V-neck t-shirt that emphasized his muscular physique. Trying to impress someone? "The unusual location tells me the elders are beginning to see the need for drastic measures."

"Such as?"

"The Regimen has your wild men, probably holding them at CSS. We can't let them take the men to Re-Ed."

Dedrick narrowed his eyes, irritated that Bolcan called them *his* wild men. "The Torva are not colony boys. But the Mosheh will take care of it. I'm sure they'll free them soon."

"Soon? Nothing happens quickly with the elders." Bolcan actually walked beside Dedrick, so close they bumped arms. "But they need to act fast in this situation, and I have the perfect plan."

"Your plans always seem to involve explosives."

"Sometimes that's the only answer."

"The Mosheh will never approve."

"I'm beginning not to care." Bolcan clenched a fist. "We destroy Re-Ed before they take the Torva there. It must be done. And I'm going to do it."

They shuffled through the gravelly remains of the cement walkway outside the warehouse. Warped plywood boards defaced with graffiti hung over the entrance doors. The one on the end was askew, showing where other Mosheh members had entered the building.

Dedrick struggled to control his irritation with Bolcan. It would do no good for the two of them to be at odds. Bolcan was right: the chaos in Aldonia warranted drastic measures or, better yet, a return to their original methods.

"You've made promises to the Mosheh," Dedrick said. "That means you wait on them. It happens when they say it does. It happens *the way* they say it does."

Bolcan reached the skewed plywood and raised a hand to it but then spun to face Dedrick. His lion's eyes held rage. "You do *not* understand." He jabbed a forefinger into Dedrick's chest. "You can't even begin to understand what that hellhole is like. You can't because you've never lived there." His gaze darted to some point over Dedrick's shoulder. "She understands."

Dedrick looked.

Two women approached, one with spiky black hair, the other with free-flowing messed up blonde hair, both of them deep in conversation and walking with a bounce in their steps. *Alix and Liberty.*

Dedrick's heart skipped a beat, and his thoughts slid from his mind. "I . . . she . . ." He turned back to Bolcan, forcing his thoughts into place. "Liberty understands the need for the Mosheh to operate secretly and with caution. She, like the Mosheh, doesn't rush into anything."

"You think you know her." Bolcan wrestled the loose plywood from the doorway and flung it aside. As it clapped to the crumbled concrete, glass tinkled and a cloud of dirt blew up. Brushing his hands together, he watched the girls approach.

They stepped off the curb and into the decaying road, still talking, not noticing Dedrick and Bolcan.

Heart beating erratically and palms sweating, Dedrick, without giving full consent to his body, moved toward her. His leather bracelet rode low on his hand, making him think of her dark hair, making him miss it.

Liberty looked up and scanned her surroundings, appearing to appreciate the sky and the horizon. Turning to the parking lot, her gaze landed on him.

He couldn't fix his gaze on her. Kept glancing away. Her disguise bothered him more than he realized. Her green eyes, the color of mist in the woods, so beautiful yet surreal, had stirred him up inside, but the deep scarlet lenses she now wore unsettled him. And the unnatural color of her hair, blonde with streaks resembling the rainbow in an oil spill . . . He missed her rich auburn hair.

Dedrick locked his gaze on her and smiled. Disguised or not, this was still her. And he loved her.

Liberty gave him the slightest smile then Alix said something and smirked, stealing her attention.

They crossed the last few yards to each other and he stopped.

She didn't.

"Are you my escort again?" she said over her shoulder as she walked past him.

"Huh?" He jogged a few paces and caught up then strolled beside her across the parking lot. He wished she'd grab his arm the way Miriam did when they walked together.

"My escort." She smiled, melting him somewhere inside. "Like in the Breeder Facility."

"Oh, yeah. If you want." He liked that she'd brought it up. Maybe she had enjoyed working with him as much as he had with her. "Everything work out last night? I saw you getting scolded outside the Breeder Facility."

Unable to reach the emergency housing or the access point last night due to trooper activity, Fulton had told them to return to the Breeder Facility. When Camilla had pulled the bus into the alley across from the facility, Dedrick had spotted a Unity Trooper chewing out another Unity Trooper, a trooper with long blonde hair who stood at attention, poised and self-possessed. He knew at once it was her, and he had whispered her name. She turned and peered in the direction of the bus, as if, despite the distance, she had heard or sensed him. The urge to protect her had nearly overwhelmed him. He had to grip the pole behind Camilla's seat to keep from bounding off the bus.

"She's fine," Camilla had said, looking both amused and annoyed at his antsy behavior.

"I know. She can take care of herself." He wished he could play it off, but everyone seemed to know how Liberty made him feel.

~~~

"Yeah, everything worked out." Liberty stared at him as they walked.

He could only glance at her mouth. That hadn't changed.

"I got reprimanded for not following orders." She shrugged. "But we saved all those women and children." Her mouth trembled until she pressed her lips together.

He lifted his gaze to her eyes, which, as he'd sensed, held deep emotion. Nothing could compare to the feeling of laying your life down for another. People called to that service wouldn't trade it for anything. How could he expect her to give up that opportunity and marry him? Maybe the Mosheh wouldn't allow new commitments for a good long time. And maybe she'd get her fill of rescues and see that marriage and family had its own sacrifices, its own rewards.

"Saving them feels good, doesn't it?" he said.

She nodded, seeming unable to answer with words.

They stepped up to the gravelly cement walkway and picked their way through the debris.

Bolcan stood, chest puffed up, next to the entrance he'd unblocked. "Alix, Liberty, watch your step." He bowed and made a sweeping gesture, inviting them to step through the frame of a once-glass door.

Liberty gave him the sweetest smile.

Dedrick bristled, jealousy flaring up. "You're going to have to rehang that plywood when we're done here," he said to Bolcan as he followed Liberty to the doorway.

"I'll leave that for you." Bolcan slapped Dedrick's chest and shoved him back. Grinning, he stepped in after Liberty.

Dedrick resigned himself to coming in last. This time.

As he stepped inside, voices carried to him, indistinct chatter. His eyes soon adjusted to the darker surroundings.

From one end of the warehouse to the other, dusty beams of light streamed in through a hundred open skylights and a few still with milky plastic infills. Forty or so Mosheh members gathered in a cleared area, pallets and damaged shelving units surrounding them. Lanterns hung from cables above and lay scattered on the dirty floor. Someone had made four tables, stacking the nicer pallets and shelves, and had set out cups, bottles, and trays. As if this were a party.

If CSS discovered them, that's how they'd roll. Members without ID implants would usher the elders to safety, while members with implants would sacrifice themselves, distracting the Unity Troopers by creating a riot and pretending they had gathered for a party. Dedrick would bet someone had even brought an assortment of illegal drugs to complete the image.

Dedrick scanned the group. Liberty, Bolcan, and Alix stood with Camilla and three other undercover agents. Several people sat in a wide circle on the floor, ready to get started but talking amongst themselves. He couldn't spot Fulton, but Fulton most likely remained below. He would keep track of Regimen chatter and warn them if necessary.

Two elders, Lukman and Rayna, sat in the only two chairs in the building, canvas folding chairs. The Mosheh respected their elders the same way colonists did. The Aldonians among them respected them, too, maybe even more so. Living in a society that rejected or disposed of everything tired and old, they had never realized the wealth of wisdom and unique gifts these men and women offered, even when infirm.

Something brushed Dedrick's elbow then an arm looped through his. *Miriam.*

A smile stretched across his face. He couldn't turn to her fast enough. Barely glimpsing her—dark hair with white streaks on the sides, a big smile, and eyes that could lift him from any mood—he pulled her into a hug.

Her firm grip gave him temporary assurance that all was right in the world, in Aldonia, in his life. She released him and stepped back. "Good to see ya."

"Yeah, I've been worried about you." He glimpsed a pink gash on the side of her forehead.

"Oh, I'm fine." She ran a hand through her hair, pulling strands to cover the gash rather than tucking them behind her ear like she usually did. "I wish things had turned out differently." She looped her arm through his and led him toward the group.

Most people now sat in a big circle on the floor. Liberty sat between Bolcan and Alix. Camilla knelt behind Alix, talking in her animated, silly way.

"So what went wrong?" Dedrick said, wishing he were next to Liberty.

Miriam sat cross-legged on the floor, using her hands to move one of her legs. Dirt or something stained her hands. A denim jacket covered her arms . . . and any other bruises or gashes.

"Grenton decided he couldn't rely on the Mosheh," Miriam said. "Decided they needed to take the girls themselves and do it before anyone else discovered the sinkhole. He thought this might be their only chance."

Dedrick took a spot on the floor beside her then leaned forward and rested his arms on his raised knees. "Grenton is a stubborn man."

She laughed. "Yup. I brought up everything I could, trying to talk him out of the idea, trying to get him to trust the Mosheh. But Grenton *is* a stubborn man." She stopped smiling. ". . . with a troop of forty armed and determined Torva. So I stuck close to them and warned you guys as soon as I could."

Dedrick averted his gaze, remembering the whimper in her voice when she had called in the second time. Someone had probably restrained her. Maybe hurt her.

His muscles tensed. She was family to him. He wanted the people he cared about safe, but half of them now flirted with danger.

"Did Ann make it yet?" he said. His sister had volunteered to assist the Aldonian girls in choosing where they wanted to live, with the Torva or in a colony. She had seemed under Grenton's spell last he saw her, but she wouldn't like this new turn of events.

"No, she's traveling with a small group from Rivergrove, not expected for another couple of days." Miriam gave Dedrick a studied glance, probably reading his mind. "She has no idea what Grenton led his men to do."

"Hmm." It gave him satisfaction knowing she'd be irked at Grenton when she found out.

Dedrick's gaze drifted to Liberty. Cross-legged like Miriam, she sat nearly opposite him in the circle listening to Bolcan go on about something. Dedrick should've pushed Bolcan back and followed her in, walked with her. He'd be sitting with her now. She'd be talking to him.

"Well, let's get started." Elder Lukman leaned forward and, with a bit of effort, got up from the camp chair. Dressed in soft leather shoes that were worn at the edges and a homespun linen tunic over faded jeans, he shuffled to the middle of the floor.

The warehouse grew silent, everyone following him with their eyes.

"We have much to talk about." White hair and beard glowing under a beam from a skylight, he scanned faces, turning and making direct eye contact with several members. "Let us begin on a positive note. You who are working undercover, I commend you. Your efforts have brought many to the assemblies. Many have begun to question the government." After praising a few individuals for spreading the word and eliciting interest in Bot's 3D games, he said, "We have something new planned for the next assembly." He nodded to Elder Rayna and returned to his camp chair.

Repositioning her long black braids over one shoulder, she stood but remained close to her chair. In the way of the elders, she also looked from member to member before speaking. "Some of you may have heard . . . if all goes well, the next assembly will be broadcast to everyone through their flexi-phones and TVs."

A collective gasp and a few whispers broke out. Liberty's mouth fell open. She glanced at Dedrick then at Alix. Alix, sitting with legs stretched out and leaning back on her arms, gave a confident nod as if she had already known.

A smile passed Elder Rayna's lips, a satisfied look. "We have a team working on this."

A young man with Aldonian hair, dark with green and blond streaks, raised a hand.

Elder Rayna noticed at once.

"How soon?" he asked.

"Very soon," she said. "Two days."

"If all goes well, that is." Elder Lukman leaned forward in his seat and clasped his hands in front of him.

"Yes." Elder Rayna gave Elder Lukman a glance, a look of concern passing between them. "Our underground members have several tasks. We still have the issue of finding our intruder."

Dedrick tensed. She meant Silver. The last he knew, Silver had neared Gardenhall and had left the message saying she wanted in. How long would she wait for a reply? What would she do without receiving one?

Elder Rayna turned her dark face to Dedrick, the commanding look in her eyes making him want to stand at attention. "We will need you . . ." Her gaze shifted to Bolcan. ". . . and you to attempt to communicate with our intruder. She threatens our safety, so we have no choice but to meet with her."

Dedrick nodded and glanced at Bolcan.

Bolcan, sitting casually with an arm draped over a raised knee, squinted up at the elder. His eyes narrowed and flickered. "I don't know."

Everyone turned to him. Someone let out a nervous laugh. No one contradicted an elder.

"We have to deal with the wild men," Bolcan said. "The Torva."

"Yes, we do." Elder Rayna's stiff posture showed she recognized Bolcan's words as a challenge.

Elder Lukman pushed up from his chair and stood beside her.

"The Regimen has them." Bolcan, still with an arm on his raised knee, got up on his other knee. "We need to act before they're sent to Re-Ed.

We need to destroy that facility." His biceps, his fists, his entire body tensed.

"Bolcan," Elder Lukman said, compassion in his eyes and tone. "I am sorry to inform you . . . they are already there. Apparently, CSS did not feel equal to holding interrogations for so many at their facility."

"No," Bolcan whispered, the word seeming to slip out. He rose to his feet like a King Cobra rearing up.

"The women who wanted freedom, and their children, are safe with us," Elder Rayna said, her eyes on him. "In time, we will provide safe passage to the colonies. The other women have been returned to the Breeder Facility. The Regimen is troubled by the disappearances. It has caused a bit of confusion, but Camilla established a scapegoat, taking the bus to Jensenville—"

"No!" Bolcan's hardened eyes shifted from her to Elder Lukman and then to various members of the Mosheh. "We must rescue them now. We must destroy that place." His voice traveled to the corners of the building.

"We will." Elder Lukman stepped forward, his voice powerful but not having its usual effect.

Bolcan did not flinch, did not back down, but puffed up even more.

Elder Lukman spoke again. "Aldonia is in chaos—"

"That chaos gives us an opportunity. We must destroy that place." Bolcan stepped toward the elders.

Dedrick jumped to his feet. Two other men he glimpsed in his peripheral vision did the same, all of them ready to subdue Bolcan if necessary.

Bolcan's gaze connected with Dedrick's. He jutted his chin, gave a crooked grin, and stepped back. "I will take care of it myself." He turned and stormed away, his boots making the only sound until he stepped through the frame of the door. Something outside banged . . . once, twice, three times.

"We will rescue them," Elder Rayna said, her eyes on Dedrick.

He nodded. "I know." Did he need to convince her of his loyalty? While no longer bound to the Mosheh by promises, he wasn't about to join Bolcan on his suicide mission. He wished the Mosheh would return to their original methods, working underground, rescuing one here and there. They had exposed themselves and only bad would come of it.

"The Regimen will interrogate them," a woman said, a colonist not in Aldonian disguise. "They will learn that the Torva came from the wilderness. The colonies will be threatened again."

"Not necessarily." Miriam leaned forward. "The Torva are proud and strong. They won't easily admit where they came from. Maybe the Regimen will think they're a group of troublemakers from somewhere within the city. I covered their tracks under the fence and outside the fence. Then I tried making it seem like they came from one of the Gray Zones."

Dedrick winced. She wouldn't mean the one Andy now called home. She would've picked a different one, one used for drug dealing and parties.

"How'd you do that?" the woman said.

Miriam raised her hands, showing everyone the red, blue, and black stains on them. "Spray paint. I sprayed messages and Torva symbols all the way from the Breeder Facility to the Gray Zone."

"Don't you think that's too obvious?" the woman challenged.

"Maybe." Miriam folded her arms and shrugged. "I didn't know what else to do."

"We can work with it," Elder Rayna said. "We will need to develop an explanation for these men without implants, men whose retina scans are not in the database. Perhaps we can link it to Jensenville."

"I got the bus there last night," Camilla said, jumping to her feet and beaming. "Got it to Jensenville. Troopers spotted me, but I dove from the bus in the nick of time."

"I should've gone with you," Dedrick blurted out, feeling guilty about letting her go alone.

Liberty looked at him. Concerned? Jealous?

"No, I had it. You and Bolcan had to move the dead weight." Camilla referred to the staff members they had sedated on the buses. He and Bolcan had carried them all into the Breeder Facility one by one.

Camilla's smile faded. "What do you think Bolcan will do?"

"Bolcan will do what he feels he must," Elder Lukman said. "We all must. We've learned that there are uprisings in cities across the continent. This may work to our advantage. The Regimen cannot fight battles on every front. Our business might go unnoticed."

"Or we might be at greater risk," Elder Rayna said, not appearing to challenge Elder Lukman so much as completing his thought. "The situation above ground grows more hostile daily, more unsafe."

Liberty's hand went up.

Elder Rayna nodded, inviting her to speak.

"Maybe Bolcan's right," Liberty said, giving her eyes only to the elders. "And we should use this chaos to destroy Re-Ed once and for all."

Dedrick gritted his teeth. Bolcan had gotten to her. Or Bolcan was right: she understood, maybe shared, his intense desire to destroy the place.

"We will keep that under consideration," Elder Rayna said.

"You know they will rebuild," Elder Lukman said. "You must change the people, which is why our assemblies, integration into society, and outreach are so important."

Elder Rayna walked to the center of the group and turned, gazing from face to face, skipping no one. "Each of you must reconsider the choice you've made to work undercover and the promises you've made to us. Today, I ask you to look inward, to think hard, to pray for discernment. If you feel threatened by this turmoil but you still want to serve, I want you below ground. If you feel called to remain above ground and have the courage to work undercover, I want a pledge of service."

Dedrick jerked back. A pledge of service? His gaze snapped to Liberty. A tingling sensation began in his chest and spread through his body, making him lightheaded. *No, Liberty.*

"In three days," Elder Rayna said, "we will meet here again. Those who wish to renew their promises or make them for the first time are invited to do so then."

Liberty stared as one transfixed, her chest rising and falling. The hint of a smile passed her lips. Until her eyes found Dedrick.

No, Liberty, he wanted to say. *Don't make promises to them.* He gazed for a moment then had to look away.

22

"I am here. Why do you make me wait?" Dr. Supero muttered, tugging his black stocking cap down over his forehead and sliding it back up. For the hundredth time. He sat with one foot on a crate, leaning against a support beam on the third story of the condemned building Guy and other miscreants called home.

Upon entering the building this time, he had received no torment. Juno, a boy with black-rimmed tawny eyes, had escorted him directly upstairs and—via rope ladder—to the third floor.

"Guy's doing something," Juno had said. "You can wait here."

Groups of young people and a few older ones, all rejects of society, sat around upside-down crates, some playing old-fashioned dice and card games, others talking. A few people shuffled from one of the rooms that came off this open area to other rooms, passing Dr. Supero without a glance. Several straggled into one room in particular, one somewhere behind Dr. Supero. He had no interest in knowing why. No one walked with purpose. Apparently, the losers wasted their days doing nothing to benefit society.

Guy's elevated voice came from the room in the far corner.

Dr. Supero gazed in that direction, but a makeshift curtain hung in the doorway, half-blocking the view, allowing him to glimpse a figure now and then. He contented himself with watching the group nearest that room.

Eight young men and three women sat in a circle on the splintered, scuffed hardwood floor, their attention on one man in their group: a bearded man in a straw hat and a long black robe. He spoke in animated fashion with eyes lit up and gesturing wildly. His devotees laughed and one of them said something, a boy with a guitar. The black robe replied.

Dr. Supero pulled his cap over his eyes and slid his hand up to the scar on his head, feeling it through the knitted fabric. He remembered this man from the Re-Education Facility. He'd had to bribe the guard just to speak with him because the man was a priest. Father Damon, they had called him. A priest in this day and age? Who could believe it? What propaganda did he have for his followers? Dr. Supero had once overheard that the man went out preaching in the streets, too. What interest did Aldonians find in him?

These people had all lost their minds.

"Because that's the way I want it!" Guy's voice, loud and angry, traveled to him. The other chatter lessened.

Dr. Supero straightened his cap and sat up.

Guy stood outside the room glaring at Juno, who spoke to him from the doorway. Bare-chested under the Regimen jacket and with a handless arm dangling at his side . . . How had this freak of a man commanded the respect of these people?

Guy's gaze caught Dr. Supero. He nodded and stuck his index finger up. "One minute," he mouthed and darted into a different room.

Dr. Supero sighed and leaned back. He had other things to do besides wait on Guy.

He had assignments to grade and lessons to plan, though that concerned him the least. He would much rather complete the research he had begun, digging deeper into the secrets of the Regimen. But now, stretched in every direction, he needed to apply himself to the breeder crisis.

He and the rest of Governor Yancy's team had spent over two hours discussing solutions for maintaining population numbers. They would have no choice but to select more women and perform tubal reversals. He did not look forward to that.

"We have no women to spare," the governor had said. "All vocations are vital to our society."

"Perhaps the women can do both," he'd suggested.

The Breeder Facility workers had gasped and muttered.

"That would be too much for a girl to do."

"Not fair."

"They would feel alone and overwhelmed with so much responsibility."

"Give Professor Supero a moment to explain," Governor Yancy had said, her pupils round and black, dilated with desire for him.

"Assign others to act as support systems to them," he'd said, his attention no longer on the governor. He needed do nothing more. He had her. At that moment, he knew that once he asked her to meet with him, she would say yes. Guy would have his meeting, for whatever reason.

"Who? What others?" one of the women had said. "That would be a new vocation and quite a commitment."

"Would the children be raised inside the facility? We no longer have the staff."

"Would they be raised outside the facility? What resources would they need?"

He knew as the conversation developed that the only real solution was something like old-fashioned marriage, the children raised by mothers and fathers with permanent commitments, but he would not be the one to suggest it.

~~~

Movement caught Dr. Supero's attention. The group in the corner broke up. The black robe strolled toward him.

"Greetings, friend," the priest said as he neared. He tugged the rim of his hat. His brown eyes and the dull coloring of his hair gave him away. Everyone must've known he came from somewhere other than a Regimen city.

Dr. Supero slid his foot off the crate and slouched forward, giving the priest a lazy stare.

"You look familiar," the priest said. "Do we know each other?"

"We do not." An image came to Dr. Supero's mind. The man lay naked except for undershorts, practically unconscious on the floor of a Lesson Room in the Re-Education Facility.

"I'm Father Damon." The priest continued to study Dr. Supero's face.

"You are not Aldonian. Where are you from?" Dr. Supero said, knowing the answer but wanting to hear the man say it.

"The past is not important. I like to think about where I am now." He sat beside Dr. Supero on the crate.

"Do you live here, now," Dr. Supero said, unable to hide disgust in his tone, "with these people in this decaying building?"

Father Damon threw a few glances around the open area. "Yes, I do. But only for a time. We aren't made for this world."

"So I cannot help but overhear when I visit this place that you go out into the city and give talks, stirring up Aldonians. One day, Unity Troopers will catch you. They will throw you back into Re-Ed. Why do you risk it? We both know you could live free outside the reach of the Regimen."

The priest chuckled and touched Dr. Supero's shoulder then rubbed his back. "I thought we knew each other. When I was naked, you gave me clothes."

Dr. Supero shrunk back at the man's touch and put up a hand. Something about the man, his simplicity, joy, compassion . . . stirred feelings of disgust and self-loathing in Dr. Supero.

The priest withdrew his hand. "Why do I risk it?" He gazed into space for a moment. Then he breathed. "I could live outside the reach of the Regimen, as you say, but would I be free? Is a man exercising freedom when fear keeps him from doing what he feels called to do?"

He stared at Dr. Supero one moment too long. "It is my calling to speak the truth. Without truth, people live in darkness. Humanity is threatened. It was silence by the shepherds and believers of past generations, fear of offending or a desire to compromise, that put us in this mess."

"What mess?"

"Do you not see the moral evil all around you? It has damaged the fabric of society, causing it to collapse, enslaving all. The culture was brought down almost without a fight."

Dr. Supero tried to tie the priest's words to his own research. Something rang true.

Ideas clashed in his mind, making his temper spike. Words flew from his mouth. "Our generation values life more than any generation previously. All life. We, as citizens of the world, are the most globally-responsible people that have ever lived. We protect the environment, the world, and every organism on it." He was doing it, reciting the propaganda. He wasn't even sure he believed it now. "We-we ensure that every baby born is healthy. That every baby . . . is-is needed." Trembling, he shut his mouth.

"You ensure the babies born are healthy, but you kill hundreds of human embryos in the process, don't you?" The priest's eyes held no malice. No curiosity. The look . . . what was it?

"It would be irresponsible to do otherwise," Dr. Supero spit. "Do you not know the defects and disease that once plagued our earth?"

"Are you and I so perfect?" The look intensified. The look . . . what was it?

Dr. Supero shook his head, unable to respond and unable to turn away. His tumor had proven he was less than perfect. He should've gone peacefully from life. He shouldn't have clung to it, desperately, as if he'd had a right to it.

"Hey, it's good to see you." Guy sauntered up to them.

Dr. Supero wrenched his gaze from the priest's and stood. "It is about time. You think I have nothing better to do than to wait on you."

Guy laughed and slapped him on the shoulder. "You're such a sport."

Father Damon got up. "I hope we can talk again," he said to Dr. Supero.

"I hope never to come here again," Dr. Supero said without looking at the man.

"I'm glad you have hope. We can always hope." The priest strolled away.

"Walk with me," Guy said. "Tell me what you've got."

Trying to regain his calm, Dr. Supero walked beside Guy toward the room in the far corner. "I have everything you asked for. And I would like to be released of my servitude." He considered whether to mention Silver.

Guy held the make-shift curtain back and motioned for Dr. Supero to step inside the room. Three men leaned against the wall on one side of a boarded-up window. On the other side of the room, Angel sat on an old wooden desk, cradling a bowl. She brought something red to her mouth, perhaps a strawberry. Her eyes turned to Dr. Supero and she smiled.

His scalp crawled, craving her touch.

"So, tell me . . ." Guy came to stand directly in front of Dr. Supero, his eyes lighting up like a child about to receive a treat.

Dr. Supero scowled for a moment, disappointed that he could not watch Angel eat the strawberry. "Very well, but you must give me a break after this. I have other things to do. I . . ." He felt foolish for admitting his weakness. "I grow weary."

"Okay." Guy nodded. "You got my word, Dr. Supero. After I meet with the governor, I won't need you for a while. Maybe never."

Dr. Supero's curiosity piqued, but he decided against asking for specifics. The less he knew, the better. "The governor will be at my apartment Friday night."

After the meeting at CSS, he had accompanied Governor Yancy to her car. "We should talk further on this," he had said. "Just you and I, perhaps at my apartment." He had been ready with an explanation as to why there, but he hadn't needed to use it.

"I understand," she had said. "Tonight won't do, though. How about Friday?" So he agreed.

As she drove away, he realized his mistake. Cam had invited him somewhere. He would have to tell her *no*.

A lopsided grin stretched across Guy's face. He waggled his eyebrows. "Your apartment, huh? Smooth."

The sleazy feelings that Dr. Supero had felt when inviting her returned to him. He was throwing himself at this woman to get something for Guy. "You said somewhere without surveillance. What was I supposed to do? How should I know what places have surveillance? Certainly, you did not mean here?"

Guy glanced at the three men against the wall and laughed. They laughed.

Dr. Supero's heartbeat quickened as he fumed interiorly, barely keeping it inside.

Guy turned back and slapped Dr. Supero's shoulder. "No, calm down. You did good." He stared into space for a moment. "I wish it wasn't Friday. That's such a busy day for me. But this is important, so I'll have to make it work."

"Do that. Because I am not setting another date with the woman."

Another round of laughter erupted.

Guy gained control and faced Dr. Supero again. "You know there's surveillance in your apartment, right?"

"Yes, I shall take care of it."

"Good. I'll send a man tomorrow, too. He can help you." Guy brushed the front of Dr. Supero's white dress shirt. "He can help you with laundry and cleaning the place, too. Help you get ready for your . . . *date.*"

Chest tensing, scar throbbing, Dr. Supero slapped Guy's hand away and took a breath. He did not want to erupt in anger. It would only incite more laughter.

"So, let's hear the scoop from CSS."

"Very well, but there is something I must tell you first." He would report Silver and make it seem as though he sided with Guy. Then he would contact CSS himself. But after Friday. He would have to wait and see what that day held in store.

23

Jogging from a tunnel, Dedrick glimpsed the Mosheh Control Center. The hum of equipment made the only sound. A skeleton crew manned the workstations, Fulton one of them. He considered asking Fulton if he had seen Bolcan, but instinct told him where Bolcan had gone.

Bolcan had come for his things, maybe to clear out for good.

Most of the Mosheh kept their personal belongings in the dorms above the Control Center. Some stayed at Gardenhall, preferring the hominess of the community or maybe liking the privacy of a sleeping pod. Bolcan had taken to sleeping here, in the room previously offered to the newly rescued. Having a toilet, sink, and cot, it gave the *rescues* a place to clean up and rest and change into something other than a hospital gown, in many cases.

Dedrick passed the "landing pad," the big mattress under the tubes that brought people from access points several floors above, and the "Superman booths," the old telephone booths that housed the hydraulic lifts they used to get above ground in a hurry.

Reaching the *rescue* room, Dedrick pulled back the sheet in the doorway.

Bolcan hunched over a military-issue canvas duffle bag on a cot on the far wall. He glanced over his shoulder. "Hope you're not here to talk me into staying with the Mosheh."

Letting the sheet fall behind him, Dedrick stepped into the room. "I like what you've done with the place."

Bolcan had updated the room somewhat. A stack of crates topped with toiletries blocked the view of the grungy toilet and sink. On the wall adjacent the bed, a low-pressure sodium lamp hung over a canvas spray-painted with vibrant colors in an angry, abstract pattern—Aldonian artwork. Under it, a sloppy spread of maps and papers lay on and under two card tables pushed together. Bolcan's clothes hung from hangers on a pipe that stretched across the wall with the doorway.

Bolcan hadn't always called this room home. For a couple of months, he'd bunked with Dedrick in the boys' dorm above the Control Center. But he suffered from night terrors. He had woken Dedrick and half the guys in the dorm several times, talking in his sleep. Or screaming. When the nightmares finally woke Bolcan, he'd stormed from the dorm not to return for the night. A few weeks of that, and he stopped sleeping there. Dedrick had assumed he moved to one of Gardenhall's sleeping pods, until he caught Bolcan heading here one night.

"So what do you want?" Bolcan glanced at Dedrick on his way to the clothes.

Dedrick stepped onto a big rag rug in the middle of the room. He briefly wondered which colonist had made it. "Bolcan, you know they need you."

"We'll see if they still need me when I'm done." He pushed clothes aside, scraping wire hangers along the pipe, revealing a shelf behind them, and grabbed a few things. "Your Torva are in there. Don't you care?"

Dedrick sympathized entirely with the impatience one felt waiting on the Mosheh. But still . . . "The Mosheh will rescue them. You know that."

"Yeah, after how long?" Bolcan crossed back to the duffle bag with an armful of things, one item looking like a sedation mister. "You don't know what that place does to a person."

"I haven't experienced it, but I know." They had access to all the cameras, the same access CSS had. Dedrick had seen what they do in there. He'd seen his mother and father in there. He'd seen Liberty.

Bolcan stuffed things into the duffle bag then spun to face Dedrick. "No, Dedrick, you don't know. You can't even begin to understand. If you did, you'd be with me."

Turning away, biting back a cutting reply, Dedrick's gaze landed on the papers spread out on the card tables. He stepped closer. "These your plans?"

Bolcan joined him. "Yeah. I don't use computers." He stood relaxed and seemed calm now. "Too many eyes on all that. No one knows about my stuff."

Dedrick leaned to inspect a map. It was a diagram of the Re-Education Facility, with details of both the interior and the surrounding property.

"So, what's your plan?" Dedrick continued to study it. Evenly-spaced red "x" marks had been drawn on the exterior walls of the facility. "This where explosives go?"

Bolcan stared as if assessing Dedrick. "I could use some help."

"If you're going half-cocked, you know I can't help you."

"You've made no promises to them. You can do what you want."

"Tell me your plan."

Bolcan fixed a hand on the card table and leaned over the map. He pointed to a section outside the fence. "I plan to drop guns here, many guns. It's close enough to the facility but far enough for when the building blows."

"Why?"

"So when the Torva come out, they're armed."

Dedrick shook his head, not getting the plan. "Go on."

"Then I'll place Semtex all around the building." He pointed to the red "x" marks.

"And security cameras will catch you doing it." Dedrick stepped back from the table, frustrated at the foolishness of the plan. "Unity Troopers will be on you before you get halfway around the building."

Bolcan's golden eyes gleamed, his pupils dilating. He grimaced. "No, I use a pea shooter and blind surveillance cameras."

Dedrick couldn't keep from shaking his head again, more dramatically. "All of them? Too suspicious."

"Once the explosives are placed, I go inside and tell them they need to evacuate."

"You're getting inside, how? There're implant readers at every door. They only open to approved people." Dedrick leaned in Bolcan's face, wanting to force him to see the holes in his plan.

Unfazed, Bolcan continued: "I'll wait for someone to come out. I've been watching their surveillance. I know which guards take breaks when."

Dedrick stomped away and turned back, his arms flying up with his frustration. "And you'll be picked up on the same surveillance you watched them on."

"CSS isn't always looking. They look when there's trouble."

"You can't rely on that."

"I'm going to rely on that, and I'll get in when a security guard steps out. I'll knock him unconscious." Bolcan tapped a canister on his belt, a sedation mister. "I'll break open cell doors and let those wild men help me clear the place."

"Meanwhile, the guards up front see you on camera. They call UT or they go after you themselves." Anxious to be understood, Dedrick had lost control of his tone and body, his face distorting in frustrated expressions, his arms flailing. "The Torva have no way of opening external doors. You're all trapped. They're sent back to their cells. And *you* get assigned a cell. Is that what you want? Back in there?"

Bolcan breathed, sucking in a deep breath that made his chest rise then exhaling loudly. "I plan to get help. Maybe someone will deliver the bomb threat. The guards will start emptying the place."

"And CSS will be contacted at once."

"And we'll be ready for them." Bolcan raised his voice, matching the anger in Dedrick's. "That's why I'm bringing guns. They'll have their silly rubber-bullet rifles—"

"And tranq. guns."

"We'll have real guns."

"It'll be an all-out battle."

Bolcan gave a single nod. "I'm counting on it."

"People will die."

Bolcan gritted his teeth but said nothing.

"So . . ." Dedrick struggled to produce a point that would change Bolcan's mind. "Who's your outside help?"

"For one, I'm going to ask Liberty."

Every muscle in Dedrick's body tensed. His hands curled into fists. "Oh, no you're not. Why would you put her in danger like that?"

Bolcan drew near, seeming to grow in height. "I need the help, and she's quite competent. You think you know her, that one day you'll have her." His eyes narrowed, filling with hostility. He inched closer, challenging Dedrick. "She's not a colony girl. She's Aldonian. She's suffered through the torture of Re-Ed. Maybe you can't see how it's changed her. But I can."

Dedrick stood face to face, shifting from one foot to the other, threatening with his eyes. "You risk putting her back in that place." His hand shot up. He couldn't help it. He flicked Bolcan's shoulder.

Bolcan retaliated without pause, slapping Dedrick's shoulder, knocking Dedrick back. "Don't mess with me."

The pain barely registered over his anger. "You. Don't mess. With her."

Then it happened. Dedrick snapped and flung himself at Bolcan, fists swinging.

Bolcan blocked and backed into his cot, avoiding all but a single glance to his chin. Then he launched a blow, an uppercut that sent a jolt of pain to Dedrick's gut.

Ignoring the stabbing pain, unwilling to let Bolcan have his way, pushing reason from his mind, Dedrick lurched forward and wrapped his arms around Bolcan's solid torso, wanting to take him down.

Bolcan shoved back, throwing Dedrick off balance, and the two of them crashed to the floor.

Dedrick landed on the rag rug and sprang into action, rolling off the rug and onto Bolcan. He hadn't been fast enough, hadn't pinned Bolcan's arms like he'd meant to, and Bolcan flung him like a colony girl's rag doll. Dedrick crashed into the card tables and papers rained down.

"You can't stop me," Bolcan spit, pinning Dedrick to the floor with solid steel arms.

Dedrick shifted his hips and caught Bolcan's leg between his own. With a sudden twist of his body and a jerk of Bolcan's arms, he flipped Bolcan's massive weight off him.

Bolcan landed on his side. Then . . . rather than shift into an offensive position, he rolled onto his back and thrust his hands into his hair, blocking his face with his arms. He groaned, letting out the deep, guttural sound of a wounded animal.

Dedrick pushed himself up on one elbow, heart racing, panting . . . wondering if their fight had ended.

"I got sent there in Secondary," Bolcan said into his arms, his voice rough. "But it started . . . for me, it started in Primary. The torture. Those little things that stay with you."

Relieved that Bolcan seemed to have switched gears and feeling guilty for having started a fistfight, Dedrick sat up. He meant to get to his feet, but Bolcan's strange mood made him wait.

Swinging his arms down, Bolcan sat up and hunched over. "I was just a kid. But the things they taught didn't make sense, and it made me feel strange inside, a feeling I didn't like." Hair in his face, he glanced at Dedrick.

Dedrick nodded, realizing where Bolcan was going with this. Never having considered Bolcan a friend, the honor overwhelmed him. And he wanted Bolcan to stop.

"I tried explaining my thoughts," Bolcan said, facing the wall and not Dedrick, twisting the frayed edge of the rug half under him. ". . . talking with other kids. We always sat in groups of four or six around interactive desks, all working together on things. The teachers, they didn't like my ideas, and when I wouldn't stop trying to explain myself, just trying to figure things out, I got sent to this desk in the corner." He sneered, then gave a relaxed laugh, as if struggling with the conflicting emotions evoked by the memory.

"Desk was old and smaller than the others, and it would rock because one of the legs was shorter. And I could only access specific lessons on it, like it wasn't linked to the main smartboard. I'd hear the rest of the class talking in their groups . . . while I sat alone. Sometimes had to eat alone, even had to sleep apart from the others. I was just a kid. They gave me a mat in the hallway." Eyes to the floor, his expression went blank. "But I kept thinking, figuring things out for myself. Most times I didn't even do my lessons, and that made them mad."

He clenched his fists and hunched more, curling his torso over his bent legs. "At Secondary things got worse. Always the group discussions, the group lessons with programs designed so you could only take the discussion in certain directions. If you tried steering it another way, the kids in your group would make you feel stupid or mean."

Bolcan turned his face and lifted his golden eyes. His gaze pierced deep, unsettling Dedrick and tempting him to look away.

"They don't send you to the corner in Secondary," Bolcan said. "They send you to Re-Ed."

Wanting Bolcan to know he listened, that he understood, that he cared . . . wanting Bolcan to release him from that gaze, Dedrick nodded.

"What they did to me there . . ." Bolcan doubled over, flung his arms over his face, and sunk his hands into his hair again. ". . . so cold and hungry all the time. Never enough sleep. The lessons . . . they felt so . . . real. More real than life. They got deep in your mind and messed with your thoughts, gave you thoughts. Took things from you that you didn't want to give."

Dedrick's heart twisted. He rubbed his face, pressing too hard. He'd never seen this side of a man. His father, after his experience in Re-Ed, had played it off, kept saying he was fine and that his faith got him through. He'd never gone into specifics, Dedrick was glad. Seeing Bolcan now, he realized he wouldn't have been able to handle hearing it from his father.

"There was this girl in Secondary," Bolcan said. "She wasn't like the others, and sometimes we'd talk. She was always in my mind at Re-Ed, in the lessons. I'd feel good, relieved, seeing her there in the lessons. It felt real and safe for a moment. Then she'd start talking, saying things she would've never said, things the teachers and nannies wanted you to believe. Lies.

"When I challenged her, she'd turn cold and hateful, and it ripped my heart. I-I wanted her in a way I hadn't wanted her in Secondary, deeply, desperately . . . physically. And it happened over and over, her saying these things and rejecting me when I didn't agree, so that all I could do was curl up like a . . . like a baby and cry." Hair hanging in his face, arms wrapped around his waist, rocking slightly . . . Bolcan had never appeared more vulnerable.

Dedrick averted his gaze.

"After lessons, between lessons—you never really knew; could'a been a lesson—I lay there on the cold, hard floor, feeling her cold, hard hatred, and aching all over, inside and out. I tried telling myself it wasn't really her, but I couldn't hold onto reality.

"Day after day this went on, not ending until I agreed with her. Every time I did it—" His gaze snapped to Dedrick, making Dedrick look up. "You know I've been to Re-Ed several times."

"I know." Dedrick's voice broke. He didn't want to hear any more. Some in the Mosheh admired Bolcan for holding the record among *rescues* for most trips to Re-Ed. Bolcan had made people think he was proud of that record because it showed his resistance to the RCT. Dedrick would never see it that way again.

"Every time I agreed, she'd come back to me and make me feel accepted, make me feel loved. And I'd rest in this false . . . ecstasy with her, trying to convince myself that I hadn't . . . I hadn't just betrayed myself."

Bolcan clenched a fist. "They took things from me," he said, his voice strangled. "They got in my head with their ideas, using things that mattered to me, and they took parts of me."

Bolcan rolled onto one knee and got to his feet. He stood with his back to Dedrick, wiping his face, maybe wiping tears that Dedrick hadn't noticed. Then, grunting, he kicked the card table that hadn't fallen in their skirmish. Papers sailed to the floor as it crashed.

"I'm sorry, man," Dedrick said. "I'm sorry they did that to you, that you had to live through that for so many years. I-I'm sorry the Mosheh didn't come for you sooner."

He climbed to his feet and spoke to Bolcan's back. "I get, now, why you're so determined. You don't want the Torva going through that, don't want them wondering if anyone's gonna come for them."

"It'll be hard for them." Bolcan twisted to face him. "The lessons, all of it so foreign to their way of life, them not being from here."

Dedrick's thoughts flashed to the Maxwell colonists that had endured it. How had they fared? He hadn't thought to ask anyone.

"Help me do this," Bolcan said.

Dedrick took a breath, wrestling internally with his own impulsive nature. "I will. But not today."

His TekBand signaled an incoming call. He fumbled with the earpiece. "We'll push this hard," he said to Bolcan, stuffing the earpiece in his ear. "We'll get the elders to make it a priority."

As soon as he tapped his TekBand and answered the call, Fulton's voice came through. "Dedrick, we got trouble."

Dedrick braced himself, hoping it didn't concern Liberty. "What'cha got?"

Bolcan grabbed the duffle bag, his biceps bulging as he hoisted the bag onto his back.

Dedrick stepped in Bolcan's way to keep him from leaving. He needed assurance that Bolcan would leave Liberty out of it.

"It's about Silver," Fulton said. "We intercepted CSS Intel. For some reason, they're tailing her."

Bolcan stepped to move around Dedrick, but Dedrick blocked him.

"Bring Bolcan in on the call," Dedrick said, holding Bolcan's gaze. He gained a shred of hope that this problem might divert Bolcan's attention. "CSS is tailing Silver," he said to Bolcan.

"That can't be good," Bolcan said. "She'll come down here."

"Right," Fulton said. "So we need one of you to talk to her. We know where she works now."

"Give it to me," Dedrick said.

"She's a community physical instructor at Aldonia's Rehab. And what's worse, even if you can keep her from snooping down here again, they're searching footage of her past activities. We've got all our underground communities on high alert, but we're going to need someone to blow up the access point she came through, the one in the warehouse nearest the old city center."

"Blow it up?" Dedrick said.

Bolcan nodded and moved toward the door. "You can do that. I'll talk to Silver."

Dedrick almost protested but decided this would work. If Bolcan went after Silver, he wouldn't be blowing up Re-Ed. Or recruiting Liberty. At least not yet.

24

Under a clear blue sky without the trace of a cloud, Holt and I marched in-step. Our route had taken us past a long vacant strip of weeds and chunks of building material, past the oldest Secondary Residence in Aldonia, and past the backside of a row of shops.

I wished we strolled along the Boundary Fence that separated Aldonia from the Fully-Protected Nature Preserves. We could be gazing at wildflowers and twisted tree trunks through the electrically-charged beams, watching little animals scamper through the underbrush, and catching whiffs of green and floral scents on the breeze.

Instead, a seven-meter-high reinforced concrete wall rose up on one side, a three-meter-deep trench on the other. A pyramid of razor wire coils, blazing under the afternoon sun, lined the other side of the trench, making my eyes water when I gazed too long at the field or the backsides of three-story apartment buildings in Aldonia. All of this, along with the occasional patrol—Holt and I, at the moment—and the surveillance cameras, made the Jensenville border impenetrable.

We both carried our helmets. I craved the feel of the brisk spring breeze on my face and neck. Sweat trickled down my back, however, tickling me and making me want to rip off the scaled Unity Trooper armor and slam myself against the cool, gritty surface of the boundary wall. It might hurt if I got carried away, scratching like a bear with its back to a tree. But it would feel good at first.

Holt glanced at his flexi-phone, as he did every few minutes, maybe afraid he would miss an important call without his helmet on. He was the only trooper I noticed who walked tall and followed procedure every moment of the day, as if a commander watched him.

Our day had been relatively uneventful. After an hour and a half at the station, the big hangar full of grounded drones, Commander Fillida had sent us out by twos. She had sent Holt and me to patrol a section of the

Jensenville border. Transported here by an open bus, we spent the morning on the western section, walking several kilometers each way. We now covered the eastern section. Another kilometer and we could head back. We had nothing to report.

According to earlier reports, there'd been a few minor explosions on other sections of the border, but the homemade bombs did little damage. I didn't understand what motivated the Jensenville citizens. The commanders said anarchists in Jensenville had unauthorized ways into and out of Aldonia and they wanted to take us over. I worried all this turbulence would threaten to delay the progress we'd made, distracting people from the seeds sown in our assemblies.

"Another kilometer and we're done," Holt said. He only spoke about work or he regurgitated Regimen ideologies, so I had given up trying to invite him to the assemblies.

Our conversations went like this:

I'd say, "Do you ever feel like the Regimen hides things from us?"

Most people say, "Like what?"

He'd said, "If they do, it's only for our safety and the greater good."

"What makes you think they have all the answers?" I once asked him. "I mean, they don't even let us consider other views."

"The entire world agrees," he said. "Why would any one of us be smarter than the whole world?"

"Have you ever wanted to do anything other than be a Unity Trooper? Like, as a kid, did you ever think about what you could be?"

"No." He'd given me a stone-cold stare with that answer. "They watch us from infancy," he'd said, as if it were a good thing. "They know the best vocation for each of us."

I transferred my helmet from one hand to the other, still keeping pace with Holt, and squinted past the glare of the razor wire coils into Aldonia.

I wished the Mosheh had communicated with me today, giving me something else to do. Not that I could think of how to break away from Holt without arousing suspicion. I couldn't think of how to disable the camera and microphone in my helmet either, again, without arousing suspicion. If the Mosheh ever called me into action, I would have to pretend I faced an emergency and that my helmet accidentally sustained damage. I doubted a trooper damaged his helmet often. The things were pretty tough. So I'd draw attention regardless.

My eyes watered from the glare of sunlight reflecting off the coils. Facing forward, I blinked and a tear ran down my cheek. I took a deep breath and closed my eyes, pretending we walked along the Nature Preserves. A smile came to my lips.

Two more days until I could make my promises.

A nervous, edgy feeling shuddered through me, the feeling I imagined I'd get standing on the rooftop of a ten-story building with my toes hanging over the edge. I knew the danger of this vocation, of becoming Mosheh. I would take risks daily to rescue people or live undercover in Aldonia. I wanted to do this.

Dedrick hadn't looked happy at the Mosheh meeting when the elders announced the commitment day. I had caught him staring at me, communicating with his eyes. I understood what the look meant. I heard his voice in my mind, him telling me the words he spoke months ago. "Don't make promises to them. Make promises to me."

A deep longing filled my heart. I didn't want to lose Dedrick, but I needed to do this. I needed to make a public commitment, to tie myself to the work of changing the culture in Aldonia. People deserved more. They deserved freedom.

"You hear that?" Holt gripped his helmet with both hands. If we saw or heard anything, we needed to wear our helmets so we could send the information back to UT headquarters and CSS and wherever else the live feed went. They could amplify whatever we picked up.

"Hear what?" I wiped my cheek, though the breeze had dried my tear anyway.

Holt donned the helmet, stopped, and faced the high cement wall. We stood motionless and silent, side by side in a sliver of shadow. The breeze kicked up, blowing my hair into my face and carrying a pungent odor . . . someone smoking weed?

Mumbled voices traveled to us. Jensenville Unity Troopers or citizens? Citizens weren't allowed to get close to Boundary Fences. Besides, they probably had a trench and coils of razor wire on their side, too.

I gripped my helmet in both hands, knowing I should put it on but feeling reluctant to do it. Instead, I turned in a circle and scanned our surroundings. The voices came from the other side of the Boundary Fence, but something felt off on this side. Squinting to tone down the glare of the shiny coils, I stepped toward the ditch and peered over the edge.

What I saw did not shock me. For whatever reason. Maybe *My Friend* had prepared me. He hadn't been communicating with me in other ways, lately. But His style changed often. I never knew what to expect.

A man sat in the bottom of the ditch, leaning against the steeply-sloped dirt wall. He rested his chin on his chest and sat with legs stretched out before him. One leg of his pants was ripped at the calf and covered in—

The blood shocked me. So much of it! I jerked back as Holt turned around.

"Better don your helmet, Amity," he said. "What have we here?"

"I think he's hurt." I fumbled with the strap of my helmet. My hair kept blowing in my face, but I slid the helmet on anyway and pushed strands out of my eyes.

"Looks like he tried to crawl under the coils." Holt, squinting, pointed to the nearest stake. Someone had untied the coils from it and stuck a board under from the Aldonian side.

The man stirred and lifted his head, his gaze rising to us. Pain and defeat showed in his eyes, the look of a man who'd run out of options.

I wanted to help him, to find a way to get him out of the ditch without him getting in trouble.

"Probably acted on a dare." Holt grabbed a nylon cord from his belt and squatted. "I'll get him out. You get his retina scan."

I nodded even though every fiber in my body rebelled at the idea. I wanted to help him, not turn him in. His friends must've abandoned him last night. Once he crawled under the coils of galvanized barbed wire—and cut open his leg—he would've fallen into the ditch. They might not have realized the ditch was right there, so close to the sharp coils. Maybe the pain kept him from calling out to his friends. Or a Unity Trooper could've driven by and scared them off. Whatever the case, he'd been abandoned.

"Razor wire's sharp, huh?" Holt shouted to the man. He made a loop with the cord and tossed it down. "You're not allowed over here, you know?"

The man looked away, wincing, and grabbed his bloody leg at the thigh.

"Get that rope around your chest," Holt said. "I don't want to come down after you."

With surrender in his manner, he did as commanded. Within a few minutes, Holt and I had dragged him groaning from the ditch. He had tried to use his hands and good leg, but pain showed in his face with every effort.

I grabbed his arm when he reached the top and pulled him to safety, getting the retina scan at the same time.

We carried him between us, with our arms wrapped around his torso and his arms draped over our shoulders . . . the way Alix and I had carried the wounded soldier in the 3D game. Only this man was heavy and much more awkward to carry. It sickened me to know that I was not assisting a comrade but rather leading him to his enemy.

Holt would follow procedure. I hadn't met anyone who followed it as strictly as he did. I got the impression he wanted to become a captain. He'd make a good one. Not because he cared about the citizens of Aldonia, but because he obeyed without questioning.

We would take this man back to the station. He would be questioned. His record would determine what happened after that. Maybe counseling. Maybe Re-Ed.

~~~

With my helmet dangling from one hand and hair blowing in my face, I strode back to my apartment on a busy sidewalk, trying to shake the feeling that I was a betrayer. I had to accept this: to work for the greater cause and keep my cover, I would sometimes have to do things I didn't like. This thought did not sit well with me. Should a person do something wrong to accomplish something right? The man had broken rules, though, I kept telling myself. He knew he'd face consequences if caught. It was his risk to take, and he took it.

Turning onto a residential street, walking into the wind now, I forced my thoughts to turn as well. I needed to focus on the good that would come from tonight. Finally, the Friday assembly!

A motorcycle rumbled in the distance, drawing my eye to the far end of the street, to a point beyond my apartment building. A group stood outside our building, my new friends. A few of them gazed up to where puffy gray clouds crept across a blue sky, threatening of rain.

Last night after the Mosheh meeting, filled with zeal for our mission, I had hung out with people from my apartment. Maybe they'd sensed the excitement in me. Every one of them had agreed to come tonight, and a few said they'd invite others.

Alix worked overtime with the Unity Troopers last night. She seemed to prefer overtime to hanging out with people after work. She claimed she got more information about the turbulence in Aldonia that way.

She would envy me today. "I can't wait for my turn at the Jensenville border," she had said. Her reason? My opinion: she wanted to aggravate the situation and help get the boundary wall down. Alix believed it would benefit us if it came down and the two cities could work together to change things. But our commander had been sending her to bust up drug parties and keep an eye on the Gray Zone that Miriam had painted with graffiti.

The motorcycle weaved past two scooters, drawing nearer to me. The rider's easy grip on the handlebars and control of the bike gave his identity away. Not to mention his honey blond hair flapping in the wind.

Bolcan pulled up to the curb. He wore a colonist-made buckskin jacket. "Hey, hot stuff."

"Hey, yourself. What're you out doing?" I stood on the edge of the curb, holding my helmet behind my back. The wind blew my hair in my face, so I turned, letting the wind blow it back again.

"I'm out recruiting." He smiled, looking my uniform over. He had toyed with the idea of going undercover as a Unity Trooper, too.

"Recruiting for what?" The things he'd said to me before the Mosheh meeting and the way he stormed out before the meeting's end had me guessing his answer.

"Oh, you know. I want to have a little bonfire at Re-Ed."

"Little, huh?" We exchanged flirty smiles.

"I've got Silver helping me." His expression turned business-like. "We stashed weapons and clothes outside the fence around the facility."

"Silver?" I tensed, worried for a moment that Bolcan had told her things about the Mosheh. But he wouldn't do that. He might not obey, but he wouldn't betray. I exhaled. "What's she getting out of it?"

"Same thing you and I will get out of it, the satisfaction of destroying that place."

I caught his insinuation that I would be working with him. "But she's never been there. Why does she care?"

"Everyone in Aldonia is one step from Re-Ed."

I nodded. He had a point. "When's this happening?"

"Now. And I could use your help."

"Why now? We've got the assembly tonight, the one Fulton's going to broadcast everywhere. People will hear the truth, most for the first time."

"It has to be now. It's all about timing." Bolcan gathered his hair behind his head, his muscles straining his jacket sleeves, then let the wind throw it forward over his shoulders. "Besides, they don't need us. Dedrick's brother and that priest will be there. They'll give their talks. Fulton will broadcast it. What do they need us for?"

Another motorcycle rumbled in the distance then came into view on a crossing street. Alix, heading home. She didn't notice us or made no show of it if she did.

"I've been trying to get people there." I glanced at the group outside our apartment building. Clouds drifted in front of the sun, throwing a shadow over them and us. The talk wasn't for two hours, but the group had already doubled in size. We had all agreed last night to walk to it together.

"Does it matter if they go? They'll all catch it on their flexi-phones."

"It'd be more effective with a big crowd. Don't you think?"

"No. I think . . . I need you." The clouds drifted away from the sun and a beam of sunlight glinted in Bolcan's golden eyes, revealing a hint of the damage that place had done to him.

Heart aching for him, I looked away.

"I need you to arrive at the facility in uniform," he said. "Get in the front doors. Then announce a bomb threat."

I stared, trying to understand his plan, trying to recall the bits he had shared with me yesterday before the meeting.

Jaw set with determination, he leaned forward and gripped the handlebars. "Get on and let's do this."

"No." I shrunk back, swinging my helmet to my side. My experience in Re-Ed had scarred me deeply. I knew this. And I saw it in him. I understood his driving need to destroy the place. I felt it myself. All the same, I believed what the elders said about the Regimen rebuilding the facility and how we needed to change the people. More than that, I wanted to join the Mosheh, and I wasn't about to risk that by doing something they had advised against. "Sorry, Bolcan, I can't risk blowing my cover, and I need to be at the assembly tonight. This needs to happen, too. And it needs to be big."

Stepping toward him, I took his hand and gazed into his eyes. My hair blew into my face, but I didn't care. "Don't do this now. Wait. Wait until I can do it with you."

The hint of a smile came to his lips. Breaking our handhold, he grabbed a lock of my hair and let it slide through his fingers. "Can't, Liberty. See ya." He gripped the handlebars, the motorcycle rumbling at his touch. And he took off.

After watching him disappear around a corner, I sprinted to the apartment building. I told the group outside I was going in to change my clothes and bolted up to our room.

"Hey," Alix said. She leaned against the doorframe of her bedroom door, wearing high black boots and a red flannel shirt that matched the red streaks in her dark, spiky hair. Under the flannel, she wore a white shirtdress. "Let's make something to eat and hang with the others outside."

"Oh, you're not working overtime?" I stopped at the boxes in the middle of the living room.

She shrugged. "Not today. I like to be there for the assemblies." She sauntered to the kitchen.

"Yeah, and we've got a good crowd out there just from our apartment building." I darted into my bedroom and yanked open the closet door, trying to remember what the colony ladies had packed for me. A few dresses and skirts. A few jeans and shirts. Nothing I would ordinarily wear.

"Yup, that's mainly your doing," Alix hollered.

I grabbed a tan long-sleeved shirt and studied it. The color reminded me of Bolcan's hair. I wished he wasn't so stubborn and that he'd wait. He was going to get himself into trouble. I couldn't see how he could avoid it.

My stomach churned, and my hand shot to it. Having eaten little for lunch, I was hungry.

Pans clanked in the kitchen. Alix mumbled something.

I tossed the shirt onto the bed and unfastened my armor. My body couldn't wait to get the sweaty stuff off. As I yanked the armor off over my head, my gaze rested on the shirt and my stomach churned again. A sense of dread came over me.

They would catch Bolcan tonight. Maybe Silver, too. Bolcan's plan . . . he wanted me to enter the facility as a Unity Trooper and warn of a bomb threat, get everyone to evacuate. That was smart. They'd get everyone out. Then Bolcan and Silver . . . did he have anyone else? Could the two of them pull this off?

I plopped down on the bed and hugged the armor to my chest. What would he do without me to instigate the evacuation? Before the Mosheh meeting, he'd said something about placing bombs.

My stomach turned to stone. If his plan didn't go smoothly, people could die. Innocent people. The residents of the facility.

Trembling now, I stood and glanced at my bedroom door. A rich, savory aroma wafted to me. Alix was making some kind of canned soup. Rather than growl, my stomach ached. The ache a person feels when she realizes she's abandoning someone in need.

I dropped the armor and shoved my hands into my hair. I couldn't go back to the Re-Education Facility, even with my disguise. I couldn't simply march inside and make an announcement. Someone might recognize me. That one guard, the one with the potato chin and black eyes, he would know me.

I grabbed the tan shirt, but it slipped from my trembling hand.

My gaze dropped to the scaled armor on the floor. I had to do this, didn't I? I couldn't let people die. Maybe I could talk Bolcan out of it. If I went along, the Mosheh would not understand. I would forfeit my chance to join them.

The trembling ceased as I reached for the armor.

25

"Please, God. Please, God. Please, God," Dedrick whispered, hands shaking as he stuffed the prongs of a timer into an outlet in the back of the crowded storage unit. He had found the old black thing in the bottom of a box in the WAG room. It hadn't seemed too reliable.

With a final push and no spark, Dedrick exhaled and slumped over. "Thank you."

He straightened and shined the flashlight on the open containers of gasoline and on the open access point. Everything looked good, so he clipped the flashlight to his belt and made for the door.

Donning his shades with one hand, he tugged the overhead door up a few feet, dropped to the cement slab, and rolled out. A strong, brisk breeze came as welcome relief from the gas fumes that had accumulated in the storage unit over the hours. It had taken him longer than he'd expected to round up the four canisters of gasoline. Way longer than expected to find the timer to make the spark for the explosion. He didn't have time to waste. He needed to get to Liberty before Bolcan did. Of course, if Bolcan found Silver last night, the elders may have given him additional instruction. Bolcan might be distracted for a time.

Dedrick yanked the overhead door down, locked it, and popped to his feet.

He scanned the grounds as he jogged away, glad to find himself alone. He wouldn't want any casualties. Four o'clock was not a good time for an explosion. Fortunately, most deliveries to and from the storage unit side of this Warehouse Zone ended around three thirty.

Nearing the twelve-foot chain-link fence that surrounded the storage units, Dedrick sprinted and leaped. The links rattled under him as he raced to the top.

He hoped the timer would work but not go off too soon, at least giving him time to get some distance. He should probably hang out in the strip of trees across the street until it he knew for sure. He'd set the timer for five minutes. If more than five minutes passed, what would he do? He'd hate to risk coming back. Maybe he could set a spark some other way. Like with his Beretta.

Dedrick gripped the top vertical bar of the fence, climbed with his feet, and hoisted himself over. He descended a few feet, toes to the links, then dropped.

In mid-turn, it happened.

The storage unit exploded with a bone-jarring bang, sending a burst of heat and scraps of metal hurling through the air. Several projectiles crashed against the fence, making Dedrick's insides jump. He hadn't waited around, though. He had taken off as soon as his feet hit the ground.

Reaching the grass and the line of trees across the street, Dedrick slowed his pace. He threw himself against a tree trunk and leaned over to catch his breath. Clouds covered the sun for a moment, then passed. The little risks of this work had never much bothered him before. But now she filled his thoughts. *Liberty.* If something bad happened, he might not ever see her again.

Dedrick tapped his TekBand to contact Fulton. "Mission accomplished."

"You got that one?" Fulton said. "Good, because now you need to get another one."

"What?" Dedrick pushed off the tree and glanced back at his work. Black smoke snaked up from big, rolling orange flames. "No, Fulton. I've got something I need to do. What's Bolcan doing? Did he find Silver?"

"No, we haven't heard from him."

Dedrick grimaced. Bolcan was moving ahead with his own plan.

"I got something I need to do first." Turning his back to his accomplishment, he strode toward a row of buildings, offices not far from the Warehouse Zone. He needed to reach Liberty before Bolcan did. She'd be getting home from her UT job right about now. Part of him wanted to help Bolcan, and maybe he would. He'd convince Bolcan to accept his help instead of asking Liberty. He'd probably miss out on Andy's assembly if he did that. Too much going on for a Friday. He'd have to leave Andy in God's hands.

"I think this is gonna take priority," Fulton said. "CSS found old footage of Silver at another access point, a manhole near the Jensensville border."

Dedrick sighed and stopped in his tracks. If he didn't destroy the access point and anyone with the Regimen investigated, they'd find Tradehall, the underground community near the Jensenville border.

"Copy that."

He changed direction and jogged toward the sun, heading for the nearest access point. He'd have to get more supplies and blow this one up from underneath, maybe just destroy a portion of the tunnel so investigators would think it had always been blocked. Dedrick made supply lists in his mind and calculated the time for the mission. He'd need time to get to the WAG room, gather supplies, and get to the destination . . . no, he needed someone to get the supplies for him and meet him there. Maybe they didn't have anyone to spare and he'd have to do it himself.

Bolcan could be at Liberty's apartment right now, begging her to join him. Would she do it? If she really wanted to join the Mosheh, she'd have to turn him down. Yeah, she'd turn Bolcan down the way she'd turned Dedrick down. Joining the Mosheh, helping Aldonia, meant everything to her. Maybe she'd talk Bolcan into doing things the right way and waiting obediently on the Mosheh. She could be very persuasive. But so could Bolcan. Would he tell her about his experience there?

Dedrick gritted his teeth. Bolcan shouldn't put her through that. She shouldn't have to go through any of this. She should be able to live free and happy surrounded by people who loved her, surround by children. Her children. His children.

He would do anything to take her away from all this and marry her.

"Dedrick, where are you?" Fulton's voice held a note of panic.

Jogging down a cracked and patched one-lane street, Dedrick focused on his surroundings. The backside of businesses rose up on his right, the afternoon sun creating angled shadows on propped open doors and crates and dumpsters. A mowed lawn stretched out on his left, the backyard of a trade school.

"I'm near Aldonia's west-side trade school."

"Okay, okay, scrap that mission. The elders have something else for you to do."

"Such as?" Dedrick slowed his pace, Fulton's unusual tone bringing up red flags.

"They want you to destroy the tunnels that lead here."

"Here?" Dedrick stopped, certain that he did not want to hear the answer. He already knew.

"Mosheh Control Center."

The clouds drifted over the sun again, but this time they stayed there.

26

The steady rumble of the motorcycle, the cool evening air on my face, and the open road gave me a sense of freedom, of flying like a bird. I liked riding alone. Laying heavy on the throttle, I went through the gears and my mind numbed somewhat. Or rather, my head cleared.

Alix had called me a fool, but she let me take her UT motorcycle. She knew she would get in trouble, too, once this whole thing went down. We'd have to change our disguises and vocations . . . if the Mosheh accepted us. If they accepted me.

I had considered trying to stop Bolcan rather than go along with him. The Mosheh would approve that action. I could sneak to the land that bordered the backside of the facility. That's where I imagined he would be right now. But as I neared the facility, I realized that wouldn't happen. Bolcan was determined to do this. He would blow up the Re-Education Facility tonight.

So my current mission was to get everyone out alive.

I raced down the last stretch of road that led to the facility, wind turbines on one side, a field of solar panels on the other. Clouds gathered overhead. And in my heart. The sun peeked out less and less, leaving me the way *My Friend* had done.

Little strokes fell great oaks. I had been certain that was the message *My Friend* meant to give me through Bot's 3D game. This would not be a little stroke. This would be a massive attack on the Regimen Custodia Terra, an attack on their methods of securing a civilization that shared a common ideology and worked toward a common goal. This would not go unnoticed. It would not create positive organic change or fell the great oak of the all-controlling government. We risked infuriating them and setting in motion a counterattack. They had the world on their side. We had each other.

If Bolcan or I got caught, they would discover many things. They would realize that someone had the ability to manipulate the files attached to retina scans. They would know that I and the colonists I'd helped break from Re-Ed still lived, whereas they thought we had drowned in the river. They would begin to realize the strength of their enemy.

"You are exceeding the speed limit," came a voice through my helmet, some kid working at the Unity Trooper headquarters.

Gritting my teeth, I rolled back the throttle. "My mistake."

I had contacted my UT captain as soon as I set out, saying I'd heard rumor of trouble on the road to Re-Ed and I wanted to check it out. They hadn't heard any similar rumors, and they had more than enough trouble elsewhere in Aldonia, so they let me go alone. I had to remain in constant contact, though.

I still wrestled with how to sever contact once I got there. I didn't want anyone with the Regimen hearing me announce the bomb threat. Real Unity Troopers and drones would arrive in a matter of minutes. I needed to buy Bolcan as much time as possible. We needed to get everyone to safety.

A high black gate and the cement-block guard tower came into view. The facility peeked over a ridge. Full daylight. Why would Bolcan do this in daylight?

I slowed the bike, but my heart beat faster. It began now.

"Name, please," came a voice through my helmet, the guard this time. "And state your business." Having the ability to read my ID implant through my UT communication system or through my flexi-phone, he would know my name already. My purpose, he might not know. Headquarters might not have contacted him.

I gazed up at the window in the tower. Clouds bathed in sunlight reflected on the window, hiding the view inside.

My name? Liberty came to mind. Nothing else for a full second. Then I saw Betsy Ross in the kitchen of the house in Mount Holly. *"I know you."* *She squinted as she approached. "Miss Amity, right?"*

"Right. My name is Amity 254-060965-101 of Aldonia. I'm a Unity Trooper. Suspicious activity was reported in the area, and I'd like to make a quick check of the grounds and facility."

"I've not been told of this."

How to answer that? Why would he be told? I never said I wanted to visit the facility. I only said I'd heard of trouble on the road that led here. "I don't doubt it. There's chaos all over Aldonia tonight. Headquarters has its hands full."

"I'll contact your commander."

My breath caught. "Where are you?" I mentally asked *My Friend*. I needed assurance. I couldn't go in there without it. Was I making a mistake? Would this all come down on me?

The gate creaked back.

I took a breath, shifted into gear, and rolled on through. Would Bolcan or Silver have seen me approach? Even if they had, they'd have no way of knowing it was me. Was there any way I could alert them to my presence? The Mosheh, most likely, watched my every move. They wouldn't like what I was doing, but they could contact Bolcan.

The driveway turned and ended at a parking lot with several scooters and one car, the staff's transportation. Second shift had begun, so fewer staff were present.

I parked the bike where the sidewalk began and dismounted. I had to get rid of the helmet. But how? The instant I did, whoever watched me would grow suspicious. Did anyone with the Regimen watch me? Was there too much chaos in Aldonia tonight? Maybe no one would notice me.

Eyes on the facility doors, glass panels with thick frames, I drew near. My heartbeat thumped in my ears, keeping time with my heavy footfalls. I would have to walk through the doors. I would have to go inside.

Every cell in my being opposed the idea and wanted to rebel. I couldn't do this. What was I going to say? Should I even be here? The Mosheh would not approve. *My Friend* remained silent, and Dedrick . . .

My eyelids and my heart fluttered thinking of him. He would not approve.

The helmet . . . I had to get rid of the helmet.

My steps slowed. Was Bolcan ready for me to do this? I didn't know anything else about his plan. I had told him I wasn't going to help. He wouldn't be expecting me unless the Mosheh had contacted him.

Ten steps to the door, I slid the helmet from my head and drew my arm back, ready to whip the helmet to the wall.

No.

I froze, clutching the helmet in one hand. No? Had *My Friend* spoken? I put the helmet back on and stared at the door. No . . . meaning he didn't want me to go without the helmet? Or no, he did not want me doing this at all? I could turn around and leave. But Bolcan would blow the place regardless. And people might die. I couldn't let that happen.

Forcing my feet to move, I took six more steps and the door shuddered open.

I counted five security guards in a well-lit, spacious reception area, three behind bulletproof glass and a high wraparound counter. One stood with a leg propped on one of the spindly black chairs that lined a wall. The fourth turned away from a computer station near the chairs. They all looked at me.

One of the guards behind the glass . . .

My heart beat out of control, riding up my throat, choking me. I couldn't tear my gaze from his hollow eyes. I knew him. He had been my guard.

"Hey, there, breeder." I heard his voice in my mind. I felt the cold floor of my cell on my legs, saw the guard standing over me, smirking at me, rubbing his big, potato chin. "You really blew it, getting yourself in here."

The guard by the computer station ambled toward me. "A surprise visit from a Unity Trooper? We've never had one of those. What gives?"

I couldn't look at him, couldn't tear my eyes from the smirking guard. Did he recognize me? No, he couldn't have. I opened my mouth to speak . . . to say what?

"Bomb threat," I said, my voice thick. "Clear the building." I motioned with my arms, slicing horizontal lines in front of me. I couldn't think of what else to do. I did it again and again, slicing, slicing the air. I must've looked crazy, but I wanted them to jump into action.

They all stared at me, blank looks on their faces.

"What do you mean?" The man by the chairs dropped his boot to the floor and put his hands on his hips. "This a drill?"

Pushing past my fear, I forced myself to the high counter and gazed directly into the eyes of the smirking guard. "This is not a drill. Clear the building."

"Amity . . ." The voice came through my helmet. The Unity Troopers at headquarters had heard me. They would now be on the alert. They would send troopers, drones. We had only minutes to get the job done. "Where are you getting your information?"

A chair squeaked behind me. Footfalls on the linoleum. Two guards ran for the front door.

"Stop!" I shrieked. I had expected them to follow procedure. "The prisoners. You must evacuate the entire building."

One of the three behind the counter, a chubby man with more badges than the others, slipped around the counter and bolted for the door.

Another guard followed suit.

I lunged for him—it was *my* guard—and wrestled him to the ground. "You can't leave these people here to die. The building's gonna blow." At some point I had grabbed him by the neck without realizing it.

He gripped my wrist and pried at my fingers. Fear showed in his round eyes, slivers of white around big black pupils.

I released my grip and raised my trembling hands to show I meant no harm.

"Please," I whispered.

He twisted away from me, shoving my leg off his, and shouted over his shoulder, "Hit the alarm. Open the cell doors. Open the back doors. Let 'em all out." Then he scrambled to his feet and ran for the door.

"Wait," I screamed after him. Then I turned to the last guard behind the bulletproof window.

His hands flew over controls. Doors on every side of the room slid open. He glanced at me once as he worked. Then he stepped back and turned eyes round with fear to me. "That's all I can do."

"What do you mean?" I raced around the counter and slipped in through the door the guards had left open. Images showed on an array of monitors. Men, women—all in gowns—raced through hallways that pulsed with red light. Some ran arm in arm as if too weak to go alone.

I remembered this . . . the day of my escape . . . and the naked man, the priest, who lay crumpled on the floor. Was there anyone here today who couldn't save himself? Who would rescue him?

"You have to search the place," I shouted, glancing around for the remaining guard.

But he had already reached the door. "You search it," he said over his shoulder. "I want to live." He fled the building.

I glanced at the nearest hallway then back at the monitors. The images now showed an empty hallway and empty rooms. But the images flipped every few seconds. How long before it flipped through all the rooms? Did every room have a camera?

I watched monitors for two more seconds and then dashed down a hallway pulsing with blood-red light. Every door hung open. I only needed to peek inside. The first room I came to . . . it-it couldn't be. I staggered back and slammed into a wall. My mind numbed.

My Lesson Room.

Men shouted in harsh voices. Women wailed. The clomping of horse hooves. Bodies, drenched in blood, lay strewn on the ground around me, tangles of brown limbs, black hair, and feathers. A fly zipped around my face. Anguish gripped my soul. This was my fault.

"Noooo!" I shrieked, falling to my knees.

As I cracked down, all went dark.

I breathed.

Blinking but unable to see, I reached into the dark and found a cold wall but nothing else. Where was I?

Yes, I remembered now. The guard had strapped me to the chair. I had struggled. But he won. This was only a History Lesson. This wasn't real.

High on a nearby wall, a ball of white burst forth from the dark.

I squinted at it, trying to understand. Then I recognized it. It was an emergency light. This was not my History Lesson. I was here to save people. It was time to break out.

Less than a second later, an explosion shattered through some part of the building. The building shook, and I stumbled.

A burst of adrenaline shot through me, propelling me to my feet. I snatched my taser flashlight from my belt and shined it into the room opposite me. The beam fell on an empty bed with open straps and, on the floor, a 3D helmet and a tangle of sensor wires. No bodies.

Another explosion rattled the building, then another. They were so near that the vibrations ripped through my chest and cut through my nerves.

The building was going down.

A thrill coursed through me. I wanted to smile, to laugh. Bolcan was doing it.

A dose of reality hit me . . . I was still in the building, me and maybe others.

I raced to the next room and the next. These were the rooms I needed to search anyway. The Lesson Rooms. If anyone couldn't leave on their own, they'd be here in a Lesson Room.

The next explosion knocked me off balance and sent me tumbling to the floor. I scrambled to my feet within seconds.

"Liberty!"

I turned to see who called my name. I needed to get him out of here. Who would know me by name? Not the Torva. Was there someone else in this place who knew me?

I sucked in a sharp breath. My eyes snapped open wide.

The wall before me burst apart. I hadn't heard the explosion. Chunks of wall and particles flew without sound. I flew, too. Flames appeared to my left, my right, everywhere. I cracked down on my back. And all went black.

27

Smoke and debris settling behind him, Dedrick sped away in a tunnel kart. His stomach turned at what he'd done.

He had tried to accomplish his task like a machine with no feelings, placing explosives in precise locations, counting off steps, flash sighting the targets and detonating them, doing what he had to do . . . destroying the tunnels that led to the Mosheh Control Center. It had felt like cutting an artery or severing a limb. They would never recover from this. Completely cut off from the rest of the underground network, everyone inside would have only the hydraulic lifts to get out. If they needed to get above, they could get to one of three nearby locations in Aldonia.

The tunnel kart's headlights opened the way as Dedrick barreled along, heading for the access point near the Jensenville border. If anyone came through that point, they'd soon stumble upon Tradehall.

Approaching a turn, Dedrick eased off the accelerator. But not enough. He cranked the steering wheel and held his breath. A brick wall zoomed up to him, then away, missing the tunnel kart by an inch. Maybe a fraction of an inch.

He breathed. He didn't need to drive like a maniac. Fulton would've contacted Tradehall, so they'd be implementing defensive measures right now. They had arms. But they were few, maybe twenty-five residents, twenty-five valuable residents who traded with secret communities in other cities and saw to the supplies needed in Aldonia's entire underground network. They were not trained in fighting.

Had Silver discovered them?

"Dedrick, you there?" Fulton's voice came through his earpiece.

He eased off the accelerator, slowing a bit to hear him better. "Yeah, what do you got?"

"Re-Education Facility . . ."

Dedrick took his foot off the pedal and touched the earpiece. "Yeah?"

"Just got word . . . an accident of some sort."

"What do you mean *accident?*"

"It blew up."

"That was no accident." He stepped on the gas and the tunnel kart lurched forward. He had to get above ground and find Liberty. He'd destroy this access point and find another way up, somewhere closer to her apartment.

"Fulton?" With the crises below, should he even ask?

"Yeah, Dedrick?"

"Uh . . ."

"Last we heard," Fulton said. "Liberty was on the road to Re-Ed."

Dedrick squeezed the steering wheel.

"We believe she went in to evacuate the facility before Bolcan . . . Well, that's all we know. And Alix called in for duty, volunteered to help out at the Jensenville border, probably doesn't know about the explosion or our trouble down here."

"Thanks for the report." He tapped his TekBand to end the call.

No good would come of anything tonight. No good would come of any of the Mosheh's efforts to change Aldonians. They had opened themselves up to failure, opened themselves big. Irreparable damage would come of it. If only Andy and Liberty would see it, too, and leave this godforsaken city. Dedrick had once felt called to help here. And he'd done his part. He'd lost count of how many people he'd rescued. He hated to feel like a quitter, but he was ready to move on, to live his life as far from this place as possible. He was ready to give up on Aldonia.

Nearing the intersection of his last turn, he eased off the accelerator and tapped the brakes. A sense of foreboding shuddered through him. He parked the kart several yards back, grabbed a pack of explosives, and jumped out.

He would take the tunnel to the left and walk the two hundred yards to the access point.

The sense of foreboding increased, making Dedrick stop at the intersection. He peered around the corner to the right and squinted into the darkness. At the end of the tunnel lay Tradehall.

Beams of light cut through the darkness at the far end of the tunnel about a quarter mile away, streaming from Tradehall. Figures appeared, dozens of people moving at the pace of a church procession. A man barked out a command that Dedrick couldn't understand from the distance.

He backed away to avoid being seen—to avoid seeing—and flattened his back to the cold tunnel wall. The pack of explosives slipped from his hand. Frustration, anger, and fear for the people of Tradehall made knots in his heart. The Regimen had found them. They would soon know about every underground community.

This is the day the Mosheh falls.

Footfalls, shuffling sounds, an elderly man's cough told Dedrick they neared.

He wiped his teary eyes and peeked again.

Unity Troopers with weapons drawn and flashlights illuminating their path flanked the procession. Two, four, six . . . how many troopers? The man in the front . . .

Dedrick squinted. His heart twisted more. *Maco, Gardenhall's faithful guardian.*

Hands tied behind him, one eye swollen shut, and blood streaking his bearded face, he walked with a limp, dragging his right foot. Maco would not have given up these people without a fight. He must've secured Gardenhall and come here to help. Gardenhall would not be safe for much longer. A day or two. The Regimen knew, now, about the underground. They would clear it out.

Back to the wall, heart pummeling his ribcage, Dedrick drew his pistol and gripped it with both hands. He would have to act fast. Could he possibly get all the troopers? No. Once he started shooting, surely one of them would turn a gun on a . . . a prisoner. That's what they were now. Prisoners. Plus, his action would only confirm that others were down here. CSS would see the live feed from the cameras in the troopers' helmets. They'd give the command for troopers to search tunnels all through the night. On the other hand, if they felt they had everyone, maybe they'd come back tomorrow to expand their search. That would give the other communities time . . .

Dedrick lowered the pistol, his arms, stubborn as stone, resisting the effort. With his heart pierced through, he turned and jogged into darkness back the way he had come. The Mosheh would not be able to remain below. None of them. They would all need to come out in the open.

This is the day the Mosheh falls.

28

"Wine and cheese?" Governor Yancy wore a sleeveless dress of bumpy off-white fabric, the latest environmentally-friendly fashion. While it exposed more cleavage than Dr. Supero wanted to see, it did not in any other way flatter her fuller figure.

"Yes, I thought you might like something to eat." Dr. Supero leaned against the wall, watching her, wondering what this evening held once Guy arrived.

Governor Yancy popped a cube of cheese into her mouth and touched her hair. She had spent time on it this evening. The top stood up in stiff tufts, while red curls—plastered to her forehead and ruddy cheeks—framed her face. She smiled as she inspected the spread on the table. Then she leaned in for a closer look and picked up a tray. "Chocolate?"

Dr. Supero lifted his hands but made no reply. What could he say? They both knew such a large quantity of chocolate could've only come from the black market. One of Guy's thugs, a muscular one who'd refused to speak with Dr. Supero, had made all the arrangements.

He had arrived early this morning before Dr. Supero had even dressed. He began by covering the miniature camera lenses throughout the apartment, including ones previously unknown to Dr. Supero. Then he gathered dirty clothes from the floor and piled it all in the middle of the oversized bed. Using the dirty sheet as a sack, he took it all away and returned two hours later with clean, folded clothes. Next, he gave the place a thorough cleaning, working quickly but efficiently, dusting, vacuuming, washing dishes, and rearranging furniture. He had even obtained drapes to hang in the balcony window and screens to give privacy to the bedroom, if it could be called that. The bed sat on a raised floor with thick columns on the corners, open to the rest of the apartment. Finally, the thug brought groceries, arranged some on the table—

including the black-market chocolate—and put the rest in the refrigerator. That, he did not clean.

Governor Yancy stuffed a square of chocolate into her mouth and sucked on it, her eyes rolling back. "Mmmm."

"I am glad you approve." Dr. Supero glanced at his wrist, forgetting for a moment that he had intentionally left his flexi-phone in a drawer . . . per Guy's instructions. He had yet to get the governor's phone from her.

"Would you mind . . ." Pushing off the wall, Dr. Supero took her hand and traced his fingers from her palm to her wrist. "I would like our conversation to remain private." He unfastened her flexi-phone without protest, stepped up to his sleeping area, and dropped it into a drawer.

"I had never envisioned the two of us as friends," she said, watching his every step as he returned to her.

"Nor had I." He did not like this game and wanted it to end, but he did not look forward to Guy's arrival. Somehow this would go bad for him. He needed to work on a cover.

"You look nice." She touched him. Touched a finger to his shirt at the chest.

While every impulse told him to draw back, he took her hand and gazed into her eyes. "I do not have words for how beautiful you look tonight."

She lifted her hand to his face, touched his cheek, and continued upward.

His heart set to racing, fear setting in. He grabbed her hand and lowered it.

"You don't have to wear that with me," she said, her eyes on his stocking cap. "I don't mind."

He tried to smile but it felt like a sneer. Releasing her hands, he stepped back and turned away from her. She must've assumed the tumor showed as a lump on his head. She would not know about the scar and bald patches.

"Are we going to trust each other?" She came up beside him and touched his arm.

No, he was not going to trust her. He would not remove the hat. He spun to her, thinking words of flattery would distract her, but the door to his apartment flung open and banged against the wall.

Men and women poured into the room. Two, five . . . seven of them, each armed with weapons and equipment.

Dr. Supero pulled Governor Yancy close as if to protect her. A part of him did feel protective. Guy had never explained his plan. Why the weapons?

While the others set up tripods, lights, and two video cameras, Guy sauntered into the room, Angel at his side and a grin on his face. He wore jeans and a shirt under the Regimen jacket. His hair had been trimmed, face shaved. He looked cleaner than usual. Angel, dressed in a long flowing shirt and dark leggings, appeared glorious.

Governor Yancy sucked in a breath and pushed Dr. Supero aside. "What is this? Who are you people?" Her gaze snapped to Guy's stump. "You . . . what happened to you?"

"Take what you want," Dr. Supero said, hoping for the shred of a cover. He could not appear to be connected to them. "I have nothing of value."

Guy stopped directly before them and looked them over. "Aw, sure you do, Dr. Supero." He winked. "You have a lot to offer. And you don't have to hide who you are anymore. Or what you've done."

Heat spread throughout Dr. Supero's body, hot blood racing through his veins. Every muscle tensed. Rage brought a white gnat into his vision. "I have done nothing." He threatened Guy with his eyes. Guy meant to betray him.

"Who are you people?" Governor Yancy shrieked, splaying her trembling hands.

"Now, now." Guy lifted his maimed arm. "We're not going to hurt you. We're going to hurt the Regimen."

Governor Yancy backed away. She *was* the Regimen in Aldonia.

Dr. Supero rushed to her side, but she shoved him away.

"We're here to tell you," Guy said, "that your services as governor are no longer required. Actually, we'd like to hear you say it." He gestured toward the cameras. "You're going to tell the citizens of Aldonia that there's been a change in leadership." He paused. Smiled. "I'm the new governor now."

Her eyes popped wide. She grasped her wrist. Her gaze shot to Dr. Supero. "My flexi-phone."

Dr. Supero shook his head, regret overwhelming him. He hadn't known why Guy wanted the flexi-phones removed. He thought it was to avoid having their conversations overheard, but Guy meant to keep her, to keep them, from calling for help.

"You might not know this," Guy said, lowering his eyebrows, showing mock-concern in his eyes, "but there are uprisings all over Aldonia right now, even as we speak. And they will continue to go on until Aldonians get what they want."

"And what do they want?" she said, throwing back her shoulders and sounding stronger now.

"They want the truth. And they want freedom." Guy paced between a column and the wall that Angel stood by. "No more forced sterilizations. No re-education. The people get to form their own government and decide how to rule themselves. They will decide upon the value of their services and establish trade until something better can be arranged." He pulled a coin from his pocket, tossed it straight up, and caught it.

"How can you ever hope to succeed?" Dr. Supero said to Guy, coming again to the governor's side. "You are a fool. You are few compared to the Regimen. And now you are exposed, and there is no turning back."

"You know these people?" the governor said, her voice a whisper and her eyes turning cold. She did not wait for an answer. Her hand shot up.

His hand shot up but not quickly enough to save himself.

She had ripped the stocking cap from his head. A burst of cool air made his scalp tingle. He staggered back, exposed and humiliated, everyone looking at him. A studio lamp turned on at that moment. And the red dot of a camera.

"The procedure was denied," she said, gawking. "Who did this?"

He covered the scar with both hands and shook his head, backing into one of the columns at the edge of his sleeping area. This wasn't happening.

"Answer me." Governor Yancy's eyes blazed.

Dr. Supero dropped his hands to his sides and let anger transform him. His expression hardened as he stepped toward her. "The Regimen did this. I did this. You did this."

Her face scrunched up with a look of disgust and confusion. She backed away.

"I have discovered secrets that every citizen needs to know," he said. "We have been living a lie. And the lie can no longer sustain us."

"What lie? Who are these people?" Governor Yancy backed into a wall.

"You think we can solve the problem of population numbers without returning to the ways of old? Every woman will need to have a reversal. They will need to be taught to raise their children. Every man will need to commit to a woman, to help raise these children. We will need families."

Guy stepped back and whispered to one of the two camera operators. Angel stood off by herself.

"This is our fault," Dr. Supero spit. "The fault of the Regimen Custodia Terra."

Governor Yancy shook her head and glanced around as if trying to assess the situation. Fear showed in her eyes. Fear of what would happen to her or maybe fear of losing power.

"Less than a hundred years ago," Dr. Supero continued, grabbing her fleshy arms and pressing her to the wall, "the world governments united for the sake of the earth. Humans had been looked upon as little more than parasites. And in some ways, maybe they were. So the parasites had to be, for the most part, exterminated . . . a concerted effort by the new government. Only a specific number were permitted to survive. And these had been stripped of all self-rule and cornered into micromanaged cities where they were placated with trivial amusements and benefits."

To get his point across, he leered at her and drew closer, into her intimate space. "Mores had been forced onto societies," he whispered in her ear, "so that the average citizen is satiated in sexual promiscuity, having no clue as to the natural purpose of sexual intimacy."

She stomped hard on his foot and slammed her palms to his chest.

A jolt of pain made him stumble back. He glanced around the room.

Everyone stared. This was being recorded, maybe broadcast live. He was done for.

What did he care? To contain it would drive him mad anyway. "So we saved Mother Earth, saved her from the devastating effects of pollution, though the climate continued to change dramatically. Animals and plants lived without negative human impact, though species continued to die out at a rate equal to the days before the Regimen. Only one life-form suffered under the new regime. Can you guess which one?"

She stared through hot, narrow eyes, her painted lips a thin line.

"Ours," he answered for her. "You may have noticed. Suicide rates climb. Populations decrease . . . despite our scientific intervention. We were not made to live like this."

"Where are you getting all this?" Her gaze flitted to the cameras. She folded her arms. "This isn't true. You've gone insane."

His gaze slid to Angel, his brain surgeon. "I may be insane. I don't really know. But I have proof, records to back me up."

"You're not insane." Angel approached, but Guy, who stood next to a camera operator, waved her back.

"And who have you shown these records to?" Governor Yancy asked, a calculating look in her eyes.

"No one, yet. But soon . . . everyone."

29

"You're free to go, if that's what you need to do," Betsy said, *gazing through big, unblinking avatar eyes. "It's always been your choice."*

I clung to the doorframe, one foot in the house, the other on the porch. "I-I'm not sure what I want to do. I need to do something to help bring freedom to these people. And I don't want to sit around and eat dinner with the enemy."

"Do you think we are ignoring this war, pretending it doesn't exist?" Her eyes narrowed. She smoothed her skirt. "No, we may be doing something little, but it will help bring about a great victory. Each of us, we only need to do our little part."

"You're worried you're not doing enough," Dedrick said.

I spun to face him.

He leaned against a wall in the shadows of the Mosheh's training room. Betsy and the house in Mount Holly had vanished.

My heart pounded and palms sweated. How long had he been watching me? "What're you doing here?"

Still shrouded in shadows, Dedrick sauntered to me and took my sweaty hands into hands warm and dry. "Who was it that said: Be who God meant you to be and you will set the world on fire?*"*

God? Did I believe in God? Who did God want me *to be?*

Heat transferred from his hands to mine and slid up my arms. I pulled away and rubbed my hands together.

Laughter erupted in the dining room. I was again standing on the threshold of the house in Mount Holly.

I snapped open my eyes and sucked in a breath.

I lay on my back on a hard floor, my head on a pillow, a dark, rotting ceiling above me. Men's low voices and coarse laughter came from nearby.

I sat up, pain rushing to my head. As I lifted a hand, I glimpsed a black box on my wrist, the Mosheh's ID implant signal bouncer.

Muted sunlight snuck around the edges of boarded up windows along one wall. A warped counter stretched along the same wall under the windows. Cans, a ratty pillow, and other debris lay scattered on a filthy floor. Two boxy seats, each on thick poles near the counters, made me think this was once an old barber shop, the kind you learned about in school when studying the past.

Someone laughed again, a woman this time. People sat on the floor in the darkest corner, ten, maybe twelve, most of them men.

A door swung open, blinding me with light. Two muscular figures stepped inside, silhouettes crunching over gritty debris. The first one squatted by me as the door shut.

"How you feeling?" Bolcan said, touching my forehead with the palm of his hand. He wore his hair pulled back. His jeans were ripped on one knee and dirt marred his buckskin jacket.

"What happened?" I asked.

He smiled and waggled his eyebrows. "We did it. Re-Ed's a pile of rubble."

"Everyone get out?" I toyed with the black box on my wrist. I couldn't bear the thought of people dying in the explosion.

"Yeah. Everyone. Even the staff, thanks to you."

"So no one died?" I allowed myself to feel a bit of relief.

"Oh, people died." The second muscular figure crunched across the room, muted beams of light playing in her silver hair. She sat in one of the boxy barber-shop seats. She tried turning the seat but it only shifted.

"Who?" I directed the question to Bolcan. "I didn't want anyone to die. That's not the way the Mosheh works."

Bolcan's jaw twitched. "Well, unfortunately, that's the way life works. It's messy. Aldonia is messy. Our mission was messy." He inhaled and sat down beside me. "I'm glad you changed your mind. Fulton told me you were on the way, so we adjusted our plan. Went back to Plan A."

"Plan A?"

"The one that saved the most lives. Once you showed up and delivered the bomb threat, they let everyone go. We didn't have to break in. I'd learned how many were in there, so we counted them as they came out. We got them all."

"Then we blew the place." Silver grinned and pushed up the sleeves on her black jacket.

"I didn't know you'd still be in there." Bolcan touched my hand, stopping me from fidgeting with the box on my wrist. "I came around to find you with the guards and to subdue them. And you weren't there. So I went in and got you." He laced his fingers through mine and lifted our hands. "Good thing you wore the helmet. You got thrown."

"Yeah, I almost took it off." I rubbed my head with my other hand. "I have a headache."

A man emerged from the dark corner and rifled through one of several backpacks. My Unity Trooper armor lay over there, too.

"But no broken bones or anything," Bolcan said. "So thank God."

The mention of God made me smile and then reminded me of the dream I had before waking. *Be who God meant you to be and you will set the world on fire?* Dedrick had said. Did I believe in God? The colonists did. Dedrick did. Even Sarkin did. And it affected the way they lived their lives. We had grown up not believing in things science couldn't prove. And, in a way, the belief still struck me as childish. But a good thing. If I believed in God, what would that mean for me and the way I lived my life?

I shook my head to stop the progression of thoughts. I'd have to think on that another day. Today, I just liked the way "Thank God" sounded coming from Bolcan.

"So I got you out of there," Bolcan said, "then Unity Troopers showed up, first a few on bikes, then a whole open transport of them."

"Then a helicopter," Silver said, her voice loud and brimming with pride. "And we stood our ground and picked them off, them with their rubber bullet guns and tear gas, us with our bombs and semiautomatics." She motioned with her hands, pretending to aim and shoot at me.

My stomach sank and my head grew light. "You killed them all?"

The man who had been rifling through a backpack approached and stuck a hand out to me. "Here, take this. It'll help." He tapped his forehead. A scraggily beard and hair hid most of his face, but his eyes were kind. And brown. One of the Torva?

I accepted the pill then the bottle of water he offered.

"What would you have wanted us to do?" Silver slid off the boxy chair and cranked it by hand, forcing it to twist around with an awful noise. "They were armed. And they wanted to take all of us."

"But they didn't have lethal weapons," I said, though I saw her point. They had to protect themselves.

She shrugged and leaned a hip against the chair, folding her arms.

"We didn't kill them all," Bolcan snapped, facing Silver. "Our intent was to save ourselves, not to murder people. We put the survivors in the shop next door with a few Torva men standing guard. Most of the Torva, though, are on their way to the border. And some went to help underground. I've been checking on—"

"Underground?" My heart skipped a beat. "What's going on underground?"

"You . . . don't know?" Bolcan whispered.

I shook my head, unable to speak and fearing the worst.

"Oh. Bad news." He glanced at Silver but didn't seem reluctant to speak in front of her. "Regimen discovered our underground network, at least part of it."

"What?" I put a hand to the wall, stood, and brushed debris from the back of my uniform pants. I didn't want to believe him. The Mosheh was a rock. It had to remain secret and forever safe.

He stood, too, and held my arm as if he thought I'd tip over. "There's not much we can do about it. Dedrick already sealed off access points and tunnels, did everything he could. The elders and the Control Center are safe."

"What about Gardenhall?" My heart went to Abby and all the people down there. *Please keep them safe*, I said internally to *My Friend*. They didn't need more trouble in their lives.

"Safe for now. But troopers discovered Tradehall and cleared our people out."

"Tradehall?" I said, feeling numb. I had visited the place once. A small, tight group lived there, good people that provided a much-needed service for the entire Mosheh. "Where did they take them?"

"I don't know." He clenched his jaw. "Not Re-Ed."

Silver laughed. "That's for sure."

"Where's Dedrick?" My heart ached for him. He had to be taking this hard. The Mosheh had been his life for the past four years. He knew these people. He loved these people.

Bolcan shrugged and walked to a window as he answered, his tone loud and angry. "Dedrick is wherever the Mosheh wants him to be. Fulton told me you were coming to help us, but that's the last I heard from them."

Silver watched Bolcan but didn't seem shocked by or curious about anything he said.

I shook my head in disbelief. The pieces were coming together in my mind. "So you told Silver?"

Bolcan lifted his hands, palms up. "This is a different game now, Liberty. All the cards are face up." He glanced at Silver. "Besides, she's been helping."

I huffed and gawked at her. Silver wanted to find a way to profit. Didn't he realize that? She was using him. The reason she snooped around the tunnels was to find secrets she could use for gain. The Regimen had probably followed her one day . . .

My eyes opened wide then narrowed as the picture became clear. Then I lost control. "You did this to them," I shrieked, dashing toward her. Wanting to take it out on her, I grabbed her by the jacket and yanked.

She stumbled forward, laughing, then shoved me away.

I staggered back, sliding on debris, and bumped into Bolcan.

"Hey, what'cha doing?" Bolcan wrapped his arms around my waist, preventing me from lunging at her again.

"This is her fault." I pried his arms from me and spun to face him.

He lifted his hands and backed off.

"She led the Regimen to the Mosheh," I said, "put all those people at risk. You've freed these men while we lost our own."

"No." Bolcan shook his head. "It would've went down that way anyway. There's no blaming anyone. It's done, and we have to figure out where to go from here."

Silver stood with her arms at her sides, staring at me, one side of her lip curled. "I am not your enemy." She stomped to the pile of backpacks on the floor, kicked bags aside, and grabbed a semiautomatic rifle and a pistol. Then she stomped to the door. "I'm outta here."

"Where's she going?" I said as the door swung shut.

"Jensenville border. They say the wall's coming down tonight."

"What?" I scooted to the boarded-up window, to where a sliver of light stole through. "Where am I?" I peeked out, squinting against the evening sunlight.

Gray clouds covered half the sky. A broken street overrun with weeds ran between this building and a row of old shops. The recycling center peeked over rooftops.

Bolcan came up behind me. "We're not too far from the remains of the Re-Education Facility. We don't have transportation for so many. So we're waiting for nightfall."

Teeth gritted, tension spreading through me, I continued to gaze through the gap between the board and the window frame. Where did we go from here? We still needed to change the hearts and minds of Aldonians. I could still place my hope in that.

I glared at Bolcan. "What time is it?"

He glanced at his TekBand. "Little after six."

I had time. I would meet up with Alix and get people to the assembly. "I'm not waiting for nightfall. I'm going now." I lifted my arm with the black box attached to the wrist. "Get this thing off me."

"Still want your implant?" He withdrew an implant remover from a jacket pocket.

"No, I'm sure my cover was blown with the building." I stuck a finger in my eye. I wouldn't need the scarlet contacts either.

"Want an escort?" The bearded Torva man who had given me medicine joined us.

"I'll take her," Bolcan said. "I've got a motorcycle."

30

Dedrick stood with one hand on the doorknob and his forehead practically touching the door to Liberty's apartment. Should he knock again? His gut told him she wasn't here, but what if . . . Could she possibly be asleep? Hurt? He wouldn't be able to live with himself if he ever discovered a single door had stood between them in her moment of need.

He took a lock pick from his belt and, five wasted minutes later, opened the door. He did not have Liberty's talent for picking locks. Or Bolcan's, for that matter. In fact, he'd been about to give up and kick the door in.

Gray evening light streamed through a window with no curtains and fell on boxes in the middle of the living room. The boxes had come from Gardenhall, packed with household items the women there thought she might need.

"Liberty?" Dedrick crossed the room and stuck his head in one and then the other little bedroom.

A tan shirt lay on the floor of the second bedroom, a wrench and screwdriver in the corner, making him think of her. Before her rescue last year, she always wore a tool belt . . . was always fixing things for people. Even last summer in the Maxwell Colony, she had spent her time on projects like designing the emergency door to the CAT cave. She seemed like a girl who needed a few tools handy to feel comfortable. He wished she needed him that way.

"Liberty, where are you?" he whispered, crossing back to the door.

Markings on top of one of the boxes caught his eye. Someone had carved words into the cardboard. *It's not tonight, so I'm going to the border. Lex.*

Lex, Alix's undercover name. Maybe Alix meant it as a message for Liberty. Fulton said she'd gone in to work. What wasn't tonight? The assembly?

Dedrick yanked open the door to their apartment and stepped into the hallway.

A siren blipped.

He stomped down two flights of stairs and pushed open the entranceway door.

Two black Unity Trooper vehicles pulled up to the curb, their orange and blue lights flashing. Car doors flew open and armed troopers bolted for the apartment building.

Heart stopping, Dedrick jumped out of the way and slammed his back against a corner of the brick wall. They were looking for her? She'd done it. She went with Bolcan and destroyed Re-Ed. And the Regimen knew it.

Where was she now? Troopers searched for her, so she hadn't been caught. Was she hurt? Or worse?

Dedrick's hands clenched into fists. Why had she gone with Bolcan? What had he said to convince her to risk her future with the Mosheh? To risk her life? Had she taken much convincing? Or was Bolcan right and she shared his driving desire to level Re-Ed.

Dedrick raced down the steps, catching the eye of the trooper who remained in one of the vehicles. He forced himself to slow his pace and wandered across the street, pretending the towering apartment building across the street was his destination. Then he darted to the shadows between buildings.

Leaning back against the wall, he raked a hand through his hair. Where was she? Bolcan—

Dedrick was going to kill him. He risked her safety. For his own personal goal.

Less than five minutes passed. The Unity Trooper vehicles pulled away from the curb and sped off down the road.

Dedrick emerged from the shadows and strolled into the road, not sure where to begin his search. He'd need transportation if he wanted to get to Re-Ed.

The rumble of a motorcycle came from the direction opposite the departing Unity Troopers. Within seconds, it drew close enough for him to make out the riders: Bolcan—he was going to rip him off the bike and have at him—and Liberty—thank God she was alive. She sat behind

Bolcan, her blonde hair whipping across her face, her hands on his hips. Neither one wore a helmet.

Dedrick stood frozen in the middle of the road, stunned as it occurred to him. Bolcan and Liberty . . . two Aldonians who had grown up in this culture of death yet had both refused to go along blindly. They both challenged it, stood against it, and suffered the consequences. And now, they had both just blown up the Re-Education Facility. They shared all this in common.

"Hey, Dedrick." Bolcan pulled up alongside him in the middle of the road. He sat atop a burly black military-grade motorcycle. The kind that can run on five types of fuel.

Where he got it, Dedrick wasn't going to ask. In fact, he couldn't even get himself to reply to Bolcan's greeting.

A siren wailed in the distance.

Dedrick's gaze locked onto Liberty, and he found himself unable to speak.

Smudges on her face, scrapes on one cheek and on her forehead . . . she had chosen to risk her life for Bolcan's mission.

Maybe Bolcan was right about everything concerning her. Dedrick came from the colonies, she from Aldonia, and differences too great stood between them. As much as he loved the colony he grew up in, the woods around it, and every trail from here to there . . . she loved Aldonia. She grew up here. And these people, the Aldonians, while messed up and confused, these were her people. She may have hated their ways, but she loved them. She would risk everything for them.

He could still picture the videos he watched when preparing for her rescue last year. He remembered her shouting at workers who disrespected the elderly in the Senior Center, coming to the aid of a drug addict in a downpour, giving her jacket and almost her socks to the children they rescued from Primary. Those were colonists. His people. Still, she put others before herself, made their freedom her priority, and risked all to do what she thought was right. He loved that about her. He just wished she didn't feel the need to do it without him.

Liberty leaned against Bolcan, gripping the sides of his buckskin jacket, and slid off the bike. "Is Alix inside?"

"No," Dedrick said.

She took two steps toward him, looking unsatisfied with the answer.

"Fulton says she volunteered for more hours," Dedrick said. "I think she's at the border."

Trouble and disappointment flickered in her eyes. Her pale green eyes. She no longer wore the contacts. She glanced at her apartment building. "The assembly's tonight. The big one. The one they're going to broadcast."

Dedrick remembered the note carved into the box in her apartment. "Oh, hey, Alix left a message. It's not tonight."

The color drained from Liberty's face. Her mouth fell open and a strand of hair blew across her face. "It has to be. We have the biggest crowd ever. We can't let them down." She turned to Bolcan . . . to Bolcan and not to Dedrick. "I have to talk to Guy and Andy. I need to get to the old city center."

Bolcan nodded and looked at Dedrick, his expression grim and communicating something Dedrick didn't understand. He wasn't rubbing it in. What was the look?

Dedrick nodded and—though it killed him to do it—he stepped back. As much as he wanted Liberty with him, Bolcan had this one. Liberty had trusted Bolcan with her life and safety, trusted him enough to go on a suicide mission with him. Maybe she liked him better. That would explain why she never answered when Dedrick had asked to see her. He'd ask her again sometime. One last time. He needed to know, needed to hear her say it. Did he stand a chance with her?

"Do you know how to get there?" Liberty asked Bolcan.

"I know how to get anywhere." A flirty grin flashed across his face then faded as his gaze turned to Dedrick.

"I hear you got the job done," Dedrick said, finally able to speak to Bolcan. "Took the *hellhole* down."

Bolcan smiled, suppressed emotion flickering on his face.

The siren wailed again, sounding nearer.

"Better go." Dedrick scooted off the road. "The troopers, they're circling back, probably be watching this area for a while."

Without shutting the bike off, Bolcan dropped the kickstand and dismounted. "You take her. I have other things to do."

Dedrick met him in the road and stood face to face. He wanted to say *thank you*, and to say he was glad Re-Ed was blown up, and that he really did care and would've helped if he hadn't had his own responsibilities. But he said nothing.

Bolcan stuck a hand out.

Dedrick slapped it, front and back, and made for the bike. Grabbing the handlebars, he threw a leg over the bike and kicked up the kickstand.

Liberty climbed on behind him, fitting her body against his and resting her hands on his sides.

"Where's your helmet?" he said, sliding her left hand over his waist.

She wrapped her arms around him and leaned closer. "I don't know."

"Step on it," Bolcan shouted.

A siren ripped through the air. Blue and orange lights flashed in the bike's mirror.

Dedrick gave Bolcan a nod to say *thanks,* shifted the bike into gear, twisted the throttle, and took off.

Before the chase even began, a black vehicle with flashing lights pulled into the road, several yards ahead and blocking the way. The passenger-side door flung open and a trooper jumped out leveling a rubber-bullet rifle.

Glimpsing an alley between high rises, Dedrick pushed one side of the handgrip and leaned for a turn. Liberty leaned with him, hugging him, her arms firm against his waist.

Something dinged behind them. The trooper taking a shot?

Dedrick gunned it, speeding through the alley, the bike sounding like a tank. They came out on a street of shops. The trooper would come after them. He'd have to slow for the turn, but his vehicle would fit through the alley without a hitch. They'd probably send another car around the block.

What to do?

A row of shops lined both sides of the street for two blocks. Beyond the shops, he remembered seeing an open area with nowhere to hide one way, but a tangle of roads and an overpass the other way.

Dedrick turned right, scanning for breaks between shops, hoping for a narrow opening that his bike could fit through but a car couldn't.

Were the troopers really looking for Liberty, or had they just looked suspicious? Troopers might have noticed her uniform, the snug black shirt and pants, though she didn't wear the armor. What'd happened to it? What had happened to her helmet? Bolcan should've seen to her safety.

Near the end of the first block, blue and orange lights flashed in his mirrors. Two Unity Trooper cars now, siren blaring.

They needed to get off main roads, find some place to hide. He could not let Liberty get caught.

He leaned, turning the corner, her leaning with him, then straightened, their bodies moving like one. They rode behind the shops, backtracking. His gaze snapped to a row of three dumpsters a few shops down. They sat close together, each of them six feet wide and six feet high.

Yeah, they could hide there. Downshifting, he headed for the dumpsters.

Nearing his destination, a dozen yards to go, a motorcycle pulled out from behind the dumpsters and blinded Dedrick with its headlight. The motorcycle revved its engine and rolled forward, its rider in scaled armor and a sleek black helmet. A Unity Trooper!

A wave of shock washed over Dedrick. Then a surge of adrenaline controlled his next move.

He dropped his foot to the pavement, squeezed the front brakes, and hit the throttle, swinging the back end of the bike around. He took off with the trooper on his tail.

Now a car, no—two cars on his tail. Lights flashing. Sirens blaring. Down one road then another, every turn taking him further from the old city center and closer to the highway. How could he lose them?

Increasing the throttle, wind pushing the bike, Dedrick sped down a curved road toward an overpass. Taking a curve too fast, leaning too low, peg scraping the ground, forgetting to breathe . . .

Feathering the throttle . . . clearing another bend, overpass coming into view, praying the troopers couldn't see him, he held in the clutch and braked hard.

He swerved the bike, skidding, heading away from the overpass and toward the sloped grass under it. The bumpy ride lifted him, lifted her off the seat, as they plowed down the side of the mound. Squeezing the brakes, he stopped in the shadows and waited.

Liberty lessened her grip and sat up.

Sirens blaring, two Unity Trooper vehicles blew by.

She pressed against him again and held on, but Dedrick waited until the sirens faded in the distance. Then, clutching the handlebars and leaning forward, he eased the motorcycle back up the slope, back to the road. No sign of a trooper anywhere.

He exhaled. They were safe. He could set his course for the Gray Zone, now, and take her where she wanted to go.

31

Dedrick perched near the top of the chain-link fence that surrounded the Gray Zone, toes stuck in the links, one hand gripping a vertical pole, shrugging out of his jacket. Last time we climbed this fence, he'd thrown his cape over the sagging barbed wires and held them down while everyone in our group climbed over.

His gallantry touched me. But I didn't need his help. I wrestled for a moment with whether I should pretend I did or just climb over. I scaled the fence as I thought about it and swung a leg over the barbed wires, my impulses deciding for me.

I thumped down onto hard-packed earth.

He jumped two seconds later and two meters away. His brown leather jacket hung open, and the breeze made his white shirt flutter against his chest. With a tilt of his chin he indicated which way to go. It was a different way than I had taken when I'd come to find Sarkin, but I trusted Dedrick's judgment.

We took off together, falling into a comfortable pace.

He hadn't said a word since I climbed behind him on the motorcycle. Other than, "Where's your helmet?" To which I'd answered, "I don't know." Neither of us had worn one, and the slope of the seat had made me lean on him, bringing my face close to his neck. We could've spoken. I wanted to know everything that had happened underground. But the raiding of Tradehall had probably devastated him, and I didn't want to stick knives in a new wound.

We jogged to a gravelly road overgrown with tall weeds that bent in the wind. Then we turned down a street.

A full moon crested the horizon, visible between rows of two- and three-story deteriorating buildings. Greenish, moody clouds streaked through a lavender-blue sky, creeping toward the sun and threatening to turn volatile. We had less than two hours before sunset.

"Think it's going to rain?" I said.

Dedrick glanced at the sky then looked at me. "Yeah . . . why . . . why'd you go with him? I-I didn't think you'd do it," he blurted out as if he'd been waiting impatiently for me to breach the silence between us.

I looked at him.

He swung his face forward. "I know you wanted to join the Mosheh. So I don't get why you did it. Unless . . ." He gave the slightest glance. "When you delivered the message at the Breeder Facility, you wished it were Bolcan who'd gone with you. Am I right? And . . . and you wanted him to take you here. And his Re-Ed mission—"

"Wow, no! Just stop, okay?" A breeze kicked up, blowing my hair and prickling my skin. Making my eyes water. Where had all Dedrick's crazy thoughts come from? "I didn't *go* with Bolcan to destroy Re-Ed. I went after, to stop him . . . but on the way, I realized that wouldn't be possible. So I went there to make sure everyone got out."

Dedrick stared for a moment then nodded as if he would've done the same.

His approval comforted me, making me wonder if his opinion meant too much to me. When it came to it, I didn't want to hesitate to do what I needed to do out of fear of upsetting him.

"Bolcan's plan was foolish. I didn't want anyone to . . . die." My voice broke.

Dedrick's gaze clicked to me. "Did anyone die?"

"Unity Troopers." I answered without emotion, though it saddened me. None of them chose their vocation. None of them chose to risk their lives for this government or to defend ideologies forced on them.

"How many?"

"I don't know. Bolcan didn't say, and I didn't see it. Before the fighting began, I was knocked unconscious."

Dedrick stopped jogging. Hand to the top of his head, he spun in a circle then faced me with a clenched jaw. "You were knocked unconscious?" He seemed unable to hold my gaze. Or hold still, for that matter.

"I'm fine."

"What if you have a concussion?"

"I don't have a concussion."

"How do you know?"

"I'm fine."

With sulky eyes and a pouty mouth, Dedrick shook his head. "He shouldn't have asked you to help. He shouldn't have put you in that kind of danger." With both hands atop his head, he resumed walking. A few steps later, he swung his arms down. "I wanted to get to him first, to help him so he wouldn't ask you."

"I'm okay, Dedrick." His concern touched me, sort of melted my heart, but I couldn't let it stand in the way of our mission. "Can you stop worrying about me?"

He gave me a look that said, "No."

We picked up our pace, jogging now.

"If there hadn't been trouble underground," he said, "I'd a' been there."

Since he brought it up, I dared to ask, "What's the damage down there?"

"Don't know yet. Troopers came through the access point nearest Tradehall and took everyone. Fulton intercepted CSS and UT communications. They'll be exploring tunnels tomorrow."

"If I had known . . ." I wished I had known. I would've done anything to keep the underground safe, not that I could've done anything he hadn't.

"I know. You'd a' been there." He smiled.

"Yeah." I smiled, and a warm togetherness passed between us.

Still jogging, we turned down an alley and crunched over debris.

"Bolcan said you sealed off tunnels," I said, "that Gardenhall and the Control Center are safe."

Dedrick gazed at the sky as clouds covered the sun and a shadow fell over us. Harsh shadows on the edges of bricks, steps, and window frames softened, everything mutating into shades of gray.

"We've got to make it seem like Tradehall was the sole underground community," he said. "The Mosheh's doing that now. But we all need to get out of here, out of Aldonia. Nothing's safe now. It's falling apart." He turned to me. "I wish you'd go with me."

"And leave everyone?"

He gave me a sad smile. "I know you won't. So I won't either. I mean, unless . . ."

The courthouse square came into view, less than half a kilometer away, and a campfire scent carried on the wind.

"You never did answer me." Dedrick slowed, walking now.

I wanted to speed up. We needed to get Guy, Andy, and that priest to the assembly by seven. What reason could they have for cancelling? Alix's message could've meant something else. We could've been wasting our time right now. Not that I minded. I enjoyed Dedrick's company. His presence tempered my anxiety.

"Did you hear me?"

I didn't look right away, trying to remember what he'd said. I wanted to assure him I was of sound mind and body, that I didn't have a concussion. "You said I didn't answer you." I glanced. "What was the question?"

"I want to see you."

My heart stirred. *That's not a question*, I almost said. *It's a statement*. But I wondered what made him bring this up now. "Do you think the Mosheh won't accept me now? Because of today?"

He shrugged. "No. They're going to need you. They're going to need all of us, not only to help with their mission but for their safety."

"Well, we're two days from commitments. You said you'd respect my promises."

"So give me two days."

Overwhelmed by the passion his words and tone conveyed, I couldn't speak at first. "Are . . . you renewing your promises?"

"No. My heart wouldn't be in it. It's somewhere else. Unless . . ."

He grabbed my arm and stopped me altogether. "Liberty, I just need you to tell me. Because I'm no good at reading your signals. You're Aldonian. I'm from the colonies. Does that matter to you? And I - I've never experienced the things you've experienced so I'll never fully understand. Is that a wall between us? I know it can't be today, but in four years, when your promises to the Mosheh end . . ." The brown of his eyes deepened, a glint of longing in them. ". . . do I stand a chance with you?"

Having forgotten to breathe as he spoke, I sucked in a breath. "I . . . of course you do. Okay? But let's run now. Let's go find Guy."

"You said *okay*? You'll see me?" His hand slid down my arm to my hand.

My skin tingled. That nervous, edgy feeling of standing on a rooftop shuddered through me again. I had felt that way recently, anticipating the day I'd make my commitment to the Mosheh. Why did I feel this way now?

"Yes, I'll see you. Want to go with me to the assembly?" I suppressed a smile. He had the motorcycle, so I assumed we'd go together. "Then we can drop by Gardenhall and visit the elders." The next two days would have us busy anyway, but we could work together. Would that be enough for him? Would it be enough for me? Would I let my feelings for him stand in the way of my mission or of making a commitment to the Mosheh?

He nodded, a playful smile on his face. "Sounds fun." Then he tugged my hand and let go. "Race ya." He took off running down a broken road, weaving around huge potholes and meter-high weeds, heading for the courthouse square.

I bolted after him, sprinting to our destination.

Once Dedrick reached the square, he stopped suddenly as if something caught his attention. Then a man in a dark suit strode out from behind overgrown bushes.

I caught up to them, panting.

"Hey, Liberty," Guy said, lifting his handless arm. With a clean-shaven jaw, short and styled hair, and a pressed suit, he looked different from how I remembered him. Had I seen him in anything but the Regimen officer's jacket?

"My lookouts told me we had visitors," Guy said. "What brings you to our turf?"

"Assembly's still on for tonight, isn't it?" Desperation eked out in my tone.

"Walk with me," Guy said, turning.

He led us through the square down a dirt walkway that someone had cleared. Sarkin and Father Damon? Is that what they were doing the other day before I had interrupted?

Flowers and weeds bloomed together on either side. A plastic wrapper skittered across our path and got stuck in a thistle. We passed a new fire pit, bricks stacked in a meter-high circle. Smoke spiraled up from it, but the flames didn't show.

Stopping near a rebuilt gazebo, Guy faced us and flung his arm out. "What do you think?"

Dedrick, staring at the gazebo, nodded. His expression gave nothing away.

Cement blocks replaced five of the eight original posts. Sheets of plywood formed the top, and strips of white fabric hung from them, flapping in the breeze. Several people worked in and around the gazebo, some arranging speakers and wires of an old-fashioned sound system. Others placing homemade lanterns and decorations among the ruins.

"Throwing a party?" Dedrick said.

"Oh, more than that." Guy draped an arm around Dedrick and stood gazing at the gazebo with him. "Me and Angel, we're getting married."

"What?" Dedrick jerked back, grinning. "You're kidding."

"No, no, I'm not kidding." Guy rubbed his smooth chin with his stump. "Shaved and everything."

Dedrick laughed and slapped Guy's shoulder. "Well, good for you. It'll be a first in Aldonia, huh?"

"Yeah, yeah, I think so. We got two other couples getting married, too."

"So where's your bride?" Dedrick said, looking around.

Guy pointed at the old courthouse. "Getting ready. I won't see her until it's time." He glanced at his watch.

"Wait . . ." I stepped in front of them. "But not tonight, right? I mean, you guys are on your way to the assembly, right? We've invited a lot of people. And Fulton's going to broadcast—"

Guy dropped his arm from Dedrick's shoulder and scratched his head. "Oh, yeah, about that . . ."

I saw it all falling apart and crashing down. "No! You can't cancel it."

"Yeah, we have to." He frowned in an exaggerated way. "Schedule got all messed up today. We were going to have the wedding earlier this evening. Wedding, then the assembly for our announcement and celebration, but I had some messy business, had to meet with the governor." A silly, open-mouthed grin stretched across his face. "Ex-governor. I'm the governor now." He lowered his brow, his mouth becoming a grim line, and stuck a hand out to Dedrick. Dedrick shook it. "We'll be making that announcement later."

"Oh, yeah? Congratulations." Dedrick's smirk said he didn't believe him.

I stamped my foot and threw my arms up. Impatience had me nearly jumping out of my skin. "Listen, we need speakers for tonight's assembly. This is the one we've been building up to, the important one, the one that can change everything. Aldonia's falling apart. Who knows what chance we'll have tomorrow?"

"Is anything more important than love?" Guy said, jutting his jaw and peering through heavy-lidded eyes.

Groaning, I thrust my hands into my hair and turned away.

Dedrick laughed and rubbed my shoulder. "It'll work out. Relax."

"Relax?"

A deep, low sound of a bowed string instrument thundered through the speakers and vibrated through my chest. Then a lower note played, followed by several more.

The chords struck me deep inside, captivating me.

Guy's crew stopped working, everyone now standing or squatting, frozen in place.

"What is that?" I gazed at big black speakers.

"That's a bass, a bull fiddle." Dedrick twisted strands of my hair.

Guy lifted his arms as a higher-pitched bowed string instrument joined in the song.

"And that's a violin." Dedrick grinned with amusement at Guy. "Pachelbel's Canon."

Eyes closed, head tilted back, Guy waved his hand and his stump in and out.

Another and another violin entered the song, each picking up the same tune and playing the long notes in sequence. The rich, harmonic melody stirred my soul, making me close my eyes, too. Dark, haunting . . . the melody tugged at my emotions.

Dedrick's hand slid down my back and to my waist.

I snapped open my eyes and breathed. My emotional mood shattered as Dedrick wrapped his arm around me. I wasn't ready for this. The music and his touch stirred me in a similar way, comforting me but also creating a deep longing. I wanted to belong to him. And him to me. Forever and complete, just the two of us.

"You guys have been ripped off." Dedrick gazed into my eyes and eased me closer. "You don't get to hear the Masters, read the Classics. None of that."

"We've heard them. In Secondary." For some reason I felt the need to defend my upbringing. Our teachers presented them to us for one quarter of one year, in a hurried course that included a variety of music, all of it presented with equal enthusiasm. And this song didn't sound familiar.

Dedrick toyed with the hem of my shirt, the snug black uniform meant to be worn under our armor, making me wish I would've changed into something nicer. For him? And when exactly would I have done that?

He dipped his head down to me. For a kiss?

A rush of heat assailed me. I jerked away. "So, Guy . . ."

The mood of the song intensified. Guy danced in a circle, arms flailing and head back. The others stood transfixed. Even Dedrick. White streamers rose and fell, twisting and snapping. Clouds raced through the sky. A plastic wrapper—the one I'd seen stuck in a weed?—sailed through the air. An earthy odor of soil and dross passed by, then the campfire scent. The music played on.

"Guy!" I shouted, frantic, using every gram of self-control to keep from shaking him.

The music reached a dramatic peak, the notes stretching out long and beautiful. Then they fell silent.

Guy dropped his arms and his head rolled forward. The others broke from the spell and returned to their work and conversations.

I exchanged glances with Dedrick. "He's crazy," I mumbled. "Or high."

Dedrick shrugged. Was that a hurt look in his eyes? Because I rejected his kiss?

A man in a straw hat and a black robe that flapped in the breeze carried a pitcher and a folded white cloth toward the gazebo. Father Damon? Another man in a black robe followed him, carrying smaller vessels. Was Sarkin nearby, too?

"What're they doing?" I said. Maybe I should've been talking with Father Damon. Did we really need Guy?

Guy lifted his head. "Oh, Father wants to get a few baptisms in."

"Well, can someone come to the assembly? And where's Andy?"

"We need him for music."

"Why? You already have music."

"Liberty, stop," Dedrick said, looking a bit annoyed. "It's not going to happen tonight."

"Yeah," Guy said. "Not tonight."

"But it has to happen tonight." Why didn't anyone understand this? Or didn't they care?

"Hey, I've got it . . ." Dedrick's eyes opened wide. "They can broadcast the wedding." He looked at Guy. "You can do that, right?"

"Well . . ." Guy twisted his mouth to one side and rubbed his chin. "We plan to make a public announcement, so . . ." He turned and scanned the area. "Yeah, we can broadcast this. Yeah . . ." He nodded, grinning. Then he grabbed my wrist. "No flexi-phone?"

I shook my head and twisted my arm from his grip. Bolcan had probably removed it so we couldn't be tracked. But so what? I didn't want to watch the wedding. I wanted to hear a talk about freedom. I wanted everyone to hear it.

Guy gave Dedrick a questioning gaze.

"Me?" Dedrick's eyes narrowed as if he took it as an insult. "I don't have a flexi-phone. I'm not Aldonian."

"Later on, I suggest you stand by someone who's got one. You'll want to catch my announcement. Then we'll broadcast our wedding." Eyebrows drawn, he nodded. "Yeah, I like it."

"Broadcast a wedding? No!" I threw desperate glances from one to the other. Were they living in a dream world? "The people of Aldonia need us. They need to know they've grown up on lies. They need to know the truth is out there and that it's beautiful. The truth is freedom and goodness and life. And it belongs to them."

I held their attention, but I strained to find understanding in Guy's eyes, in Dedrick's eyes. A tingling sensation struck me and tears welled up. "When they hear the message tonight, the words will speak to their hearts. They will recognize the truth, and truth will set them free. They will demand freedom from the Regimen. Everything will change." My voice failed me, and the last words came out in a whisper.

"Liberty." Dedrick took my hand. "Sometimes the truth reaches us through the little things."

A tidal wave of hard emotion struck me, throwing me back. "What? Why did you say that?" My head grew light, thoughts sailing through it but nothing within my grasp. "Why did you say that?"

"This is important to them," Dedrick said. "They're making a lifelong commitment. And it's bound to have an impact on everyone who knows them. Maybe good will spread from it."

"No." I pushed him aside and sprinted back the way we came. I was wrong. I was wrong about everything. *Experience is a better teacher, My Friend* had said. Better than words?

"Where're you going?" Dedrick called after me.

My feet flew over the dirt walk, barely touching the ground. The world shook in my vision, flowers and cement blocks, clouds heavy with rain.

Where was I going? I didn't know. Where did I belong? What was my part in all this? What was I called to do?

32

"Jensenville border. That's where you should go." Guy pointed in the general direction. "Liberty's friend Silas will be there."

"Silas?"

"You don't know about him then. Dark hair, red eyes . . ."

"Oh, you mean Sarkin." Dedrick got a bad taste in his mouth. How did Guy know Liberty knew Sarkin? Unless she'd met Sarkin here. Dedrick resisted the temptation to question Guy about it.

"Well, he's Silas to us," Guy said. "And he's probably reached the border by now. I mean, you two are welcome to stick around here." He spun a finger in the air. "But she . . ." Mouth open, head tilted, Guy squinted in the direction Liberty had taken off in. "What's up with her? She's wound pretty tight, huh?"

Dedrick bounced on his toes and glanced over his shoulder, anxious to take off after her. "Yeah, I'd better catch up with her. Best wishes, man."

He slapped Guy's shoulder and bolted after Liberty, kicking up dirt as he raced down the fresh path.

He hated this emotional turbulence. When Liberty had first gotten on the bike with him back at her apartment, he struggled to believe he stood a chance with her. Then they got here and she agreed to see him. At least for two days. He could've been airborne on a dirt bike; she'd made him so happy.

Then, once she realized Guy's change of plans, her mood had crashed. Dedrick had felt compelled to comfort her and found himself reaching for her. She hadn't seemed to mind his touch at first. Then the music played and she closed her eyes, visibly moved by it. He couldn't keep his hands off her, needed to hold her. But when he'd pulled her close, she tensed. She didn't want his affection.

What did she want? Had she met up with Sarkin here? What did he mean to her?

Dedrick raced down the alley they came through, retracing their steps at top speed but not seeing her anywhere.

Then the fence came into view . . . and Liberty racing toward it. *Man, that girl can run.* She leaped and latched onto the fence, the links rattling at the impact.

Tonight's assembly meant too much to her. She couldn't accept that it wasn't going to happen. Maybe she'd give the talk herself. She could probably do it.

"Hey!" he shouted, closing the distance between them, heart racing out of control, lungs screaming.

"Where're you going?" he said, chest heaving as he sucked in air.

She'd reached the top of the fence but jumped back down and spun to face him, her hair fanning out. The hints of color in the blonde accentuated her pale green eyes and flushed cheeks. She stepped toward him and turned a palm up. "Let me have the key to the motorcycle."

"What? I'll drive." He grabbed the fence and stuck a toe in the links. "Where're we going?"

"I can handle a motorcycle."

His jaw dropped. He couldn't believe her. "So you're going to leave me here?"

She shrugged, her expression cold. "Stay and watch the wedding. You seemed excited about it."

Irritated and a little hurt, Dedrick huffed then climbed over the fence and mounted the bike.

She hesitated, but once he cranked the key and revved the engine, she climbed the fence and got on behind him.

"You're not fair," he said, taking off. "I'm only here to help you."

"I'm not fair?" She wrapped her arms around him then pulled back and propped her hands on his hips. "I was content trying to learn something from Bot's 3D game, but everyone kept insisting I join the rest of you and *do* something. So I'm trying to do something!"

"Not me. I sure didn't want you working undercover." He rode a bit too fast through a bumpy field, making them bounce in the seat. After weaving to avoid a scraggily bush, he shot out onto a quiet street.

Her grip on his waist lessened. "Ha! You begged me to help at the Breeder Facility."

"That was a one-time thing." He turned his head and glimpsed blonde strands whipping around her face and shoulders. "I never wanted you to pose as a Unity Trooper. Talk about the most dangerous job in Aldonia."

"Whatever. I was learning something in that game, and I left before I fully understood." She spoke quieter and with less attitude. "I thought I understood. But now . . . I don't have a clue."

"What did you think you were learning?"

Towering apartment buildings hid the sun, making shadows that covered the street.

"I don't know." She leaned against him, maybe by accident but it comforted Dedrick. "History repeats itself. If we take an honest look at the past, we can learn something. And I was learning something."

"Maybe you didn't like what you learned." Squinting against the setting sun, sitting loose on the motorcycle, Dedrick rode easy.

Liberty made no reply, so they rode to the grumbling of the motorcycle through a residential area, past a hospital, and onto an open road that led to Jensenville. Dedrick bit back the questions he wanted to ask about her and Sarkin. She did say she'd see him so he shouldn't worry about it. Of course, he'd poured his heart out to her and she simply said he stood a chance.

Should he tell her Sarkin would be at the border?

A few minutes later, they neared an intersection and rows of rundown shops and offices. Streetlights blinked on. Scooters came from both directions. People walked down the middle of the road in groups.

Dedrick shifted into a lower gear and weaved around pedestrians. They passed another and another group, some people carrying coolers and backpacks, others carrying bags. Guy was right. Something was going down tonight.

"People will be gathering for the assembly," Liberty said over his shoulder. "They'll be mad when no speakers show. We'll lose their trust."

"Looks like everyone's on their way to the border." Dedrick happened to glance over his shoulder—then he looked again. A jolt of anger flowed through him, and his body tensed.

"No way." He pulled to the side of the road, stopped the bike, and twisted to see behind him. He wanted to keep in his sight the woman responsible for exposing the Mosheh. "Quick, get off."

"What? Why?" Liberty dropped her feet from the pegs, gripped Dedrick's jacket, and swung a leg off the bike. She peered into the crowd, looking in the direction Dedrick looked.

"It's her." Dedrick waited for two men to pass then pushed through the rest of the group. He glimpsed Silver's wild hair as she passed under a streetlight. She and seven others—were they Guy's people?—carried a long carpet roll, four on each side. More of Guy's people walked behind and beside them, carrying twelve-foot boards. Sarkin was not among them.

How long had Dedrick searched for that woman? Months? And here she was. Flames burst to life in his mind, debris raining down, tunnels and access points blowing up, explosion after explosion. He could see the residents of Tradehall led between armed guards. He could see Maco, bruised and limping.

She brought this upon them.

Dedrick smacked into a man twice his width and practically bounced off his body. He staggered back and lifted his arms to show he hadn't done it on purpose.

"Watch it," the man growled, walking past.

"Sorry." Unwilling to let Silver get away, Dedrick weaved through another group.

Then a hand landed on his bicep.

"What're you doing?" Liberty tugged his arm, making him stop. "Are we just going to abandon the bike? And we're not exactly heading for the border now."

"It's her. Silver." Dedrick pointed. Dressed in a short gray jacket, leading the way with the carpet and making the load appear effortless, she was a mere eight yards away.

Liberty searched with her eyes and apparently found her. "So? I mean, I know you've been trying to find her in the tunnels but—"

"No, don't you get it? She's responsible for what happened at Tradehall. She's the reason the Regimen knows about us now. She led them down there. Maybe not on purpose but . . ."

"Did you know she helped Bolcan with Re-Ed?"

"No. Why would she?" Dedrick watched Silver walking away. He remembered Bolcan's emotional state last time they spoke. Bolcan might've solicited her help, but he wouldn't have betrayed the Mosheh.

"I don't know why," Liberty said. "But let's go. Let's get to the border. I have to do something. I just don't know what."

A rowdy group passed, kids shouting and waving bottles overhead, blocking his view of Silver. He leaned one way and then another.

Liberty looped her arm through his, the way Miriam always did it. She brushed his chin with her fingers, maybe to turn his head, but she didn't use force.

Lured by her touch, he faced her. "Silver's responsible . . ."

The setting sun sparkled in her misty green eyes, mixing up his emotions and making him lose his train of thought.

"What can we do about that?" she said. "It's done, right?"

He combed a hand through his hair, then let her drag him back to the bike. What would he do if he confronted Silver? He'd at least like to tell her what she'd done. Maybe she already knew. Maybe she was working with the Regimen. Or maybe Bolcan had given her a story and Dedrick would risk contradicting it if he said anything. Yeah, he should keep his mouth shut until he knew more.

~~~

The crowd had grown too big, so Dedrick parked the motorcycle and we walked. Laughter, chatter, and excitement filled the air. A few teens pushed through the slow-moving group, racing to get through first.

Dedrick and I shuffled along with the crowd as it funneled between two apartment buildings, bumping people around us, bumping each other.

My fingers brushed his.

His head turned toward me but he didn't look up. Maybe, even after my mean remarks and cold attitude, he thought I wanted to hold his hand. I was confusing him, hurting him, but I couldn't stop myself. What did he want with me anyway? I couldn't give him what a colony girl could. That's what he really wanted. I'd never become the sweet little wife in his home hidden in the wilderness, giving him love, children, and endless days of peace. Growing old together.

Emotions tangled in my heart, making my eyelids flutter. I wanted that, too, but my life was destined to be chaos. I was Aldonian. I belonged to these people and could not sever that relationship to please myself.

Something stirred inside me, something small like a single note. Small but important. I tried to hold onto it, to understand it, but it disappeared. Was it *My Friend*? He hadn't spoken to me in so long.

"Come on." Dedrick tapped my wrist, making me realize I had stopped walking and that people pushed past me.

Resisting the urge to take his hand, I walked with him.

We stepped beyond the apartments, and a gust of wind carried the foul odor of a campfire and burning rubber. The clouds had turned into dark streaks in an orange sky, hiding the moon at the moment. The setting sun hung like a yellow ball over a jagged line of buildings along the horizon.

The chatter and shouting rose, voices competing with each other, none of them clear. People ran or stood crowded together. I glimpsed a faraway campfire. A group I couldn't see chanted something over and over. This was not the organized, informative assembly setting. This was wild, everyone doing whatever they wanted.

The crowd spread out, revealing a distant sea of Unity Troopers—must've been every trooper on the force—with full masks and stun batons. Shields up, standing shoulder to shoulder, they formed a barricade to a section of the chain-link fence that marked the off-limits area, the strip of grass that ran up to the protected border wall. Did the crowd really want past them? How could anyone get over the stacked razor wire coils? Then they'd have to cross the trench only to reach a seven-meter-high reinforced concrete wall. Maybe everyone was expecting someone else to do something.

A trooper lifted his shield higher. Something clanked against it. More and more shields lifted, troopers protecting themselves from whatever people threw at them.

"Is that . . . ?" Dedrick squinted in the direction of the apartments we'd passed.

A group of five men strolled along the backside of apartments, a good distance away from us but drawing nearer. One of them wore the long black robe of a priest. The others wore black jackets. And one of them had dark skin and a scruffy little beard.

"That's Sarkin," I said, taking a step in their direction. I had expected him to take part in or at least attend the ceremony at Guy's place.

"Hey, over there." Dedrick took my hand and held it firmly. He led me toward one end of the line of Unity Troopers.

I glanced a few times over my shoulder, trying to see where Sarkin headed.

Dedrick sighed. "We'll catch up with him later. Let's go talk to Alix."

As we neared the line of troopers, I glimpsed the fence behind them. A section hung open and mangled. Several campfires burned on this side of the fence. People with hoods shrouding their faces stood around them. One campfire burned on the other side, too. A group of men stood and crouched around it. How had they gotten through? Why hadn't anyone gone after them? Maybe the troopers felt they had enough to handle with the growing mob and had let the stragglers go.

The chanting became louder here. "We want truth! We want truth!" They had shouted the same thing at the assemblies. They silenced for a moment and voices traveled on the wind, shouting and singing coming from over the wall, from Jensenville.

Frustrated and not knowing what to do with myself, I felt tempted to join the Unity Troopers in the line. I liked the idea of throwing myself into something. But did I want the wall down, or did I want to stop this chaos? What would be better for Aldonia? What did Jensenville want with us?

We squeezed through the crowd, drawing nearer to the troopers.

"Torva," Dedrick said, stopping. "What are they doing? This isn't their fight."

I looked where he looked, to the men around the campfire on the other side of the chain-link fence. A single trooper approached them. The sea of troopers stretched out, thinning, side-stepping, trying to cover more area.

A trooper without a helmet broke ranks and sprinted toward us.

I shrunk back, thinking we should merge into the crowd to keep from being recognized.

Dedrick squeezed my hand. "It's Alix."

"Hey," she shouted, almost upon us. "Took you long enough to get here. You should be helping." She jabbed her thumb over her shoulder then stood hands on hips. "Where's your armor? Your helmet?"

"Where's yours?" I said.

She smiled. "Had to take it off. I've been bossing other troopers, trying to add to the confusion, and headquarters picked up on it. Told me to stop giving orders." She shrugged. "So I lost the helmet."

"I lost mine at Re-Ed."

"You're lucky you didn't lose your life," she said, Dedrick nodding in agreement.

"So you got my message about tonight," Alix said. "I told our neighbors and everyone I could to come here instead."

"We went to see Guy." I exchanged glances with Dedrick. "Tried talking Guy into holding the assembly anyways. But he has . . . other plans."

My gaze caught something in the distance, a man in a gray Mosheh cape and shades, maybe night vision goggles. A few more glances showed me more Mosheh in capes at various distant points. Dedrick rarely concealed his identity anymore.

"Yeah, well," Alix said, "this is pretty big. You know this wall is coming down. And our own governor's not leading. No one's heard from her. UT are making their own calls. You'll notice few troopers are armed with anything more than taser batons and flashlights." She yanked her flashlight from her belt and shined the beam at me. "They didn't want to appear threatening and escalate the situation." She laughed and clipped her flashlight to her belt again. "So we're pretty much unarmed out here."

"Doesn't Jensenville have troopers on the other side?" I said.

She shrugged.

"What about drones? They could drop tear gas or something, send everyone home."

"The drones have been grounded for too long. They aren't ready to put into operation tonight." Her eyes went to Dedrick. "I went in to see where they took our people, the people from Tradehall."

"And?" Dedrick's hand tensed in mine.

"They're in holding cells at CSS. But it's packed, so they'll have to find somewhere else. That's when we'll get them back. No problem."

"You sound confident," I said to Alix.

"We'll get them," Dedrick said.

"I'm getting back to work," Alix said, stepping away. "Join me if you want." She jogged away, returning to the line of troopers. I imagined that "work" meant confusing the troopers.

"Amity."

I recognized my partner's voice and turned to see him.

Lifting his face mask, Holt marched from the line of troopers and up to us. The chanting intensified. Projectiles sailed through the air, something whizzing right past me.

Dedrick threw an arm over my shoulder and forced me down into a crouch.

Holt crouched, too, his knee bumping mine. "I heard double rumors about you."

"Oh, yeah?"

"Yeah. One, you tried to warn Re-Ed about a bomb threat. And the other, you've turned against the Regimen and helped rebels destroy the place."

"Uh . . ." Was he about to report me? The troopers had chased us from my apartment, and now we were all here, together at the border.

"Several officers died in that. Thought you were one of them." Holt smiled. "Glad you're not."

I exhaled and smiled back, a bit touched by his concern and relieved that he seemed to have decided I was legit.

"We need you tonight. You and I'll round up the rowdies that made it past the fence." His gaze shifted to Dedrick as if he'd just noticed him. Holt had lifted the face mask, but he still wore his helmet and could easily do a retina scan. His eyelids flickered. He began to straighten, his hand snapping to the holster at his side.

Dedrick lunged from a crouch and threw Holt down on his back. Grunting and grabbing, they wrestled.

I stumbled back and looked up. The other troopers didn't seem to notice. No one approached.

The electrical buzz of a taser ripped through the air. Holt's taser. His body jerked and lay still.

Dedrick pushed himself up and got to his feet, his eyes on me. "Maybe we should get out of here."

"No, I—"

A soft buzzing sounded all around us, the sound of hundreds of flexi-phones receiving a call. The chants, shouts, and chaos ceased. It was rare that we all received a call at the same time.

Someone had a message for all Aldonia.

I squatted and unfastened the flexi-phone from Holt's wrist. Words scrolled across the screen: *The 6-6-6 plan!*

Then a colorful 3D image of tiny balls appeared. They projected upward from the screen and burst into red, yellow, and green fireworks.

I straightened and Dedrick came to my side, standing closer than necessary to see the message.

As the fireworks fizzled out, a face appeared, a middle-aged woman with short red hair and curls on her forehead. Distress showed in eyes that darted to one side and back to the camera. Her trembling red lips parted. "I, Yancy of Aldonia, am no longer your governor."

Mumbling spread through the sea of people then silence as the governor spoke again.

"Aldonia is under new leadership, and I will do everything in my . . . power . . . to ensure a smooth transfer of authority." She turned her head and sneered. "I introduce your new governor, Guy."

I stared without blinking, finding this hard to believe even though he had told us.

Guy's smiling face with heavy-lidded eyes appeared in the projection. "Thank you, governor, former governor. That was lovely." His gaze turned to the camera, to us, and he stripped off the Regimen jacket, revealing a clean white shirt. "My name is Guy. There are no numbers after my name. And I have no implant in my . . ." He lifted his handless arm and glanced at the stump that stuck out from the pushed-up sleeve. He dropped his arm. "Well, I have no implant. You and I, we are no longer children of the Regimen."

People muttered all around us in questioning tones. Governors had no real authority. They followed the directives of the world-wide government. How could he hope to accomplish this?

"There is a new way," Guy said, "an old way, a true way that will become the sure foundation of a solid society. If Aldonia's Regimen officers resist, we will shut down everything. Under cover of night, we have gained control of many operations in Aldonia. We have taken over the commissaries, factories, hospitals, and power stations."

"How much of what he's saying is true?" Dedrick said.

"You know of the attack on the Breeder Facility," Guy went on. "You will soon learn that the Re-Education Facility no longer exists."

"He's taking credit for things we've done." Dedrick's eyes shifted to me. "What you've done."

"You're right. But who would know?" I noticed Guy insinuated but didn't exactly lie and say he was responsible.

"Aldonia changes today, and my armed men will see to it." Several men with guns came into view and stood behind him.

"We are all equal. Greater than other living things, you know, like a polypore mushroom or an agate rock snail. But we are equal to one another." He spoke with his head tilted back and chin jutted out, looking confident with the authority he claimed. "We have rights that belong to us naturally, rights that a government has the duty to protect and can in no way violate. Among these rights are life, liberty, and the pursuit of happiness."

His words made me think of Bot and the old documents he'd once told us about, and about things I'd learned from the game.

"Our government has overstepped its boundaries. It has failed to protect our rights and has become the chief violator of them. So it is our right, our duty, the duty of the people of Aldonia to abolish our government and institute a new one. We lay the foundation for our new government on the principles that can bring about a respect for our natural rights. The security of our future depends upon it. This is a new day." He smiled.

The image shifted to one side, shrinking, and a new image popped up in its place. People around us began talking all at once, the noise climbing upward in crescendo.

"That's the gazebo." Dedrick placed a hand under the hand in which I held the flexi-phone.

The full moon, a pale orange disk, hung in a moody sky of orange streaks and black clouds, peeking over the silhouette of the gazebo. Torches burned along the dirt path and between the gazebo's pillars, flames flickering in the wind. Streamers attached to the roof, twisted and flapped, glowing yellow in the light of the flames, making an erratic background.

The chatter increased around us, confusion and curiosity.

The image switched to a woman in a long, slender dress. *Angel.* Streamers, like the ones on the gazebo, hung from the low waistline of her dress and from her hair. They twisted and flapped, sailing and circling around her in the strong wind. A flurry of movement around her still, elegant figure. The image zoomed in on her somber face, her dark almond-shaped eyes, and shapely, grim lips. A dark-blonde tress blew across her face.

Then a deep, rich note played. The first note of Pachelbel's Canon.

The voices and chatter stopped. Hundreds of people stood motionless, staring at their flexi-phones.

Angel sauntered forward, two other women behind her, the wind playing with their long dresses as they processed toward the gazebo. The three of them carried bouquets of wildflowers. Angel sauntered to Guy, the other women to other men, and together they approached Father Damon.

Father Damon spoke, invoking God, and holding down pages to read from an actual book. Then he closed the book and spoke of love and commitment, the love of a husband and wife, the love of God for his people. He spoke of the sacrament—as they referred to it—that these couples were about to receive, and the gift of children to bless their marriages. The two that become one. The two that become three. The gift of life that comes from love, freely and completely given in marriage. He spoke of family.

A breeze kicked up, sending my hair into Dedrick's face and prickling my skin. Warmth and peace rushed through me, making my head grow light and my knees give out. *My Friend . . .*

Dedrick's arm slid around my back, steadying me. "You okay?"

I didn't answer. The feeling of the single note stirred inside me. Enrapt, I turned my attention inward. Another note arose inside, playing with it.

Then a third. The three formed a beautiful harmony. It brought to mind the encounter I'd had with *My Friend* in my deepest despair in Re-Ed. Three tongues of fire had leaped from the heart of *My Friend*. The three notes had to do with Him, with me. With love.

"I, Guy, take you, Angel . . ."

I breathed and opened my eyes. Guy and Angel stood facing each other, holding hands.

". . . for my lawful wife to have and to hold from this day forward, for better, for worse, for richer, for poorer, in sickness and health, until death do us part."

Angel repeated similar words to Guy. Then the priest said another prayer and the couples placed rings on each other's fingers as they whispered words to each other that the audio didn't pick up.

"What are they doing?" I whispered.

Dedrick's face hovered near mine. "Exchanging rings. It's a symbol of their marriage bond, represents their undying love for each other. They'll wear them forever."

I felt his gaze on me and not the image of the ceremony, but I couldn't get myself to look at him. I knew what I'd see in his eyes, but I didn't know what my eyes would tell him. I recognized the strength in the union of a married couple, the promises of forever, and the forming of families. We didn't have that in Aldonia today, but we once did. The Regimen must've feared strong families. That's why, in the early years, they'd destroyed them.

I wanted this with Dedrick, this forever love. Family. But it still scared me.

When I focused on the image from the flexi-phone again, Guy and Angel were kissing. Then the image faded, and no image replaced it.

A drop of rain hit my face. Then more drops.

People groaned and began mumbling then talking louder. Then the flexi-phones all buzzed again. This time it showed a new message in the mailbox.

My breath caught in my throat.

A message from Dr. Supero?

"Open it," Dedrick said, squeezing my hand. We still held the flexi-phone together.

"I can't. I don't know Holt's password. We'll have to see what it's about later."

The crowd did not seem interested. A group resumed chanting, "We want truth!" People shouted. A mud ball flew past me, toward the Unity Troopers. A few troopers had lowered their shields. One and then another walked away from the line.

"Whaddya think they're doing with that?" Dedrick shielded his eyes from the rain and squinted at a group approaching the line of Unity Troopers. They carried a long carpet roll, Silver in the lead.

"I don't—"

A bomb exploded, ripping apart a section of the high cement wall. Chunks flew. A cloud of dust rose up. People gasped and shouted. Unity Troopers broke formation, some turning toward the wall, others running. Five troopers charged the group with carpet. Chaos ensued. Another bomb went off. The bonfire in the stretch of grass leaped.

"Yes, I do know," I shouted, the reason occurring to me. We could help change Aldonia by doing one little thing. I grabbed Dedrick's hand. "Let's go help them."

Pushing people out of the way, weaving through bodies in motion, we reached the group. The carpet lay on the ground. Several from the group stood at a distance, a Unity Trooper threatening them. Two troopers flanked Silver. Then she swung a fist and cracked one of them in the jaw. The other two troopers had merged into a rioting crowd. The kids carrying the boards snuck past everyone.

The rain poured now, making rivulets down my face and the neckline of my shirt. I stopped by the long carpet roll, wondering if Dedrick and I could move it ourselves. Four straps made of twisted plastic bags held it together and provided handles for the people who had carried it. "We need to throw this over the razor coils," I shouted to Dedrick, "so people can get across. They'll use the boards to bridge the ditch."

"Why?" Dedrick stood at one end of the carpet, water dripping from his nose, looking ready to stoop for it but also like he needed convincing.

"The wall's coming down." I smiled. "And I think it's a good thing. I mean, it's not just us; it's not only Aldonians who want freedom and are willing to fight for it. I think that's what *they* want, too." I swung a hand out to indicate Jensenville, and another bomb went off.

Once the debris settled, I saw the damage. This one did it. A five-meter-wide section had caved.

Dedrick stooped for the end of the carpet. A Unity Trooper I didn't recognize threw off his helmet and grabbed it, too. The rest of the group came back, including Silver with wet gray hair plastered to her head. I didn't see what had happened to the troopers that had confronted her, but they were nowhere in sight.

Together we hoisted the carpet roll and charged through the pouring rain. The line of Unity Troopers had grown thin. Silver let out a guttural battle-cry, and we all joined in. The Unity Troopers glanced at each other and scooted out of the way. We ran through the opening in the chain-link fence and crossed the stretch of grass, running like a well-trained unit. Reaching the razor coils, we slowed. Silver cut one of the bands that held the carpet in a roll then reached and cut another.

"Why don't you toss me that knife?" Dedrick said to Silver, hostility in his eyes.

Silver glanced at the knife and laughed. "It's yours anyway, huh? You can have it." She tossed it to him.

He caught it and sliced the other two bands. Together we all worked the carpet up over the coils. The carpet unrolled, flopping down and creating a mound that people could walk over. The planks were put in place over the ditch as the smoke settled.

Torches flickering in the rain appeared on the other side of the wall, visible through the hole the bomb had made. A more studied look revealed not only the torches but the people holding them. They climbed over the ruins, singing and carrying a huge flag that the wind struggled to own.

I caught fragments of their song. Something about the flag of the free. A standard forever. A banner of the right.

Dedrick grabbed my hand and pulled me back, out of the path of the Jensenville rebels.

The rain lessened. As the flagbearer reached the top of the pile of debris, a torch threw light on the flag. And tingles ran down my spine. With red and white stripes and a blue square with white stars, it reminded me of the American flag in Bot's 3D game and the flag Betsy Ross had made, and even the flag I'd found in the bunker last year.

The Aldonians crowded into the stretch of land and stood silent as raindrops, a welcoming party for the Jensenville rebels. The Unity Troopers stood defeated, back by the chain-link fence. The Jensenville party crossed the boards single-file then climbed awkwardly over the carpeted coils, which bowed and shifted with each step. The Aldonians cleared a space but surrounded them. Questions came from here and there.

"Who are you?"

"What happened to the Regimen in Jensenville?"

"Why do you want in Aldonia?"

A tall man in his thirties with a long face and hollow cheeks answered the questions. "We've broken the power of the Regimen in Jensenville. We're taking our freedom back. We've been silent for too long. And we're inviting you to join us."

Uncertainty showed on the faces of the Aldonians. They needed a leader. Would they accept Guy?

"We have a new governor," I shouted, drawing attention.

The man smiled. "Yeah, we saw that." He brought up his wrist, showing his own flexi-phone. Apparently, the message had gone farther than Aldonia. "We'd like to meet him. You might not realize this . . ." he shouted, looking from face to face, ". . . but we were once united, fifty states in one country, free to come and go, free to live our lives the way we felt best. We'd like for Aldonia to unite with us now. Together we will secure our freedom and become again the United States of America."

"I'll take you to our governor," Silver said, stepping apart from the crowd.

I shook my head, staring in disbelief. I'd never know how to take her, friend or foe, help or trouble.

The crowd parted to allow Silver and the group through then closed up again.

Peace rested in my soul. *My Friend* had once assured me, "we will conquer."

It began today. I could see now that the work of freedom would continue. Many wanted it. Many had yet to learn what it meant. Many would be called to the service of restoring and protecting freedom. I could see it happening, not overnight, but happening in time.

I didn't need to feel so driven and anxious. I could have the things I deeply wanted, too. In some way, faithfulness to my little part, to my calling, to the things I wanted deeply, would help bring about true freedom. I didn't need to do something big. I could carry a carpet roll or deliver a message. I could live my life as a wife and mother, raising children and teaching them truth. And courage. That's what we needed in addition to freedom. In addition to truth. We needed courage.

Dedrick grabbed my hand again and pulled me to his side, away from the moving crowd. "We don't have to go with them, do we?"

"Don't you want to? This is history in the making."

"Not really. We were going to check on Gardenhall and the Mosheh Control Center, right?"

"Oh, yeah, our date." I stood facing him.

He smiled. "I've only got two days with you. I don't want to waste them."

"Well, about that . . ."

"No, you're not changing your mind. It's two days." He flung the hand not holding mine in a frustrated gesture. "Then I have to wait four years and hope you don't fall in love with someone else in the meantime. Like . . . like Sarkin. He's Aldonian. You're Aldonian. Not sure why he's back in Aldonia when I saved his butt two years ago, but . . . you're anxious to see him again, aren't you?"

He shut his mouth, and his Adam's apple bobbed.

I laughed and grabbed his flailing hand. "Sarkin's a seminarian studying under Father Damon."

"Huh?" Dedrick blinked a few times then turned and peered towards where we'd last spotted Sarkin.

"He said he's got a few more years before ordination, then he hopes to go on a mission to Jensenville." I tugged Dedrick's hand.

He returned his troubled eyes to me.

My heart pounded and something fluttered in my stomach. I had in mind what I wanted to say next. Was I really going to say this? Did I really mean this? I couldn't say it and not follow through. I'd confused him enough already.

Dedrick stared, but my gaze kept slipping away.

In a moment of determination, I squeezed his hand, looked him dead in the eye, and blurted out, "I've decided not to make promises to the Mosheh."

The rain had lessened to a sprinkle, and clouds drifted away from the moon.

Dedrick's lips parted but he didn't speak. He looked down, then lifted our hands and weaved his fingers between mine. "Oh yeah? So does that mean . . ."

I released the breath I'd held for what felt like an eternity, and my chest heaved as I sucked in a new one. "Maybe we can raise a family and work on changing the culture in a different way."

His mouth fell open. The hint of a smile passed his lips. Then hope filled his eyes and he nodded. "You're gonna . . . you're gonna marry me?" He pulled me close and wrapped his arms around me.

A surge of love and joy swept through me. "Well, there's one thing I need to ask you."

"What?"

"Can we live in Aldonia? Raise our children here?"

His eyes opened wide, and he jerked back. He glanced to either side, at a crowd that had grown loud and wild again and milled around us.

Resignation showed in his face when he looked at me again. "If that's what you want. We can have Father Damon marry us."

He sunk a hand in my hair and gazed at me with intensity. "I love you, Liberty. I want to spend the rest of my life loving you. But I've always known that your heart is here with these people. So I'm gonna learn to love what you love. Yes, we can stay here and raise our children here."

Tears filled my eyes. My heart overflowed with love for the brown-eyed colony boy who had rescued me from the Breeder Facility, from Sid, from an eagle's nest outside Re-Ed, and even from myself. At this moment, I knew he would never give up on me. We were meant to be together, to become one.

I tiptoed to see him eye to eye. "You'd do that?"

Tears glistened in his eyes, too, but his gaze kept sliding to my mouth. "I'd do anything for you."

33

Moonlight streamed in through the balcony windows and fell on Dr. Supero. He sat on the floor leaning against a wall, alone in his apartment. The curtains that covered the windows earlier lay strewn across an overturned armchair and on the floor. The privacy screens that Guy's thug had also brought lay twisted and torn at Dr. Supero's feet. It had surprised him to discover they were made of recycled cardboard. If he would've had a lighter, he would've set them to flame.

Governor Yancy's white sweater, lying crumpled in a corner of the room, appeared to glow under the moonlight. Leaving in haste, she had forgotten it.

After Guy had asked Governor Yancy—at gunpoint—to introduce him as governor, he released her. "Go on home and watch the news," Guy had said, as if he spoke to a friend. "See what's going on. You'll have a chance to decide if you want on the right side. Or if you want to go down with the other Regimen supporters." He smiled as if he had not meant it as a threat.

Yancy had blanched and fled.

Guy had returned to the camera where he took a few minutes to explain the new government in Aldonia. Then he and his thugs had packed up their equipment.

"You did good, Dr. Supero." Guy had come out to the balcony where Dr. Supero stood wondering what injuries he would sustain if he jumped from his third-floor apartment. "All that research you did. I had no idea. You should've told me. In fact, I'd like to get together sometime. I'd like to know what you know."

"Yes, well, I only wanted to dissuade you and your lover from your warped plan."

"Hmm. What plan was that?"

"Never mind. If you are done, if you are finished with me, please go."

"Well, okay." Guy had handed Dr. Supero a bottle of wine and a wine goblet. "Thought you might want to celebrate. I'd loved to celebrate with you, but I've gotta be somewhere. It's an important day for me."

"Good. Then go." Dr. Supero had dropped the goblet over the edge of the balcony and held his breath until glass shattered into a million pieces.

Guy laughed, slapped Dr. Supero's back, and finally left.

Dr. Supero had taken the wine bottle inside. He'd no sooner set it on the counter when he snapped. A deep, guttural groan escaped him. Stars clouded his vision. He lunged for the table and—with one broad swipe— cleared it of dishes, cheese, and chocolate. Rage propelled him to the privacy screens, his bedding, drawers, even the new curtains. Months ago, he had struggled moving the overstuffed armchair into the apartment. Today, it seemed to weigh next to nothing when he had hurled it across the room.

Crashing, smashing, ripping, cursing . . . he had trashed the place.

Once done, standing in the midst of the destruction, heart beating outside his chest, he couldn't say he felt any better. He'd sunk to the floor, to where he sat now. He couldn't have felt any worse.

Within a few hours, he had become absolutely nobody. His rant to the governor—ex-governor—would appear on every TV and flexi-phone, all his secrets laid bare. If the Regimen kept control of Aldonia, he'd have no job. They would send him to Re-Ed. He who was once the Head Physician of Aldonia Hospital, who once oversaw everything concerning the hospital, including giving judgments to the board on who would or would not benefit from costly treatments, who would live or die.

If Guy, somehow, managed to control Aldonia, chaos would rule. How could it be any other way? The man belonged in an asylum.

A knock sounded on the door.

Dr. Supero ran a hand through his stubbly hair, slowing as he reached the smooth skin of the scar.

The door creaked open. "Professor?"

A curvy, feminine silhouette eased into the doorway. "Is that you?" The voice sounded like Cam's.

"What do you want?" He had stood her up. Why would she look for him now?

"Oh, there you are." She tripped on something then crunched on ceramic shards as she crossed the apartment to him.

He considered picking up his stocking cap from where it lay in the middle of the room. It wouldn't take much for him to reach it. He could hide his ugliness. Or he could let her see it.

"Are you okay?" She squatted, peering at him, then sat down beside him and leaned against the wall. "I had a time figuring out where you lived."

"Why are you here? You had somewhere to go?"

"You were going to go with me."

He stared at her through tired eyes.

Moonlight illuminated her high boots and bare legs, her short skirt and loose sweater, her round eyes gazing at him, and her hair up in a ponytail.

"Why don't you wear your hair down?"

"Will you come with me if I do?" She tugged the band off and shook her hair. Gorgeous waves cascaded over her shoulders.

He gazed at her for a moment, taking in her beauty. "Why do you care if I go? What am I to you?"

She shrugged. "I don't know. I care about you."

"How can you?" A knife stabbed his heart. This made no sense to him. He turned away, tears coming to his eyes.

She grabbed his hand and held it on her lap. "The city is falling apart tonight. There's chaos everywhere."

"So I hear." A tear rolled down his cheek, but the emotion had passed.

"Come." Still holding his hand, she stood and tugged his arm. "There's still time to get there."

He twisted his hand from hers. "No. I don't understand." Self-pity and anger wrestled in his mind. "I am twice your age and, as you can see, I am pieced together, a mess of a man."

She got down on her knees and sat back on her heels. "So? I still care about you."

He shook his head and turned away, struggling to accept her compassion.

"And don't forget that you're often grumpy. And you can be very rude."

He looked.

She smiled. "Okay?" She offered her hand to him. "So, let's get going. You and me. Neither one of us perfect."

"Are you and I so perfect?" Father Damon had said. That look in his eyes . . . she had it, too.

He took her hand and stood. Together they crunched and scuffed through the mess, toward the half-open door. Whatever she wanted him to experience, he would accept. She possessed something he did not understand, but he would be open to it. He would believe what she wanted him to believe, do what she wanted him to do. He would be for her what she wanted him to be. He would be a new man.

"Wait." He released her hand. "There is something I must do." He stepped to the table and yanked the tablecloth the rest of the way off. Then he tapped the edge of the table to turn on the computer. The desktop took a moment to appear. Another moment and a few taps on the desktop, and he had accomplished his goal. He sent out the files he had discovered. To everyone. Tomorrow would indeed be a new day for one and all. They would have the truth.

"Okay?" She reached out to him again.

He placed his hand in hers, his heart warming at her kindness. Perhaps she did not think of him as a lover. He did not care. He would take whatever she wanted to give. He would not ask for more.

A shadow fell in the hallway outside the door then the door swung open to a figure in black. A figure in a mask.

"Are you Dr. Supero?" the man said, his voice digitally altered.

Dr. Supero's heart pounded. "I am."

Cam stepped forward. "Who are you?"

Dr. Supero yanked her back . . . just in time.

The man had lifted a gun, not the rubber-bullet kind or a stun gun. A gun that Dr. Supero remembered seeing in the history lessons at Secondary. A gun that kills.

A shot rang out.

Dr. Supero fell back, landing hard on shards of ceramic and glass. His chest grew warm, a slight burning sensation that spread.

Another shot sounded. Or his mind made it seem that way.

Cam's face appeared over his, her brown tresses falling onto his neck and brushing his cheek. "Professor! Supero!" Tears fell from her eyes, becoming great drops as they landed on his face.

Her voice came distant now. "No . . . no . . ." she wailed. "Don't die."

He wanted to comfort her, but his vision failed him . . .

34

Dedrick strode toward his destination carrying a bouquet of pink and pale-green hydrangeas in hands that grew clammier by the minute. Light from the Mosheh Control Center ahead gave a dusty sheen to rough tunnel walls and floor, guiding him. The scuffing and clomping of his boots kept anxious thoughts at bay. He'd taken a tunnel kart to this point, so his heart had no business racing the way it did.

Abby had helped him with the bouquet. "The pinks and greens will complement her eyes," she had said as she cut bloom after bloom and arranged them in Dedrick's hands. She'd been the first to learn of their engagement.

After the chaos at the border, Liberty and Dedrick had raced to Gardenhall. They found the underground community in a somber mood, everyone mourning the loss of Maco and the others to the Unity Troopers. "We'll get them back," Dedrick had promised the dozen or so elderly that had crowded round. Then he and Liberty had helped serve tea and sat down with Abby. Liberty told her everything, talking until midnight, Dedrick mostly watching, basking in the joy in her eyes, her voice, her body language.

She was going to marry him.

Dedrick brought the hydrangeas to his nose and inhaled. Too bad they didn't smell like anything. He would've liked to give Liberty something with a pretty fragrance.

Stepping from the tunnel and into the Mosheh Control Center, he dropped the bouquet to his side and made a sweeping scan of the workstations. He didn't want anyone to notice him with the flowers until he met up with Liberty. He'd never given a girl flowers in all his life. Except for his mother. Liberty would like them, wouldn't she?

One of the hydraulic lifts sighed and groaned, someone going above. Boxes and stuffed backpacks cluttered the "landing pad," the big mattress under the tubes attached to above-ground access points, tubes they'd never have a reason to use again. Two women carried boxes down the ramp that led from the upper level, probably carrying their belongings. Three Mosheh men shuffled around the workstations, checking things, stooping for things, taking long looks around, and talking.

A melancholy mood had gripped them all week, ever since the day after the wall came down. Days had passed in confusion, none of the Mosheh knowing what the future held, no one in Aldonia knowing what the future held.

The elders assigned members various tasks, necessary things or maybe just busy work. Dedrick spoke with Liberty every day, but he hadn't *seen* her all week. He'd had the grueling jobs of reopening one of the underground tunnels to the Control Center—the one he'd just come through—and of spying on Regimen agencies to see how they handled the change in power. Liberty had been helping people from Re-Ed transition, everyone except for the Torva.

The Torva wanted to meet the girls. The elders allowed eight of them to live underground to care for the girls and their children, but the rest had to find a place above. They made camp in the warehouse where the above-ground Mosheh meeting had taken place.

For two days, Guy had met with people from Jensenville and people in authority in Aldonia, working out temporary arrangements. He wanted the citizens of Aldonia to make the decisions. Unfortunately, the citizens had been too stunned to decide anything.

Yesterday, the elders finally met with Guy. All of them. Even Elder Dean in his wheelchair. That was a project, getting him and the chair above ground. They had met at a neutral location, a greenspace near the hospital several stories above the Mosheh Control Center. Bolcan, Miriam, and Dedrick had accompanied them.

"I'm excited to finally meet you," Guy had said, shaking each of their hands, pausing at Elder Dean. He wore the Regimen jacket again over a clean, pressed shirt and dress pants. "I always hoped someday we could help each other." He sat in the camp chair beside Elder Dean, though his people had tried directing him to the opposite side of the seating arrangement. "I'm thinking we're going to need you as advisors. We're going to need your wisdom to get this all going. Would you like to serve in that capacity? Aldonia needs you."

The elders had readily agreed. "I had never expected to see so much change in my lifetime," Elder Lukman had said, stroking his white beard. "We will do all we can. The time has come for us to join you in Aldonia . . . above ground." Everyone chuckled.

"I still can't believe this is the end." Fulton, the sole person sitting at a workstation, sat with his chair turned, his baseball cap in his hand, and his thin black arms waving in the air as he spoke to the three others. His voice carried. "All this time I been here . . . this is my life, man, my home, my brothas. What if I don't want to leave?"

"Yeah, well, we wanted to be there for Aldonians, right?" Arc said, squatting by a mess of cords. "Their needs are different now."

"It's a good thing, Fulton," another man said, shutting off a station and stuffing something into a front pocket of his jeans. "Handle it."

"A good thing? I don't know." Fulton laughed, positioning his baseball cap on his head with two hands. "You may've wanted to be here for Aldonians. Me? I just like the challenge of keeping our people safe while they're out there. I can get anyone, anywhere, under any circumstance."

He spun his chair, and his dark eyes snapped to Dedrick. "Ain't that right, Dedrick? What am I gonna do with myself now?"

Dedrick had meant to scoot over to the hydraulic lifts where Liberty said she'd meet him. But he shared Fulton's opinion and had gravitated toward him. He struggled to accept that he'd have no reason to wander the tunnels again. No one would. They would be forgotten. "I'm sure they can use you up in CSS." Dedrick swung the bouquet behind his thigh and propped his other hand on Fulton's desktop.

"CSS? Shoot." Fulton glanced at Arc. "No way I'm working for them."

"They're not the same," Dedrick said, though he wouldn't want to work for them either. "They don't spy on citizens anymore. They watch for outside threats. At least that's their directive."

"Their directive from that one-handed dude, their new governor? How long they gonna take him seriously?" Fulton folded his arms across his chest and rolled his chair up to his desk. He gave Dedrick the once-over. "What you hiding back there?"

Dedrick squirmed and lifted the bouquet.

"Yeow." Fulton raised his eyebrows and nodded. "Nice. We all heard about you and Liberty." He shoved a fist at Dedrick.

Dedrick bumped it with his own fist, heat sliding up his neck. Once he and Liberty had told Abby, everyone found out. She must've told the others in Gardenhall, and it had spread from there. Not that he minded. He just couldn't shake the feeling that she'd change her mind and not go through with it.

"You set a date?" Fulton said.

"No, not yet." He wanted to talk to Liberty about that. Maybe they could sneak away today and see Father Damon. Get things started.

Footfalls sounded behind him, from the direction of the ramp. "Flowers?" a woman said.

Dedrick tuned.

Elder Rayna strolled toward him, a big smile on her face and her eyes on the bouquet. "They're lovely, Dedrick. I'm very happy for you. You and Liberty make a wonderful couple." She patted his hand, took the flowers from him, and arranged three blooms. "But I'm not sure you want to give her these." She handed them back.

"What? Why?" Dedrick inspected them, wondering what Elder Raya saw. They rarely had bugs in Gardenhall's garden.

"Have you thought about a ring?" Elder Rayna walked past him and weaved through the workstations. She stopped at a desk.

"Where am I going to get a ring in Aldonia?" Dedrick continued to inspect the bouquet. He glanced at Fulton, who then shrugged. "It's not like I have credits."

"Guy's people do a bit of trading, don't they? You must have something you could trade." Elder Rayna picked up a few items from a workstation and stuffed them into a side pocket of her long homespun tunic. "I'll see you above ground." She strolled away, back toward the ramp.

Alix and Camilla stomped down the ramp, greeting Elder Rayna as they passed.

Dedrick jerked the bouquet back, feeling the urge to hide it, but Camilla's face had lit up, her eyes growing wide and mouth falling open. She saw it already.

She jogged down the ramp and to him. "Oh, how pretty. For Liberty, huh?" She shrugged out of an overstuffed backpack and dropped it to the ground.

"Yeah."

Alix approached, shaking her head and scowling. "Flowers?"

"Yeah."

Thumbs stuffed in the straps of the backpack she wore, Alix hefted the load higher on her back. "You know she really misses the tools she gave up when she went into the Breeder Facility last year."

"Tools?"

"Yeah, Guy's got that black market. I bet you could find some there." Alix nodded.

"Maybe even some of her own," Camilla said to Alix.

Both of them nodded, looking serious.

Dedrick shook his head. Why would a guy give a girl tools? Maybe they were joking. He decided to change the subject. "Is that all your stuff?" He indicated Camilla's backpack with a glance. "Where're you guys headed?"

Camilla bounced on her toes, her ponytail swinging behind her, her eyes lighting up again. "I've been volunteering at Primary, same one your little sister was in. I just love being around all those children. I told them I'm going to be their big sister now."

Dedrick smiled. "You're perfect for the job." He looked at Alix. "What about you?"

She shrugged. "I'm sticking with the Unity Troopers until the elders give me something else to do. All this chaos has brought out the criminal in everyone. People smashing shop windows and stealing stuff. Vandalizing. Fighting." Her gaze connected with Camilla's and they both turned sullen.

"What's happened?" Dedrick looked from one to the other.

Camilla pursed her lips, a look of sadness flickering across her face.

"The doctor died, or professor, whatever he was," Alix said. "Dr. Supero. Someone shot him last week. With a real gun."

"Wow, I wonder why," Dedrick said.

"Did you read the email he sent to everyone?" Camilla said, almost whispering. "Someone probably wanted to stop him from sending it. It's all about what the government did to the people. Bad things."

Dedrick had read it. Dr. Supero had uncovered documents that showed exactly what the government had done over the years and continued to do to control the people: destroying the family, faith, and freedom; reducing populations by evil methods; indoctrinating the young; and criminalizing anyone with opposing ideologies.

"Dedrick," Bolcan shouted, coming from the direction of the hydraulic lifts, from the direction of his room . . . with Liberty at his side.

Liberty's hair, back to its original auburn color, fell over one shoulder. She wore an oversized cream-colored shirt, slim black pants, and ankle boots.

Dedrick sucked in a breath and clenched his jaw, watching them approach. How long had they been in there together? In his room. And why? Had they been working together, hanging out together all week? Had Liberty changed her mind about getting married? Maybe Bolcan had something to say about it.

"Better get that jealous look off your face before your woman sees it," Fulton said. "You gotta show her you trust her."

"What?" Dedrick faced Fulton, feeling flushed.

Fulton spun a finger at his own face. "Lose the sneer."

Dedrick forced his muscles to relax and forced himself to smile, bracing himself for rejection. Maybe she had agreed to marry him in the heat of the moment as the border wall came down. She'd had time, now, to think about it. Time to change her mind.

Clutching the bouquet in one hand, Dedrick raked the other through his hair.

"Hi," Liberty said, smiling and glancing at the bouquet. She stopped two feet from him, Bolcan on her heels.

"Hi." The fear of rejection kept him from kissing her. Especially with so many people around. He pushed the bouquet into her hands.

"Oh." Her smile faded and her eyebrows climbed up her forehead. She tipped the bouquet over and stared at the stems. "What happened to them?"

"Uh, what do you mean?"

She looked at him, blinking. "They're cut off from their plants."

Dedrick threw furtive glances at the others, catching Alix's and Bolcan's smirks and Camilla's wistful look. "Well, yeah. I wanted to give them to you."

Bolcan let out a derisive huff and put his hands on his hips. "Are you for real? Who gives an Aldonian girl flowers? That's akin to murder. Besides, you're engaged. Get her a ring."

Liberty glanced at him over her shoulder, the hint of a smile on her face.

Burning heat washed over Dedrick. "Where am I gonna get a ring in Aldonia?" He knew what Bolcan was going to say. Everyone had the same advice for him.

"Guy's place," Bolcan said. "I'm sure the black market's still open, probably gonna be thriving."

Dedrick nodded. "Okay, I messed up."

Liberty smiled at the hydrangeas then at him. Bouquet in hand, she stepped close and wrapped her arms around his neck, sending warmth all through his body. "I love you," she said. Then she kissed him, a quick firm kiss that sent his heart spiraling out of control.

She backed up just as quickly and smiled at the flowers again.

Dedrick breathed. She hadn't changed her mind. She was going to marry him.

"I guess I was wrong, huh?" Bolcan said.

"About?" Dedrick still couldn't push all the jealous feelings away.

"You're not too much of a colony boy for her."

Liberty turned to Alix and laughed.

"So when's the big day?" Bolcan said.

Dedrick shrugged and looked at Liberty. He assumed they'd have to schedule it with Father Damon.

"Oh." Liberty's expression turned business-like. "I'm working on a gate for the Boundary Fence so the Mosheh can come and go easily. There's no electricity running through it, so it's just a matter of design and supplies. It'll probably take us another week."

"Miriam's waiting on you," Alix said to Dedrick. "She'll be leaving with the Torva and breeders."

Dedrick bristled at the word "breeders," but it was true. Miriam had volunteered to accompany them back to the Rivergrove Colony. Ann and other Torva planned to meet them at the Boundary Fence so they could help on the journey. Ann wanted to ensure that the wild men treated the women properly and didn't force them into relationships they didn't want.

"So after that?" Dedrick said, wanting Liberty to commit to a date. "We should probably talk to Father Damon. We could do that any day. We could do that today." He was sounding desperate, he knew, but he couldn't stop himself.

"Oh." She stared at him for a moment, her misty green eyes making her irresistible. "I was thinking . . ."

Dedrick tensed. "Thinking?"

"Wouldn't your parents like to see their oldest son get married?"

His mouth fell open. His mind went blank. Then he grabbed her and pulled her close. "We're going to Rivergrove?" He hoped she answered quickly because he was one second from kissing her.

"If you want to."

35

I stood with arms stretched out at my sides and eyes closed, inhaling a fresh, green, earthy scent that made me feel warm and alive. Beams of sunlight warmed my face and turned my eyelids orange. The slightest breeze stirred, bringing goosebumps to my arms and rustling leaves, a faint sound I would've ordinarily missed. Birds called in the distance. A white-throated sparrow leisurely sang nearby. *My Friend* rested in my soul, heightening my senses and stirring me to thankfulness and praise.

I had come to realize that *My Friend* was somehow related to God. Either the voice of God speaking inside me or a messenger of God, ever by my side.

How had I ever gotten here? Here in the wilderness. Here in faith. Here with Dedrick, my future husband, my future family. Free.

Everyone in Aldonia would soon have what I had. Something to live for. Something to die for. They would all have the freedom to make families, to spend their lives caring for and protecting them, seeing to their security and happiness. Loving them. And soon, Aldonia would become a stable society. A strong society.

A female voice, high and angry, broke the peaceful moment. A man's angry voice followed.

I opened my eyes and scanned the woods, turning in a slow circle, the euphoria fading.

A figure stood in the distance, visible between tree trunks.

Careful to avoid snapping a twig, I drew near.

Faded jeans, olive t-shirt on an athletic body, short brown hair that stood up on top . . . Dedrick leaned an arm against a tree trunk and peered at two figures farther away.

Picking my steps as I drew nearer, I soon recognized the figures: the Torva leader in a buckskin vest and Dedrick's sister Ann in a ponytail and denim dress. Bits of their shouted conversation became clear. Ann, waving an arm in anger, said something about his boys learning a thing or two about courtship and respect. The Torva leader, gesturing with both hands, said something about the ways of his people.

Less than a meter from Dedrick, I leaned and whispered, "Hey!"

"Huh!" Dedrick jumped and spun to face me, exhaling when he saw my smile. He shook his head and glared. "Why'd you do that?"

"You're spying on people." I grabbed his hands, lifted them, and laced our fingers together. "You're not Mosheh anymore, so you don't get to do that." A sneaky smile on my face, I pushed his hands toward his shoulders.

He pushed back, using a fraction of his strength, still peering through narrowed eyes. "That's my sister."

"Yes, we met."

"And that's Grenton." Dedrick's square jaw twitched.

"Met him, too." I pushed harder, forcing one hand toward the trunk behind him.

Biceps bulging from under his short sleeves, Dedrick swung our hands down and brought them behind my back. "Grenton is chief of the Torva. Or he will be, anyway, when his father steps down."

Dedrick gave me a peck on the lips, released our hands, and peered around the tree again.

I stood beside him, folding my arms even though I wanted to put an arm around him. I couldn't imagine ever feeling comfortable initiating contact.

Ann stood with folded arms, too, glaring up at Grenton while he spoke. Now she said something while shaking her head, throwing an arm out, turning away, turning toward him. Grenton stood with legs spread, shoulders slumped, and occasionally swinging an arm out. They were talking about marking the girls, whatever that meant.

Dedrick swallowed hard, his Adam's apple bobbing.

"Are you worried he'll hurt her?"

Dedrick turned away and leaned his back against the trunk. "No. I guess not." Eyes to the ground, he took my hands again and rubbed his fingers against mine, pressed our palms together, and slid his hand up and down mine.

The pleasant sensation distracted me, so I laced our fingers together again and squeezed.

He lifted his gaze to mine. "There's something I have to tell you."

"Okay."

His mouth opened. He breathed, closed his mouth, and narrowed his eyes. "Well, first I have a question. Why were you in Bolcan's room?"

"What? You mean last week, the day you gave me flowers?"

"Yeah."

I wriggled my fingers from his and folded my arms. "He wanted to talk to me. It was private."

Jealousy flickered in his earthy brown eyes. "We're getting married. We shouldn't keep secrets."

"It's not my secret. It's Bolcan's. He confided in me."

When Bolcan and I had crossed paths, he'd asked to speak with me privately. His room was near, so we went there. A broken card table lay against a wall, a clutter of papers on another table. We sat side by side on the bed, and after a moment of him dipping his head and shoving his hands through his hair, he'd told me he was sorry for risking my life. He realized he'd been so fixated on destroying Re-Ed that he hadn't thought of anything or anyone else. Then he said he felt like a fool because if he had waited, the fall of Aldonia's government would've taken care of it. But I told him that Guy might've needed the destruction of Re-Ed to happen first. It gave him credibility.

Bolcan had stared for half a minute then nodded and kissed me on the cheek. "Dedrick's a lucky man. But he's good for you, too. He's a good man. He'll never do you wrong." A lopsided grin came to his lips. "Don't tell him I said that."

I threw my arms around his muscular shoulders and hugged him, tears and laughter threatening to erupt, a mess of emotion struggling to come out. I identified with Bolcan in more ways than I could count, the experience of Re-Ed being the most traumatic.

It still affected me at times. Would it keep me from being a good wife and mother?

"Fine," Dedrick said, looking at me through sulky eyes. "Don't tell me."

"Are you going to be mad?"

He shrugged then traced a finger across my folded arms. "No, I'm not gonna be mad."

"Well, nothing went on between us, if that's what you think." I unfolded my arms and started to clasp my hands, but he grabbed them.

"I know, Liberty. I'm sorry. I do trust you."

My heart filled with the love he transmitted through his eyes, his touch, his words. I wanted to be worthy of his love. I wanted to return his love. Could I?

"Dedrick, there's something I have to tell you, too."

"Okay, you can go first." He stared, giving me his complete attention.

I pulled my hands from his and stepped back. "It's not a fun subject."

He folded his arms but didn't look hurt. "Mine won't be either."

"It's about Re-Ed." I waited for his expression to change, but it didn't. "It messed with my mind. Big time. And sometimes it still messes with me. Things push into my thoughts and dreams, making me freak out, panic. Maybe stress brings it on." I paused, wanting the next words to soak in. He needed to really think through his desire to marry me. "I'm not the girl you first met."

He waited a moment, gazing at me. "In ten years, Liberty, you're not going to be the woman you are today. But I'm going to love you anyways. I love you. I love every bit of you. Even the messed-up parts."

My eyelids flickered and tears welled up. My entire body tingled like I might pass out. "Your turn."

Glancing away, he took a breath. "I should've told you this before I asked you to marry me."

That shocked me. He had something to tell me that might affect my decision to marry him, something worse than the effects of Re-Ed on me?

Voices rose in the distance, in the direction of our camp, making us both look. Ann and Grenton had gone. Someone shouted. A baby cried.

Dedrick and I took off together. We sprinted side by side down a deer path and past canvas tents.

A teenage Torva boy by a roaring campfire gripped a long stick and stood defensively. Two Aldonian women and five toddling children sat around the fire. More women and Torva men were on the opposite side of the camp, several of them talking at once.

Miriam's voice rose above the others. "His name is Bot. He's a friend."

The group parted, letting Miriam and Bot through.

Bot wore a leather sack draped over one shoulder and a backpack. His red hair stood up in unruly tufts, the way I remembered it. He wore baggy beige pants, probably homespun by the colonists, and a blue button-front shirt. Even while mumbling something to Miriam, he noticed Dedrick and me at once. "Hey, hey!" he shouted, stomping to us.

People gathered around the campfire. A girl holding a baby peeked out of the nearest tent. "I can't stand all these bugs," a young woman said, stomping past us.

I wondered how many girls wished they would've stayed in Aldonia. Since Guy had become governor, the vocation of breeder no longer existed, so the elders gave every woman the choice of remaining in Aldonia or leaving with their children and the Torva. Out here, they would still have the choice to live in a colony or wander with the Torva. The number of women that chose to leave Aldonia surprised me.

"What are you doing here?" Dedrick motioned for Bot to have a seat around the campfire then he sat down.

"I'm going back to Aldonia."

"Really? Wow." I sat on the ground beside Dedrick.

"Sure, this is a historic moment. How could I not be there? Besides, starting up a new government of the people, by the people . . . they're going to need someone with my abilities."

One of the Torva men came around with mugs. He offered one to each of us.

"I've been doing my research." Bot sipped from the mug. "And I have an idea for another game."

"Yeah?" Dedrick glanced suspiciously at the contents of the mug and gave me a little headshake.

I brought the mug to my nose to smell it, but Dedrick touched my hand as if to stop me from drinking.

"Did you know," Bot said, "that there was one man in the history of the world who had an impact on civilizations, cultures, and individuals even long after he died? Or I should say, after he rose from the dead."

We listened to Bot explain the concept for his new game and tell us his plans for building a solid but not overbearing government in Aldonia. And he had more to say, but I lost my ability to focus.

I watched the Aldonian girls interacting with the Torva boys. The boys seemed eager to please. The girls seemed shocked. A Torva boy with an unruly goatee held the hands of a baby just learning to walk, both of them seeming amused. The mother smiled, watching them.

I leaned and whispered to Dedrick, "They seem happy, don't they?"

"I told Dedrick once . . ."

I jumped at the sound of Grenton's baritone voice and found him staring at me.

Dedrick, sitting beside me with arms resting on raised knees, turned at once to face him.

"We bring women into our tribe by force, but they stay because they want to. They learn who we are, they see how we treat them, and they are satisfied." Grenton grinned, his gaze sliding from me to Dedrick, a bit of I-told-you-so in his eyes.

"How many days until we get there?" a pregnant woman said, rubbing her belly. "I can't walk the whole way."

The Torva man next to her whispered something in her ear. She rolled her eyes, looking disgusted. "I'm too heavy for you to carry." Then she bumped his shoulder, a smile coming to her face.

"Do not worry," Grenton boomed. "Help arrives tomorrow, more of our people and carts. The journey will be easier but several days long."

Dedrick shifted, accidentally kicking the mug at his feet. "Uh, Grenton, who's bringing the carts? Who's coming tomorrow?"

Grenton gulped down a drink and laughed. "Yes, she is coming." He spoke louder than necessary, but maybe he wanted everyone to hear him. "She will not be happy to meet your new friend."

Dedrick rocked back and glanced at me.

"What does he mean?" I said. "Who is *she*? Who's your friend?"

Dedrick grabbed my hand and we stood. "Come on. We have to talk."

Grenton's laugh rose above other sounds as we plunged into the woods.

We stood by a tree in a clearing, alone. Voices traveled from the camp, making a soft background noise.

Dedrick bit his lip and played with a tuft of his hair. He took a few steps one way then another, finally stopping two meters away and facing me. "Okay, so the Torva have some strange practices."

"Okay." I gave him my full attention, focusing on his eyes. The sunlight played in them, making warm shades of brown that I could lose myself in.

"So . . . I've got this mark on my shoulder." He rubbed his upper arm.

"I know. I . . . I saw it. It's like a letter *S*, right?" I had seen it several months ago when tending a wound on his arm. He had seemed very uncomfortable about it, so I never mentioned it.

He rolled his eyes and took a deep breath. "Yeah. It's an *S*. Stands for Shaneka."

"Oh. Old girlfriend?" An unexpected streak of jealousy flared inside me. I tried to keep from grimacing. He must've been close to the girl to have gotten a mark like that on his body.

"No." He glared. "She was never my girlfriend." He turned away and rubbed his face. "It's this thing the Torva do. They sort of mark people. Men mark women usually, like a man might mark his cattle."

"Mark your cattle?"

He faced me, shaking his head. "Well, Aldonians probably don't, but cowboys used to take a hot iron . . . never mind. It's a branding that tells other people to stay away, that they . . . own you."

I pressed my lips together, trying not to smile. But the way he squirmed trying to explain himself made him endearing. "Are you telling me that girl owns you? Shaneka?" I took slow steps toward him.

"Well, no. A person can't own a person." He watched me approach, his gaze roaming up and down me.

"Can I see it?"

He averted his gaze for a moment then connected with mine. "If you want." He reached for the hem of his olive-green t-shirt.

Suppressing a smile, I grabbed his hands to keep him from stripping his shirt off.

He opened his mouth as if to say something then he closed it and pushed up his sleeve. And there it was. A big brown scar on his smooth skin.

I touched it, running my finger along the swirls that came off the *S*. The humor left me, replaced by irritation that someone had done this to him. "I bet that hurt when she did it."

He nodded.

"How'd she do it?"

"Well, I didn't let her, if that's what you're asking. She . . . her brothers— she has seven brothers. They drugged me, and she took a hot branding iron . . ."

"Oh." I pressed my hand against it, biting my lip, trying not to imagine the pain he'd endured. "That's terrible."

He nodded. Then he dove in and kissed me, quick and rough.

A rush of warmth spread through me, making me dizzy.

He jerked back and turned away. "I just wanted you to know what it means." He paced a few steps away and stood talking with his back to me. "The Torva consider me her property. They think . . . she thinks I'm gonna marry her." He turned to me and flung an arm out. "I already told her it's not gonna happen. But they're pretty persistent. So if you marry me, we'll have that to deal with, until she gets over it." He glanced away. "*If* she gets over it."

"Hmm." I came up to him, a sneaky smile on my face.

The look in his eyes said he wrestled with various emotions.

I didn't want him thinking this changed things between us. I slid my hand up his sleeve and touched the scar again. "Any way we can turn that *S* into an *L*?"

He dipped down and kissed me again, softer and deeper this time, making me want to lose myself in him. Then he drew back. "I'm no girl's property, but I give myself to you."

My lips burned, and the message that had come with his kiss whispered in my mind. We would face all challenges together. I was no longer Liberty 554-062466-84 of Aldonia, a child of the Regimen Custodia Terra. I was a child of the Creator, of God. And I would no longer simply be Liberty, free but alone. Soon I would be Liberty Ryder. Bound to Dedrick for as long as we lived.

I had a family. I belonged.

I would be his and he would be mine.

Forever.

Did you enjoy this book? If so, help others enjoy it, too! Please recommend it to friends and leave a review when possible. Thank you!

Every month I send out a newsletter so that you can keep up with my newest releases and enjoy updates, contests, and more. Visit my website www.theresalinden.com to sign up. And while you're there, check out my book trailers and extras!

Facebook: www.facebook.com/theresalindenauthor/
Twitter: @LindenTheresa

ABOUT THE AUTHOR

Theresa Linden is the author of award-winning *Battle for His Soul* and *Roland West, Loner* (Catholic Press Association Book Awards, 2016 & 2017). Raised in a military family, she developed a strong patriotism and a sense of adventure. Her Catholic faith inspires the belief that there is no greater adventure than the reality we can't see, the spiritual side of life. She has eight published novels, including a fast-paced dystopian trilogy that tackles tough moral questions of our day, and two short stories in *Image and Likeness: Literary Reflections on the Theology of the Body* (Full Quiver Publishing). She holds a Catechetical Diploma from Catholic Distance University and is a member of the Catholic Writers Guild and the International Writers Society. A wife, homeschooling mom, and Secular Franciscan, she resides in northeast Ohio with her husband and three teenage boys.

Made in the USA
San Bernardino,
CA